Natalie Chandler is the bestselling author of *Believe Me Not*. She w... ...d ... has a professional background in behavioural education. Natalie shares her sofa with her fiancé and a collection of cockapoos, and divides her time between London and rural Lancashire. She enjoys greeting every dog she meets.

Also by Natalie Chandler

Believe Me Not

WHAT WE DID

NATALIE CHANDLER

ACCENT

First published in 2023 by Headline Accent
An imprint of HEADLINE PUBLISHING GROUP

1

Cataloguing in Publication Data is available from the British Library

ISBN 978 1 4722 9175 2

Typeset in 11.25/15.25pt Bembo Std by Jouve (UK), Milton Keynes

Printed and bound in Great Britain by Clays Ltd, Elcograf S.p.A.

HEADLINE PUBLISHING GROUP
An Hachette UK Company
Carmelite House
50 Victoria Embankment
London EC4Y 0DZ

www.headline.co.uk
www.hachette.co.uk

To my fiancé Lee, who was absolutely no fucking
help at all in the process of this book, but who did write his
own dedication. Love you forever, to Versailles and back.

And for Indy, who has brought more to our lives than
he will ever know.

*'The sins of Britain's most secretive school. My campaign
to uncover the hidden truths' by Amy Donald*

Halewood House School, hidden away in idyllic rural Essex, was
regarded as one of the best in the country in its heyday. Run by a
small but influential religious order renowned for its scholars, the
school had a reputation for academic excellence. Parents clamoured
to beat the admission policy, especially after the school decided to
admit girls in the mid-nineties. However, behind the oak doors and
mullioned windows, a dark side of Halewood House was hidden
from the public eye.

Known by pupils as Cell Block H, Halewood House was dogged by scandals over the years, most of them hushed up by leaders
desperate to deny they were at fault. One thing they couldn't hide,
however, was the death of a student, declared at the time to be a
tragic accident. The eighteen-year-old boy was found in his dormi-
tory, having overdosed on amphetamines, later discovered in another
student's belongings.

Desperate to protect the Church's reputation, the tragedy was
covered up by senior teachers, with pupils warned that anyone
caught speaking out would face immediate expulsion. Charges were
never brought against any party and stricter procedures were hurriedly implemented by the Order in an attempt to deflect from their
failings.

Scrutinised only by the Independent Schools Inspectorate, whose
sole focus until as recently as 2012 was the quality of education rather
than welfare, the school flew under the radar. The autonomous

Brothers were a cloistered group, removed from the outside world, and they were determined that the authorities did not glimpse the true nature of Halewood House. It wasn't until 2002 that minimum standards of safeguarding and welfare were established for boarding schools but, ultimately, it was too late for Halewoodians.

By the noughties, Halewood House was attempting to reinvent itself. The Charities Commission had finally banished the Order, although those in power blocked the school's closure and established a new leadership team. The irony of its new name – Milton Hall, after education reformer John Milton – seemed to go unnoticed, and the school retreated from the headlines for a fresh start following the Nolan Report.

Milton Hall closed its doors for the final time just this year when another tragedy rocked the school. The suicide of former student Olivia Seabrook, leaving a note blaming Halewood House for the psychiatric illnesses that had dogged her for the rest of her life, triggered an immediate Ofsted inspection. This time, the school's sins could not be denied, and immediate action was taken amid scandalous revelations about just what went on in the boarding houses.

Few have mourned the demise of an institution that, although once renowned for its league-table highs, gained its academic prowess at the cost of children's safety.

Chapter One

This morning is different to all the others. Today is the day Jenna's fears breach daylight and begin to destroy the walls of her carefully constructed world.

The usual sounds of Loki's cheerful panting, the percolator's steady drip and rushing, heavy footsteps thumping against the upstairs floorboards, all of it has faded into the background. Their unwelcome replacements seem louder: blood pounding hard enough to burst an eardrum, the unsteady rasp of breathing not quite under control, the rhythmic drumming of fingers against the worktop.

It has been a long time since Jenna experienced a panic attack, but she is on the verge of one now, and the unexpected intruder has robbed her of competence. She tries to count, an old habit taught by a long-banished shrink, but all that does is remind her how late she is. She hates being late as much as she hates the well-concealed anxiety it inevitably causes.

Weekday mornings in the Taylor household run strictly to a schedule. There is much to be organised in the short time before their exodus and efficiency is a necessity. Procrastination is the enemy at all times for Jenna, but especially on a Monday.

'Love? You OK?' Zach's voice is soft as always, heavy with sleep, but it's enough to break through the intruding sounds.

Out of the corner of her eye, Jenna sees him survey the chaos of the kitchen-diner, the pristine pearl of their home, today cluttered with last night's plates, unironed laundry, disorganised paperwork, dirty glasses.

'Why are you tapping like that?'

She counts the words in her husband's sentences. *One, two, three* . . . She hasn't done so for years, not since the urge had gradually faded at university, but it comforts her now, as it did before.

'Jenna?' More insistent, Zach moves towards her. His expressive face shows concern for her, for her pallor, the dark circles swelling beneath her eyes, the sharp, frantic movements as she tries to collect herself. He is still damp from the shower, never bothering to make sure he is fully dried, and she skirts away before his moist skin can touch hers.

Loki launches himself joyously on his playmate, giving Jenna a chance to take control of her agitated movements. She manages to slow her breathing, forces herself to look at him.

'Sorry. Miles away.'

Zach grabs the day's crumpled newspaper from the dining table, oblivious to Jenna's flinch as she glimpses the headline again. He flips straight to the sport, a careless scan of the pages.

The bold black print burns into Jenna's eyes. The words feel contaminating, her skin crawling as if she needs to scrub it clean.

'You don't look well,' Zach observes quietly.

'Neither would you if you'd had no sleep.'

Zach blinks, taking a step back, allowing her personal space from his towering height looming above her. 'I didn't hear you tossing and turning.'

'You wouldn't hear a particularly localised tornado ripping through the bedroom,' Jenna mutters to avoid the question, wincing internally when she sees Zach's shoulders droop in response to her sharpness. She hates herself for the way her words so often hurt the only man who has ever been able to love her. She wishes she knew how to stop the cutting remarks, how to tell him just how deep her feelings run beneath her polished veneer. She means it when she tells Zach she loves him, but no one ever taught her the way to show it.

Unable to think of a way to apologise, she deals the percolator a sharp smack as it grinds to a premature halt.

Zach rallies himself, gently steering her aside, and takes the machine to task with a little more compassion. She offers him a conciliatory smile, as if it could ever be enough after everything he puts up with.

'You should've woken me if you couldn't sleep,' he chides lightly. 'I'd have kept you company.'

Jenna turns away, the smile sliding from her lips as they tense. How can she wake him, with her limbs paralysed by invisible bonds, the oxygen sapped from her lungs and her heart about to pound itself to arrest? She is forty years old and terrorised by the fear of a young child.

'Want to talk about whatever's keeping you awake?'

She shakes her head, not trusting herself to speak, eyes firmly focused on the ham-and-cheese sandwich before her as if she will make a terrible error if she dares look away from it.

Maybe she will never want to talk about it.

The open bottle of wine next to the hob calls to her, just to get her moving, and she nearly reaches for a glass before common sense intervenes.

No. She will not become like her mother.

'Maybe you should make a GP appointment? Ask for some sleeping pills?' Zach suggests, forming his words too carefully, so they sound rehearsed. Maybe they are. 'You haven't slept properly in far too long. Ever since Olivia's funeral.'

'Don't!' Jenna's voice rises sharply.

She cannot have that conversation. She can't acknowledge just what the death of beautiful, wild, brave Olivia, a friend whose loyalty knew no bounds, has caused.

Zach takes another step back, a chasm of distance between them.

'Just leave it, Zach,' she begs. 'I've too much to do. I don't have time for this.'

He absently scratches his pot belly, an unwanted fortieth-birthday present earlier in the year, and jerks his hand away as if shocked to find the small pouch of fat on his otherwise angular frame.

'We'll make time this evening, then.'

It is meant to be a comfort, but it feels like a threat. Jenna doesn't reply, for Zach's sake. She keeps her back turned until he has retreated upstairs, Loki bounding after him, to make sure neither of them glimpses the tears shining in her eyes.

She blinks them away.

She never cries. The past wasted too many tears.

The newspaper is abandoned once again on the worktop, and she finds herself reaching for it, a compulsion she can't control. A small headshot of the journalist, Amy Donald, sits beneath the article, an attractive blonde with piercing eyes, arms folded, chin tilted just slightly upward. She looks effortlessly capable of achieving whatever she sets her sights on. She looks like the person Jenna tries so hard to be.

4

For just a moment the Sabatier in Jenna's hand, wicked blade stalled above the block of Cheddar, is too tempting. She imagines herself running it gently along the velvety underbelly of her forearm, watching the skin part and swell with crimson as the release flows from her.

The old scars are mostly faded now. It would be easy to make new ones.

By the time her son erupts into the room, she has placed the paper and the knife beyond arm's reach and is carrying on with her tasks. Lando throws his kit bag casually aside, not noticing that the thud of it landing makes Jenna jump. He attacks an apple as if it has offended him, crunching so hard little slivers fly into the air with each enormous bite. He is taller than her now, destined for Zach's height, a presence that seizes both space and air.

She has no idea how her little boy has become this shaggy-haired savage, hands and feet too large for his body to coordinate, limbs constantly creeping out of the ends of shirts and trousers, his father's walnut eyes prepared for mutiny. Their mutual love of sci-fi makes his chosen name rather more appropriate than it had felt when Zach had begged and Jenna had given up caring.

He is Zach, through and through. At a glance, or with more consideration, few would pair them as mother and son. Lando had been her slip-up baby. A careless night of drinking leading to the precious slip of tiny pills remaining snug in the bedside drawer and, before she knew it, a life was dependent on her. So dependent.

'I heard you shouting last night,' Lando says as he rifles through the fridge, as casually as if telling her it was raining.

Jenna angles her body so he can't see her face. 'I wasn't shouting.'

'It woke me. You kept saying "I don't want to".'

'Must have been a nightmare, I don't remember it.' She should apologise for disturbing him, but the words don't come.

Lando shrugs, massacring a brioche with slaps of a Nutella-loaded butter knife. 'Will you write me a note saying why I haven't done my maths homework?'

'Why haven't you done your maths homework?'

He rolls his eyes, the answer apparently obvious. ''Cos I was too tired from you waking me to get up early and do it!'

Jenna is about to argue, be a better parent and tell him he'd had plenty of time for homework the previous evening and he will have to accept the consequences of not having done it.

She can't summon the energy for the rebuke. She doesn't care about maths homework or teaching responsibility this morning. There is very little she cares about this morning.

She writes the note.

It is a manic dash through the Islington traffic to deliver Lando to the outstanding-rated state school they had finally selected for him, rising above the inner-city comprehensive jungle with its middle-class beacons of rugby and Latin.

Zach had clamoured for a private school, but Jenna had been immovable. The world had changed since their education; extortionate fees no longer equalled success. They lived in a good neighbourhood with decent schools – that's why they had chosen the house, after all – and they should support their community.

None of those reasons are the real one, not even close, but they make her feel better, more in control. Lando won't need to hide the sort of secrets she guards so closely.

'Have a good day,' she remembers to say before the passenger door is flung open. 'Remember you have swimming after school.'

A dramatic eyeroll. 'When do I ever forget swimming?'

Lando escapes the Audi without so much as a wave and disappears into the throng of grey blazers. Jenna lets the engine idle as she flips down the visor mirror and begins slapping on make-up, layering too much concealer and foundation in an attempt to hide her burdens. One eye streams furiously as the unsteady mascara wand jabs it, smudging the liquid eyeliner, and her lipstick breaks as she tries to trace the outline of lips too generous for her square face.

'Fuck it!' she shrieks, causing several passing kids to leap away from proximity to her car.

She hurls the make-up back into her tote, not bothering to zip it safely into its own bag. Her powder will leave perfumed crumbs all over the silk lining. She doesn't care.

Her hair is usually sentenced to being perfectly straight, unruly waves banished by GHDs, but she has forgotten the daily ritual. She drags it into a messy bun she tells herself is deliberate, the honey hues that deny her natural mousy tones dull and brittle. She takes hold of the steering wheel, getting a grip both physically and mentally.

Work is just off Upper Street, a short drive too long to endure. Horns beep as she makes careless manoeuvres; cyclists yell curses when she strays into their assigned lane. Addison Residential has its own parking, awkward bays even on a good day. Eventually she abandons the car across two spaces.

'Jenna! I need you!' Of course Hugo would choose today to show his face. The self-titled chief exec prefers to spend his time haunting the newer Clapham branch these days, trusting Jenna to run the north London office in his absence.

'Be right there,' she calls, this time managing to bite back the less amenable words that rise to her lips. She finds it easier to control her sharpness at work, where her acting skills are used for influence rather than to conceal.

Hugo is safely behind his large desk, deliberately bigger than hers. He is the sort of attractive man who doesn't need to try, but effort shines from his perfectly tailored suit and handmade loafers, matching his expensive haircut and gleaming smile, smooth skin bronzed as much from regular sunbed usage as his frequent jaunts to the Amalfi coast.

On the gleaming walnut surface, another daily paper glares up at her and, as hard as she tries not to look at it, the words leap out at her.

SEX, DRUGS AND SCANDAL AT TOP PRIVATE SCHOOL

'Jenna!' It appears Hugo has been speaking as she was attempting to read the article upside down.

'Have you read that?' she demands.

His expression tells her he hasn't even looked at it.

'It's our school, Hugo.' She grabs it, thrusting the headline into his face. 'Halewood House is being exposed in a national campaign.'

'Exposed for what?' He snatches it but doesn't even glance at the story before tossing it back on to his desk.

'All the shit that went on.'

Hugo hisses a sigh between his perfect teeth, his broad shoulders straightening as he tenses. 'Get a grip, Jenna. School was decades ago, and it's the last thing I want to talk about. Can we keep our minds on more urgent matters? This is a bloody important day!'

She has no choice but to snap back to attention, pretend she is at the top of her game. Hugo has been her friend for more years than she cares to remember but, technically, he is her boss and it matters that she maintains her professional edge in front of him. He can't be allowed to see what lurks beneath.

Addison Residential is a boutique estate agency, representing only the top echelons of the housing ladder, and multimillion-pound properties are as awkward to sell as their prospective owners are to assure. As senior partner, the pressure to close deals is intense, unyielding, but Jenna wields her reputation proudly, carrying the weight with a smile and a bounce in her step that fall away the moment she signs off for the day and the motivation of her career fades.

She is just wondering what makes today so important when Hugo coughs pointedly, flying hands creating words of their own as he indicates his own face. 'Have you used a mirror this morning? You can't greet a prince looking like that!'

She can't let him see she has forgotten all about the minor Middle Eastern royal keen to snap up a Knightsbridge pied-á-terre for his summer jaunts. She never forgets.

'Have you been out drinking all night?' asks Hugo.

'I've been having trouble sleeping,' she sighs. 'I'll grab an espresso and redo my make-up, all right?'

'A Xanax wouldn't go amiss either.' Hugo is a firm believer in the power of tranquillisers.

'Can I take the paper?'

'You can do whatever you want, as long as you sell that bloody flat.'

Jenna already knows it will take too much effort to shift the tired apartment at such an optimistic asking price. Another blow to her professional pride.

Dismissed, she shoves the paper into her capacious handbag and escapes to the Ladies to assess the damage. Worse than she'd thought. Lines that have appeared seemingly overnight battle for space, competing with swollen shadows almost meeting her high cheekbones. Usually, her forget-me-not eyes are her best feature, and she regularly exploits them to her full advantage to dazzle uncertain buyers, but today they are as dull and lifeless as her complexion.

Frantically chewing gum to rid her mouth of the bitter tang of fear, she attempts a rapid repair job, shaking hands hampering her progress until she finally gives up. She can claim illness, a sudden onset she is prepared to gamely battle through for her client.

Maybe she *is* ill. Would that explain the sweat-drenched pillow and the erratic heartbeat? Could illness be the cause of all this?

'Jen?' The door creaks open to reveal Hugo's face. 'Sure you're OK?'

'I'll be fine.'

'Sorry for snapping. And for saying you look like shit. Do you want me to take the appointment?'

Jenna makes herself smile in reply. She and Hugo are too similar to have an easy relationship, but they have steered Addison through turbulent waters since he persuaded Jenna to leave Foxtons. She can't afford for them to fall out now.

'As if I'd trust you with such a big sale.' She forces lightness into her tone.

'We can both have the rest of the day off if you get an offer.'

And what, exactly, would she do with a day of no distractions?

Chapter Two

Usually, Jenna's spirits lift as she drives down the wide avenue lined with handsome Edwardian terraces. They are uniformed by bay windows that glow with warm, welcoming light, white sashes and golden brickwork. Even the front paths of terracotta mosaic tiles meeting the pavements are identical, in upkeep as much as design. The avenue basks in its appearance, assuring each resident: you are safe here.

Except now she isn't sure she is.

The silence as she closes the door is deafening. Jenna finds herself craving company and solitude with equal desperation. Loki's ecstatic welcome would have been wonderful, but Zach's trendy office is dog friendly, so Loki happily goes to work each day and plays with his friends, human and canine.

She shouts a greeting to Lando, receives no response, as usual. He returns home independently, either from school or swimming training, and shuts himself away for his gaming fix. She wonders if the pressure of competitive swimming is getting to him, but she doesn't know how to ask him in a way that won't result in another blazing row.

She moves swiftly about the ground floor, flicking on the TV, the kitchen radio, setting the washing machine off half full and loading the dishwasher without a thought for careful order. Anything for noise.

The wine hasn't moved since morning. She had half hoped it would have tactfully shuffled off to a corner, but there it is, waiting for her. There is only a large glassful left; it would get her through the lonely hours until Zach returns and Lando emerges from his lair.

Turning on her heel, reminding herself how decisive she is, she leaves the kitchen and strides up the stairs. Admittedly, her resolve weakens as she tentatively enters her son's room, forcing herself to knock but not waiting for an invitation.

She perches on the edge of Lando's duvet, running her palm over the cartoon images he hasn't yet grown out of in pretence of smoothing it down. She counts each character until her hands no longer shake quite so noticeably.

Lando spins in his gaming chair, brow knitted at the presence of his mother. He smells of chlorine and too much deodorant, his hair still damp and curling wildly. One hand clutches a controller while the other feeds mounds of popcorn into his mouth, his hunger insatiable.

His finger jabs a button, and his dual screens immediately go black as he snatches off his oversized headphones.

'What?' he asks after a moment.

How can she explain that she just wants to see him, to remind herself that this home is where she belongs, that she has everything she needs within these walls?

'Just wondered how swimming went today.'

He shrugs, as if it is no big deal that he has been selected to

12

train for the under-fourteens national championships. He doesn't seem to mind the punishing schedule elite sport demands – three early-morning sessions, three afternoons, only Sundays off – but he doesn't discuss his new-found passion with his mother. It is Zach who gets the details, the high and lows and the difficulty of tumble turns.

'The head coach was there today. He said my times were good.'

'And was school OK?' she tries.

An impatient sigh, another jab at the game controller to silence the sounds coming from the headphones. They sound more like human conversation than video-game weapons.

'I learned how to say "fuck" in Lithuanian.' He is much less keen to be in a classroom than in a pool or on a pitch; it was a constant battle to keep his attendance acceptable.

'Useful for the future, I'm sure.' She curses herself the moment the words leave her and she sees her son's face shut down instantly, his eyes flashing retaliation.

'We were stuck in the hall most of the day doing a stupid workshop. This woman banging on about what we should do if someone asks for nudes or if we get touched up and all that shit.' Lando's cheeks colour, beyond his control.

'That's important.'

'We're not idiots.'

'It happens more easily than you think.'

'Like you would know.' He rolls his eyes.

Jenna's mouth opens to shoot back a response, but the words don't come this time. Saliva catches in her throat, making her cough violently, inadvertently saving her from making another mistake.

'Mum, what do you really want?' Lando asks, a noticeable bite in his tone.

'Who's your next rugby match against?' she gasps, eyes streaming from the coughing fit, or something more painful.

A shrug. He knows she is grasping at straws for a conversation topic. 'School in Hackney. We're on the Marshes. You coming?'

'If you want me to.'

'Not bothered either way.' His walnut eyes study her and, for a moment, it seems he will ask what's wrong.

Abruptly, he spins back to face the waiting screens.

'What's for dinner?'

That is her dismissal, and she has no option but to return downstairs, to turn the radio volume up further and close all the curtains against the menace of the dark. The bottle invites her again, a sly offering, but she fights the instinctive reaction just long enough to convince herself that she is in control. Only then does she allow herself to pour the glass.

She pulls Hugo's newspaper from her bag, crumpled and stained with sprinkles of her face powder. The pages have been folded hurriedly and it is not Amy Donald's revelations that look up at her but another article entirely.

'Righting the Wrongs' – Drew Merchant on education, tradition and the twenty-first century

Andrew Merchant ruffled a few feathers when he was appointed head of one of London's most exclusive public schools, doing away with straw boaters and boarding-house initiations in favour of coeducation and international qualifications. A rising star in the world of education who gained recognition for turning around some of the

UK's worst comprehensives, Merchant always intended to return to the elite school system, and he continues to build his reputation at the helm of an institution where time has stood still for centuries. Rumours, however, are beginning to circulate of simmering political ambitions and the fiercely ambitious Merchant may not wait long to swap the classroom for the House of Commons.

Andrew Merchant. Jenna knows that name. Another ghost from too long ago. She looks at the accompanying colour picture. It has been taken in a cobbled quadrangle, surrounded by Georgian buildings every bit as handsome as the man smiling up at the camera, his features instantly recognisable.

He is surrounded by children of all ages, heights and races, all dressed in expensive uniforms and grinning cooperatively. Close by his side, the youngest child, a little girl with a serious face and a pixie haircut, seems about to slide her hand into his, a trusting acceptance of her headmaster.

Jenna holds the paper closer to her face, her heart jolting as she realises she knows the girl as well as the man. Her pulse continues to pound as she searches for an answer to why the picture makes her feel so uneasy, but nothing is forthcoming. She picks away at it, even after she banishes the newspaper to the recycling, but it remains beyond her reach, shrouded.

By evening, another bottle of Malbec is becoming harder to ignore. Dinner is a hasty pasta bake she slaps on to the table, not even accompanied by a salad. Lando pokes at a sliver of red pepper in disgust but stops short of complaining after seeing his mother's clenched jaw. Even Loki has abandoned his usual post, sitting on Zach's feet under the table, for the safety of his basket. Zach looks as puzzled by his dog's wariness as he is by the slapdash meal.

'Still tired, love?' he asks, forking huge mouthfuls of tasteless penne, dropping tomato sauce on his white T-shirt. The daily race between father and son to see who can eat the fastest is not the source of tension this evening, but Jenna still catches herself waiting to deliver her usual rebuke, despite her best intentions.

She nods shortly, unwilling to voice a reply. She is counting the words in each sentence again, listening to the beat rather than the content, the old habit becoming stronger. She doesn't stop herself.

'I've lost my goggles,' Lando declares, as if new ones will appear immediately.

It takes a moment to understand the statement is directed at her. 'You haven't lost them; they're in the utility room, where they always are.'

'I've looked, they're not there.'

'You'll have man-looked, like your father when he can't find his keys on the key hook.'

'You're not allowed to use gender-related generalisations now.'

Zach nearly chokes, laughing so hard his eyes well with tears of mirth. Jenna forces a smile. It's funny, she knows it's funny, to hear such words from the mouth of her thirteen-year-old, but she can't summon a laugh.

'Oh, mate, that was class,' Zach declares when he finally calms down. 'Wasn't it, love?'

Jenna forces another smile in her son's direction. He is too busy eating to notice. She doesn't use terms of endearment, sticking rigidly to proper names. Zach peppers his speech with 'loves' and 'pals' that sounded warm and genuine alongside his flat vowels and insistence on calling rolls 'breadcakes', easy affection to make up for her inability to be demonstrative.

'Did you get the offer you wanted today?' Zach asks, determined to keep the conversation flowing.

'Not even close.' She hadn't bothered to persuade the young royal to raise his price. She had counted his words too – he had used too many.

'Damn, that would have been a decent bonus for you.'

Jenna doesn't know what to say so settles for a shrug, fingers tapping against the underside of the table in time with her counts. Her earnings are not to be sniffed at, but it is Zach who makes the big bucks doing God-knows-what in IT that mostly seems to involve long lunches on Old Street. Occasionally he tries to explain what his job actually entails, but she has an unfortunate habit of switching off thirty seconds in. Zach no longer commands her attention.

'Why don't you go for a bath and an early night? We'll sort the kitchen out, won't we, pal?'

Lando looks about as keen as the prince had but nods reluctant cooperation after a beat too long. Jenna needs no further encouragement to abandon her untouched plate.

Her son's head rises from his second helping as she passes his chair, just long enough to make her bite down on her lip. Unease flashes across Lando's face and he quickly focuses on the food again.

'I'm just tired,' Jenna whispers to the back of his unruly mop of curls, identical to Zach's when left untamed. He doesn't look up again, and she doesn't know how to reassure him, so she just creeps out of the room.

Upstairs, the bath proves to be an effort too far. She can barely summon the energy to brush her teeth.

The bed welcomes her, cocooning her in soft, comforting warmth. The band around her ribcage eases at last and she drinks in deep breaths as her jaw unclamps. Exhaustion begs her to sleep, but she forces her weighted eyes to remain open, directing their focus, counting objects.

She can't defend herself once they are closed. Open eyes mean control, and control has been the most important element of her adult life. She clings to it now, her self-taught crutch, even as her brain begs for rest.

Rigid once again, she continues her numerical mantra.

Her name is being called, over and over again, insistent, refusing to be ignored. A hand grabs her, forceful, shaking her, and she shrinks away with a gasp.

'Jenna, wake up, love.'

Another gasp, as though icy water has been thrown over her. She feels herself catapult bolt upright, drenched not in water but in sweat. Her limbs are no longer restrained, but she grips the covers so tightly she can't persuade her fingers to release.

Blinding light, painful to her raw, tender eyes. She hears a cry escape as she tries to shy away from it. Hands grasp hers and she tries to rear away from their hold.

Zach tilts the bedside lamp down, softening its glare. The room is familiar, bringing her back to the present, sending the other room retreating. She forces herself to take in each detail, counting them, feeling her heart racing. The ornate ironwork of their big, soft bed. The Moroccan throw unsuccessfully haggled for in a sweat-soaked souk. The olive-green walls, one adorned by a canvas of three people, together yet so very apart, and a speckled blue roan puppy drawing them closer.

'You're safe, love, I'm here,' Zach whispers from beside her, his warm body pressed close against hers, trying to be reassuring but inducing only claustrophobia in her. She wrenches herself free, hugging her knees. 'Here, drink some water.'

A glass is pushed into her hand. It is warm and stale, but she gulps it, spilling some down her chin in her haste. She is gasping for air again by the time she drains it.

'You scared me. I thought you were having a fit or something.'

She feels her cheeks burning feverishly. Her entire body aches as if she has been in a fight for survival. She can't reply.

'What did you see?' Zach asks, so gently she nearly sobs.

She shakes her head again, clamping her mouth shut.

'Tell me, Jenna. I can't help you if I don't know.'

'I need more water.'

She can see his hesitation to leave her. Protective instinct or a reluctance to let her distance herself? At last, he climbs out of bed. She hears the tap running in the bathroom, water pounding against the basin. The floor will be damp from the splashes, but for once she doesn't feel the urge to go and mop up the water.

The fresh glass is cold, wonderfully soothing to her raw throat, and she sips it slowly, buying more time. Zach doesn't get back under the covers, instead perching on her side of the mattress, body angled towards her.

He reaches for her hand and she fights the instinct to pull away. It isn't his fault. Zach avoids treading on snails because he thinks they mate for life and apologises to Loki any time he has to tell him off. It is wrong to make him feel rejected and yet she

19

can't stop herself. She has never known how to prevent her instinct for self-preservation, not since it became a necessity.

'I was in a tiny room,' she whispers, staring into the water glass. The sweat has cooled too much; she feels chilled to the bone. 'Someone came in, in the night. They were standing over me, watching me.'

'Anything else?'

She tries to remember, think beyond the piercing pain stabbing through her skull, but there is only fog. 'I was scared.'

She jerks free and grabs her pillows, stacking and punching them into shape so she can sit upright and attempt to open her lungs, trying to draw in enough air to negate the feeling of suffocation. Zach watches her until she has to close her eyes, desperate to escape his scrutiny. Eventually, he returns to his own side of the bed, pulling the duvet up so it covers her more securely.

'Can I do anything?'

She shakes her head. 'Go back to sleep.'

She keeps her eyes tightly closed, staying perfectly still until she feels Zach shuffle on to his back, his breathing deepening within moments. He sleeps the sleep of the unencumbered, and she envies him for it. Her own nights are very different. Even when she isn't aware of anything bothering her, she still struggles for more than a few hours of restful slumber.

Even though she knows it is the wrong thing to do, she unlocks her phone and scrolls through various social media, trying to find a distraction. She opens the news app, flinching as an article leaps from the screen.

'BOYS TREATED US LIKE PLAYTHINGS' – THE GIRLS FAILED BY THEIR ELITE SCHOOL, by Amy Donald

The same headshot of the reporter, the same accusing gaze, and a hot flush runs through Jenna's body as if she is guilty. Somewhere beyond her reach, there is a dawning sentience. She has buried it deep over the course of many years, building a thick, impenetrable skin to keep it hidden and unacknowledged.

Now it is beginning to force its way back to the surface, and she doesn't know if she has the strength to inter it again.

Chapter Three

Drew

D rew Merchant is late for dinner.

Natasha does not tolerate lateness, but sometimes it is unavoidable, impossible not to get caught up in the convenient excuses of overrun governors' meetings or budget discussions or training analysis as he attempts to manage his packed schedule. They ensure his whereabouts are rarely questioned, delays easily explained, and he relies heavily on the demands of his job to cover for him.

It helps that their Wanstead home, chosen for greenery and artisan bread shops, is too far from his Hampstead workplace and the A406 easily doubles an hour's journey, especially if he happens to be returning from somewhere other than school.

Drew usually abandons his X6 wherever he comes to a stop, but today he takes his time, slowly circling the little pampasgrass roundabout so the gravel doesn't spray wildly across the sprawling driveway, parking next to his wife's Mercedes. He strides through the double front doors, making an immediate left into the dining room. The shutters are already closed against the dark, making the chandelier sparkle softly, even though it has been rejected in preference to tall, thick candles spaced precisely along the length of the table like an Orthodox Church service.

Natasha and Elena are halfway through their first course, at opposite ends of the table. There is no conversation between them, the only noise the chink of cutlery against china and the soft notes of Prokofiev drifting from the concealed speakers.

'So sorry I'm late, darling, the meeting went on for hours.' Drew moves to kiss his wife's unyielding cheek first, before doing the same to his daughter. Elena at least bothers to tilt her face to accept his greeting.

Natasha takes a tiny sip of blood-red wine, watching him skirt around to an empty seat in the middle. The housekeeper appears on cue, Drew's plate warm with baked garlicky mushrooms and home-made sourdough. He smiles his thanks and pours more wine, including Elena without needing her glared demand.

'How was your day?' he asks his daughter.

'Boring,' she pronounces, dragging out the single word in a way that makes her sound too young for her eighteen years. 'Can I spend the whole summer in Russia this year? I could stay till I start uni.'

'I was thinking a couple of weeks in the Maldives.'

'Mama.' Elena shoots a look at her mother.

'She'll be fine in Moskva,' Natasha murmurs, her accent lightened by her years in England. 'We have plenty of staff to look after her.'

It isn't the caregiving that bothers Drew. Moscow is danger and adrenaline and uncertainty, beckoning Elena into its alluring clutches, just as it had once done to him. He knows it well; he had been easily seduced in the early years of his marriage. Every holiday spent in the glittering properties of Natasha's family, as untouchable as his in-laws, before he had grown tired of being a pet in a gilded cage and his old desires had risen again.

'We'll see,' he says, concentrating on his food.

Natasha rises to relight a candle blown out by his movements around the table. She carries herself at attention, neat feet barely seeming to kiss the floor, her aristocratic features as expressionless as they are beautiful. Icy blue Slavic blood courses through her veins, as much in her character as her upbringing. She will make the perfect MP's wife; she understands discretion is as important as confrontation, lessons learned from her golden cradle bought by bloodshed.

'I would prefer the Seychelles,' she says, the voice that had once entranced him still lower and deeper than her appearance suggests. A voice that will not be ignored.

Drew doesn't bother to argue. One sweep of Natasha's Prussian eyes is enough.

'Can I go to the Black Sea as well?' Elena slips effortlessly into her second tongue to address her mother.

'We'll arrange it, sweetheart. Sochi or Anapa?'

Drew grits his teeth. His is an analytical, scientific mind: he has never found fluency in the Russian language, able to handle only the basics even after all these years, and his ignorance is regularly exploited.

'Speak English!' he thunders.

Identical scornful gazes flash at him before the conversation continues at even greater speed.

'For God's sake!' He slams his closed fist on to the table, making the crockery rattle alarmingly. Silence falls, broken only by the gentle waves of piano.

'Apologies, darling.' Natasha's red lips curve. 'Would you like more wine?'

He nods curtly and is immediately served, the wine matching the colour of his wife's long, immaculate fingernails.

'Tell us about your day,' Natasha invites, returning to her seat and placing her cutlery neatly together, food barely touched.

'You don't want to hear about it.'

Natasha does not deny it.

'The new French teacher is terrible,' Elena declares, drinking her wine too fast, as usual. 'No one understands a word she says.'

'Would that be because she's actually French?' says Drew. 'You're still a pupil, Ele, not on the school board.'

Elena rolls her eyes. 'What's with you tonight? You're in a stinking mood.'

'Perhaps it would be nice to come home to enjoy a relaxing conversation with my family.'

'We're talking, aren't we?'

Drew looks up sharply as his wife rings the bell for the main course, hurriedly forking the rest of the mushrooms into his mouth before the plate is removed, but Elena has already cast her eyes down, heaving a sigh as beef stroganoff replaces the starter. Neither parent gives her any attention, focusing on each other instead. Natasha raises her glass in a silent toast, her head tilted towards Drew, a reminder of the deal that is their marriage. A reminder that, without her, none of this privileged life would be possible.

Drew ignores her and pours again, draining what little remains of the bottle.

25

Chapter Four

Before she can change her mind, Jenna checks the WhatsApp group for signs of life. The Unholy Trinity, three friends united by their boarding-school days. The group used to have a different name, when there were four of them, but one of them is now lost forever.

Ava Vaughan has been Jenna's best friend since the mid-nineties, along with Seb Byron, a fellow inmate in their education gaol who left for Broadway and drifted out of contact, until the death of their friend drew them back to the safety of each other.

Olivia Seabrook's life had ended in such an un-Olivia-like way, quietly slipping away, alone in her flat, the needle still in her vein. A deliberate, massive overdose had ended her suffering.

The tabloids and the coroner had spoken of her addictions, of her hedonistic lifestyle, of her mental health sections and unstable behaviour. They never portrayed *Olivia*, how she lit up every room she entered, her fierce mind and her generous soul, who could make anyone smile with one flash of her impish grin. The person had been overshadowed by her demons, her true self denied by the reports and the headlines. The person who had tried so hard to keep Jenna safe but had spent the rest of her days consumed by her own guilt.

Hugo has never been part of the group chat. He insists he doesn't like to cling to the past, and she can't blame him. He had never liked Olivia, and Ava and Seb actively avoid him. It is easier for them to deny his existence.

The Trinity are far from their adolescent selves now, in their carefully polished London lives, and they take care not to speak of the bad old days when they meet weekly for lunch, wine, cocktails or all three.

You two free after work?

Unusually, a reply pings almost immediately.

Ava: Name the place. Mario's?

Somewhere more private.

Sounds ominous, what we done?

It's the anniversary today. Olivia's been gone for a whole year.

This time, the response takes longer, the 'typing' notification remaining for several minutes.

I didn't forget.

We should mark it. She deserves that much.

Another extended pause.

Come to mine.

Jenna counts the ticks of her office clock until the hands show five o'clock, typing then deleting property details, inputting wrong amounts into spreadsheets. She leaves without saying goodbye, striding past the juniors' desks as if on emergency business, knowing they won't question her.

Seb opens the door to Ava's Camden warehouse apartment.

'Hi, gorgeous.' He envelops her in a hug. Like Zach, he towers above her, tinted eyebrows as perfect as his dewy skin and cosmetic dentistry. He wears a delicate watch and a fine neck chain that makes the ropey muscles of his forearms and throat look even more defined. Appearance-wise, the years since school have been kind to him.

He ushers her into the incense-heavy living room, taking her coat, even though she knows perfectly well where the hooks are. Iggy Pop plays quietly in the background and bowls of wasabi peas and cashew nuts are artfully arranged on the low coffee table.

Ava appears, her long, sinuous body enveloped in a silk Japanese kimono, raven hair glistening from the shower. She has been a constant in Jenna's life for so many years, a force to be reckoned with even as a teenager, and one of the only people who has breached Jenna's defensive walls. Ava was there before they were built.

Jenna accepts a kiss of greeting without flinching, allowing herself to be steered to the sofa. 'Is Adeline here? I saw a school picture of her in the newspaper.'

'Cute shot of her, wasn't it?' Ava smiles at her daughter's first glimpse of fame. 'She's still at the childminder's. I'll tell her you saw the article.'

Ava wages a constant battle with childcare while her husband, Simon, swans around the Far East for his shipping company. Simon is very good looking, very wealthy, and uncompromising in every way. He barely knows his four-year-old daughter and is equally ignorant that his wife's best friend is fully aware of the pre-nup Ava signed, swearing the marriage would be child free. Adeline had been a shock arrival, Jenna stepping in as birthing partner when Simon's flight from Hong Kong had, apparently, been delayed.

Jenna privately thinks their separate lives suit the couple. Ava can raise her daughter the way she wants, and Simon can pretend to be single in Macanese casinos.

'You didn't tell me Drew Merchant is the head of her school.'

Ava looks mystified. 'We've never discussed her school.' Confusion slows her words. 'You've never shown any interest. It's a small world, I'll give you that, but it honestly never occurred to me to tell you Drew is the head. Besides, he's always up at the senior school. I don't think he ever goes near pre-prep, except for Speech Day.'

'Is Adeline OK?' The question bursts out before Jenna can form it adequately to sound casual.

A crease forms between Ava's eyebrows. 'Why wouldn't she be?'

'Is she happy? At school?'

'As happy as Adeline ever is. Why are you asking? What's wrong?'

Jenna holds her breath for a brief moment, fighting to stem the flood of fears rushing through her. 'She just looked so serious,' she says weakly.

Ava's shoulders visibly relax. 'Doesn't she always! Never been a smiler, has she?' She reties her kimono, tutting at the clock. 'I need to nip in to check on the Lyric before she's dropped off. She's started playing up whenever she comes with me.'

Ava's time is in high demand throughout the West End, and she effortlessly holds court as she touts the talents of her ever-expanding stable of actors, voice artists and directors. She also, as a favour, represents Sebastian Byron, when he controls his sertraline doses enough to brave a studio. So far, Seb has provided voiceovers for breakfast cereals, a talking air freshener, a Dalmatian and a

Bavarian beer, though rumour has it he's in the running for a role in the latest Disney offering.

'Do we need cocktails?' Seb asks Ava as he returns to the room.

At her nod he bustles off, pleased to have something to do, comfortable enough in Ava's home to take over her kitchen. He spends more time here than he does at his own flat. He feels safe here, the fears and anxieties that dominate his life left at the door.

Ava regards Jenna as she lights another ever-present cigarette, her mood sobering. 'Something's bothering you. You're all jittery. Is it because of the anniversary? It's still hard, isn't it, without her.'

Seb returns, precariously clutching three Martini glasses and an extra tumbler of his usual single-malt chaser, depositing them carefully on the coffee table. 'I can't believe it's been a year already.'

'It feels like it happened last week.' Jenna focuses on the drinks, unable to look at her friends. Her hand shakes as she picks up her martini. 'I miss her. I wish we'd been able to help her.'

'It had gone too far for that,' Ava murmurs.

'It wasn't her fault. She blamed herself but it was all of us, not just her. We should have found a way to make her understand that.'

'She wouldn't have listened, even if we had,' Seb says softly. 'She wasn't really Olivia any more. We'd already lost her to the drugs and the breakdowns.'

They fall quiet for a long moment, considering the demons that had stolen their friend.

'To Olivia,' Ava says, raising her glass, the wobble noticeable in her voice.

'To Olivia,' the other two intone, in unison.

Jenna takes a large mouthful of her drink, almost choking at the strength. Seb doesn't believe in using measures. They sit in reflective silence, lost in their own thoughts and memories, the atmosphere growing still and heavy. Tears prick at Jenna's eyes, and it feels as though a chasm has opened inside her again, a missing piece now lost forever.

She takes a deep breath, blinking hard, bracing herself.

'Have you read about Halewood House in the papers?' she asks.

Ava raises one eyebrow at the sudden sound of Jenna's voice in the quiet room. 'What about it?'

'A journalist has written an exposé.' The closing line still echoes in her head: Amy Donald urging other female ex-pupils to stand up to those who had wronged them. To show a united front of defiance. 'You know it's been closed down?'

Silence. Seb and Ava study the contents of their glasses as if fascinated by the clear liquid, their faces tensing.

'I've been having dreams,' Jenna says, carefully precise. 'About school.'

Seb grimaces, dropping down beside her and draping an arm around her neck in a reassuring squeeze.

'No one wants Cell Block H rearing its ugly head.' Ava pinches the stem of her glass between finger and thumb as she sips the liquid dynamite without any reaction to how strong it is. Without asking, she reaches for Seb's whisky and takes a large mouthful before returning it. Seb smiles indulgently, turning the glass to avoid her lipstick stain.

Jenna forces her constricted lungs to take a deep breath. 'I dream I'm in my third-form room. In the middle of the night, someone comes in and tells me to be quiet.'

Seb and Ava's spines unconsciously straighten. Seb's face drains of colour as his eyes spark with some unreadable emotion, and he instinctively draws back against the opposite end of the sofa, wrapping one arm around his middle.

Ava grinds out her cigarette and lights a new one, even though the last was only half smoked, never looking away from Jenna as she does so.

'Jenna, we swore we'd never talk about all this again. We put it behind us, remember?' She speaks as if explaining to a young child, leaning forward over her knees.

Jenna ignores the rhetorical question. 'It's been happening since Olivia's funeral. I'm scared to go to sleep.'

'Have you tried sleeping pills?'

'Drugging myself doesn't stop them!' Jenna cries, making both her friends jump at the sudden increase in volume.

Seb spills what remains in his whisky glass, leaping up with a curse to blot ineffectively at the wet patch on the sofa cushion. He shoots off to the kitchen to get a cloth, hurrying back.

'Sorry, mention Cell Block H and my nerves are shot to bits,' he laughs weakly as he dabs a tea towel against the stain. 'Not good memories for any of us.'

Ava draws heavily on her cigarette, taking her time expelling the smoke from her lungs. 'I know this must be horrible for you, but being sleep deprived will be making it feel much worse.'

Jenna gulps the rest of her cocktail, hoping there will be another forthcoming. She will abandon the car in Ava's unused space. Ava's little hatchback rarely leaves its spot outside her office building.

Ava reaches across, squeezing her hand. 'I've got some diazepam. Why don't you take a few home with you? You'll feel better after some proper sleep.'

'Ava, this isn't going to get better.'

'Why not?'

The words have burst from Jenna's throat before she has a chance to think, to brace herself.

'Because we can't just keep pretending it didn't fucking happen.'

She closes her eyes. She can't bring herself to see Ava's expression, the wide eyes and flaring nostrils, the forehead crumpled despite her regular Botox.

'But we all agreed,' Seb whispers, as if fearing she will bolt like a frightened horse if he speaks at a normal volume.

'What's set it all off again?' Ava has forgotten about her smouldering cigarette and gives a cry as it burns the delicate skin between her fingers.

'Olivia, obviously!' Jenna's fingers find a scatter cushion and grip it as if it will protect her. 'I've spent half a lifetime blocking it out, leaving it behind me. I thought I'd managed to bury it, until Olivia died. Now I keep seeing the articles about Hale wood House and it's eating away at me all over again. Lando came home from a safeguarding talk, and it hit me – what if it happened to him? All the old fears started up.'

Seb grasps at his neck chain, worrying the links like rosary beads. 'How has Zach reacted?'

Jenna stares determinedly at the faint wisps of smoke rising from the incense sticks, counting her pounding pulse beats. 'I've never told him. None of it.'

'Not even about what happened to you?'

'How could I? Then everything else might have come out too. It was too much of a risk.'

All three are suddenly teenagers again, afraid and uncertain, terrified of their tangled web of secrets being exposed.

'Jesus, we were fucking idiots,' Seb declares, leaning forward to grasp both her hands in his.

'We didn't mean to cause such a mess.' Ava's eyes are shiny with tears. 'We were just kids – we thought we were going to make it better, not worse. We didn't set out to do something so awful.'

Jenna can't help but wonder if Ava is trying to justify their actions to them or to herself. That has always been her instinct – self-preservation – the polar opposite to Olivia.

'It makes you scared to trust anyone, doesn't it?' Seb says gently.

A sob rises in Jenna's throat, threatening to erupt, and she chokes as she tries to swallow it, coughing until her face burns from the effort. It gives her the chance to pull away from Seb's hands, unable to bear anyone's touch. 'Even now, I keep people at arm's length to feel safe. Even my own family.'

She is Jenna's oldest friend, the first person ever to accept her. Ava had made Jenna feel loved at a time when Jenna had been sure no one else gave a damn about her.

'I think you should tell Zach.'

'How can I? How can I tell him now, after all these years together? It was part of our vows – to never keep secrets from each other.' Yet another solemn promise she has broken.

'What good will telling him do, anyway?' Seb shakes his head too fast. 'It'll only lead to more questions.'

'It'll *stop* him asking questions,' Ava insists. 'I'm not saying tell him *everything*.'

'No.' Jenna stands too quickly and the room swims before her, black spots dancing across her line of vision. 'I can't. I can't do it.'

'But . . .'

'Ava,' Jenna practically snarls, 'I won't tell Zach anything about what happened at school.'

'I understand your reasons why—'

'No, you don't.'

'Then tell me!'

Jenna snatches up her coat with shaking hands. She needs to escape.

'Because if I do, I have to admit responsibility for what we did.'

Chapter Five

The narrow room was just big enough to contain a single bed, a rickety wardrobe, a chair, and a desk engraved with the names of previous inmates. She was three months into a five-year sentence of striped blazers, evening prep and daily chapel to absolve the sins that were committed behind closed doors.

She found her new environment unnerving, from the ghostly Brothers silently walking the grounds in their dark brown habits to the feverish classrooms and intense teaching. The Order was hailed by the Church for its academic pursuits, and the devout, disciplined men wanted to pass their learning on to their students despite the gulfs that existed between them.

The knowledge that she was supposed to be grateful to be here, in this small, highly selective school desired above all others by religious families up and down the country, made her insides churn. She had long since accepted she didn't believe in God. It made her surroundings hard to stomach.

She hadn't expected a single room — they were traditionally reserved for sixth-formers — but boys dominated the school population and the four-bed dorms were already occupied. Seeing it for the first time, two weeks previously, she had been reminded of a cell, not helped by the tiny window attic rooms always had. By necessity, the girls had been banished to the top floor, their arrival causing logistical issues as much as the traditional ones.

She had been left to haul her luggage up the stairs alone, her parents driving away with barely a backwards glance. An older boy had appeared just in time to save Jenna's belongings from harm, effortlessly sweeping the heavy cases from her shaking hands.

'Let me,' he had said with an easy smile when she attempted to help but only succeeded in getting in his way. 'My name's Drew. I'm a lower-sixth prefect.'

Such was his beauty that she had stumbled embarrassingly on the top step as she tried to hurry ahead to open the door he directed her to, but Drew had just given her a reassuring wink and offered a large hand to help her up, unlocking the door for her. His presence in the tiny room had somehow made it brighter, almost welcoming.

'Can you show me where the dining room is?' she had dared to ask, terrified of getting lost on her way to the welcome tea and biscuits promised in the information pack that she was clutching in sweaty fingers.

'Sure, I've got rugby practice, but they'll let the captain be a few minutes late.' Drew had winked at Jenna again.

He had pointed to the cross attached to the wall above her bed.

'You a believer?'

'No. Are you?'

He huffed a laugh. 'The only believers around here wear habits. Come on, have your map ready. This place is a warren, unless you've got God to guide you.'

The tour had been whistle-stop and the tea and biscuits mortifying, as she tried to find something to say to the small number of girls whose

37

educational path had been diverted as Halewood House expanded its intake to both genders for the first time. Most, like Jenna, were fresh from prep school, though a handful had arrived for sixth form. A couple were fourth-formers, noticeable as the only ones to have left their previous schools without having had a natural break in their education. They had already paired up, and their confident laughter had drawn Jenna's gaze as they wolfed biscuits and whispered in one another's ears.

She hadn't had the courage to say hello to them, even though she had wanted to. A cocky lower-sixth boy had tried to engage her in conversation, but she hadn't known how to respond to his cutting humour and it had been a relief when he had finally been dragged away by a laughing Drew.

Safely back in her room, she had been grateful for the solitude. Only days later, the isolation would come to terrify her.

The door handle creaked, in need of oil, clicking quietly as it closed. The dark shadow stood at the end of her bed, completely still. The moonlight at his back ensured that his face remained in shadow. She always slept with the curtains open, afraid of the dark but too embarrassed to submit to a night light.

The clear night sky provided enough light for her to see firm shoulders and long legs, a suggestion of a chiselled jaw and floppy hair. The scent of a recently smoked cigarette mixed with citrus deodorant and the faintest whiff of chlorine, at odds with the peaty tang of whisky. She nearly screamed as his featureless face loomed over her, a flattened, fleshless face that couldn't possibly be human, surrounded by wrinkled folds of white skin.

It was then she realised that he was wearing a fencing mask, the mesh dark enough to disguise him, although she could see the feverish gleam of his eyes through the material.

The moonlight reflected off something on his hand as he raised it to adjust the mask. A signet ring on his little finger. A small gold square, intricately engraved, surrounding a black stone. A beautiful work of crafts-manship, in any other circumstance.

She focused her gaze on it; anything to avoid looking at the terrifying void hiding his face.

She watched the ring.

Chapter Six

Jenna only realises she has cried out when Zach jerks upright. His eyes are wide, the tendons in his neck almost bursting from beneath his skin as he automatically reaches for her.

She opens her mouth to speak, but he wraps his arms around her before she can find the words to deny or dismiss, drawing her into the safety of his warm body. His hands envelop hers, squeezing gently, but all she can focus on is trying to free herself from him.

She can't bear the unintentional invasion of her personal space. Her mind screams, ordering her to protect herself, even from a man who will never be a threat to her.

'Tell me,' he urges.

Jenna's breath rasps in her throat, incoherent thoughts screaming inside her head. Abruptly, she recognises she is going to be sick. She shoves Zach aside as she scrambles for the bathroom, only just making it in time. Her stomach writhes and clenches, the spasms continuing into dry heaves that seem to last for ever. She barely feels the hand rubbing comforting circles between her shoulder blades, but she still jumps at his proximity.

'You're OK,' Zach whispers. His arms close around her again, lifting her to her feet and guiding her to the sink, and she doesn't have the strength to resist. He sponges her clean as if she were a baby, even putting the toothpaste on her brush for her.

He almost carries her back to their bedroom, laying her down as if she is the most delicate china, drawing the covers over her shivering body. Her instinct is to push him away, but she somehow manages to control the kneejerk reaction.

'You were crying out, begging someone not to hurt you. You kept telling them to stop.' Zach's face is pale, his lips compressed. 'Jenna, talk to me. Has something happened? A client?'

His expression telegraphs his thought process, imagining her with a lone male, viewing an empty house.

Jenna shakes her head frantically. She can't focus, can't get her thoughts under control.

'Go back to sleep, Zach.'

'Please, love, don't shut me out. I know something's wrong.'

'I don't want to talk any more. Tomorrow, maybe.' She squeezes her eyes shut against the ache in her chest, waiting for him to admit defeat. She needs time to rebuild her walls, strengthen her defences.

He stays still for what feels like for ever, refusing to give up on her, just as he always does, but eventually he has no choice. He moves around to his side and she hears his sigh as he lies down. Her heart wants to reach out to him, an apologetic touch without needing words, like any normal couple, but she can't.

Her brain won't let her bridge the gap.

The moment she hears Zach step into the shower Jenna flies out of bed. She had managed to convince him she was deeply asleep when he tried to gently nudge her awake, and now she has to escape before he emerges from the bathroom to ask questions she dare not answer.

Lando will already be at morning swimming training. He has recently announced he will take the Tube rather than suffer the indignity of being dropped off, and he doesn't bother to say goodbye before he leaves. His parents have been easily swayed by the lure of precious extra sleep.

Downstairs, she hurries to gather her belongings, whispering useless apologies to Loki when he skitters behind her, pleading for his breakfast. She leaves a note for Zach next to the kettle, telling him she will collect Lando from swimming.

The schedule, usually followed to the letter, says it is Zach's day to drop him at school, but Jenna needs a reason to leave the house early. Collection remains a necessary chore; their son can no longer be trusted to take himself to school, recently evidenced by a sudden scattering of unauthorised absences gravely reported by his form tutor.

Zach always does the mornings after swimming training. His pride in Lando's sporting prowess beaming from every pore, Zach is eager to watch the last minutes of the session and hear his son's times. Lando much prefers Zach's pick-up days, discussing super-heroes with his father and walking Loki on the Heath before they set off for school, rather than the sleepy silence of Jenna's.

Safely in her car, she gulps in deep breaths, her back teeth finally unclenching. Her mobile pings.

Zach: *Why are you collecting Lando?*

She considers not replying until she reaches the office, claiming she hadn't noticed the message, but if she doesn't give him a reason for her early departure it will only fuel his suspicions.

Felt guilty. Never seen where he swims.

Out of the blue . . .

The implication stings. She furiously types several replies, deleting each one, before switching the engine on and putting the car in gear. It is only then that she remembers she has no idea where the pool is. She is forced to ask Zach for the postcode.

Are you OK? Followed instantly by: *I know you're not.*

I'm fine. Sorry for snapping last night.

Talk more about it this eve?

See what time I get home. Remember Loki needs worming.

Sure you'll be all right today? He isn't distracted by the boring domesticity, as she had hoped.

Sure.

It's easy to lie via text.

Love you.

She stares at the last message for several minutes, sees he is still online, waiting for her response. She sends him a kiss emoji.

How much easier her life would be if she could communicate solely in emojis instead of having to force painful attempts at the real emotions other people can show with such ease.

The pool's location turns out to be Hampstead, in the grounds of a public school. It sits at the very edge of the school's land, with a separate driveway, but the grand Georgian buildings atop the hill boast their glory above the more modern building.

Jenna pays little attention to her surroundings as she parks. She doesn't know the protocol and it discomfits her. Does she wait out here for the kids to emerge or does she have to make her presence known to prevent Lando camping out in the changing rooms?

He has been part of this squad for over three months, and this is the first time Jenna has collected him from morning training. She chooses not to dwell on that, tells herself it's just the way scheduling has demanded, with her starting work earlier than Zach.

She waits fifteen minutes, watching athletic, long-limbed teenagers spilling down the front steps in identical tracksuits, kitbags thrown over their strong shoulders, before her patience runs out and she strides for the door.

The moist air and smell of chlorine assault her as she steps inside. The narrow corridor is deserted, but the chlorine gets stronger as she walks down it, guiding her to the frosted glass door at the far end. The light changes, becoming fluid from the reflection of the water gently lapping at the edges of the pool, and sounds become amplified, echoing off the tiled surfaces.

Lando stands by the diving blocks, one foot resting on the rail. Clad only in his jammers, the skin-tight swimming shorts running from waist to knee, his defined, lean physique makes him look so much older than his thirteen years. He grasps at the towel thrown casually around his neck, laughing at something a man in shorts and a white polo shirt says. Jenna can't remember the last time he laughed with her.

'Lando, you're going to be late,' she calls when he doesn't notice, or refuses to acknowledge, her presence.

He spins round, the smile falling from his face. He hadn't known she was there.

'What are you doing here?' His voice is hard.

'Making sure you don't get another detention for being late,' she fires back before she can stop her instinctive response to his tone.

'Jenna?' the man asks. 'Jenna Alcott?'

Lando's brow creases. 'You know her?'

The man steps past Lando, moving closer to Jenna.

'Drew,' she breathes.

A smile softens his features. 'I had no idea Lando was your son. The surname.'

'Are you coaching him? I thought you were a headmaster?'

'This is my school, but I'm the director for the London regional youth squad.' Another smile. 'I could never bring myself to walk away from swimming.'

'You made it to the Olympics,' she remembers.

'And so will Lando if he keeps this up.' Drew throws a smile over his shoulder and Lando visibly blushes at the praise. 'I don't have the time to make every session, but I'm here a couple of times a week and Lando always proves himself to be the standout in his age group.'

Lando ducks his head, avoiding looking at his mother. Jenna recognises, too late, that she should have praised him too, acknowledged his achievement, but the moment has already passed.

'Go and get changed,' Drew tells him. 'You don't want to be late for school.'

Lando leaves without argument, his lips quirking as Drew thumps him lightly on the shoulder.

Drew shakes his head once he and Jenna are alone. 'I can't believe he's yours – so unexpected.'

'Looks nothing like me, does he?'

'Double of his father. Zach, isn't it? He always collects him in the mornings. How long have you been married?'

'Too long. We met at university.'

'I can hardly think about how many years it's been. You never came to any of the school reunions.'

Jenna's muscles clench. 'No,' she forces out, trying to sound casually dismissive and certain she is failing.

'What do you do now?'

'Hugo Addison started his own estate agency; I'm his second-in-command. And you're Britain's favourite headteacher, so I read.'

'Don't believe everything you read, though it's handy to have this at my disposal.' He indicates around him before his attention is drawn to his wristwatch. 'I'm going to be late myself.'

Jenna is already moving towards the door. 'It was nice to see you again.'

'We've hardly had any time to catch up.' He checks his watch again as if it will reveal his full schedule. 'Meet me for a drink. It's been so long. After work?'

She is trying to form a rational excuse when he reaches into his polo-shirt pocket and produces a business card, his details embossed on thick, expensive paper.

'I'll be finished by five. You live in Islington, Lando said? I'll come to you. Queen's Head?'

Almost before she knew it, Jenna has accepted the card and nodded her agreement, and Drew has given her a peck on the cheek and departed.

He was exactly as he had been at school, entirely assured that he would get his own way.

Chapter Seven

Drew is already waiting by the time Jenna walks into the familiar pub. He stands with a smile, pulling out her chair for her before settling himself on the other side of the small table.

'I ordered a bottle. Hope that's OK with you?' He shows her the label for approval before he pours.

The wine is a deep, rich red that uncomfortably reminds Jenna of blood. Her fingers unconsciously stroke her sleeve, tracing the faint paths of the scars beneath her clothes.

'Cheers.' Drew reaches to tap his glass against hers. 'I'm glad you agreed to meet me. I wasn't sure you'd want to.'

Jenna drinks too quickly, glancing around her to focus on anything but him. She wonders how much he remembers of that night all those years ago and what suspicions he might have had. He had never voiced them at the time, but she had been convinced he knew more than he said.

The paranoia is biting hard and she is struggling to silence its sly whispers.

His eyes sweep over her, appraising. 'You look amazing. You've changed so much since school.'

Despite herself, she is flattered to be complimented by this attractive man who is catching admiring glances from bar staff and customers.

'School was a long time ago.' She searches for a change of conversation. 'Do you have kids?'

'Only one, my daughter Elena. She's just turned eighteen; she'll be going to UCL in September if she stops buggering about and gets her grades. I married a Russian, Natasha. Oligarch family.' His lips tighten, barely perceptible. 'I guess she could be described as high maintenance.'

'Zach's the opposite, so laidback he barely reacts to anything.'

'Lando thinks a lot of him.'

'Has Lando told you that?'

'Sure, we chat whenever I make it to training. He's a great kid, got a bright future ahead of him.'

She can't bring herself to ask if Lando has ever mentioned his mother. She knows the answer. 'Lando's very close to his father.'

'Is that why Zach always collects him instead of you?'

Jenna doesn't like this casual analysis of her family, the threat it poses. 'Zach's schedule is more flexible than mine.'

'Yes, I imagine estate-agency life must be demanding. How is Hugo these days? Poor guy had it rough. I was always surprised he stayed on at Halewood House, after everything.'

Jenna takes too big a mouthful of wine and nearly chokes. She takes her time swallowing bit by bit. 'He's doing okay. Addison has been very successful in the last few years.'

'Did you always stay in touch?'

'No, not at all. I suppose you could say he headhunted me when he found out I was in his line of work.'

'How flattering.' Drew grins. 'And what about the others?

Ava, Seb, Olivia? I see Ava occasionally. Her daughter's in pre-prep here.'

Olivia's name hits like a punch to Jenna's sternum and she nearly gasps at the power of the blow. 'You don't know?'

'Know what?'

'Olivia died. It was her first anniversary this week.'

'Oh God.' He squeezes his eyes shut momentarily. 'I'm so sorry, I had no idea. What happened?'

Jenna reaches for the wine, but her hand is shaking too much to pour. Drew takes it gently from her and tops up her glass before his own. The bottle is already empty and he signals for another one to be brought.

'I can't talk about it. None of us can. It broke us. I haven't slept properly since she died. Seb came back to London for the funeral and had a breakdown.' She gasps a laugh, shaking her head. 'Ava takes enough anti-depressants to cheer up Eeyore. It's all such a mess.'

'Christ, that sounds awful. Is there anything I can do?'

'Not unless you can turn back time.' And not just the last year, she thinks. Much longer than that. Turn back two decades and stop us being so bloody stupid.

Drew takes a slow sip of his wine. 'I still think about that night at school, you know. Waking up to all that panic. Police and paramedics everywhere.'

'It was horrible.'

'Were you scared?'

Jenna doesn't like the way he asks the question. 'Why would I have been scared?'

'Not just you. Ava, Olivia, even Seb. I remember you all looking terrified.'

Her mind races. Drew can't know for sure. No one ever had any proof of their sins. 'We were still high from the night before, that's all. Everyone was paranoid, not just us. Especially when the rooms started getting searched.'

Drew gives a conspiratorial smile. 'I had to rush and hide my own stash.'

She smiles back, even though she feels no humour, relieved that his focus seems to have shifted. 'I could do with some of the old gear now. I can't remember the last time I felt relaxed.'

'Lando picks up on your stress, you know.'

Jenna's barriers immediately react to the insinuation, closing down sharply. 'He doesn't notice.'

'That's not what he says.'

'I'm glad he can talk to a stranger when he can't talk to his mother,' Jenna snaps.

'Maybe he finds it easier to speak to someone who isn't directly involved,' Drew suggests, his voice gentle. 'A lot of kids do.'

Jenna grits her teeth. 'If you say so.'

'I didn't mean to upset you. Teenagers are difficult at the best of times, let alone when you're struggling. Let's talk about something else.'

The silence as both try to think of an alternative topic goes on too long for comfort.

'How long have you been in education?' Jenna blurts out, finding her wine glass empty again.

'Since I finished my masters, so over twenty years. I'd hoped my swimming career would last longer, but it didn't work out.'

'Why not?'

'Too many injuries. My own fault. I should've stopped skiing, but I loved the adrenaline too much. I wasn't selected for the swimming Worlds and the sponsors started dropping off. I had to let it go.'

He lightly catches hold of her hand and guides her fingers to his left shoulder, moving them along the length of his clavicle. 'This has caused me problems for years. Fractured it in two places on a black run, showing off.'

She touches the misshapen fissure in the smooth bone before she jerks away, pulling her hand free and using it to manically sweep invisible hair from her eyes, trying to conceal her jerky movements.

'Sorry,' she mumbles when she sees the confusion in his expression. She imagines few women pull away from him. 'I'm not great with being touched.'

He raises his palms. 'Won't happen again . . . unless you want it to.'

From nowhere, a jolt of electricity runs through Jenna. His eyes are deep and warm, pools of rich, liquid chocolate that draw her helplessly to them. He is dangerously attractive, and he knows it.

The wine is beginning to buzz, and when Drew pours again, draining the second bottle, Jenna doesn't hesitate to drink deeply. He holds eye contact as he sips what must be only his second glass. No wonder she is feeling distinctly tipsy.

'Do you find you and Zach lead mostly separate lives?' he asks softly. 'My wife and I barely spend any time in each other's company. I suppose all marriages drift apart when you're together for so long, once the kids have grown up and don't need us as much. You lose that connection, don't you?'

Jenna nods, captivated by his understanding of her marriage. If she had thought about it, she would have imagined his relationship to be passionate, intense, two alpha personalities clashing and making up with equal fervour. It makes her feel just slightly better to know she and Zach aren't the only ones who are merely coexisting.

She knows the wine is the reason she doesn't pull away when Drew reaches across the table and rests his large palm on top of her knuckles.

'I have a little place my wife doesn't visit. Would you like to come for a drink there?'

Her brain screams at her to say no, to insist she has to get home, back to her family.

Her mouth says yes.

They drive west in Drew's car, to the 'little place' that turns out to not be quite as modest as it sounded.

Their teeth clash as their first tentative kiss of exploration turns feral within moments. For a heartbeat, Jenna freezes, sweat breaking out under her arms as he grips her hair too tightly. Trapped, she lashes out, backing away with fast, jerky movements the moment he releases her.

'What's wrong?' Hurt and confusion crease Drew's handsome brow. 'What did I do?'

Jenna grips the back of a chair, fighting for breath. She is shaking so badly even her lips are quivering. Her pulse roars in her ears.

'Jenna?' He moves towards her, slow and careful, reaching out his hand.

'I'm sorry,' she gasps. 'I've never done anything like this before.'

She lets him take her hand and draw her against his strong chest. He strokes her back with long, tender caresses and, despite herself, her rigid muscles begin to relax. She doesn't have to pretend here. She is free to be damaged and antagonistic and she needn't apologise for it, because they are both here for one thing and they don't require emotions for that.

'We've got as much time as you need,' he murmurs, thoughtful without being suffocating. 'Come on.'

Drew leads her through to the en suite bathroom, filling a sunken jacuzzi she automatically labels 'feature' in her professional mind. When it is hot and bubbling, he undresses her, slowly peeling away her clothes, dropping featherlike kisses that make her squirm with pleasure in spite of herself. They sink beneath the surface together and he holds her like a newborn, lathering soap over her limbs and torso with strong, sure hands until she is melting under his touch.

The sex is frantic, a battle for dominance, rapid rhythm and ragged breaths and feral sounds. She doesn't climax but lets him think she did. Afterwards, she lies in his arms, lulled by the gentle pummelling of the jets and the scent of pomegranates, until he finally rises with a reluctant groan and lifts her effortlessly from the tub.

He wraps her in a soft bath sheet, patting her skin dry as his lips graze her ear. She allows him the contact, no tension, because this is purely physical, with none of the intimacy that ignites her deepest fears. It doesn't threaten her. She is in control, able to walk away whenever she wants, a control she can't have in her own world.

In the bedroom, they skirt about each other, each preparing to return to their lives. Jenna re-pins her hair, checking it hasn't got wet, assessing her skin for any incriminating marks. Drew dresses more methodically as she perches on the edge of the mattress to try to drag her tights back on under her pencil skirt.

'I could take your number,' he says softly, 'if you might like to do this again.'

He holds out his phone and, although she hesitates, the delicious ache he has left behind convinces her to type in the digits.

She can't help but watch him as he carefully knots his tie, his long fingers sure and nimble with the silk. He slides on his jewellery, and she idly notes the understated elegance of his watch, wedding ring, cufflinks as she stands to wrestle her tights up. He turns to embrace her, stroking her hair from her face, the band of his ring cool against her flushed skin.

'I feel bad for wearing my wedding ring,' she murmurs.

He gives a wry shrug. 'I usually remember to leave mine in the car.'

She pretends that this didn't confirm that he brought other women here. 'Yours is beautiful. Did you get it in Russia?'

'No, it was handmade in London.'

She traces the ornate engraving with her little finger. Abruptly, her heart begins to pound and the hairs stand up on her arms, goosebumps springing to the surface as a chill sweeps over her. A steel band clamps around her lungs, making deep breaths impossible. Nausea swells from her stomach, rising in her throat.

This isn't the first time she has seen this signet ring.

She recognises it. She remembers.

But it can't be. It isn't possible, she tries to tell her brain as it kicks into fight-or-flight mode, emotions shutting down as it prepares to protect her.

She has to leave.

She almost slips in her stockinged feet as she rushes for the kitchen, scrabbling to gather her coat and bag, spilling half the contents in her haste. With a sharp cry, she drops to her knees, feverishly grabbing for lipstick, keys and loose change.

'What is it?' Drew follows her, crouching down to try to help gather the scattered items, his lips pursed in consternation as her fevered hands bat his away, unable to tolerate his touch.

'I've . . . just realised something.' She is about to be sick, all over the pristine floor. She can't stay here a moment longer. 'I've got to go.'

'Tell me what's wrong,' he pleads.

'I've got to go!' she screams, stumbling upright.

She runs down the hallway, fingers slipping on the lock, and when she slams the door shut behind her she has to grab the wall to remain standing, her breath coming in desperate gasps. At the kerb, she doubles over, dry heaving into a gutter that smells of cigarette butts and the previous night's takeaway offerings.

Passers-by stare determinedly ahead, refusing to acknowledge the spectacle.

Jenna closes her front door silently as if trying not to disturb her demons, desperate not to draw attention to herself in her own home. She is whispering to herself, trying to summon explanations, justifications, but the panic retains its choking grip, and she is unable to count herself to calm.

The house is empty. Zach will have taken Lando out to eat rather than cook. The surfaces are cluttered with the remnants of their breakfast and she falls upon the distraction activity, busying herself dealing with the mess in a manic rush. She is on autopilot, robotically going about her usual chores, her brain still too shocked to summon emotion or rational thought, and she takes comfort in the familiar routine.

Untidiness makes her fizz with unease, just as it has since her earliest childhood. She can still hear her mother's acid tongue, blaming Jenna for a mess she hadn't made.

She seizes a cloth, wiping down the worktops with small, fast strokes. This is her penance for her overwhelming need for control, her refusal to employ a cleaner and let a stranger into her home. Lando's sandwich for tomorrow is constructed like an architecture task, even spreading of the butter and mayonnaise, aligned slices of smoked ham and carved Cheddar, as if she can make up for her myriad faults as a wife and mother with food.

Again, the honed knife makes its quiet appeal and she has to place it out of reach. With the immediate danger removed, she calms, her pulse slowing, her breathing gradually settling to a steadier rate.

Turning up the volume of Radio 2, she eyes the blank screen of her phone, no longer capable of decisive action. She opens the Google app, but it is several minutes before she can summon the courage to type Drew's full name.

A professional headshot pops up, immediately recognisable, but she doesn't need to see him as he is now. She scrolls hurriedly, turning back the years. She eventually finds him as a broad-shouldered teenager sliding across the try line, triumphant shout captured by a newspaper photographer twenty-five years previously.

After that, it doesn't take much effort to uncover what she needs. A photo of four boys in blazers and grey trousers, identically posed, each with one hand on his neighbour's shoulder. Forelocks flop over insolent eyes as they gaze at the camera, daring it to challenge them. At their feet, a propped sign declares them to be the fifth-form Fives team. Drew is in the middle, chin slightly raised and full lips pursed, a sixteen-year-old Adonis.

In an act of self-flagellation, she flicks between the headshot and the old photo. Drew has aged well. His hair is shorter but flecked with only a few glimpses of silver that suit him. The determined jawline remains firm and the dark eyes gaze steadily at the camera with what could have been amusement or impudence or, mostly likely, both. He is still as devastatingly attractive now as he was the first day she met him on the stairs of Raleigh House.

Jenna pinches her fingers over the old photo, zooming in to his hand atop the adjacent boy's slim shoulder, a touch that looks almost proprietorial. The signet ring on his finger blurs with the resolution, but it is enough to see the black stone set into the gold.

The shadow has finally become flesh and blood and knowing it was him brings only more sickening disbelief.

They got it wrong. All those years ago, they got it so badly wrong.

The sound of Zach, Lando and Loki crashing through the front door without a care in the world startles her badly. She drops the phone, wincing as it bounces off the flagstones.

She hears Lando thump upstairs as Zach comes to see what the noise was.

'What's wrong?' Zach stoops to retrieve the phone at the same time as she does and Jenna flinches away from him touching her.

'You made me jump,' she snarls, snatching the handset from him. 'Can't you just come in quietly like a normal person?'

Zach shrinks away from her ire, crouching to hug Loki to him. 'Are you OK?'

She doesn't think anything will ever be OK again, not after the terrible understanding that has now dawned upon her.

'I wish you could tell me,' Zach says sadly as he straightens up, skirting around her to make tea. 'I know something's happened. I know you too well, love, whether you like it or not.'

Jenna squeezes her eyes closed, clenches her fists. She isn't strong enough for this, not at this moment. Her walls are crumbling and she doesn't have the capability to shore them up.

'Please, Zach.' The plea comes out as a whimper.

The next moment, he is holding her with infinite care, as if she is made precious porcelain, and he is so safe and warm that she can't prevent the shock from spilling out as her brain's limbic system floods her with emotions she doesn't want.

'Something did happen,' she mumbles, her face buried in his chest as much to muffle her words as to hide her face. 'But not recently. Years ago. At school.'

She hears Zach swallow hard, bracing himself. 'What was it, love?'

He's going to make her say it.

'I was abused.' It is the second time she has uttered that sentence in her entire life and it costs her just as much as it did the first time. Maybe she will never say it again, but the agony those words have brought will remain, indelible.

Zach's whole body flinches, even his head recoiling. His mouth opens and closes, the start of words emerging but trailing off before they can be completed.

The retching takes Jenna by surprise, doubling her over her knees even though nothing is coming up, beyond her control. Her heart pounds so hard its hurts, a sharp ache in the middle of her chest.

She never thought she would say it out loud again. Twenty-five years have passed, but the pain is every bit as urgent; time has failed to dull it.

Zach catches her just in time, before her legs fold beneath her, his own movements slow and clumsy with shock.

'I don't understand,' he finally whispers, his face begging her to tell him it isn't true, that he is mistaken in his interpretation. He has begun to shake his head unconsciously, and Jenna counts the motions back and forth until he speaks again. 'Who? A teacher?'

'No, an older boy.'

'Who was he?'

She shakes her head wordlessly, not daring to answer the question, not yet. 'I can't tell you.'

'But you did tell someone at the time?' he croaks.

'Seb and Ava. And Olivia.'

She sees a flash of hurt in Zach's eyes. 'But not me, in all these years?'

'It's not a competition!' Rage flares in her gut that he can feel rejected even as she tells him her most devastating secret, the ultimate reason she is the way she is.

'I didn't mean it to sound like that. Jenna, I'm sorry.'

'Bit late now,' she snaps. She turns away from him. It has cost her so much to admit to him and, unwittingly, Zach has now robbed her of more.

Unable to look him, afraid of what she might see in his eyes, Jenna seizes her coat and Loki's lead, whistling for him as she strides to the door. Loki watches her struggle to snatch at the lock with numb fingers but follows her dutifully out. His speckled face reflects confusion: Jenna never walks him alone.

'Sorry,' she whispers as she struggles to clip on the lead. Even their dog doesn't believe he can rely on her to take care of him.

She hears her name being called after her, but doesn't look back, doesn't slow her rapid pace.

The park is empty, a heavy mist settling over the damp grass. She drops on to the nearest bench, not caring when the icy moisture creeps through her leggings. Loki hovers, unwilling to leave her side for his usual explorations. She has no idea why she's come here. Her only thought had been escape.

It's only when Loki jumps up alongside her and tries to snuggle into her coat, his little body shivering, that she realises how long she has sat staring at nothing and how low the temperature has dropped. She has solved nothing, her brain able to focus only on the image her dream has left imprinted, visible every time she closes her eyes.

There is nothing to be gained from staying here. Mumbling apologies, she leads Loki home, heaving a sigh of relief at both the silence and the warm air that greets them.

'You didn't take your phone.' Zach appears at the end of the hallway, drying a dish unnecessarily.

'No,' she agrees. She had hoped to sneak upstairs without him hearing.

'I was worried.'

'I was safe with Loki.'

Zach risks coming closer, touching her cold face with his warm fingers. 'Love, why did you run like that?'

'I couldn't breathe. I needed air before I suffocated.' Jenna forces a smile she doesn't mean and that doesn't fool Zach for a moment. 'Can I have a cup of tea?' She doesn't want it, but it gives Zach something to do other than ask questions she cannot answer.

While he is distracted, she escapes to the dining table, opening her laptop, determined to find a distraction from her paranoia. She can't remember the password she's had for over ten years. Her fingers catch in the keyboard as she attempts to let them work by instinct, but finally they find their own way just before her simmering temper boils over.

She barely notices Zach place a steaming mug beside her and quietly continue with the chores he never does.

'What are you doing?' he eventually asks.

'Nothing,' she mumbles. 'Research.'

'Can we talk about . . .'

'No!' she almost shouts.

'But I need to know, love. I need to understand.'

'I can't.' Her voice drops to a plaintive whisper. 'I don't know how to. Just give me time to think, Zach, please.'

'I'm not trying to force you to do anything you don't want to. There's just so many questions.'

'I know.' She wants to tell him she is sorry, for rocking his world to its core, for keeping him in the dark their entire marriage, for every fault she has, but she doesn't have the words. She can feel the pain emanating from Zach, his own internal struggle to process it, but she can't help him any more than she can help herself.

She doesn't hear him give in and leave the kitchen. She hunches over the screen, speed-reading badly, clicking on link after link, scrawling notes in a hand that looks nothing like her own neat script.

A message illuminates her phone screen an indeterminable amount of time later.

Please come to bed.

She almost ignores it but eventually types 'soon' in appeasement and sets the phone aside. Other messages follow but go unread.

'Jenna.' She hasn't heard Zach pad back downstairs and her reaction to the shock of his voice sends the untouched cup of cold tea spilling across the table.

They both swear, Zach leaping into action with a tea towel while Jenna sits frozen, unable to decide what best to do. She rescues her laptop, snatching it free from Zach as he tries to lift it to safety.

'Still researching?' he asks carefully.

She shrugs, angling her screen away from him.

'What *are* you doing, then?'

Jenna holds her breath, swallowing the angry, hurtful retort that rises. She shoves her notes across the table, slamming down her pen. 'I'm researching repressed memories.'

A crease appears between Zach's eyebrows, and she has to interrupt him before he says something that will tip her over the edge.

'It's actually a condition called dissociative amnesia,' she parrots, trying to sound robotic and emotionless, as if she hadn't felt darts of agony stabbing at her throughout her reading, hope and denial combining into a Molotov cocktail. ' "If trauma is experienced in childhood, the brain blocks out the disturbing memories to allow the person to function." '

His hand is gentle on her shoulder, but she still jumps at the touch. 'This isn't helping, love. Come to bed. You're losing enough sleep without deliberately adding insomnia to the mix.'

'Not yet,' she insists, unable to bear the prospect of them sitting side by side in bed. 'You go up. I won't be much longer.'

She returns to scrolling, soothed by the repetitive tap of the down arrow, until she hears Zach's reluctant footsteps padding back upstairs. Loki hovers, momentarily torn, but as usual chooses Zach and bounds off in pursuit.

It is a relief to be alone again. Tonight, she prefers the stillness of the silent ground floor, in complete contrast to her usual desire for noise and life. Silence means safety at night. No one can sneak up on her unnoticed; she is alert to every sound, every creaking floorboard or moving door handle.

She is safe, she tells herself.

Chapter Eight

J enna takes refuge in her office, door closed and blinds tilted. This morning, she had fled the house before Zach had even stirred, switching her phone off in a futile attempt to hide from what she had told him. She hadn't meant to say anything. She had intended to deny and now she is irate at her loss of the control she has fought so hard for.

In her bag, the bottle of Malbec, bought ostensibly to go with the evening meal, whispers quiet implorations. She shakes her head, attempting to dislodge the urge, keeping her eyes fixed on the property description she is failing to write.

Hugo strides in without knocking, leaving the door open, his long legs covering the space between them too quickly for Jenna's comfort. She sits as far back in her chair as she can as he perches on the edge of her desk, feeling as if he is pinning her still with the dark, beguiling eyes he uses to their full advantage.

'The prince's people sent feedback on the appointment,' he announces, too loudly. 'It wasn't positive.'

Jenna winces at the thought of the rest of the office hearing his strident tone. 'He decided against the place from the moment he had to walk up the stairs to it. There was no point putting on a show for him.'

'You could have bloody well tried! You knew how important that sale was.'

'I couldn't have sold him that flat if I'd thrown in a free Ferrari. I can't work miracles.'

'You've barely been working at all recently.' He lowers his voice, leaning forward confidentially. 'What's going on with you? Are you taking something?'

'No, Hugo, I'm not on drugs,' she drawls with as much sarcasm as she can muster, fighting the urge to slide her chair back against the wall.

'Then what exactly is making you like a zombie? This isn't you! You're the most together person I know.'

'I'm just finding things a bit tough at the moment. I'll be fine. I'll sort myself out.' She forces a smile. 'Promise.'

'Can I do anything?'

'No.' She barely manages to stop a humourless laugh. 'There's nothing you can do.'

She manages to last until lunchtime. When she notices she has eaten her way through an entire box of Maltesers and her hands are shaking, she reaches reluctantly for her phone and takes it off aeroplane mode. She messages Seb's number rather than the Trinity group.

Meet me for lunch. Don't tell Ava.

Several texts pile in: Drew pleading for an explanation for her abrupt departure. She ignores Zach's, along with the rest, the guilt sitting like a stone in her stomach.

'I'm going to take photos of the Russell Square apartment,'

she tells the few juniors who are at their desks as she leaves, in case any of them cares.

'Where are you actually going?' Hugo catches up with her the moment her feet touch the pavement.

'To see Seb.'

Hugo's nose wrinkles. 'Still hanging around, is he?'

'Grow up, will you? You sound like you're jealous of him.'

'As if I'd be jealous of a man like Sebastian Byron. I don't like him, simple as that.'

'You're the only one.'

'He clings to you. It's pathetic, at his age.'

Jenna can't help but laugh. 'You actually are jealous! What, do you want to be my only male friend? Can't you bear to share me?'

'Get over yourself. He only came back because he wanted Ava Vaughan to save his career. Now he uses you for ego support like he uses her for a paycheque.'

It is almost a relief to focus on an issue other than her own, and a wave of protective instinct rises in her chest. 'He came back for Olivia. You know that.'

'He'll have had his own reasons,' Hugo says dismissively. 'Why are you defending him?'

'Because someone has to! I've got to go. I'll see you after lunch.'

'Jenna!' he calls after her as she strides away, but she ignores him. She's got enough to deal with without Hugo's insecurities.

As usual, Seb is late and arrives in a flutter of apologies and tales of unavoidable delays. The waiter eyes him appraisingly as menus are presented and drinks orders taken, but Seb doesn't have the confidence to meet his gaze. Jenna experiences a disconcerting sense of relief when Seb asks if she'd prefer a bottle rather than a glass.

'I've told Zach,' she says the moment the waiter has left them.

Seb's eyes widen. 'What did you say?'

'Almost nothing. I didn't mean to . . . it just came spilling out.'

'What does he know? Did you mention—'

'No,' Jenna interrupts before Seb can inadvertently cause more damage to her defensive walls. 'He can never know that.'

'How did he take it?'

Jenna shrugs, torn between wanting to tell him how badly Zach's reaction had hurt and the stronger urge to protect herself by pretending she didn't care. 'He didn't understand.'

'Maybe you shouldn't have said anything.'

'Thanks for your support, Seb,' Jenna ground out, her back teeth clamped together.

'We're on your side. You know that!'

'How would you feel, in my position? Didn't we stand by you, when you were struggling? Didn't we tell you to stay in London and we'd help you?'

Seb's eyes narrow as he looks away. 'This isn't about me. Don't make me talk about that, Jenna, please.'

'I want you to remember how you felt then, leaving New York.'

He regards her just long enough for her to be sure he will withdraw, refuse to engage; his own defence mechanism.

'I was broken,' he whispers to the table. His fingers reach for the cutlery, arranging it precisely, lining it up until it is perfect. 'I couldn't cope after Olivia died. Everything got too much. I didn't know how to make it better.'

'And now I'm in the same situation.'

'It's not the same!' His eyes fly to hers, burning with a flammable combination of panic and anger. 'Don't belittle what I went through!'

Her pulse quickens until, finally, he regains control and sits back, arms folded, chest rising and falling. She sees he is on the verge of tears and, in spite of maelstrom churning in her stomach, she feels sorry for him.

She reaches to rest her hand briefly on his tense forearm, the best comfort she can offer him. 'It's OK.'

'It's never really OK, though, is it?'

Jenna shakes her head. 'I feel so out of control. I don't know how to get a grip of myself.'

'I know what that's like.'

Seb distracts himself by scrutinising the menu, pausing only to sample the Rioja as it is delivered and nervously declare it excellent, even though Jenna is certain it is merely acceptable, judging by its position on the wine list. The waiter accepts the compliment as if he has personally crushed the grapes.

'How do you feel?' he asks, almost reluctantly.

'A mess,' she admits, because she can't find the energy to pretend otherwise. 'Everything's blurry and muddled. There are things I can't remember at all, until I'm asleep. Then I see it all.'

Seb watches her carefully. 'Jenna, you've kept this secret for twenty-five years. Wouldn't you remember the details, no matter what? How could you forget?'

Jenna grips her head in her fingertips, counting the throb of her pulse beneath them. 'I didn't understand what was wrong with me, not until I did some research.'

She delves into her bag and retrieves her notes, laying them on the table. She watches Seb's expression as he skims the lines and is sure she sees excitement illuminating his eyes.

'This has happened to a lot of people!' he gasps, his grip tightening on the pages as he waves them at her.

'Guess it's nice to know I'm not alone.'

'And prosecutions have been brought after victims have recovered repressed memories!' His free hand grasps his wine glass, and he drinks urgently. He rakes his fingers through his hair, then catches himself and hurriedly restyles it in the reflection of the water jug, as if he will be judged for his messy locks. 'There are so many things I'd love to forget.'

Jenna keeps her eyes fixed on her cutlery as she builds up the courage to get to the real reason why she wanted to meet.

'Seb, I didn't tell Zach who it was.'

He pauses at her tone. 'OK . . .?'

'I couldn't. I'm not sure any more.'

Seb's forehead creases. 'What do you mean, you're not sure? We know who it was.'

Jenna grips the edge of the table as a wave of vertigo threatens. 'What if we were wrong?'

'We weren't wrong.' A rare firmness enters Seb's voice.

'I think we might have been.'

'Jenna, what are you talking about?'

The panic is beginning to build. Her fingers are tingling with numbness and her breath is coming in snatched gasps.

She can't do it.

'I'm sorry.'

She is on her feet, snatching her belongings, stumbling over her own feet with her need to escape.

'Jenna!' Seb yells after her.

She hears his chair topple over as he leaps up. She can't look back. She is almost running as she hurries away.

She can't go back to work. Can't risk Hugo seeing her fragile control shattered. The panic attack doesn't stop. As she walks with no direction, not caring where she is going, it envelops her completely. The familiar sounds of traffic, conversations, her own footsteps, are indiscernible over the sounds echoing inside her head.

Eventually, without meaning to, she arrives home. She goes straight to the fridge, pulling a chilled bottle of Riesling free. She hesitates momentarily as she hears the creak of Lando's floorboards through the ceiling as he shifts his chair, but the call is too strong. She glugs a large amount into a glass lightly stained with lip marks. There are no clean ones and the lack of order makes her want to scream. Zach has forgotten to load the dishwasher again.

She finishes the wine in a couple of mouthfuls, and she has to do something to prevent herself gulping down another glass. In the utility room, she fills a mop bucket with hot water and the artificial lemon of antibacterial solution while she shoves dirty clothes into the washing machine.

Back in the kitchen, she douses every surface in bleach spray, its pomegranate odour fighting with the lemon for supremacy, and leaves it to work as she attacks the floor, sweeping up the toast crumbs, Weetabix remnants and Loki's shed hairs. Gripping the mop like the throat of her enemy, she scrubs until the tiles are shining.

That done, she dices onions, juliennes peppers and carrots, finely chops garlic and ginger, the steady thud of the chef's knife against the wooden chopping block calming her as she counts along to its reassuring rhythm. The chicken thighs are already marinated in their umami bath of soy, oyster and mirin, nestling alongside a star anise and Szechuan peppercorns, and she slides the dish into the hot oven. Lando will happily tolerate the spices, even if he will pick out the vegetables.

She adds sesame oil to the hot wok, enjoying the hiss as the vegetables hit its surface, agitating them until each piece is coated and sizzling. As they begin to soften, she plucks coriander and basil from the pots on the windowsill, the knife effortlessly reducing them to neat green ribbons.

Her ringtone trills out, making her heart leap into her throat. She stabs at the slider, not getting a chance to speak before Zach is shouting cheerfully down the phone for her to open the front door; his damn key is buried God knows where and he has no spare hands.

Jenna steps out on to the terracotta tiles in her bare feet. The shock of cold doesn't help to clear her fuzzy head, as she had hoped. A vice closes around her forehead as she sees Zach isn't alone. Close behind him are Seb and Ava.

'Look who I ran into.' Zach looks relieved to have found back-up. 'We've brought Thai and beer.'

'I cooked,' Jenna says woodenly.

'Oh.' The smile falls from his face. 'Sorry. You haven't been making dinner recently . . . I didn't think you'd feel up to it.'

'Doesn't matter. Never mind.' She moves aside.

'If you don't have gin, I'm leaving again,' Ava announces, delivering swooping kisses to Jenna's cheeks before making a beeline for the drinks cupboard, leaving behind a wave of grapefruit scent strong enough to cause a swell of nausea. She is trying too hard to be cheerful; Jenna can see that her teeth are gritted and her shoulders are rigid.

'Are you OK?' Seb stoops to wrap her in a hug. She feels him flinch as he catches his own reflection in the hallway mirror. No matter how good he looks now, he is still haunted by his struggles with his eating disorder.

'Not really,' she whispers.

'I was worried you were going to do something stupid.' He drops his voice. 'We came to look for you, but you weren't home. Zach saw us checking the pubs. He insisted we come back with him.'

'I don't know what to tell everyone.' The panic is rising again, closing off her throat, and she struggles free from Seb's embrace, unable to breathe.

'Lando!' Zach yells as he discards his shoes and coat, making more noise than is necessary. 'Food's here! Come say hi to Seb and Ava.'

The clamour brings Lando to the top of the stairs. He frowns a reply in Ava and Seb's direction, delaying his descent until they have all clattered into the kitchen.

Zach shoulders his way through with the takeaway bags as Seb pauses to attempt a selfie of them all, to fulfil a compulsive need to post daily on his various socials. 'Twitter won't die out without your updates,' he says.

'It's all about Snapchat now.' Seb apes giving an adolescent eye roll, trying too hard for approval. He blushes as he draws an appreciative laugh from Zach. 'Right, Lando?'

Lando grunts, his eyes boring into Seb's phone.

'Bloody social media,' Zach grins, a firm devotee of the various platforms. He has even persuaded Jenna to download

Snapchat so he can send her pictures of Loki throughout the working day.

Jenna lets them roam through her kitchen, grabbing bottles and glasses, ice and corkscrews. She turns off the hob and the oven, unable to find any concern about the food waste. Their fake cheer is making the dread worse. She sits down at the dining table, unnoticed, tearing at her cuticles with her teeth. Her feet tap against the chair leg, offering a counting rhythm that she can't manage to focus on.

Lando crunches prawn cracker after prawn cracker until Zach wrests the bag away, attempting to establish who has ordered what at increasing volume. Finally, plates are distributed and a chicken pad Thai is slapped unceremoniously in front of Jenna by her son, half a spring roll sticking out of his pursed lips.

'Do I have to eat down here?'

'You can take yours up to your room.' She can't allow the inevitable conversation in front of her son. She must protect him from all this. It's the least she can do.

Lando wastes no time leaving the room, and the adults choose places at the table, sharing out cutlery and dipping sauces, still making far too much noise.

'I'm glad you told Zach,' Ava whispers as she leans across Jenna for a cracker. 'Bless him, he's really cut up about it. He was almost in tears.'

'Discussed me on the way, did you?' Jenna demands, her animosity effectively concealing the tidal wave of fear threatening to drown her. Seb keeps his eyes fixed on his plate, shying away from the conflict.

'We asked how you were, that's all!'

'Then had a good gossip.'

'We're all worried about you.' Ava looks across the table to include the two men.

Seb puts a forkful of his soy-and-ginger seabass down untouched, swallowing hard. His fingers grope for his neck chain, tucked neatly into his shirt as always, and begin to tug insistently at it, his own calming method.

Jenna gulps half a glass of wine, concentrating on winding noodles around her fork as her brain tries to find the right way to tell them without revealing her sins. The words lodge in her throat like a piece of the chicken she has yet to bite into.

She tries to speak calmly, as if it is of little consequence, but her voice breaks, betraying her. Her defences have failed, despite her best efforts. 'I think I know who it was,' she finally says.

From Ava's expression of dread, Jenna knows Seb has already briefed her on her lunchtime behaviour. Ava half closes her eyes, her entire body tense, as if waiting for a blow.

'Didn't you know who it was back then?' Zach almost whispers.

Jenna can't look at him. She keeps her eyes fixed on Ava. 'He wore a mask. I never saw his face. But I remembered a ring. He wore a signet ring.'

No one speaks. They are frozen, holding their breath without realizing it. Ava's knuckles are white as she grips the stem of her gin balloon. The ticking of the clock is the loudest sound in the room.

'I think it belonged to . . .' She can barely bring herself to say his name. A sob rises in her chest at the taste of those two words on her lips and she only just manages to contain it. '. . . Drew Merchant.'

Ava's breath explodes as she exhales. 'Drew? Adeline's head-teacher, Drew Merchant?'

Jenna can only nod, each use of his name like a knife stabbing into her gut. Each time she hears it, she fears her heart will stop, damaged beyond repair.

'I know that name,' Zach stammers. 'Why do I know him?'

'He's Lando's swimming coach.'

'You think Drew Merchant abused you?' Ava croaks. 'I don't understand . . . how can you think it was Drew? Where has this come from?'

'I saw him wearing the ring. When I went to collect Lando.' Her ability to spin a tale, even in her current state, almost makes her wince at the deception she is capable of. It sits, unpalatable and bitter, on her tongue.

'And you got a look at the ring?' Seb asks.

'When he pointed at the pool, it was right under my nose. I recognised it immediately. The memory has come back so strongly.' Jenna sucks in a ragged breath, her pulse racing as if she has sprinted for her life. 'I googled him afterwards, looking for pictures. I found this one.' She summons it again and passes round her phone. 'That's the ring I saw.'

All three stare at it with an intensity strong enough to crack the screen. Seb takes his time, moving his finger to zoom in as if taking in every detail.

She braces herself for the inevitable questions about the coincidence of Drew suddenly appearing at the same time as such a damning memory returned to her, but they are distracted by the complexity of the web she has woven for them, too busy trying to understand to be suspicious.

'How can you be so certain, just from a ring?' Ava asks.

Jenna sees Zach is nodding uncertainly at the question.

'You need to be careful, love,' Zach agrees, choosing each word carefully. His voice is strained, fingernails worrying at the label of his beer bottle. 'You just said you were never able to identify the guy who hurt you. Are you sure you can suddenly understand who it was from a flashback? Your mind isn't functioning well at the moment. What if you can't trust what it's showing you?'

'Maybe it's the only thing I *can* trust,' Jenna shoots back, the spark of anger enveloping the exquisite pain of knowing that the person she should be able to rely on most is doubting her.

'Half of wealthy London wants to send their kids to Drew's school these days,' Ava says, bringing Jenna back from the edge of inferno. 'He's got a lot of influence. He won't just lie down and take something like this.'

Something is bubbling up within Jenna, a clawing fear that douses her rage. 'What if Adeline isn't safe? Drew was in the newspaper photo with her; she was trying to hold his hand. What if—'

'Adeline is perfectly safe, Jenna.' Ava puts her hand on top of Jenna's, squeezing gently. 'Try to focus on one thing at a time. You can't be certain it was Drew just because of a ring. I bet loads of Cell Block H boys had signet rings.'

'Why are you so convinced that I'm being a fantasist?' To her horror, Jenna feels her eyes fill with tears. She blinks them away before they can be seen. 'I thought you'd believe me.'

'Oh, darling.' Ava's agitation falls away at the rare sight of emotion. 'I'm not attacking you. Please don't feel like that.'

'I want to go to the police,' Jenna says abruptly.

Ava's body goes rigid. 'Is that a good idea?' she asks carefully.

'I need to. I feel hollow inside, like it's eating away at me.' She can't think of any other way to explain the sickness that is coursing through her, the true depths of the terrible knowledge that has haunted her for so many years.

'Jenna, just be sure before you make any decisions. I'm trying to protect you. You could ruin Drew's life with an accusation like this,' Ava says.

'You need to talk to someone,' Zach states.

'That's exactly what I'm going to do.'

'He means a doctor or a therapist,' Ava intercedes. 'You've said yourself, you're not sleeping. It's all getting on top of you.'

'Will you two stop?' Seb slams his palm onto the table and all eyes turn to him, so unusual is any form of outburst. 'You've no idea what she's going through!'

'Neither do you!' Ava cries.

Jenna throws down her fork, her food barely touched. The room shrinks, the walls looming threateningly close, robbing the atmosphere of oxygen.

She looks first at Ava, then at Seb. She sees their fear. Their secret is threatened by her, and they can no longer trust that she is stable enough to keep it.

But Jenna can't deny what she knows, and what Zach must never find out.

Twenty-five years ago, they made a deadly mistake.

And now Jenna is the one who must atone for it.

Chapter Nine

'*Hello? Are you OK?' The female voice came through the crack in Jenna's door. 'I heard you crying. Are you homesick?'*

A white-blond head appeared, framed by light from the corridor; she must have switched it on. Jenna nodded then shook her head frantically, trying to indicate that she was OK and not homesick. There was nothing to be homesick for.

It was too late for her to move from where she was huddled in the furthest corner of her room, limbs pulled in as tightly as she could, trying to press herself into the wall as if it could conceal her.

If the visitor noticed anything strange about Jenna's position, she was considerate enough not to show it. 'I'm Olivia. Olivia Seabrook. You're Genevieve, yeah?'

'Jenna,' she managed to say.

'Third form?'

'Yeah.'

'We're fourth.' The girl slipped inside, followed by another girl, with raven-black hair, and a tall, lean boy who leaned against the door to close it. 'This is Ava Vaughan and Seb Byron. Seb's lower sixth, but he's cool. We made friends hiding from chapel behind the sports hall!'

She paused momentarily for breath robbed by her rapid speech pattern. 'It's OK for us to come in, isn't it? Nothing worse than being on your own when you're upset.'

Ava raised a hand in greeting. 'Shall I put a lamp on? Feel like I'm talking to a black hole.'

Jenna squeezed her eyes shut as the yellow light dimly illuminated the room in a sickly glow. It took a lot of courage to open them again, to find Olivia Seabrook staring curiously at her. She was tiny, elfin – a pointy face, long waves of hair and huge blue eyes – and she fidgeted constantly, gnawing at her nails and stretching up on to her tiptoes.

'Come on, bed's a little more comfy than the floor.' She parked herself on Jenna's duvet, crossing her legs and patting the space next to her. 'I won't bite, promise.'

Jenna stood on legs that felt incapable of supporting her, wobbling over to the bed, sure she would be sick at any moment.

Ava and Seb took her place on the floor, leaning back against the lifeless radiator. Ava looked like a Spanish flamenco dancer Jenna had once seen on a magazine cover, radiant olive skin, sparkling eyes the colour of juicy raisins. In contrast, Seb was pale, as if any colour had been washed from him, unremarkable with his mousy hair and darting blackbird eyes. He appeared much younger than his sixteen years, sitting close beside Ava as if relying on her to prop him up. While she looked around the room with curiosity, he kept his eyes on his shoes, his head tilted down.

Olivia extracted a tin from her waistband, the scent of cannabis immediately reaching her Jenna's nostrils as her visitor flicked open the scarred lid and produced a ready-rolled spliff. She held it out to Ava, then extracted two more, one for her and one for Seb. Jenna saw the tremor of his fingers as he reached to take it.

'You don't mind, do you?' Olivia asked.

79

Jenna wasn't sure if she did, but she didn't want her visitors to leave, so she nodded her permission quickly.

'Better open the window,' Olivia mumbled as she gripped the roach between her lips and fired a lighter. Ava jumped to yank the sash up just in time for the first lungful of smoke to be expelled. 'Got any incense sticks?' Jenna shook her head. She'd never had a need for incense sticks.

'I'll get you some. Here, have a good drag. You look like you need to chill out. Have you tried it before?'

Another headshake.

'Don't say much, do you?' Olivia held the smouldering joint out, pushing it between Jenna's fingers when she hesitated. 'It won't hurt you. Might feel a bit sick the first time, but maybe not – it's good stuff. You've turned fourteen, haven't you? Wouldn't want to start you too young, not like I did.'

Unable to get a word in even if she wanted to, Jenna nodded confirmation of her age. She wasn't sure what difference an extra year made, especially since her birthday, early in the term, had been largely ignored.

'What if we get caught?'

Seb snorted gently, the first sound he had made. 'The Brothers are all at vigil.' He rolled his eyes. 'They don't notice anything we get up to.'

'Reckon they really think we're praying and reading bibles before lights out?' Olivia giggled. 'Go on, Jenna, give it a try.'

Jenna stared at the gentle curls of fragrant smoke before slowly bringing the roach to her lips.

'Suck it in and hold it for a few seconds,' Olivia instructed, nodding in approval when Jenna did as she was told. She and Ava grinned as Jenna broke into a coughing fit. Seb looked away as if embarrassed for her. 'Hang on. Try it this way. Watch us.'

Olivia got on to her knees and shuffled forward, beckoning Ava towards her. Ava laughed and stepped closer, her own spliff balanced between her lips. Jenna watched, enthralled, as Olivia leaned closer and carefully put her open mouth around the lit end of Ava's spliff. Ava blew, and a cloud of smoke erupted from the glowing tip into Olivia's mouth.

Olivia's eyes slipped closed in ecstasy for a moment, and Ava giggled too loudly. Jenna's stomach twisted, a strange envy churning at the easy intimacy of the two older girls. Olivia turned to repeat the act with Seb, but he shook his head, drawing away from her, wrapping his arms tightly around himself.

'Oh, sorry.' Olivia was completely unabashed. 'I keep forgetting you don't like being touched.'

Seb gave Jenna a weak smile. 'Personal space is important, right?'

She nodded uncertainly, beginning to piece together his hand tremors, his nervous twitches and inability to hold eye contact, glimpsing anxieties and fears barely concealed below the surface, a boy who was not cut out for this competitive, masculine environment.

'Your turn.' Olivia turned to Jenna, stretching out to catch her hand and tug her nearer. She plucked the other roach from Jenna's limp fingers, taking it in her lips. 'It's OK, you'll love it. Trust me.'

Jenna looked down at the tiny hand holding hers and, without hesitation, copied the pose. The smoke billowed into her mouth and she drew it in greedily.

This time, she felt it. Warmth spread up her limbs, lazily stroking her muscles until it reached her knotted, aching stomach, instantly soothing the tension. The band around her chest finally loosened.

Olivia beamed, inhaling deeply again before blowing a smoke ring towards the ceiling. Jenna watched her, fascinated, but Olivia seemed careless of the scrutiny.

'What happened to your hand?' Ava asked suddenly. 'Is that what you were crying about?'

She reached for Jenna's other hand, examining the little finger, scrutinising the swelling and bruising Jenna had been trying to hide beneath her sleeve. She tried to pull away, unable to prevent herself letting out a cry of pain.

'That looks horrible!' Seb cried.

'It got trapped playing hockey,' Jenna lied. 'It's fine, honestly.'

'Urgh, I hate Wednesday afternoons,' Olivia declared.

'You need to go to Matron. It's definitely broken.'

'I don't want to,' Jenna protested.

'Don't worry about Matron, she's OK,' Ava said. 'She's not affiliated with the Church at all. She's put us both on the Pill. Imagine if the Brothers found out!'

Jenna began to shake her head but recognised they wouldn't give up or, worse, they would become suspicious if she kept protesting. She nodded pretend cooperation instead, watching as the older girls carefully extinguished the remains of the spliffs and stored them away.

'Want us to come back in the morning and go with you?' Seb offered, as if he could sense her fear. Maybe he could, his own issues giving him an empathy others couldn't find.

'I'll be OK.'

'Offer's there if you change your mind.'

Jenna remembered to say thank you just in time. The room seemed too quiet once Olivia and Ava had bounced out and Seb had crept after them, carefully clicking the door shut behind them.

The sound made her flinch.

The next morning, the pain drove her to the sick bay. The underlying reek of TCP dominated the other, more comforting smells — fresh bandages, Germolene and clean sheets. There were four beds, crisp linen and hospital corners, and Jenna could barely contain the urge to curl up on one of them and hide herself away from everything that threatened her.

82

'How did you do this?' Matron asked, examining the distended finger.

'Hockey.'

'Happens a lot. Are you in a lot of pain? You're very pale.'

Grasping the easy explanation, Jenna nodded rapidly.

'I'll find you something a bit stronger than ibuprofen. Keep the ice on it.' The woman patted the nearest bed. 'Sit yourself on here. You'll be OK.'

Jenna watched the woman bustle around, gathering equipment and blister sleeves of pills. Her heartbeat finally slowed and she felt her jaw soften, her molars sighing in relief. This was what she had always craved when ill at home: a quiet space, a caring touch, reassurance as gentle as the hands tending to her now.

Tears began to fall at the knowledge she felt better being looked after by the compassionate stranger than by her own mother.

'Don't cry, love.' Matron reached to smooth wisps of hair back from Jenna's hot forehead. 'I know it hurts, but I'll get it sorted out for you, don't worry.'

Jenna squeezed her eyes shut until she was sure she wouldn't release the sobs welling in the pit of her stomach, breathing deeply.

'Do you feel sick?'

'A bit.'

'It'll pass once I've got the splint on. Keep your eyes closed while I give your finger a little pull.'

The pain was white-hot, shooting through every bone in Jenna's hand and up her forearm, but it was over in moments and the splint taped in place.

'How are you finding it here?' Matron asked as she began clearing up.

'It's OK.'

'Any problems so far?'

'No,' Jenna whispered.

'Made many friends?'

She was about to lie, then she realised she may not have to. 'A couple. Seb Byron in the lower sixth. And Ava and Olivia in fourth form.'

Matron laughed. 'The Trouble Twins, I call them. Make sure they don't lead you astray.'

Jenna didn't know what to say in reply so she settled for staring at the splint.

'You're very thin, love. Are you eating enough?'

'I don't have much appetite.' She couldn't mention the purging. Shedding weight had become her tactic, to make herself as unattractive as possible. Who could bear to touch someone whose bones were barely contained by translucent skin? 'I get enough.'

'Sure nothing's bothering you?'

'It hurts,' Jenna whispered, eyes still fixed on the splint.

'It'll ease soon, I promise.'

Jenna wondered if the real pain would ever get any better, but she nodded as if reassured and slid off the bed.

'I'm always here if you need anything, even just a chat.'

Yet another nod, a smile she hoped would be dismissed as distress from the fracture rather than anything more sinister.

'And be careful around Ava and Olivia. I'm sure they're great fun, but they're no innocents, those two.'

Jenna didn't care if they had the devil within them. She had made friends. That was the only thing that mattered in that moment.

'Thank you, Matron.'

Chapter Ten

'What if Drew knows what we did?' Jenna asks.

Ava and Seb wince in unison and raise their glasses to their lips in perfect synchrony. The busy saloon bar, full of Saturday afternoon drinkers, seems to increase in volume around them. Zach has stayed at home, wanting to be with Lando and Loki and prove to himself that his family isn't hanging by a thread.

Ava's lips compress. 'He won't know. Even if he suspected something, he can't prove it.'

'His word might be enough to cause questions.' Seb has gone grey. He bites at his cuticles until pinpricks of blood swell to the surface.

'It's too late for that. It's been so many years. Even if he makes noise now, who's going to listen?'

Jenna stares down at her hands, palms flat against the table. She raises the misshapen little finger, crooked against its neighbours. 'I made too much noise once.'

Ava frowns. 'You broke that finger playing hockey.'

'That's what I told the nurse.'

'You told us as well. It was the first night we got to know each other.'

'I couldn't tell you what had really happened.' Jenna can feel still the acidic heat of frantic breath on her neck.

Ava shifts uncomfortably. 'Poor Zach seems torn up.'

'He'll learn to deal with it, just like we all had to.'

She's being unfair to her husband, she knows she is, but she doesn't know how to explain how it really is, how she has watched Zach's contented little bubble collapse around him as her hidden past finally sank in.

'And he doesn't even know half of it,' Ava murmurs.

'Nor will he, as far as I'm concerned.' She can't make Ava understand how much it had cost her to trust her and Seb with the truth. To let another person, even her own husband, into the true depths of the secret web would break her. Her walls are already crumbling, and she is sure they will fall if one more brick is removed.

'Shall we talk about something else?' Ava offers, eyes huge with a mix of sympathy and desperation. 'Look, Adeline's in *The Times*! They picked up the article about her school.'

She pushes the folded newspaper across the table so Jenna can see the photo. It is the same set-up as the one she had seen the other day, but this photographer took their shot a few seconds later.

Adeline has slipped her hand into Drew's and is smiling shyly up at him, her little eyes shining.

Jenna thrusts the paper away, a swell of nausea erupting in the pit of her stomach. The trust in Adeline's expression, her complete acceptance of Drew as a role model, is too much, and Jenna's mouth floods with acid that she struggles to swallow.

'Sorry, that was tactless.' Ava reaches to take the paper back but is unable to tug it free from Jenna's death grip. 'Jenna? What is it?'

'What if he does it to someone else?' Jenna whispers, her throat constricting as she thinks of Adeline, of Lando, of anonymous schoolchildren in neat uniforms and tiny rooms with creaking floorboards.

'Darling, I know you're convinced—'

'I saw the ring!'

'How can you be sure it's the same ring if you've only just remembered it?' Ava inhales the rest of her cocktail. 'Sorry. I didn't mean it to sound like that. I'm going for a smoke.'

Seb watches their friend hurry away, cigarette gripped between her lips before she even reaches the door.

'I'm making such a mess of this.' Jenna grips her temples.

'You're doing the best you can in the circumstances,' Seb corrects gently.

Ava's copy of *The Times* lies on the table, and Jenna feels a punch to her sternum as she glimpses the picture again. Something breaks deep inside her, like a rubber band stretched too far, and she physically recoils at the white-hot sting of it.

Seb watches her carefully as he reaches for another onion ring, to break into pieces and scatter around his plate to make it appear he has eaten.

'I don't want any more lives ruined by him, Seb. What he did destroyed me. He made me this person who doesn't know how to show her own son affection, who can barely stand to let her husband touch her.' Jenna's hands tighten into fists of their own accord and she fixes her eyes on the fine, corded muscles jumping in her forearms. 'I keep everyone at arm's length, never let them see any weakness, in case I get hurt again. It's a half life, and I don't think it's ever going to change. The damage is done.'

'Everyone copes in their own way. I'm a fan of drink and drugs, personally.'

Jenna doesn't even pretend to be amused by his forced glibness. 'If I do nothing and someone else has to suffer like I have, even if it's not Adeline or Lando or anyone I care about, then it'll be my fault.'

Ava returns, calmed by nicotine, clutching another cocktail already half drunk. She sits beside Jenna and squeezes her hand. 'Sorry,' she repeats. 'Just needed to calm down. Are you OK?'

Jenna automatically starts to say yes, because she always has to be OK, but finds herself shaking her head. 'Not really.'

Ava's fingers are playing with the edge of the paper, folding and curling it. 'I read the articles, about Cell Block H. The journalist is absolutely fierce.'

'Amy Donald. She seems to be driving the whole media campaign.' Jenna's words freeze in her throat. 'Oh God, do you think she might dig up too much?'

'She's focused on the girls, not any of the other stuff,' Ava says, trying and failing to sound reassuring.

'Have you actually read the other articles in her series, the ones not about Halewood House?' Seb asks.

'Some,' she says, defence making her tone too sharp.

'One of the schools she investigated was also in Essex. Nowhere near Cell Block H, but still.' Seb has grabbed his phone, tapping the screen feverishly until he finds what he is looking for, and spins it round for Jenna to see.

He allows her a few impatient moments to read, but Jenna fails to grasp the point.

'The detective in charge of the Essex case is named!' Seb cries. 'Here. Detective Sergeant Beckett, Chelmsford Public Protection Unit.'

Jenna's eyes follow his insistent finger, realisation slowly dawning. 'Do you think he'd listen to me?'

'If he's already investigating similar cases . . .'

Jenna grips the phone too hard. 'Why are you encouraging me now?'

'Because I want to find out who did those awful things to you.'

'You said we already knew who did it,' Jenna protested. 'You were completely sure.'

'The police will find Drew innocent if he didn't do anything wrong. And it takes the spotlight off . . . anything else he might say . . . right?'

Jenna nods as if she knows for sure; anything to keep Seb on her side. She feels like that lonely schoolgirl again, desperate for friendship, for someone to care about her.

'You'll have to tell them you knew it was Drew all along, otherwise they'll start asking awkward questions.'

'Seb, this is madness!' Ava finally chimes in, finding her voice again. 'Why are you encouraging this? We were all there. We know what happened.'

Seb juts his chin forward, more determined than they have ever seen him. 'We have to protect ourselves. This is the best way to do it. Drew can't start throwing accusations around if he's got his own to answer to.'

'But . . .' Ava starts.

'We were wrong, Ava!' Jenna almost snarls. 'Can't you see? We made the worst mistake possible, and now I have a chance to put it right.'

'By accusing a man who none of us, not even for a moment, has ever suspected of hurting you? How is that rational?'

'Sometimes they don't find anyone guilty,' Seb says, his timbre lower than natural, words scratching at his throat.

'What do you mean?' Jenna asks, bemused by his sudden declaration.

His face shuts down, eyes cast low, jaw rigid. 'I told you. I know what this feels like.'

'It happened to you too?' she gasps.

'Not like this, but it hurt just as bad.' He flashes a smile that is more like a grimace. 'I'm never going to get justice.'

'Why not?'

'Because no one can outrun death when it's their time,' he says dramatically. 'No, don't ask me any more questions. We're talking about you, not me.'

'But . . .'

'Jenna!' It is a plea, as tears flood his eyes and his old hand tremors reveal themselves again.

She dare not push him any further. Whatever he went through, he isn't ready to share it, and she, more than anyone, knows that sometimes it is better to leave Pandora's box unopened. Seb's jaw clenches, his full lips twisting in a way that momentarily makes his handsome face irredeemably ugly. She sees he is struggling to keep a grip on himself, surrounded by ghosts he had not wanted to resurrect.

'But what if this detective says you need evidence?' Ava interjects, giving Seb the opportunity to recover his composure.

'I need to focus on the waking memories, the ring. That's my evidence, not the dreams.'

'You're not going to tell them about the dreams?'

'There's no need. They're all flashbacks. I'm just not awake for some of them.'

Ava plays uncertainly with her cocktail straw, her grip too tight on the flimsy item.

'You're absolutely sure about this, Jenna?'

The two women observe each other for a long, suffocating moment.

'I know you don't like the police,' Jenna says to Ava. 'Olivia was always terrified of them too.'

'God, please don't mention Olivia. I don't have enough head-space for that.'

Seb looks rapidly between them, his jaw clenching as if he is chewing the inside of his cheek. He rubs at his eyes with a closed fist, dropping his head. All three fall silent, avoiding looking at each other.

Abruptly, Jenna seizes her phone, typing in a Google search. She shows her friends the phone number.

'Shall I make an appointment while I've got Dutch courage?'

Seb's smile is only slightly forced. 'I've always believed that's the best type of courage.'

Chapter Eleven

The earliest appointment is Monday morning. Jenna calls in sick, telling Hugo she has a vomiting bug. Not entirely a fabrication, given she had spent the whole of Sunday feeling too nauseous to eat.

The police station is brighter and fresher than Jenna had expected, smelling of subtle citrus air freshener. The room she is taken to in reception has comfortable chairs, mini bottles of water and a frosted-glass window that lightens an atmosphere that still feels oppressive. The clock ticks loudly, the only sound in the silent room, and Jenna counts gratefully, focusing on the rhythm as cold fear begins to creep over her.

Just as she is about to stride from the room and declare she's made a mistake and she'd like to leave, a man arrives, preventing her exit with his presence as much as his size. He shows her an ID badge she forces herself to study declaring him to be Detective Sergeant Nick Beckett.

'I'm part of a team called the Public Protection Unit.' He sits opposite her, leaning forward over his knees. 'We deal with things like child protection, sexual assaults, domestic violence. I specialise in cases of historic abuse. I believe that's what you've come to speak to me about?'

DS Beckett has kind eyes. It is the first thing she notices after she hands back the ID and accepts her chance to walk out has passed. Nothing else matters much after that. It doesn't matter that he is well dressed but his tie is a careless knot tugged away from constraining his throat, nor that his shoulders are broad enough to strain the seams of his suit jacket. It is irrelevant that he habitually runs his fingers through close-cut dark auburn hair that fights to curl despite being too short to allow such dissent and that his voice is softer than his appearance suggests.

Jenna takes a steadying breath, wishing she'd reached for one of the bottles of water before he'd arrived. Her hands are shaking too much now, but her mouth is full of cotton wool, and she has a searing thirst. Yet again, she must repeat the sentence she once thought would never be put into words.

There. She's said it. No going back now.

Beckett nods encouragement and makes his first note on a form. 'Who was your abuser?'

'His name is Andrew Merchant.'

Another note; no sign of reaction; no recognition of Drew's name.

'Can I ask why now, Jenna, after all this time?'

She takes a deep breath. 'Because it's haunting me. I'd blocked it out for so long, I don't want it to break me again.'

A gentle nod. 'I'll ask you a short series of questions. You can have a break whenever you want. Some will be uncomfortable, and you may not want to answer them, but I need as much information from you as you can manage. We call it the first account. Would you like someone to sit with you?'

Jenna shakes her head. She couldn't bear anyone else to be witness to this.

'Where did it take place?'

'Always in my dorm room, late at night.'

'How often?'

'A few times a term.' Now she has begun, anger has replaced the fear and it seems to burn through her veins, bolstering her courage. 'Sometimes it would stop altogether for a while. Weeks without anything happening, then it would start again.'

'Were you friends with the abuser before it started?'

'I suppose I looked up to him.'

Beckett's expression remains professionally neutral. 'Have you seen him in the intervening years?'

'I hadn't seen him since school, until this week. I found out he's the head coach of my son's swimming team.' She grits her teeth, resisting the urge to sit on her hands to stop the tremors. 'I agreed to meet him for a drink.'

'And why did you agree to that?'

'Curiosity, I suppose. I think I wanted to see what he was like now, after all these years.'

'You've kept quiet about it for a long time.'

'I was so afraid, when I was younger. As I got older, I just wanted it to go away. I repressed the memories for a long time, most of my adult life.'

'This was the trigger that made them rise up again?'

'Yes, and there's a journalist – Amy Donald – I keep seeing her articles.'

Beckett nods, a muscle momentarily twitching in his jaw at the mention of the name. 'There's been a lot of women coming forward recently with similar experiences to you.'

'The flashbacks have been getting stronger and more frequent – daily now. I've never forgotten it happened, I've always carried it with me, but the details had got lost.'

Beckett follows her gaze and slides a bottle of water across to her. It takes several attempts to get the cap off and she spills some down her chin as she gulps, not stopping until the bottle is empty. Beckett opens another, placing it in front of her.

'Tell me more about the school. Did you live nearby?'

'No, we were from Guildford. My parents are very religious; they'd intended Halewood House for me for years.'

'It was a religious school?'

'Run by an Order affiliated to the Benedictines. The teachers were all Brothers who lived at the abbey attached to the school.'

'Monks?'

'Sort of. They took vows to spend their lives at study or at prayer.'

'How did you feel about that?'

'I didn't give it much thought. It was what it was. I suppose I found them a bit intimidating at first, then vaguely ridiculous as I got older. They were from another world. Another century, it felt like.'

'What about yourself, Jenna? You're married, I see. Is your husband supportive of your decision to report your abuse?'

Jenna glances at the reminder of her wedding ring. 'Of course.'

'Have you discussed it with him?'

'Some of it. Not in great detail. It doesn't feel right.' Too many things about this don't feel right.

'Have you told anyone else?'

'Just my friends from school, Ava Vaughan and Sebastian Byron. We're still very close.'

She drinks more water, even though her stomach feels swollen and taut as the skin of a drum from how quickly she drained the first bottle. She opens a third bottle, the discomfort a welcome distraction from the chaos inside her head. Has she got all the details right? Will Beckett be less likely to believe her because she isn't sobbing uncontrollably?

'I don't cry,' she finds herself explaining. 'I learned to stop myself years ago, and now I find I won't, even when I want to. The tears come to my eyes, but I can never let them out.'

'Were you an emotional child?'

'Very. I couldn't stop it, even before . . . it . . . happened. It was my little victory, learning to control it.'

Beckett makes a final note before putting his pen away. At the indication it is finally over, a rush of air leaves Jenna's lungs, as if she has barely breathed through the entire interview, and her body slumps. She's done it.

'What happens now?' she asks, her throat raw and sore despite all the water.

'I'll meet with the rest of my team to establish the investigation and plan what we need to do next—'

'So, you will investigate?' she interrupts, not sure what she wants to hear.

'With accusations such as these, it's rarely easy to prove guilt,' Beckett says carefully, 'which means prosecution can be tricky. However, in the current climate, we'll look into establishing any evidence that may persuade the CPS to press charges. Do you understand what that means?'

'Perfectly, thank you.' Jenna bristles at the words but realises he hadn't intended to patronise her, more like gently inform her that the chances of going to court are slim. She isn't sure if she is relieved or not.

'We have to do what we call an ABE interview, in a specially designed suite with cameras, otherwise we won't be able to proceed any further.'

'OK, fine,' she says, too quickly. She can't bear the thought of allowing them to glimpse her secrets, to plunge deep into her private world.

The past has already permeated her present too much. It has opened a gaping wound she has battled to heal for many years. The scars may not be visible, but they still hurt as badly as they did back then. Answering questions, just being here, she knows that will leave more scars, and these might be more obvious, especially to those she wants to conceal them from most.

'I'll be in touch soon, then.' Beckett stands, hands her a business card that she fumbles with, before extending a large hand for her to shake. She takes it from arm's length, worried he will smell the terror emanating from her pores. His grip is gentle, deliberately so for a man of his size, and she feels compassion rather than rejection. 'You've been very brave, Jenna.'

Or very stupid, she thinks.

Chapter Twelve

The multiple pitches are full of anonymous boys crashing into each other, shouts echoing across the Hackney Marshes, and it takes Jenna too long to identify Lando's match as she picks her way around puddles. Finally locating Zach's rangy frame, she wraps herself tighter in her pashmina, as much for security as for warmth. Her heeled boots sink into the boggy ground, sending flecks of mud up her tights. Such a tiny inconvenience, but it brings hot, angry tears leaping to her eyes that she blinks furiously away. When Loki's welcoming paws add their own streaks, she shoves him away so hard he nearly falls over.

'He's only saying hello!' Zach crouches to comfort his dog and Jenna feels a stab of guilt on seeing Loki's beseeching eyes. Yet another soul she has managed to inadvertently hurt.

'Sorry,' she mumbles, to both of them. She feels hung over, her mouth gritty and foul, her head pounding. What has she done? Now it's too late to stop the runaway train that threatens to career out of her control.

'Didn't think you were going to make it.' Zach stands upright, attention already returning to the action.

Jenna waves to Lando as she spots the maroon-striped number ten jersey, pretending she hasn't heard. Lando takes a few seconds to raise an acknowledging hand, his expression shielded by scrumcap and mud. On the field, as in the pool, there is none of his clumsiness. He is transformed, agile and coordinated and a lifetime away from the little boy who had once asked Jenna why she never read him his bedtime story.

'How was work?' Zach asks, eyes fixed on his son.

'I didn't go to work. I went to the police this morning. They've agreed to investigate.'

Zach spins to face her. 'Have you formally accused Drew?' he asks, his voice rising.

Hissing between her teeth, Jenna drags him further away from any other spectators. 'Do you want the whole world to know?'

'What did you tell them?'

The urge to lie is strong, but she isn't sure of her ability to keep up the pretence to both DS Beckett and Zach. It is already exhausting, and she doesn't have to share a bed with the detective. She will slip with Zach; she knows she will. An unguarded moment or a thoughtless comment. As much as she doesn't want to admit it, it is better to do it now and face the wrath, let him get over it before he is interviewed.

'I told them I always knew it was Drew,' she mutters.

Zach inhales so sharply in his need to respond that he chokes, and his coughing allows Jenna a brief, merciful moment of thinking time.

'I had to do this, Zach, can't you see?'

'But how can you be so sure about this ring, love?'

'I wouldn't be doing this if I wasn't absolutely certain. You don't see it! You don't have to sleep every night knowing you're going to relive the most awful things that happened to you.'

Zach's face is bright red, either from the coughing fit or his own internal struggle, his absolute morals versus his unquestioning loyalty to his wife. 'I know how terrible this is for you,' he says weakly.

'You don't, though, do you?' Jenna's resolve roars and she sees him flinch at her venom. 'That's the point. You'll never know, so stop trying to understand and question everything.'

He takes a step back as if worried she is going to strike him. 'Maybe I should give you a bit of space to calm down. You stay and watch Lando. I'll see you at home.'

'I'll go. You stay.'

'You never get to see him play.'

'Is that meant to be another dig?'

'No! I didn't mean . . .'

'Mum?'

Jenna jumps violently as a towering, sweating teen has appeared behind her. Half-time has arrived, unnoticed.

'What's up?' Lando gulps water from a filthy sports bottle.

'I'm not feeling too good, mate,' Zach intercedes. 'Think I'd better head home. Your mum will stay for the second half. You're playing great.'

Lando looks from one parent to the other, worrying at the bottle's spout with his teeth.

'Proud of you.' Zach thumps him on one padded shoulder. 'I'll sleep off this headache and we'll watch a film later, OK?'

'Are you winning?' Jenna asks awkwardly as Zach and Loki stride away.

'Didn't you see me score?'

Jenna winces. 'Sorry.'

Lando drains the last of the water. 'Doesn't matter.'

He jogs back to his teammates. He doesn't glance her way again.

Guilt drives Jenna to a pizza restaurant with unlimited Coke refills, so peace is at least restored between her and Lando by the time they arrive home.

Her son wastes no time disappearing to his room but, for once, Jenna is glad of the distraction his sodden kit provides. She takes her time rinsing it in the utility-room sink, watching the rivers of mud swirl down the drain, counting the drips as she wrings each piece out. The tap running at full blast drowns out the call of the wine rack and gives her another task once the washing machine is on, wiping down all the splashes.

Zach is so quiet she doesn't hear him come downstairs until he enters the kitchen. She imagines he'd hoped she'd be in the living room, and his expression of dismay stings when she turns to look at him, her jaw clenched, ready for battle. She loves Zach. He is the only man she has ever loved. The only thing they have in common is a mutual ambivalence to Marmite, yet somehow it works.

At least, it used to.

Zach begins making tea, movements slow and deliberate.

'I want you to get justice, love,' he says quietly, 'but I want you to do it in the right way.'

'This doesn't feel like the wrong way to me.'

He grips the kettle too tightly. 'That's why I'm worried about you.' His eyes regard her, Lando and Loki mixed into one gaze that can spike guilt instantly. 'Let's go to bed.'

'I'll be up soon,' she feels she has to say.

She is still staring after him when her phone rings, sending a jolt running through her body. Ava's name flashes on the screen, refusing to be ignored, no matter how great the temptation.

'How did it go?' Ava asks tentatively.

'They agreed to investigate.'

A silence that seems to go on for ever. 'How do you feel?'

'Scared,' Jenna admits. 'It was awful.'

'I bet. It took a lot of courage.'

'The police will want to speak to you and Seb.'

She hears Ava's sharp intake of breath. 'What for?'

'Because you were there.'

'But what do I say?' Ava's voice wobbles. 'I don't want to talk to them. The police still terrify me.'

'I feel the same. The detective is nice. He's not investigating you.'

'We were so young,' Ava whispers, as if to herself. 'We had no idea what to do when the police came.'

'They didn't speak to you at the time,' Jenna reminds her, as her own mind is uncontrollably drawn back to that terrible night at Halewood House, the night their world fell apart.

'Thanks to you.'

Jenna tastes blood as her teeth worry her bottom lip. 'So you'll do it?'

A long silence, followed by a soft sigh.

'I'll have to. I owe you too much, don't I?'

Chapter Thirteen

The sound of footsteps outside her door made Jenna instinctively shrink back against her pillows, pulling her duvet up to her near-concave chest. She held her breath as the handle dipped, helpless to stop the whimper that forced its way out of her clenched lips.

'You're not going to sleep, are you?' Ava asked, poking her sleek head in.

'No,' Jenna gasped, releasing a rush of air.

'What's up? Are you ill?'

'I don't feel too good.'

'You look terrible – no offence. I've brought you something different to try. It'll make you forget about feeling rough.' Ava thumbed over her shoulder to a tall figure standing behind her. 'This is Hugo, if you guys haven't met.'

'We spoke at the welcome meeting at the start of term,' Jenna said.

She had seen Hugo Addison around school plenty of times since and had always said a polite hello when he had greeted her, but she wasn't quick witted enough to respond to his witticisms and generally became tongue-tied within moments. Hugo was too cool for her. He stood out from the lower-sixth boys with his diamond ear stud and Doc

Martens, hair dyed the deepest blue-black, blazer sleeves rolled to his elbows and tie shortened to a stub. She always wanted to ask him how he got away with so many uniform violations but didn't have the courage.

He nodded hello as he closed the door, assessing her. His eyes were an unreal shade of ice blue and Jenna realised he was wearing coloured contact lenses. He carried a glass of amber liquid, sipping it slowly as if demonstrating his superior maturity to the girls.

'And this is his cousin, Rory. He's a new starter this year too.'

Rory, standing shoulder to shoulder with Hugo, was so similar in features to his cousin that they could have been brothers, but he seemed to be taking care to blend in with the crowd. His uniform was perfect, hair short and neatly styled, brogues polished.

'Got to serve his time as well.' Hugo thumped his cousin in the upper arm, unbalancing him. 'You've had it easy at your old school, cuz.'

Jenna was sure she saw a flash of rage darken Rory's eyes, his face momentarily contorting into ugliness, before he laughed and shoved Hugo back.

'We didn't have as many extracurricular activities as you seem to have here,' he drawled.

Olivia bounced in a few moments later with Seb in tow. Jenna was sure she saw her friend's jaw tense when she noticed the boys' presence, and Seb actually turned as if to leave.

Olivia caught hold of his wrist. 'Oh no you don't. You're staying with us.'

Hugo smirked. 'Your little harem look after you well, Byron.'

Seb shrank away, fixing his eyes on the carpet as he whispered a barely audible 'Fuck off'.

'Leave him the fuck alone, Addison,' Olivia snarled.

'Play nice, children,' Ava warned. 'I've got something good.'

'Mouth on Legs will get us caught.' Hugo's eyes flashed in Olivia's direction.

'My money's as good as yours,' Olivia shot back, flipping him a finger. She grinned at Jenna. 'Popping your cherry tonight, gorgeous?'

'She doesn't have to try it if she doesn't want,' Seb dared to say. 'You've got weed, haven't you, Ava?'

Jenna drew her shoulders back, still not prepared to leave the safety of her duvet but desperate to show willing, to be part of this handsome group. 'I want to try it.'

Olivia gave a whoop that drew a black look from Hugo and had Rory darting to the door as if certain they were about to be caught.

'Not here,' he said. 'We'll go to the cricket pavilion. Someone will make too much noise.'

'It's safe here,' Ava insisted. 'Jenna's not on the radar. No one ever comes to check her room.'

'Not like ours,' Olivia declared, as if the victimisation was completely unfair.

'I'm not staying here.' Hugo held out a large hand. 'Give us a tab each and we'll go. Fuck knows why you had to drag us all the way up here in the first place.'

'Most people prefer company while they're tripping,' Ava retorted, but she palmed him something with practised ease and he handed her a banknote in return.

'I prefer to choose my own company.' He nodded to his cousin, who smirked back. 'People who can be trusted to have a bit of subtlety.'

Olivia settled herself crossed-legged on Jenna's bed. 'Come on, Ava, hurry up! Let the party poopers do what they want.'

'Do you ever shut your mouth?' Hugo snarled.

'Only when I'm smoking!' Olivia laughed, entirely unconcerned by the aggression in his tone.

Hugo strode for the door, Rory following close behind. 'You need to be more selective in your customers, Ava.'

'And give my competitors the edge? I don't think so.'

'Make sure she's safe.' He nodded his head towards Jenna, and she felt a tiny glow that her wellbeing mattered to him.

Once they were alone, Ava handed out tiny squares of blotting paper stamped with purple smiley faces. Olivia whooped when she saw the design.

'I love these ones!' She threw her arms round Jenna's neck in delight and even though Jenna flinched at the sudden movement she hugged her back to stop the embrace ending too quickly. 'Stick your tongue out!'

Jenna did as instructed, closing her eyes as Olivia's fingertips traced the outline of her lips before a tab was dabbed gently on her tongue.

'Close your eyes and enjoy the ride.'

Chapter Fourteen

Drew

Drew has arrived home too early. A visit to Whitehall hadn't taken as long as he had intended, and although he drove back to Wanstead in a good mood, hopeful of his private ambitions, it hasn't lasted. He shuts himself in his study, away from his daughter's demands and his wife's scrutiny.

He logs on to the school system, checking the minutes of meetings, following up emails. He strives to keep on top of his many duties; he is aware he is young to be in such a position and he still feels the need to prove himself. His predecessors had all been elderly, venerable men, dignified in their beards and fondness for lunchtime port, academic gowns billowing as they strolled around campus. Drew has since made gowns non-compulsory for teaching staff, mostly because he can only stand to wear one once a term himself. It amuses him that some of the old-timers still cling to them as if they are a shield from the modern world.

The school has stood in all its splendour since the 1700s, imposing Georgian buildings overlooking Hampstead Heath, offering excellence for the children of London's elite. Drew shook the ancient foundations when he won the appointment, the dark horse from the state sector no one had expected to triumph over the establishment.

Absorbed in the documents, he doesn't hear the crunch of tyres on the gravel outside his window. The thick curtains soften the sound of footsteps and he only reacts at the imperious peal of the original doorbell. He waits for the housekeeper to answer, but the sharp clicks on the hallway tiles warn him that his wife has been disturbed moments before the office door sweeps open.

Natasha is, as always, wearing full make-up and high heels even though she hasn't needed to leave the house that day.

'There's a police officer here to see you.'

Drew frowns. 'What's happened?'

'He won't say.' Natasha's lips purse. 'He'll only speak to you.'

'Show them in here, would you? Thanks.' One of his first lessons in teacher training, all those years ago, was to always follow a request with a thank you rather than a please, indicating that you expected it to be complied with.

Natasha shows her disdain with a flash of her icy eyes, turning sharply on a red stiletto that matches her long nails. Drew stands, having skirted around his desk to greet the man who strides confidently towards him. Natasha closes the door loudly, but there is no sound of her heels clicking away.

'Andrew Merchant?'

'Yes, that's me.' Drew automatically extends his hand to shake, noting the firm grip and straightforward gaze of the police officer. 'What can I do for you? Are you here about a student?'

'No, sir, I need to speak to you about a different matter. My name's DS Nick Beckett, I'm a detective from Essex Police.'

'Essex?' Drew frowns. 'Sorry, do have a seat.'

Beckett takes one leather armchair, waiting for Drew to do

the same. Drew's seat is too close to the open fire, and he begins to sweat almost immediately. He undoes a shirt button.

'So, DS Beckett, what can I do for you?' He is uncomfortably aware that it is the third time he has asked and he is yet to receive an answer.

'Before we go any further, I need to caution you. At the moment, I don't require a formal interview with you, but the caution is to protect us both.' Beckett rhymes off the familiar statement, recognisable from TV dramas, as he places a mobile recording device on the low table separating them. 'I'll be recording our conversation, if that's OK?' He is polite enough to make it sound like a question rather than the statement it really is.

'Caution me for what?' Drew grips the arms of his chair, his pulse beginning to throb. 'What the hell is going on?'

Beckett produces a notebook, a Biro primed. 'Were you a pupil at Halewood House School in Essex?'

'Yes. Why?'

'Did you know another pupil called Jenna Taylor, née Alcott?'

The pounding of Drew's heart increases. 'Has something happened to Jenna?'

'Mrs Taylor has made an allegation regarding historic sexual abuse. She has named you as her abuser.'

The damning sentence is delivered so matter-of-factly that Drew barely reacts at first. He continues to wait for the next question, until it finally hits him. He feels the breath rush from his lungs, the sudden loss of air making his head swim. He hears himself gasp, his limbs tingling with pins and needles.

'She's done what?'

'She's made a statement alleging that she was repeatedly molested by you at school while you were her house prefect.'

'This is madness.' Drew forces himself to speak calmly, even though he is struggling to draw sufficient breath. His chest feels as if it is being crushed. 'Are you arresting me?'

'At the moment, no, not while we're making initial inquiries. I'd like you to attend a voluntary interview tomorrow, at Chelmsford police station.'

'What about work? And my role with Swim England?'

'You'll need to inform your chair of governors and your designated safeguarding lead. I imagine you'll be required to be absent from school and training until this matter is resolved.'

'But I haven't done anything wrong.' Drew remembers abruptly that he hasn't denied the accusations, has made no protest of his innocence. 'I've never harmed Jenna!'

Beckett makes a series of notes. 'When did you last see Mrs Taylor?'

It takes Drew too long to focus enough to produce an answer. 'Just the other day. For the first time in years. We went for a drink, had a good catch-up.'

'Was your wife with you?'

'No, she has her own engagements. And I don't like what you're implying.'

Beckett doesn't seem to hear. 'Can I have your wife and daughter's names, please?'

'Why?'

'Thoroughness,' Beckett says casually.

'Elena is my daughter – she's just turned eighteen – and my wife is Natasha.'

'Does Elena attend your school?'

The tightness in Drew's chest returns with a vengeance. 'Yes. Does that matter?'

The question is ignored. 'Where's your wife from? Her accent sounds Eastern European.'

Drew frowns. 'How is that relevant?'

Beckett gives an apologetic smile. 'Every detective's flaw, I'm afraid. We're constantly nosy.'

'Natasha is from Russia. She's lived in England since she was twenty-one, in case you were wondering.'

'Beautiful country. I went to St Petersburg years ago. Loved it.'

'Natasha is a Muscovite.' Realisation dawns. 'If you're thinking I'll flee abroad, I assure you I've no intention of running away and I don't have a second passport hidden anywhere.' Other secrets, yes, but not a false passport.

'I'm only trying to get an idea of your life, Mr Merchant, nothing more sinister.'

'So I don't have to answer your questions.' Drew makes it a statement rather than a question, trying to re-establish his familiar, comforting position of authority. 'In which case, I'll say nothing further until I attend your station tomorrow with my solicitor.'

Beckett shrugs, as if it doesn't matter either way, and closes his notebook. 'I'll just need to speak to your daughter before I leave.'

'What the hell for?'

'I have a duty to check she's safe. I won't alarm her.'

'No.'

'Will you get her now, thanks?' A direction, phrased exactly as Drew himself would phrase it. 'It'll only take a minute.'

For a long moment, Drew stands his ground, gripping the arms of his chair. Beckett waits, all the time in the world, glancing pleasantly around the room as if approving the decor.

Hissing out a sharp breath between his teeth, Drew grabs his phone and messages his daughter, rather than risking a long conversation upstairs and leaving the detective unsupervised. The blue ticks give their confirmation and, moments later, Elena barges into the room.

'Have you ordered it?' she asks eagerly before spotting the visitor.

'Ele, this is Detective Sergeant Beckett.'

Elena's eyes spark with curiosity. 'Police? Why?'

'I just need a minute of your time, if that's OK?' Beckett smiles, his manner entirely different now, no hint of threat or steely determination. 'Mr Merchant, if you could leave us for a couple of minutes, thank you.'

Drew leaps to his feet. 'You have no right to—'

'Thank you,' Beckett repeats, tilting his head towards the door.

Barred from his own study, Drew can do little else but step out into the hallway. Natasha leans casually against the wall, head still tilted. They make eye contact momentarily before Drew turns his back. He strains to hear the conversation, but Beckett has dropped his voice and all he can make out is odd words. Elena speaks unusually quietly, as if mimicking the detective's tone.

The instant his watch hand ticks round to two minutes, Drew clears his throat loudly and strides in. Beckett's jaw tightens momentarily, but Elena moves towards her father, bewilderment making her sculpted features soft and innocent.

'I don't understand. What's going on?'

'I'll explain everything, darling.'

'Dad . . .'

'Go back upstairs. I'll be up as soon as I've seen DS Beckett out.'

Elena's confusion is reflected in her lack of argument, and she follows the instruction without protest. Fortunately, there is no sound of her acknowledging her mother's presence, betraying Natasha's snooping.

Drew squares his shoulders, hoping his tension can't be detected. 'I'd like you to leave now.' He speaks too loudly, a warning to his wife. 'I need to reassure my family.'

As the detective stands, shrugging into his overcoat, Drew hears the rapid tap of Natasha's shoes retreating. He opens the study door, about to call the housekeeper to show the visitor out, then decides to do it himself. He wants to watch Beckett drive away.

Drew stands perfectly still in the doorway until the unmarked car pulls out of the driveway. He barely resists the urge to lean back against the front door as he closes it, barring entry to his home.

'What the hell is happening?' Natasha appears immediately.

'You heard everything from the bloody hallway,' Drew retorts, fear making his temper shorter than he usually allowed.

'Not enough. We should get thinner doors if you're going to continue having police visitors. They're accusing you of sexual abuse?'

'Keep your fucking voice down!' Drew grabs her slender arm, not caring how hard his fingers dig into her flesh, and hauls her into the study.

Natasha wrenches herself free, refusing to rub the sting away. She draws herself up to her full height, only inches shorter than him.

'Did you do it?'

'No, I fucking didn't!'

'Then why has this Jenna Taylor said you have?'

113

'I don't know why. I have no clue why she would do this.'

'Did you fuck her?' Natasha asks, one eyebrow tilted.

Drew clenches his teeth. 'Natasha—'

'No, even you would not be so stupid,' Natasha agrees. 'So, what will we do?'

'Do?'

'To prove your innocence.'

'You make it sound so simple.'

'Every problem has a solution, darling. You know that.'

'How can you be so blasé? I have to ring Swim England, and the chair of governors. Can you imagine how this will seem?'

'No one will think you're guilty.'

'Don't be so sure.'

'What about Ele?'

'I'll speak to her after I've spoken to the chair. Hopefully that fucking detective didn't give too much away.'

'She's listening at the door,' Natasha announces calmly.

'Fuck!' Drew strides across the room to find himself face to face with his daughter. Elena is pale, tears glistening in her eyes. 'What have I told you about eavesdropping?'

'I'd never know anything if I didn't!' Elena cries. 'You tell me nothing.'

'Did you hear everything?'

'A woman has said you . . . did things to her . . . when you were at school.' Elena's attitude and confidence fall away, revealing a much younger child.

'It's nonsense, Ele, I promise you. What did the detective ask you?'

'If everything's OK at home. If there was anything I wanted to talk to him about. If I felt safe here. If I was worried about anything. It was so weird, but now I understand why he was asking.'

'It's just procedure, darling, it didn't mean anything.'

'It meant he had to check if you've abused me.'

Drew flinches at the words sullying his daughter's rosebud lips.

'Are you going to be sacked?'

'Of course not. An innocent man can't be sacked.'

'What if you go to prison?' Horror sends Elena's tears spilling over as her gilded life flashes before her eyes.

'That's not going to happen. Tomorrow, I'll speak to the police and sort all this out.'

'It's that simple?'

'Probably not,' Drew admits. Elena is not stupid, despite her carefully crafted vacuous demeanour. 'There'll have to be an investigation, but it'll find me innocent.'

He can see the calculations running through Elena's head as she weighs up the potential for disaster.

'We'll be fine, *solnyshka*,' Natasha murmurs. 'If we need to, we can go home. We'll always be taken care of.'

'There won't be any need to run away,' Drew grits his teeth at the Russian endearment Natasha likes to bestow on everyone except her husband. 'And I'm perfectly capable of continuing to take care of you both.'

The glance exchanged between mother and daughter is so perfectly translatable that Drew has to turn away and swallow the heat that rises uncontrollably in his throat.

Chapter Fifteen

Tuesday morning necessitates Jenna's invented vomiting bug to last another day, to allow her drive to Chelmsford again.

DS Beckett arrives to collect her from reception with a woman in tow; young, severe ponytail, clutching a file too tightly as she looks Jenna up and down. Her movements are akin to a bird's, quick and darting, bright eyes always on the move. A complete contrast to Beckett's stillness and subtle observations.

'Sorry you've had to take time off work,' Beckett greets her.

'I said I had a vomiting bug,' Jenna admits. 'My boss, Hugo, is another old school friend.'

She daren't tell Hugo the real reason for her absence, not yet. She can't cope with his questions as well as the police's.

'Have you interviewed Drew yet?' she asks.

The woman answers before Beckett can, a clipped tone that doesn't quite disguise her Estuary accent. 'Tomorrow. We need to make sure we've got as much detail as we can first.'

'Try not to worry,' Beckett says, his eyes crinkling at the corners as he smiles. She notices their chameleon quality – sea green in one light, coffee brown in another, enhanced with an inner core of amber that illuminates with amusement or anger. 'We'll make this as smooth as we can for you.'

She is shown to an interview suite deep in the station, carpet scored with fresh vacuum marks, paper and pens arranged neatly on the coffee table with a new collection of water bottles. The yucca plants don't quite distract from the camera equipment or the large mirror that must be two-way. Beckett directs her to the sofa and he and his subordinate take the armchairs opposite.

The second officer disappears momentarily into an anteroom concealed by the mirror, muttering under her breath as she returns to her seat, pen poised. Beckett adopts a more relaxed position, leaning back as if having a chat over coffee. His voice resonates as he states his name and collar number, the date and location, and introduces DC Rebecca Nixon, who gives no reaction.

'Please state your full name for the recording,' he requests, softening his tone as he looks to Jenna, nodding his thanks as she complies.

'This is what's known as an ABE interview – achieving best evidence – and this is our ABE suite. I'll be asking you to provide as much detail as you can regarding your allegations. This is your best chance to tell us everything that could help us pursue a conviction. I'll ask questions to clarify or explore further but I want you to tell your story in your own words. Do you understand?'

Jenna can't swallow the huge gulp of water she has just taken so has to nod frantically.

'You can pause for a break at any time. I understand this will be a difficult process for you.'

'I'll be fine,' Jenna manages to say, immediately wondering if that sounds too dismissive. 'I need to do this.'

'Can you start by telling me why you're here today, Jenna?'

Jenna stares at a dark spot on the carpet, a previous spillage that couldn't be erased.

He makes it sound so simple. Just tell the story.

She is sure the young DC's frown is one of disbelief as she describes the night-time visits, the smell of stale sweat emanating from the fencing mask, the cold touch of the signet ring.

When her careful, stilted words run out, Beckett leans forward over his knees, his movements loose and fluid. He holds eye contact easily, without a sense of pressure.

'Tell us about yourself at thirteen. What were you like?'

'No self-confidence, struggled to make friends. Scared of my own shadow, really.'

'Any particular reason?'

Jenna shrugs, slowly threading the cap back on to the half-empty water bottle to avoid the question of her upbringing. She can't open that box as well.

'It made me an easy target,' she says, moving on without giving him a reply. The slight frown tells her it hasn't gone unnoticed. 'He knew I wouldn't be brave enough to stop him or tell anyone.'

'If he wore a mask, how can you be sure it was Drew Merchant, apart from seeing his signet ring?'

She can't say his aftershave, because half the sixth form had worn the same scent, Hugo and Seb included – one of their cohort had been heiress to a famous perfumery and determinedly generous with her gifts. She can't say the peaty scent of whisky and cigarettes, because most students had a bottle and a packet of Silk Cut stashed in their room, trying to prove they were adults, but she has to find something to convince the detective that her identification is correct.

From nowhere, her panicked mind latches on to a vague recollection. It is not old knowledge, far too recent for that, but surely it's better than nothing. 'His collarbone. He'd once broken his left collarbone and it was misshapen under his skin.'

Beckett and his junior colleague both make notes this time. DC Nixon's eyes barely leave Jenna, even as she scribbles diligently.

'Did the abuse start as soon as you joined Halewood House?' Beckett asks.

'A few weeks into my first term.'

'Was there any reason it stopped?'

'I don't know.' She can't admit the reason she had always believed.

'How old would Mr Merchant have been when it started?'

'Seventeen. His birthday is the second week of September.'

'You remember his birthday?'

'It's the week before mine. Early in the school year.'

'Was Drew a popular student?'

'Very. Everyone liked him, staff and pupils. He was confident, good at everything, always smiling.'

'And how would you describe him now?'

'Powerful,' is the only thing Jenna can think of.

'You said in your initial statement the abuse occurred sporadically, with no particular pattern.'

'It was never predictable.' She could still feel the absolute tension of that time, the dread of waiting almost as bad as the acts themselves, her feeling that it was certain it couldn't be over just like that. 'The longer it went on, the angrier he seemed, until it felt like he only did it when he'd reached boiling point.'

'Did you deny consent?'

'Of course I did. I told him no every time.'

Beckett reaches forward, indicating the neat pile of plain paper. 'Can you draw your dorm room for me? It helps us to visualise the scene and we can give it for the jury if it comes to court.'

Jenna flinches at the prospect of standing in a witness box, Drew's eyes boring into her as she gives evidence. She grabs the pen and dashes off a quick sketch, outlining the furniture, every piece as clear as if she had stood in the room recently, even though the recollections are not coming from her waking mind.

'And can you do a map of your boarding house? Where the staff accommodation was, how far Drew's room was from yours, that sort of thing.'

That took more concentration. It was a long time since she had walked the narrow corridors of Raleigh, a draughty and dim Victorian building with irregular walls and ornate, cobwebbed cornicing.

'Was it usual for the houses to be mixed?'

'It was the first year girls were admitted so I suppose it was a case of trial and error, since there weren't many of us then. Raleigh was the house with the fewest students, so it took the girls. The boys were on separate corridors from us – we had the attic floor – but our housemaster was in his own world.'

'The genders mixed quite freely, even though it was a religious school?'

'The students weren't exactly devout. They were there because their families were affiliated with the Church, not because they were believers.'

'You didn't have a school boyfriend?'

'I wasn't too keen on boys,' Jenna snaps, the first time she has allowed her defences to show. She controls the reaction with difficulty, sitting more upright, pulling her shoulders back. The armour she wears is easily mistaken for arrogance; she knows that. An effective shield against intimacy that she wishes wasn't necessary. It is a bad impression to give a detective.

'I'd like a break now, please. I'm feeling light headed.'

She sees DC Nixon tense, begin to shake her head, but Beckett is on his feet, holding the door open for her, offering coffee and directions to the Ladies.

'Take as long as you need,' he says.

The problem is, the longer Jenna takes, the longer she will have to hold it together, and she is already in real danger of losing her grip.

She barely makes it to the loo before she vomits.

Chapter Sixteen

Safely back in the anonymity of London, Jenna drives straight to Ava's Camden apartment.

'Are you OK?' Half of Ava's face appears on the intercom screen.

'Not really. Can I come up?'

There is an odd hesitation. 'I'll come down. Meet you at the corner café.'

Ava crashes the entry phone back into its holder, the screen going blank in denial. Jenna has no choice but to take a table outside the coffee bar a hundred yards up the street. The wrought-iron chairs are cold, but she doesn't want to sit inside and risk the conversation being overheard.

Jenna is halfway through her cappuccino before Ava finally joins her, cigarette clamped between her blood-red lips and tripping over her unwieldy flip-flops.

'It's freezing,' Jenna can't help but point out, indicating Ava's bare toes.

'I'm hot.' She is sweating, little beads scattered along her hairline.

'Are you ill?'

'I was doing a workout.' Ava waggles her fingers at the waitress, her numerous bangles jangling loudly enough to secure immediate attention. 'Why didn't you text? I'd have come to you.'

'I was interviewed again this morning,' Jenna says abruptly. 'Drew is due tomorrow.'

A sheen slides over Ava's eyes. 'Will he be arrested?'

'They said he'll be attending voluntarily. They'll want to speak to you and Seb next.'

Ava traces her finger across the ornate metalwork of the table. 'God, this is awful, isn't it? I always liked Drew. He was so much nicer than those other morons in the 1st XV.'

'Like Hugo and Rory, you mean.'

Ava flinches. 'Are you here to ask what I'm going to say to the police?'

'More to check you're going to be OK with them.'

'I won't like it. Honestly, I'll hate every second of it, but I'll do it, for you.'

'You do believe me, don't you?'

'I believe you were abused, of course I do.'

'By Drew?'

Ava thanks the waitress as her drink is delivered, taking too long arranging it precisely on the saucer. 'I don't think we got it wrong back then. I find it hard to think Drew is capable of something like that.'

'Did we ever know what anyone was capable of at Cell Block H? Look at Olivia. Look at Rory . . .'

'Don't talk about Rory!' Ava knocks over the little vase holding a single pansy as she reaches for a sugar sachet. She hates sugar in coffee.

Jenna squeezes her eyes shut. 'I'm sorry,' she grinds out. 'I don't mean to be a dick. I'm so on edge I feel like I don't know what I'm doing any more.'

Ava stirs her coffee too fast and taps agitatedly at her phone screen. 'Shit, I'm late! I need to collect Adeline, and the bloody car's still parked at the office.' Ava is never disorganised, always on time and in control of her hectic schedule.

Jenna's face flushes hot as she realises Ava will be going to Drew's school. 'I'll take you to get her,' she offers, too quickly. 'Nip up to the flat and grab her car seat.'

'Will you?' Ava's facial muscles soften slightly, not noticing the sweat gathering at her friend's hairline. 'They fine parents for late collection. Simon will go mad if I get another one.'

It is a quiet journey, Jenna counting the taps of her fingers against the steering wheel. She wants the opportunity to catch a glimpse of Drew in his ivory tower, to see if other people understand what he truly is.

A parking space becomes available just as they pull up at the mouth of the wide school drive, flanked by towering gates and high brick walls forbidding the less privileged glimpsing a view into a world they will never know.

Ava barely waits for the handbrake to be applied before she is out of the car. Jenna is forced to trot behind her to the group of women awaiting their offspring as blazer-clad children begin to appear at the other end of the driveway. The women are very much a collective: styled hair, Burberry overcoats, pastel heels, confident voices competing with each other. Some clutch briefcases; others twirl 4x4 keys on the end of their polished nails.

'Wonder what's keeping Mr Merchant.'

'No Drew today?'

124

'Not like him to be late.'

'Wonder if he's ill.'

'He'd be out here if he was in school.'

'He might just have a meeting, no need for hysterics.'

'Who's being hysterical?'

Jenna tugs Ava's arm, moving several yards away. 'Why are they all asking for him?' she whispers. 'There's no way any news could have leaked yet.'

'He comes out at the end of every day, says goodbye to the kids and chats with the parents.'

Jenna looks from one parent to another, seeing the frisson sparking among them as their gestures become more urgent and the volume of their conversations drop as if secrets are being shared.

'Everyone adores Drew,' Ava says quietly.

'Appearances can be deceptive.' Jenna is saved from having to form a coherent argument by a teacher walking out with a gaggle of small children, too young for their staid uniforms. 'There's Adeline.'

Adeline, four years old and the oldest soul Jenna has ever met, regards both women with her usual serious expression, her watchful eyes huge under the straight fringe of her pixie cut. There is no kiss for Ava, no handing over of belongings for safe-keeping. It is an event, her mother meeting her at the school gates, but she shows no pleasure at the change of routine.

''Lo, Auntie Jen,' she says dutifully.

She squirms away when Jenna feels obliged to kneel and offer her a hug. Ice courses through Jenna's veins as her mind whispers recognition of the child's instinctive rejection of physical contact.

She has done the right thing. If the unthinkable has happened to Adeline, Jenna's actions have made sure she will be safe.

'That's not very polite, Adie.' Ava gives a brittle laugh.

Adeline shakes her head, barely perceptible. 'Don't like hugs. Will Daddy ring tonight?'

The skin around Ava's eyes tightens. 'Who knows, darling.'

As the child fastidiously smooths down her blazer, Jenna can't help but observe that Adeline has inherited few traits from the father whose attention she craves. She would have expected his child to have bright red hair and a generous smattering of freckles, but Adeline is bronze skinned and golden haired, a true sun baby.

The noise level has risen as more students emerge from the school grounds. Although the age groups have three separate entrances to their different buildings, they all congregate together as they leave, spilling out on to the wide pavement in a cacophony of laughter and chatter.

The sharp cry is barely discernible above the noise, and Jenna fails to spot the white-blond head slashing through the crowds towards her.

'I know who you are!'

The words reach her at the same time as her sleeve is seized and she is forcibly spun round to face a teenage girl. Out the corner of her eyes, she sees Ava grab Adeline, hustling her swiftly further down the street to the car, abandoning Jenna to her fate. The sound of the doors slamming is barely audible above Elena's voice.

'I don't know what you mean,' Jenna stammers, her usual bravado shocked into retreat by the suddenness of the girl's approach.

'I'm Elena Merchant. My father is the man you're making shit up about.'

'You're Drew's daughter?'

'Yes, I am! How dare you show up here?'

'How do you know who I am?'

'Don't ask me fucking questions!'

'If you calm down, we can talk about this sensibly.'

'Who the fuck are you to tell me to calm down?'

'This isn't the place to do this.'

'Because you don't want people to know the truth about you!'

'Because your dad wouldn't want all these people hearing his private business,' Jenna says quietly, dropping her voice so Elena is forced to lower her own in order to hear. 'If you want to talk to me, get in the car.'

'As if I'm going anywhere with you, you lying bitch!'

Finally, Jenna's inner core of fire decides to ignite, shielding her from the verbal attack. 'You clearly want to discuss this, and I'm not prepared to have a screaming match with you on the pavement.'

'There's nothing to discuss! You're a sick fantasist, and that's the end of it! You'd better change your story, or you'll be sorry!'

'Don't threaten me.'

Elena spits out a bitter laugh. 'Don't think I don't know people. People who can sort you out. My mum's got a lot of friends.'

'No one's going to "sort me out".'

'My dad never did anything to you! Why the hell would he ever want someone like you?'

'This really isn't any of your business.'

'It affects my life too!' Elena howls.

Another well-groomed teenage girl in an identical navy blazer and tartan skirt approaches, taking hold of Elena's hands, pulling her back from Jenna.

127

'What's going on? Why are you screaming?'

'She's why I'm screaming!'

'What's she done?' The girl eyes Jenna up and down.

Elena snatches herself free. 'I can't tell you!'

'Look after her, please,' Jenna implores the other girl, seizing the opportunity to move away. 'I didn't mean to upset her.'

'You'll be fucking sorry for this,' Elena hisses.

As Jenna gets back in the car, her body is wracked by shakes so severe she can't put her seatbelt on. Ava is in the passenger seat, her face so pale even her lips seem drained of colour. Adeline sits motionless in the back, her little arms wrapped around her middle.

'Shit, that was awful,' Ava finally breathes. 'I didn't even think about Drew's daughter being here. How did she know who you were?'

'We need to go,' Jenna grinds out, smacking the button to start the car. She has no idea how Elena Merchant recognised her but she can't calm her thoughts sufficiently to address the question.

'Are you ok? The kids were videoing it on their phones.'

Jenna struggles to grip the steering wheel, all strength draining from her body. 'I need to let DS Beckett know. He'll make them delete the videos or something.'

'They'll be all over Snapchat by now!'

'Ava, you're making this worse!' Jenna cries. 'Please, just be quiet!'

'Drive up to the main building. We can let one of the teachers know.'

'I can't go into Drew's school!'

'Do you want to be splashed all over the internet?'

Jenna swings the wheel so hard Adeline is flung against the

128

door. She whispers an apology to her, unable to look at the little girl.

'I'll come in with you,' Ava says as they draw up outside the studded double front doors of the main entrance.

'No.' Jenna can't bear any further humiliation to be witnessed. 'Stay with Adie.'

She wrenches open the door and shoots inside the foyer as if being pursued by teenagers and their smartphones. Inside, the marble floors and pillars bring a sense of calm and entitlement, admittance into a fiercely guarded world.

A middle-aged woman sits behind an oak reception desk, eyes narrowed at the sudden arrival, already preparing to deny entry.

'I need to speak to a member of senior management,' Jenna raps out before the woman can speak, fear making her voice louder and more forceful than she intended. 'Urgently. It's about a pupil.'

For a moment, it seems her demand will be ignored until, finally, the receptionist picks up a phone and speaks quietly into it.

'Your name?' she asks.

'Jenna Taylor.'

'You don't have a child here.' A statement, not a question, but Jenna confirms the answer anyway.

The woman studies her for a long moment and Jenna pretends she doesn't cringe at the scrutiny.

'Please take a seat.'

Jenna has barely perched on a polished bench, its gold plaque dedicated to a long-dead headmaster, before a man in a severe suit and bad shoes appears.

'Can I help? I'm the deputy head.'

Jenna stands to meet him, feeling the sweat running the length

of her spine, chilling her. 'Some of your pupils filmed me arguing with someone just now, outside the school.'

A frown. 'Why would they do that?'

'The headmaster's daughter confronted me.'

'Elena? Confronted you?'

'She was upset. It got out of hand.'

'For what reason?'

'It's a private matter.'

Realisation dawns in the man's eyes. 'Are you . . . ?'

'It doesn't matter who I am,' Jenna cries, struggling to draw
enough breath to speak in complete sentences. 'You need to
make your pupils delete the videos.'

'I'm afraid I don't have that power,' he snaps. 'I'd like you to
leave the premises, please.'

'If I need to involve the police, I will.'

'From what I gather, the police are already involved. Please
leave now. We don't need any further disruption to our students'
education.'

Hot anger rises at the unfairness of his dismissal, overtaking
the cold terror of the confrontation. 'Clearly you don't have
much control over them, disruption or not.'

'I won't ask again.'

She can do nothing but accept that arguing is pointless, only
degrading her further. Flushing hot, unable to look at the gawk-
ing receptionist, Jenna spins on her heel and stalks out, pretending
she doesn't hear the urgent, whispered conversation behind her.

Chapter Seventeen

*J*enna had avoided the dining hall for the evening meal. She was no longer losing weight fast enough and, although she was starving, she had to be strong. She needed to be in control of her eating, the only thing she had any autonomy over.

She sat beneath the cover of one of the enormous oak trees, hugging her bag against her chest like a shield. No one bothered to notice her. It was a warm evening and she could hear the crack of leather on willow as the 1st XI practised in the distance. So quintessentially English, the sort of schooldays Enid Blyton had depicted with such fondness, for an audience who had craved the gentle tales. If only they knew the reality.

She riffled through her bag, looking for chewing gum to attempt to fool her appetite. Instead, her fingers found her maths equipment. She pulled out the compass, staring at it as if she had never seen it before. As if beyond her direction, the pad of her index finger pressed down on the sharp point.

Jenna winced as it bit into her skin, leaving a tiny pit.

She did it again, harder this time.

'Hi, Jenna,' a male voice said, breaking the spell.

She curled her hand around the compass, feeling the metal warm in her palm as Seb appeared beside her and folded his long legs into a crouch.

As usual, he was alone. Wearing just his white shirt, he looked like he didn't have an inch of fat on his honed frame. She had seen him obsessively working out in the fitness suite, a boy possessed, trying to exorcise his demons.

'Just wondered if you were OK after dropping the smilies.'

'I was fine. Good, really. I liked it.'

'Sometimes the first trip can be bad.'

'I saw a few scary things, but most of it was OK.'

'My first time was awful. Took me ages to find the balls to try it again.' *He shook his head as if trying to eject the memory. 'The shit I saw.'*

'Like what?' *She was curious enough to ask.*

'Stuff I try to block out. Things about my mum.'

'You don't like your mum?'

'I hate her.' *His voice wobbled and there was real vehemence in his words. He had told her he was the youngest in his year, not seventeen till the end of July, and at that moment, it showed.* 'I wish she was dead.'

She wasn't sure how to respond to such an extreme statement. 'I don't get on with my mum either.'

'How bad is she?'

'She drinks. When she's pissed, she tells me she wishes I'd never been born. I don't think she loves me at all.'

'Mine loves me too much.'

'Is that a bad thing?'

'Oh yeah.' *His jaw was rigid.* 'I can't wait to get away from her for good, soon as I leave school. Lead my own life.'

'You've not long to go,' *she offered, trying to sound hopeful for him.*

'No.' *He touched her hand, which was still concealing the compass.*

For some reason, she felt compelled to show him the implement.

'Make sure you disinfect it first,' *he said.* 'And clean the cut with Dettol afterwards. They get infected easily.'

132

He tugged at his shirt sleeve, rolling it up to his elbow. Jenna saw the lines in various stages of healing littering his skin.

Wide eyed with realisation, she stared at him. 'Why do you do it?'

He glanced away, as if the sudden intimacy was too much for him. 'It makes me feel better.'

He looked back to her again, still holding her hand in his much larger one. Their fingers intertwined of their own accord and Jenna found herself leaning into him, wanting his comfort, his understanding. He slid his arm around her, drawing her closer. It felt like the touch of the protective big brother she had never had.

'Put her down, Byron, she's too young for you!' came a mocking shout.

Hugo was walking along the path with Rory, both carrying rugby kitbags over their broad shoulders. Rory didn't acknowledge them, but Hugo strolled over, leaving his cousin to carry on alone. Jenna hurriedly pulled away from Seb, tugging her hand free to conceal the compass again.

'All right, folks?' Hugo asked amiably.

Jenna mumbled hello, all her old shyness returning in his presence.

'We've just played a friendly. Got battered.'

'Sorry you lost,' she stumbled out, not sure what else to say.

'Mind if I join you?'

'If you want.' She watched Seb uncertainly, who had scrambled to his feet as Hugo approached.

'I'd better go.'

'No need to leave on my account, Byron. I'm sure Jenna can talk to both of us.'

Seb ignored him completely, shifting from one foot to the other, tapping one hand rapidly against the outside of his leg. 'Bye, Jenna.'

'Thanks for talking to me,' Jenna said, trying to make amends.

His lips twisted in an odd smile. 'I should thank you for talking to me.'

'Why wouldn't I?'

'Not many people do.'

'Ain't that the truth,' Hugo drawled as Seb slunk away, head down to avoid any chance of confrontation.

'Why don't you like him?' Jenna asked.

'Weirdo.'

'You mean he's not like you.'

'Scared of his own shadow. Always banging on about how depressed he is.'

'It's not his fault he's got problems.'

He gave a shrug, as if it couldn't matter less. 'He needs to man up.'

As tempting as it was to just nod and side with the popular, well-liked Hugo, Jenna felt a flash of loyalty to Seb.

'I like him.'

'Is that because you don't have any friends either?' He grinned to show her he was teasing.

'I do!'

'Ava and Olivia? Be careful around those two. Ava had to change schools for selling a dodgy batch of pills.'

Jenna felt her eyes widen. 'I didn't know that.'

'No one died or anything, but the kids she'd sold them to were ready to lynch her, so she played the bullied card and persuaded her parents to send her here.' A derisive snort. 'She doesn't come from money – she's here on a scholarship – so she keeps dealing to top up her piggy bank. Makes her a risky person to know, trust me.'

'What about Olivia? She's so clever, she's top of fourth form.' Jenna was desperate to prove herself academically, to show her mother.

Hugo rolled his eyes. 'She might be a genius, but she's a pain in the arse, and a junkie at that. I know — pot, kettle and all that — but, seriously, she takes so much she's never sober. She got kicked out of her last school. Her housemaster found her passed out in her dorm, completely off her face. Even her straight-A★ predictions couldn't save her.'

He grinned and barked a laugh.

'Halewood House will take anyone guaranteed to help them in the league tables.'

Chapter Eighteen

Drew

Natasha had insisted he wear his Savile Row suit. After only a few minutes in the airless, grey interview room, the heavy material is making Drew sweat profusely.

So far, no one has spoken to him. The officer supervising him as if he were an errant child hasn't even deigned to glance up. Drew's solicitor has disappeared, saying he was going to discuss 'disclosures' – presumably whatever the police were willing to say about the allegations. Drew hasn't even been offered a cup of tea.

He adjusts his tie so he can undo the top button at his collar, wondering whether to abandon the jacket altogether, but the detectives would notice the sweat patches on his pale blue shirt. Would it make him look guilty?

It seems a long time before the solicitor returns, and he is shaking his head as he dismisses the supervisory officer.

'They've given me almost nothing.'

'What does that mean?' Drew demands.

'It means they have nothing or they're not willing to share what they do have. Either way, it doesn't help us.'

'Jesus, Henry, this is madness.'

Henry Rycroft busies himself unpacking a neat laptop, a leather-bound notepad and a Montblanc, arranging his own silk-lined jacket fussily on the back of the uncomfortable chair next to Drew. He looks as if he'd rather wipe down the table before he entrusts his belongings to it.

'Well, this is quite the situation,' he says as he checks the cleanliness of the chair and finally sits down.

All these years of friendship, and that is the only thing he can say.

'Where has all this come from, Drew?'

'My guess is as good as yours.'

'Upset anyone recently? Strayed from home, maybe?'

'Keep your bloody voice down! I've had no contact with this woman for years before last week, for Christ's sake.'

'You've no idea of what's driven her to make the report?'

'None. I can't think of any reason she'd want to discredit me, or seek revenge, or . . .' Drew's voice trails off and he is reduced to shaking his head repeatedly. 'I haven't done anything to her. Not ever.'

'This current elite-school scandal is causing all sorts of issues.' Henry blows out a frustrated breath in sympathy.

'So what happens now?' Drew asks.

'They'll interview you, ask if you have any knowledge of the alleged offences, that kind of thing.'

'You make it sound like this is a casual, everyday occurrence.'

'Keep calm, old chap, I've got a plan.'

Drew grits his teeth at the term of endearment. Henry has a habit of speaking as if they exist in a Le Carre novel.

'Then tell me what it is!'

'We'll prepare a statement from you, which I'll read to the officers. You'll then give a no-comment interview, thank them for their time, and we'll go and have a damned good whisky.'

'As simple as that.' Drew rubs his eyes, overwhelmed by tiredness. 'What sort of statement?'

'Your denial, an explanation of your good character and standing, your response to the supposed victim, which will be sympathetic but firm. We don't have anything to answer for, since the detectives have chosen not to give us anything.'

'So I don't reply to their questions?'

'Absolutely not. That would only land you in trouble.'

'Why would it? I'm an innocent man, and I want to make that clear.'

'They'll try to trick you into answering, make you feel compelled to defend yourself or explain something unnecessarily. That will only give them further ammunition. Say nothing. Every time you open your mouth it increases the chances of you saying something they can use against you.'

'But I haven't done anything wrong.'

'Of course not.'

'Doesn't this make me look guilty?'

'It makes you look like a well-educated man who will not be intimidated or coerced into overlooking his legal rights. Trust me, Drew, they have no evidence, and we won't be helping them to uncover any.'

'There's no evidence because nothing happened.'

'Of course,' Henry repeats his favourite phrase. 'Right, let's get to this statement. I'll handwrite it; looks more personal if it comes to court.'

'Court?' Drew almost shouts.

'Which we won't, of course.'

Drew nearly roars at him to stop saying 'of course', as if his lawyer were a disruptive fourth-former caught swearing. He holds his breath until the urge subsides, and it dawns on him that Henry is as nervous as he is. Another flash of heat crashes over him as he sees that even one of his oldest friends isn't sure whether or not to believe him.

Henry writes quickly, his pen filling the page with his flamboyant scrawl, nodding and making encouraging noises but keeping his eyes firmly fixed on the paper in front of him.

'I'll tell them we're ready.' Henry stands as soon as the statement is finished and makes for the door, straightening his tie unnecessarily.

He returns within moments, accompanied by two others. One Drew recognises as Beckett, the detective who came to his house. The other is a twitchy younger woman with an intense stare he immediately finds disconcerting.

The officers remove their suit jackets and busy themselves opening notebooks, pushing buttons, settling in their seats on the other side of the scarred table as Henry faffs around with his papers. The woman's gaze burns into Drew.

The beep of the recording device seems deafening and lasts for ever. Beckett speaks without missing a beat, efficiently issuing the necessary identifying details. Drew finds himself staring at a brown stain on the wall behind the detective's head. Coffee? Dried blood? Or something worse?

'Mr Merchant?'

It takes him too long to register that he is being addressed. The caution has been read again and Beckett is checking his understanding.

He clears his throat, pulling his shoulders back. He has to concentrate. Why has his capable brain chosen now, of all times, to desert him?

'We will now give you a prepared statement, Detective Sergeant Beckett,' Henry intervenes smoothly, 'following which my client has been advised to respond "no comment" to your questions.'

Beckett's eyes betray that this course of action has already been predicted. 'Go ahead, Mr Rycroft.'

Henry reads without his usual tendency to inject a flair of erudition. His voice is clear, level and emotionless, as if he has already decided the situation is nonsense and shouldn't be afforded the slightest consideration. Drew finds himself breathing a little more easily as he listens to his friend's calm words.

I deny the allegation made by Jenna Taylor. We boarded at Halewood House School together in the mid-nineties and I knew her reasonably well. I never engaged in any sexual activity with her at school, consensual or otherwise, nor have I ever threatened her with harm. Jenna and I had not seen each other since school until recently, when we arranged to meet at an Islington pub to catch up. She showed no distress at being in my company, nor did she speak to me regarding her claims.

Jenna suffered from mental health difficulties at school, and it is possible she has relapsed, as I cannot think of any other reason for her to make such an outlandish allegation. I know she was previously under the care of a psychiatrist and was considered a suicide risk. She had a drug problem and self-harmed.

I have worked in education since graduating from Cambridge and am shocked and dismayed by this accusation. I am well

respected in my career and am very concerned at the potential impact
on my good name, as well as that of my school and my family, and
hope that this matter will be resolved as quickly as possible.

Beckett nods as Henry finishes reading and tidily presents the statement, but Drew can see that the detective's attention is entirely focused on him.

'This is a voluntary interview, Mr Merchant. You're free to leave at any point. I understand that you've been instructed to answer "no comment" to anything I may ask you, but this is your best opportunity to tell your side of the story, to make your voice heard.'

'We've already explained our position,' Henry states mildly, as if pointing out that Beckett has taken his pint by mistake.

Beckett's gaze doesn't waver from Drew. 'I'll ask my questions anyway. Whether you choose to answer is up to you.'

Drew stares stonily back, his chest tight once again.

'Are you guilty of the allegations I've put to you?'

Henry's leg presses briefly against his. Drew swallows his instinctive reaction to answer in a timely and succinct manner and instead says, 'No comment.' The words sound crisp and decisive, in spite of the lump in his throat.

'How do you know Jenna Taylor?'

'No comment.'

'Did you attend school together?'

'No comment.'

'Are you friends? Do you meet up regularly?'

'No comment.'

'Have you ever had a sexual relationship with Jenna Taylor?'

He hopes his flinch isn't noticeable. 'No comment.'

The questions fly at him with barely a pause for his monotonous reply. He stops listening to the content, relieved to see Henry's pen flying across his legal pad.

'Have you any idea why Mrs Taylor would make these allegations?'

Drew tunes back in for what seems to be Beckett's last question. He's got to hand it to the detective, he's tenacious. They've been sitting here for nearly an hour.

'No comment,' he says, allowing weariness to creep into his voice. Henry glances pointedly at his watch.

Beckett looks to his female colleague for the first time, and Drew feels his shoulders drop as the scrutiny is finally off him. The woman, whose name he took no notice of, gives a twitch of her head, her lips tightly compressed.

'Interview terminated at three forty-two,' Beckett states for the recording, though he makes no move to leave the table. He leans back casually, stretching powerful arms above his head until his spine audibly cracks. 'Thank you for coming in, Mr Merchant.'

'You'll be wanting to see me again, I presume?' Drew finds it odd to say something other than 'no comment'.

'Once we've made further inquiries.'

'So I'm free to go? No conditions?'

'Please do not attempt to make any contact with Jenna Taylor, be it in person, over the phone or via social media.'

'I wouldn't be so stupid,' Drew lies between gritted teeth.

After all, he has already been stupid enough when it comes to Jenna Taylor.

Henry drives him home. He wouldn't have been capable of operating a car safely even if he had taken his own. He remembers nothing of the journey, staring blankly as Henry pulls into the driveway of Drew's home and extends his hand, as if the concept of a handshake is entirely foreign.

'Try not to worry, old chap. It'll all come to nothing, mark my words.'

Drew knows he should invite his friend in for a glass of whisky, but he can't bring himself to do it. He needs to be alone. He doesn't even bother to wait for Henry to pull away before letting himself into the hall, blissfully cool after the literal and figurative heat of the interview room.

The house is silent. Elena is out with her friends after school and Natasha is off doing God knows what with her platinum card. He rarely has any idea where his wife is. The housekeeper follows him to the study, offers coffee and retreats immediately upon his curt refusal.

He seems to have lost the ability to blink. He stares at the floor, clenching and unclenching his fists. The tightness remains in his chest, an ache that seems to penetrate through to his shoulder blades. His mouth is dry – even the large cut-glass tumbler of single malt isn't helping.

He is terrified.

His mobile rings and he winces when he sees the caller is Sir Ian Weston, chair of the board of governors and esteemed former pupil of the school, now highly respected in Westminster and Drew's personal guide to navigating his own route to politics.

'Good afternoon, Drew, how are you?'

Drew gathers the strength to sound like the competent, measured professional he is held to be. 'As well as can be expected, thank you. How are things at school?'

'Those in the know are very shocked, naturally. The original plan was to keep it quiet from the pupils but let the staff know – you know they'd only find out for themselves, and it seemed better to limit the gossip – but that has been somewhat derailed.'

'In what way?'

'I'm afraid your daughter was involved in an altercation. She was rather loud and surrounded by other students and parents at the time.'

Drew freezes. 'What did Ele do?'

'Confronted a woman she identified as your accuser. She attracted rather a lot of attention, I'm afraid.'

'So now the entire school community will be throwing rumours around.'

'It would seem that way. Probably best to have a word with your daughter, impress upon her the need for discretion.'

Drew rubs his forehead. 'Yes, Sir Ian.'

'Terrible business, all this. You have our full support, naturally . . .' Is that an awkward pause Drew is sure he hears? '. . . but we can't be seen not to be following all the proper procedures. You know how education is these days, not like in my time, when we'd have quietly dealt with such matters in-house . . .'

'I understand that procedure needs to be followed,' Drew interrupts. 'We have to protect the reputation of the school.'

'Exactly. Glad you agree.'

'Surely I can work from home, keep abreast of things. I'm hoping the investigation won't run on too long.'

An unnecessarily long throat-clearing. 'I'm afraid you can't have any involvement with the school until the accusations have been dropped. Not our choice, you understand. Damn procedure. Try not to worry, though, we'll keep the place afloat until you come back.'

'But—'

'Drew, I'm truly sorry. Maybe this is the perfect time to write that book you've always talked of, take your mind off things.'

Drew can't imagine being able to focus on a Sudoku, let alone craft a novel, but the finality is clear. 'You'll keep in touch, Sir Ian?'

'Absolutely. Obviously, I can't update you on any school business, but I'll check in regularly and I'll make sure the SLT do the same.'

Drew feels his jaw tighten as he thinks of his deputy, a loyal man, but with shoulders too stooped and narrow to carry this burden of responsibility. The other members of the senior leadership team are too busy trying to get ahead of the pack in the race for further promotion to offer him much support.

'I'm sure all this will be cleared up in no time,' Weston is saying. 'You'll take care, won't you?'

'Yes, I'll be fine, thank you.' It doesn't feel like he will ever be fine again, but he has to play the game.

'Good man. Speak soon. Best to the family.'

With that, Weston is gone, back to his seat in Parliament and his country house, and Drew is horrified to find tears welling. He swipes roughly at his eyes with a clenched fist, shoving himself up to stand at the window, his back turned in case Natasha returns and deigns to come looking for him.

Chapter Nineteen

*S*ummer *term, nearing its end, had brought droughts and heat waves, but Jenna shivered uncontrollably, her emaciated body unable to provide her any protection from the insidious cold creeping through her veins.*

She scuttled into the far corner of the room, her instinctive hiding place, as the door handle suddenly moved again. He never came back. Why was he coming back? Had she made too much noise?

'Holy shit, what's happened?' Olivia hurried inside as she saw Jenna's shaking figure. She dropped to the floor, reaching out and embracing the younger girl. 'Are you OK?'

Jenna pressed her face into the slim curve of Olivia's neck, breathing in her perfume, her apple shampoo.

'Have you taken something? Are you having a bad reaction?'

'No,' Jenna managed to say. 'Nothing like that.'

'What, then? And don't tell me "nothing".' Olivia sat back on her heels, grabbing both of Jenna's hands in hers. 'I know I seem a total flake, but I'm a good friend, honestly. You can trust me.'

Jenna felt her eyes darting as she realised Olivia wasn't going to give up this time, that she needed to give a reason that would satisfy the older girl.

She turned her wrist over in Olivia's hand, showing her the fresh scores.

'Oh, babe,' Olivia breathed. 'You shouldn't start with that shit. Once you get the habit, it's harder to stop than coke.'

'Probably a bit late,' Jenna whispered, trying to smile, desperate to reassure her friend that she was all right.

Olivia's finger gently traced the deep scratches. 'Just be careful, OK? I couldn't bear anything to happen to you.'

Like a frog, she leapt to her feet, as if she couldn't possibly remain still a moment longer. She pulled Jenna upright and steered her to the bed, flopping down beside her.

'Fuck, I definitely need a smoke now.' She produced the tin, lit one spliff and inhaled deeply before handing it to Jenna.

As she took the spliff back, she reached out a long, slim finger to touch a patch of skin just below Jenna's throat. 'You've got a bruise coming through.'

Jenna recoiled instantly. Her heart beat a manic flutter against her ribs.

'Did someone hurt you? Are you being bullied?'

Jenna gritted her teeth and shook her head hard, fixing her gaze on the floor.

'You can tell me, it's OK.'

'It's never going to be OK again,' Jenna whispered. Her hand was shaking as she reached for the spliff again. Her lungs were too tight to keep the smoke in this time, so she took several quick draws in succession. It made her head spin, but she kept inhaling.

'Take it easy – that's strong stuff.' Olivia gently removed it from her fingers. 'You should talk about it. It'll help.'

'Nothing will help till it stops.'

'Till what stops?'

Jenna found her eyes being drawn upwards, to meet Olivia's open gaze.

She took a deep breath.

147

Chapter Twenty

Jenna lurches awake, gulping air into lungs that feel barren, the sheets cold and damp around her shaking body. Zach has already jerked upright and is watching her from his side of the bed with an expression that suggests he is dreading what might come next. She sees his hand twitch, as if he instinctively wants to reach out and comfort her, but he grips the duvet instead.

'You were calling out names. Ava and Olivia. Who's Rory?'

Jenna feels her body go rigid, as if she has turned to stone. 'He was at school with us.'

'You kept begging Olivia not to do it. What did she do?'

Her mind is still fogged, trapped in the remnants of the dream. 'Nothing.'

She can never let Zach know what Olivia did, because to admit Olivia's actions is to face her own guilt.

She scrabbles for her phone. Notifications fill the screen, a slew of tags and emojis and comments.

'Don't watch that video again,' Zach begs.

'I have to.' It is already a compulsion, only hours after seeing it for the first time. She checks the retweets. She doesn't have

TikTok so she can't see how many times the original has been shared, but Twitter is doing enough by itself. Her account had been discovered within minutes.

With a defeated groan, Zach rolls to his other side and pulls the duvet to his ears to hide from the glow.

As the ghosts of Olivia and Rory fade, the sweat dries and the metallic taste from biting the inside of her cheek fades, Jenna props herself up on her pillows, covers gripped tight to her chest. She frantically scrolls, her thumb damp against the phone screen. She hears snatches of her own panicked whispers escaping her compressed lips at each sickening comment.

She watches the video yet again. Elena Merchant's tear-stained face, make-up still perfect despite her sobs. A huge bed, white duvet artfully crumpled atop silk sheets, soft backlighting. The screen held close for Elena to whisper into the camera, biting her bee-stung lower lip. Her ice-blue eyes are open to their fullest, innocence personified.

'My life was perfect,' she whispers. 'My dad's life was perfect. Until a bitter, jealous bitch decided to try and fuck it all up for us.'

She pauses to dab delicately at the tear-tracks. Her eyes close momentarily, a deep breath before her body visibly tenses and she raises her head again, thrusting out her chin.

Her nostrils flare, her cheeks flushing red. 'Her name is Jenna Taylor,' she hisses. 'And she is a fucking liar. My dad is the best man you could ever meet. He would never do the shit she's accusing him of. The bitch wants to ruin my dad for her own gain. Don't trust her. Don't believe her. Jenna Taylor *lies*.'

The final word, just before the screen goes black, is spat with such venom that Jenna recoils, even though she has heard it too many times already. Panic hits her like a tidal wave, enveloping her each time she fights to take a breath. The impact shocks her with its strength, its ferocity.

Her heart pounds and her eyes fail to focus. She tries staring at a spot on the floor, battling to focus, but it spins like a carousel. She is about to lose all control.

It is the alarm that saves her, startling her out of the swirling vortex that beckons. By the time she has jabbed it into silence and dropped the phone on to the bedside table, pretending she has gone back to sleep so she can attempt to calm herself, Zach has stirred and Loki has launched his morning greeting. Usually she bats the dog off, but today she holds him close, accepts his joyous, reassuring licks until Zach opens the bedroom door and she is abandoned.

She can't fight the need to look at her phone again as she hears them clatter downstairs for Loki to pay his morning visit to the neglected rose bushes. Zach will present the Pedigree Chum with his usual announcement – 'Breakfast is served, sir' – and come back upstairs to shower while Loki eats. The same routine, as if nothing has changed. As if the life they know isn't teetering on the edge of disaster.

'Are you still reading Twitter? Just delete your account.' Zach perches on the edge of the bed and she lunges away in case he tries to take her phone. His expression tells her the thought had never crossed his mind. 'Love, please, you're only doing yourself more harm, giving the trolls an audience.'

She flinches as he puts his arm around her, his bare flesh warm and slightly damp. He smells of crystal-clear oceans and bracing waterfalls, of freedom from city shackles and internet demons.

Another wave of terror grips her. 'They know where I work.

They've seen my photos – they know what I look like and which bars I drink in. What am I going to do, Zach?'

His big hand closes over hers as she clutches her phone. She can feel his pulse, as steady and reassuring as Zach himself. She begins to count, feeling her grip loosen until she allows Zach to take the phone. His thumb flies across the screen, competent, in control.

'There's support for you as well, love. Women are replying to the trolls in your defence. Look.'

'I don't want to see. Just get rid of it all.'

'There. Gone.'

'That won't stop it, though, will it?'

His expression agrees. 'No, but it'll safeguard you from it.'

'Is Lando on Twitter?' she demands.

'No, only Snapchat and TikTok.'

'Will he follow Drew's daughter on them, or whatever it is they do?'

'How would he know her?'

'Maybe Drew's introduced them – I don't know! What if someone else he knows shares it?' She is lurching from one panic to another, unable to break fear's icy grip.

'Do you want to tell him?'

'No!'

Zach shrugs helplessly. 'I can't imagine he'll stumble across it. His social media world revolves around swimming, gaming and rugby. And porn, I suppose.'

Jenna doesn't want to give that prospect a second thought. 'What does that girl think she's doing?'

She hurls the phone on to the duvet, unsatisfied by how easily the goose down absorbs her violence.

'You're going to be late for work.' Zach's voice is muffled as he pulls a shirt over his head without bothering to undo the buttons. Jenna stares at the creases from his lackadaisical use of hangers.

She leaps out of bed, suddenly galvanised.

'What are you doing?'

'I need the detective's card. I need him to make her take her post down.'

'It's too late for that . . .'

'I can't find it!' she hisses, upending her tote bag. 'Fuck! Where's it gone?'

Zach doesn't bother urging her to calm down. 'Where did you last see it?'

'On my dressing table! It can't have vanished!'

A thorough search of the bedroom yields no card.

'Google the station's main number and leave a message for him,' Zach suggests.

The solution doesn't quell her anger. Any event, however small, that goes beyond her control is guaranteed to bring all the old terrors flooding back, overwhelming her. She kicks off the duvet and stalks into the bathroom, slamming the door hard enough to make her shampoo bottles tumble. Zach is gone when she emerges, much earlier than he usually leaves, and the guilt surges, poking at her until she feels bruised.

It takes too much effort to urge Lando from his pit, her temper fraying more with each increase in volume, even as she tries to speak calmly, encourage rather than direct. When he deigns to appear, shirt already stained with toothpaste, tie absent, he stops dead in front of her. His eyes take in her blotchy skin, puffy eyes, lips bitten and chewed to soreness. She watches him notice the clenched fists, rigid body, shallow breaths.

'I'm going to be late,' he says as he turns away from her. His broadening shoulders seem to fill the hallway and her hand twitches to reach out, to smooth his wild curls, stroke his long spine, something, anything, to prove they are mother and son.

Instead, she grabs her keys and gives up. The car journey is silent, Lando absorbed in his phone's world. Every time his thumb scrolls, Jenna's breath freezes and the lump in the centre of her chest grows bigger until he smirks a reaction or rolls his eyes in contempt.

It is the longest time before he unfolds himself from the passenger seat, throwing a 'bye' over his shoulder as he strides away. She watches him store the phone safely in his blazer pocket as he joins his friends and her shoulders slump in brief relief.

Her secret is safe a while longer.

Hugo is already in when she arrives, the door of his office pointedly left open. The junior staff have yet to arrive, so there is no excuse not to follow the implied invite.

'Have you seen Twitter?' he gasps.

Jenna remains hovering in the doorway, unwilling to cross the threshold. 'I can barely bring myself to look.'

'What are you going to do about it?'

'I don't know what I *can* do about it.'

'The company is mentioned. This office is mentioned.'

'I'm sorry.' For once, Jenna's armour isn't doing its job. She feels exposed, vulnerable to the world. 'I didn't intend all this to interfere with work. How did you find out?'

'Weren't you going to tell me?' Hugo seems almost hurt, but his eyes gleam with panic, presumably at the prospect of his beloved company being tarnished by her ills.

'How could I talk to you about something like that?'

'But Drew? I knew he was a cad – it was his dream come true when the girls arrived at the school – but I didn't think he was fucking depraved.' Hugo shakes his head as if he is trying to dislodge something. 'It's crazy, absolutely insane. Mr Perfect was as fucked up as the rest of us beneath his golden exterior.'

'I can't believe the place kept going for as long as it did.'

'The Brothers were all right. They never hurt anyone, not like others in their sphere. They just didn't look past the end of their Communion wafers to see what really went on after hours.'

'Maybe none of this would be happening if they'd bothered with basic safeguarding,' Jenna spits.

'Come off it, Jenna, it wasn't just their fault. People like Olivia—'

'I wish everyone would stop bringing Olivia into it!'

Hugo rolls his eyes, a schoolboy's disdain. 'She was out of control. I hated how she egged you on, getting you hooked on the skunk. All those fucking times she was wasted, behaving like she could do whatever she wanted.'

Jenna's restraint has gone and she is a small child again, desperate to escape the cruel words that seem to be all she ever hears.

'Don't say it like she was to blame for everything! She helped me cope! She stood by me. As if you were any better, lording it about the place.'

'No need to take it out on me! I know Cell Block H could be rough but it wasn't that bad.'

'Hugo, you have no fucking idea!'

'So what I went through was nothing, was it? I lost someone close to me, too.'

'Everyone knew the risks!' Jenna almost yells.

He reacts as if she has slapped him, his neck tensing as though it has absorbed a blow. It seems to bring him back to the present. His voice softens. 'You look awful. I can see how much you're struggling. Do you need some time off?'

'No!' As soon as the offer is made, Jenna is desperate to cling to the life raft of her career. The dread of earlier that morning is forgotten at the prospect of losing her security. 'Work is the only thing I can focus on.'

Her phone startles her. She is tempted to reject the call, but it will save her from the current conversation.

'I got your message, Jenna,' DS Beckett says.

Ignoring Hugo's hands flying into the air at missing out on the conversation, Jenna hurries into her own office and closes the door.

'Can you do anything to stop the posts?'

'Unfortunately not.'

'But I've been named! Surely that's a breach of privacy or something.'

'No details of the alleged crime have been shared.'

'Not yet. It's slander! I'm being called a liar, and that's just the lesser accusations.'

'I agree it's unpleasant, but no laws have been broken. I'll contact Mr Merchant and speak to his daughter about removing the content, but it's already been widely shared.'

Jenna sits down heavily at her desk. 'This is madness.'

'I'm sorry it's happened, but social media makes it hard to maintain privacy these days. Have you deleted your accounts?'

'Yes,' she says dully.

'My best advice is to stay offline for a while. These things flare up quickly but die down just as fast. It'll be over in a few days, I expect.'

'Not before most of my acquaintances know about it. What do I tell people?'

'Tell them you can't discuss an active investigation. I'll be directing Mr Merchant and his family to do the same.'

'Too late!'

Beckett's silence is calm, unruffled. 'We'll continue our inquiries, Jenna, and let you know when we need to speak to you again.'

'Has Drew denied everything?'

'As expected, yes. We need some time to investigate further.'

'What do I do in the meantime?'

'We advise you to try to live your normal life, as much as you can. Go to work, meet your friends, do what you would always do. Locking yourself away will only make it worse. Talk about it. Don't shut down on those you trust.'

She tunes out, letting his words wash over her. If only it could be that easy. She shut down decades ago.

Surely so long has now passed that she will never be able to unlock her true self again.

Chapter Twenty-One

Jenna calls her normal greeting up the stairs, not pausing to wait for an answer that won't come. As usual, she is met by the realisation that she only has herself to blame for the daily silence. The immediate thump of footsteps freezes her. Lando never comes to say hello. He prefers to avoid her, and she can understand why.

The next moment, he is in the hallway, standing too close to her. His size almost makes her take an involuntary step back before she stops herself. This is her son, for God's sake.

Lando's fists are balled tight, his knuckles wide. When he meets her gaze, his eyes are burning. He speaks with rare slowness, almost deliberate in his words, as if they have been carefully chosen and rehearsed continuously.

'What did you do, Mum?'

Jenna opens her mouth to reply before realising she has no idea what to say.

'There are videos of you on TikTok.'

'Videos?'

'You and Drew's daughter screaming at each other.'

'How do you know Drew's daughter?'

'She swims too.' Lando rolls his eyes impatiently. 'What have you done to him?'

'What?' she repeats stupidly, cringing at the memory of the pupils filming her exchange with Elena Merchant.

'She was shouting about you doing something to Drew. What did you *do*?' Force enters his tone.

'Lando . . .'

'Do you know how embarrassing it is when the whole world knows your mum's been up to something and you don't have a clue?'

'It's not something you need to worry about.'

'You think?' Lando snatches his phone free from his pocket as if he is about to thrust it in her face as evidence of his involvement.

DS Beckett's business card falls to the floor, unintentionally pulled out along with his phone. Lando tries to snatch it up, but Jenna beats him to it.

'Why have you got this card?' she demands.

'Found it,' he mumbles.

'In our bedroom?'

'Can't remember.'

'*Lando*.'

'You must have dropped it! I picked it up off the hallway floor and just shoved it in my pocket to put in the bin later. I forgot I had it, OK?'

He turns away, striding back upstairs before he can be accused of anything more.

Jenna has Beckett's number stored in her phone now. She doesn't expect him to answer, but he picks up on the third ring.

'It's Jenna Taylor. There's more videos, and they've been shared God knows how many times.'

'I know. I've seen them.'

She wants to ask how, but it seems unlikely he will tell her.

'Going to Mr Merchant's school wasn't a good idea, you understand that, don't you?' Beckett continued.

'I wasn't intending any confrontation.'

'You need to keep your distance from the Merchant family. You're only jeopardising your case.'

'My son has seen the videos taken outside the school. How can I tell him what this is all about?' She doesn't know why she's begging a relative stranger for guidance.

'You and your husband will need to make that decision. But be aware that he'll mostly get his information online if you choose not to tell him anything. That could have a bigger impact than explaining it tactfully yourselves.'

'We can ban him from using the internet.'

'Come on, Jenna, you can't believe that would work with a teenager.'

He's right. Lando has many of Zach's IT smarts and all of Jenna's stubbornness; he would see a ban as a challenge.

'I'll talk to him,' she says, defeated. 'Thank you for taking my call.'

'Let me know if anything else happens.'

She promises to do so and hangs up. The talk with Lando will have to wait until she has wine's courage to help her. She doesn't even check the bottle she selects, glugging the golden liquid into the nearest glass and slugging two long draughts before refilling and forcing herself to slow down. The buzz is immediate, a warm blanket of comfort enveloping her.

As she finishes the second glass, she catches her reflection in the shiny fridge door and recoils from the image of her mother staring back at her. Temporarily chastened, she yanks open the door, deposits the remains of the bottle to chill and strides upstairs before she can change her mind.

Lando's door is closed. Only six months ago, he wouldn't have cared about leaving it open but now it is always firmly shut. She nearly loses her courage, turns away to go back downstairs, but then she hears Lando's voice, on the phone or talking into his headset, not realising how loud he is.

'Yeah, I know the girl. Her dad is my swimming coach. She's on the under-nineteens.' A laugh. 'Whatever. He says I'm the most talented swimmer he's seen in years. Says I'm even better than he was. He's going to help me get to the Olympics.'

A pause to listen to the other side of the conversation.

'As if I know. Mum's been batshit recently. Who else has seen it?' Another pause. 'Why's it getting shared so much? It's not that interesting.'

Jenna doesn't give the other person a chance to reply, barging into the room as noisily as she can. Lando drops his controller, cursing loudly.

'What the fuck, Mum?' he yells.

This doesn't seem the right time to tell him off for swearing. 'Who are you talking to?'

'No one!' He snatches off his headphones.

'Your friends don't need to know my business!'

'Too late to keep it a secret now!'

'What's that supposed to mean?'

His mouth twists and he grabs his wireless keyboard, banging out a command. One of the computer screens fills with Elena's tear-stained face, the fairy lights mocking Jenna with their innocent beauty.

160

'Turn it off!' she cries.

'Why? You've seen it already, haven't you?'

'I mean it, Lando! Turn it off!'

He resists for another moment, enough for Elena's sobbing to become deafening to Jenna, before finally smacking another button and pausing the video. The still Elena glares at Jenna through overflowing eyes.

'What did you lie about?' Lando's tone is almost a snarl.

'I haven't lied. And please don't talk to me like that!'

His voice becomes vaguely mocking. *Jenna Taylor lies.*

'Stop saying that!'

'Then tell me what you've done! Are you having an affair with Drew? I know you met up with him the other night. He told me.'

Jenna recoils, her skin burning. Her heart pounds so loudly she's sure Lando can hear it. Does he really think that little of her, to be able to ask her such a devastating thing with ice-cold casualness? Is this what she has made her son? A careless, unfeeling shell of a human being, starved of a mother's nurture?

She had promised him she would never become like her mother, a promise she knows he remembers. She has failed spectacularly.

'Of course I'm not having an affair with Drew!' she manages to say.

'What, then? Or shall I message him and find out?'

'Do not contact Drew!' she orders as he reaches for his phone. 'You'll compromise everything!'

That stops him. 'What is there to compromise?'

Jenna takes an unsteady breath. 'Come downstairs with me. I want to show you something.'

Lando scowls, about to refuse.

161

'Five minutes, that's all. Please.' Deep inside, it devastates her that she has to plead with her own son.

He stomps down the stairs behind her, his reluctance clear in each heavy step. She wishes Zach were home. He has always known how to communicate with Lando. His family believe in hugs and encouragement, in building people up, in empathy and solidarity. Zach is as much a product of his upbringing as she is of hers.

In the kitchen, she plucks one of the newspapers from the recycling box. She spreads the creases out of it out on the breakfast bar, beckoning Lando closer. She sees that he's curious in spite of himself.

'This story here, the elite-school scandal. Read it.'

His eyes dart, skimming across the pages, his lips moving silently. He is a fast reader. He would be a real success at school if he ever applied himself. If Jenna ever encouraged him to apply himself.

He can't know the reason she wants him to be anonymous within his school community, to not stand out and draw attention to himself. She tells herself it is better to let him think she just doesn't care about his education. It will hurt him less than her real reason.

He reaches the end and looks to her for an explanation, and she is reminded that for all his size and attitude, he is only thirteen and he can't interpret this for himself.

'Women are coming forward saying that inappropriate things happened to them at my school,' she says. 'They were abused by boys. Do you understand?'

'OK . . .' he breathes, waiting for her to continue.

'It happened to me when I was your age.' She clenches her fists so tight she feels her nails cut into her palms. 'It was Drew.'

Lando's intake of breath is razor sharp. He is silent for a moment, and she can almost hear his brain whirring, trying to process it. She sees confusion, pain and fear flash across his features. When he looks up again, unexpected belligerence has darkened his eyes.

'Why would he do that?'

The way he demands an answer takes her aback. 'You think I'd make it up?'

'Is this why Drew wasn't at training this afternoon?'

'There's a police investigation underway.' She attempts a patient tone, but from the way Lando's jaw clenches she knows she has fallen short of the mark yet again. She wants to apologise, to try to make it right, but she can't. Her walls cannot be compromised, not even by her own child. 'I imagine he won't be able to go to school or swim training until it's concluded.'

'Until you get him sent to jail, you mean,' Lando growls. His phone chimes with a notification and he snatches at it, his face turning bright red as his eyes skim the screen. 'Now this shit is all over Snapchat!'

'But I never share anything on Snapchat!'

Lando hisses in frustration. 'Someone Snapped your name in a tweet and now everyone's sharing it. All my swimming team knows!'

Skirting around him, she stalks to the fridge, grabbing the bottle of wine. Lando sneers as she pours and gulps.

'So much for never becoming like Granny.'

That hurts. She has been honest with him about her mother's alcoholism since he started senior school. It seemed important to open his eyes before he got to the age of experimentation. She never thought he would use it as a weapon against her. Though can she blame him, when she is his example?

'Why are you being like this?'

'Because I'm tired of it.'

'Of what?'

'You. The way you are. Why can't you be like other mums? I know you never wanted me, but you could at least pretend sometimes.'

Jenna opens her mouth to retort before she has fully absorbed the words. As they find their mark, she can only gape at him. If his comment about her mother had floored her, this is the stamp to her head as she lies helpless on the ground.

Her chest burns as if he has punched her in the solar plexus, making her eyes water uncontrollably. Breathing feels like inhaling sharp gasps of air that doesn't contain enough oxygen, and her vision swims as she fights for control.

'Lando, I . . .'

'Don't bother.' He doesn't wait for her to find the words. His footsteps up the stairs are heavy enough to shake the house.

Chapter Twenty-Two

Drew

'That wasn't a clever thing to do, Ele,' Drew says between gritted teeth.

His daughter, just returned from school and lounging on a breakfast-bar stool, throws back her head in indignation. Natasha observes from the other side of the island, silently sipping an espresso.

'I did it for you!'

'It's not something for you to get involved with.'

'That woman's trying to destroy our lives!'

'My life,' Drew corrects with more force than he intended. 'How the hell did you know who she was?'

'There's this thing called Google? Her Twitter account was unlocked. Easy.' Elena rolls her eyes and takes a savage bite from the apple she has been playing with for too long.

'You can't use this to gain more likes!'

Elena looks in disgust at the fruit and discards it with a toss of her hand. 'That's not why I'm doing it!'

'Clearly you can't be trusted on the internet. You look like a spoilt child.'

'You've seen it?'

'Of course I've seen it! Colleagues have been sending it me, Elena, for God's sake!'

'I'm showing my support for you,' Elena insists. 'Look! Look how many people are backing you!'

She shoves her phone in his face, one manicured nail tapping repeatedly at the screen to get his attention. Her triumph is clear in her posture. The hashtag #Drewmerchantinnocent draws a wince from him; the tweets that quote it make him feel sick. An outpouring of mostly male vitriol, complete strangers throwing abuse at Jenna and women in general, though he spots familiar names as Elena scrolls for him. Several school parents among them, a few members of the junior swimming squads, even some contemporaries from Cambridge. The secret is truly out.

'Did you start that hashtag?'

'No, someone else did – I don't know who. That's how quickly people have joined in!'

'You're exposing us. Hardly any of those people actually know me; they have no idea who they're supporting. They're just jumping on a bandwagon.'

Outrage tightens Elena's smooth face. 'Mama!'

Natasha shows no immediate reaction to her daughter's appeal, making her wait several beats. 'Your father is right.'

Elena hadn't been expecting that, and it robs her of her planned retort.

'Is Jenna tagged in this?' Drew demands.

'She must have deleted her account.'

Natasha interjects before Drew can ask any further questions. 'You have interfered in your father's personal business. You've compromised us.'

'I have not!' Elena cries.

Natasha silences her with a single shake of her head, an impatient slash of movement. 'Delete the post.'

'Why should I?'

'Because I told you to. This issue is private; it's not for the internet to discuss.'

'Too late,' Elena smirks. 'That bitch already got exactly what she deserved.'

'Delete it,' Natasha orders, making the smile instantly vanish from her daughter's face.

Elena resists for only a moment longer before she snatches her phone up and does as she's told. Natasha holds out her hand, demanding proof without needing to speak. She nods approval before returning the phone.

'No more, you understand?'

Elena gives a short, furious nod.

Drew doesn't believe her.

His daughter storms from the room, her inappropriate shoes clicking rapidly against the floors. Natasha raises one eyebrow and finishes her coffee, leaving the tiny stained cup for the housekeeper to ferry to the dishwasher on her return from the butcher's.

'Take a shower, Drew,' she instructs. 'I can smell you from here. Like a trapped animal.'

He looks down at his shirt, seeing the sweat stains. The tang of dried fear emanates from his loosened collar.

'You need to stay in control,' Natasha continues.

'Not the easiest task,' he retorts.

'An innocent man would not be so worried.'

'You make me sound guilty.'

'You make yourself look guilty.'

He leaves the room before he says something he will later regret. On the first floor, he is tempted to knock on Elena's closed door, try to reassure her, but he has no reassurances to give. A tension headache squeezes his skull as he creeps past to the master bedroom. Everything is neat, in perfect order: the Egyptian cotton draping the bed crisply ironed, Natasha's dressing table organised into various stations, books arranged squarely on bedside tables and water glasses refilled.

No one but the housekeeper would ever guess the state she finds the room in every morning, when Drew has to step over Natasha's discarded clothes, avoid knocking over any lipstick-stained glasses or tripping on flung stilettos as he attempts to escape the room without disturbing her.

He resists the temptation to let his own clothes fall to the floor as he undresses, tossing them into the laundry basket as he walks naked to their en suite. The water turned as hot as it can go, he stands under its scorching stream for what feels like hours, until his flesh tingles and he becomes dizzy and weak from the relentless heat. When he can take no more, a savage twist of the dial brings a shock of cold, robbing his lungs of air and making him gasp painfully. He is waiting for the anger, the rage at what Jenna has done to him, to replace the numb disbelief he is currently suspended in. The shower self-flagellation is a way of feeling in the meantime.

When he returns to the bedroom, barely able to find the energy to rub a towel across his tender skin, he finds Natasha waiting for him. They face each other, almost nose to nose. In her highest heels, she is barely shorter than him and she tilts her head to suggest he is the one looking up at her.

He waits for her to speak, but she remains silent, her icy eyes dancing over his face almost in amusement, as if they are playing a game she finds vaguely entertaining. He holds her gaze, refusing to be the one to crack.

Her finger traces the outline of his mouth, her nail sharp and dangerous. Her tongue dances over her own lips, a challenge. Something ignites within him and he hates how easily she can control him, but he is powerless to prevent himself.

Seizing her shoulders, he spins her round. He forces her over, so her feet remain firmly planted on the carpet in her ridiculous heels while her forearms brace against the mattress, made to take her weight. Shoving her dress up to her hips, he enters her from behind. He feels her tense at the first thrust, but she doesn't make a sound and, although he has made sure he can't see her face, he knows it will be expressionless. Bored, even.

It takes only minutes for him to climax, his fingers digging into Natasha's rigid flesh as his body shakes, breathing shallow and ragged.

He collapses on to the edge of the bed as she casually draws herself upright and strolls to the bathroom without so much as a glance at him.

He hears her soft laugh, mocking him, as she closes the door.

Chapter Twenty-Three

Her working day finally over and another hasty meal shoved into the oven, Jenna sits at the dining table, counting the ticks of the oven timer. Her hand reaches across the table, almost of its own accord, to grasp the pack of staples Zach abandoned days ago because he couldn't persuade them to fit into the stapler.

She pulls one free, such a small, insignificant piece of stationery, and stares at its tiny prongs. Straightening her fingers, she slowly, deliberately, pushes the staple prong beneath her fingernail. Then again, pressing hard this time. A few tiny droplets of blood appear. She repeats the action, closing her eyes at the sensation she now remembers so well.

The doorbell sings, an impatient sound demanding immediate attention. She ignores it. A delivery, maybe. Zach is forever receiving Prime orders.

Another urgent peal. The sound is setting her teeth on edge.

Throwing the staple safely into the bin, she strides to the door, snatching it open to demand to know what the emergency is to deliver yet another Funko Pop.

A voice recorder is shoved within centimetres of her mouth by a blond, polished woman wearing a Barbour coat. There is something familiar about her, but Jenna can't immediately identify what.

'Jenna, my name's Amy Donald. I'm an investigative reporter. Do you have any comment about the accusations you've made against Andrew Merchant?'

Jenna is blindsided. She has no idea what to say. Her mouth opens and closes, but no sound comes out. She wants to run back inside, but she is frozen, unable to do anything other than grab the doorframe for support.

'How did you find my house?' she manages to gasp, her breath coming in desperate snatches.

'How do you feel about the backlash on Twitter? Must be awful to read those sorts of comments about you.'

Jenna stares past the woman to see she is accompanied by a small flock of people, all clutching voice recorders.

Finally, her body galvanises itself into action. She slams the door, leaning against it as if she expects the reporters to force it open. Her breath comes in painful gasps and she is convinced she is going to be sick right there on the tiles.

It takes several moments to convince herself she isn't going to vomit, and several more until she can trust her legs not to collapse beneath her. She wobbles down the hall to the kitchen to grab her phone.

'There are newspaper reporters on my doorstep,' she cries when Beckett answers. 'Can they do that?'

'They can't identify you, but they can speak to you, ask you for quotes, etcetera.'

'But they've already identified me from social media!'

'The law won't allow them to print your name. Best bet is to lock your door, close your curtains and ignore them. They'll get bored and bugger off. They always do.'

'Is that all you can say?'

'It was bound to happen, Jenna. I'm afraid the press rarely miss a social media scandal these days.'

'Can't you just make them go away?' She hates herself for begging.

'Not unless they break the law. They won't hang around long once they see they won't be getting a story from you. Don't get drawn into conversation with them. If they become too intrusive, call your local station and explain the situation. They may be able to deploy a PCSO.'

Jenna forces herself to count, tapping her foot against the floor to give herself a rhythm. Her body responds automatically to the comfort, her racing heart beginning to slow, her grip on the phone and the edge of the table loosening.

'We may have different ideas of the definition of the term "intrusive",' she says, calm enough now to have an edge to her voice.

She ends the call. There is no point in continuing the conversation. While the phone is in her hand, she rapidly texts Zach a warning, because she can't bring herself to have the same discussion again. She can already hear the accusations echoing in her ears, even though Zach takes care not to apportion blame. Maybe they are in the voice of her mother, or her father, or even the housemaster, who found it easier to ignore problems; it's a disorientating swirl that feels like vertigo.

'Lando!' she yells up the stairs, before realising the journalists may be able to hear her. She hurries up to his closed door. 'Can I come in?'

172

'No.'

She tries the handle anyway but it is locked. She wants to bang with her fist, ram her shoulder into the wood, project her own panic even though she knows it is wrong to do so. 'Why have you locked the door?'

'To keep you out, obviously. What do you want?'

'Don't go near your window. There are reporters outside.'

A moment's silence, then the squeak of his computer chair and the snick of the lock being released. He stands in the doorway, blocking the entrance.

'Aren't you going to talk to them?' There is no animosity in his tone; he sounds almost curious.

'The police said not to.'

'They're not the boss of you.'

'I don't want to talk to the press. They'll twist my words, make everything worse.'

'It can't get much worse. Have you seen Twitter?'

'You need to stay off social media.'

He rolls his eyes and shows her his phone. He has created a Twitter account – @calrissian_gamer08.

'Are you joining in with this madness?' she gasps.

'I want to know what people are saying. Look at the hashtag.'

He jabs his finger at the screen. Nausea rises in Jenna's throat as she sees #Drewmerchantinnocent and the stream of tweets referencing it. It is like being violated all over again, this time by strangers hiding behind the safety blanket of the internet.

'You shouldn't be seeing this,' she manages to say, struggling not to let him see her horror.

He shrugs. 'I want to see what they're saying about Drew. I've got a right to know.'

173

It is such an adult statement that she is momentarily lost for an answer. 'Why is he so important to you?' is all she can think to ask. What has she done? What has she allowed into their lives, when they were already struggling so badly?

Another shrug. 'He believes in me.'

'We believe in you. Both of us.'

Lando smirks. 'Whatever. Can I get back to my battle now?'

'Do you need to lock your door again?'

'Dunno. You gonna barge in on me again?'

'No,' she says, unsure why she is abashed by her thirteen-year-old son.

He closes the door on her, but she doesn't hear the lock engaging. The banging on the front door begins again as she goes slowly back downstairs.

'You're not allowed to be here! You can't identify me!' she shouts through the painted wood. 'I've called the police.'

'We're just doing our jobs, Jenna,' comes Amy Donald's voice, and Jenna can picture her pressing her ear against the door to hear.

'Go away!' she shrieks. 'I won't talk to you!'

There is a sudden babble of voices, the sound of heels against the terracotta path, followed by silence. Jenna holds her breath, praying to a god she doesn't believe in that they have gone away.

She jumps violently at the firm knock.

'Jenna? I'm Natasha Merchant.' The Russian accent silences her before she can yell again. 'I'm alone. I've told those damn press people to fuck off.'

Jenna can't help but give a slightly hysterical laugh. Natasha Merchant as her saviour. The irony is unsettling. She opens the door on the chain, peeking through in case of ambush, but there is only one tall, graceful figure on the doorstep, wrapped in a sleek woollen coat.

'Are you going to let me in? I promise I won't behave like my daughter or the press.'

Jenna has little option but to step aside and allow her entry. Natasha sweeps past as if Jenna were a Mayfair doorman, straight to the kitchen, as though she is a regular visitor rather than someone entering the house for the first time.

'How did you find out where I live?' Jenna trails helplessly after her.

Natasha gives a tiny laugh. 'It was not difficult.' She offers no further explanation as she slowly unbuttons her coat. 'I want to apologise for my daughter's behaviour towards you. She has so little self-control.'

'It was a little more than poor behaviour,' Jenna snaps, anger disguising her panic at having her private sanctum invaded by this polished stranger.

'I have made her delete the post.'

'After it's been shared countless times.'

'As I said, I apologise. She shouldn't have done it, and she knows she was wrong to do it.'

'Bit late for that. What can I do for you, Mrs Merchant?'

Natasha sits, uninvited, at the head of the dining table, forcing Jenna to choose another seat. 'I would like to talk about my husband.'

Jenna refuses to look at the other woman, the only control she has in the situation. 'I can't discuss the case with you.'

'I do not wish to discuss the case. Where is your husband?'

'Zach's still at work. My son is upstairs.'

'This must be as difficult a time for him as it is for Elena.'

'He isn't spreading shit about me all over the internet.'

'I don't condone Elena's actions. Neither does Drew. In truth, he is disgusted by what she has done.'

'Only because his name has been dragged through the mud along with mine.'

'You have seen that people believe him? Most without question. Drew is not always a good man, not like outsiders think. He has dark corners of his mind, but I don't think he is an abuser.'

'You didn't know him back then.'

'True. But I know his weaknesses and his faults, and he has plenty of both. I would have seen if he had these sins in him. I am not defending him simply because he is my husband. I am not blinded by love or loyalty.'

'I don't believe you.'

'Our marriage is more an arrangement than a romance. Drew and I both have ambitions for our future and this . . . unpleasantness . . . is quite inconvenient.'

'It's a bit more than an inconvenience to me. And don't you dare dismiss this as "unpleasantness"! My life fell apart after I was abused, not that it was fucking rosy before. The effects impact me every single day, even after all these years. You can never understand what this feels like.'

'I'm not doubting that you were harmed, Jenna.' Natasha raises her voice, demanding to be heard. 'What happened to you must have been an awful experience. But you are accusing Drew without solid evidence.'

'You don't know that!'

'I do. I do know that. But, like you, I cannot prove anything.'

'Don't say we're in the same boat.'

'We are, though. Your reputation is being damaged just as badly as ours. As you've seen, the internet has mostly sided with my husband. He's led an unblemished public life until now and it seems people are prepared to stand by him. It makes your situation even more difficult.'

'What do you want?' Jenna repeats, more forcefully this time.

'I would like us to reach an agreement. We will decide on a sum of money and I will transfer it to whichever account you choose. And you will withdraw your complaint.'

For several moments, Jenna can't articulate her words, struggling to spit them out as they crowd from her brain to her mouth.

'You think you can bribe me to make this go away? You're not in Russia any more!'

'Bribe? No. This is to help you. Maybe you would like to move, somewhere out of London, more freedom for your son and your dog?' She is looking at the photos on the wall, a series of Lando and Loki through the years, their bond shining from their eyes. Jenna's fingers twitch to tear them down and hide them from sight. 'Perhaps a private psychologist to help you recover. Whatever you want.'

'What I don't want is your money.'

Natasha purses her lips, tapping her talons against the tabletop. 'Can't you see how much better it would be for everyone if all this just went away? Don't you regret unleashing this hell?'

'It was the right thing to do,' Jenna insists, her vision clouded by images of Adeline and Lando and anonymous children, a tall, strong figure towering over them. She has to swallow hard to prevent herself being overwhelmed by nausea.

Natasha's expression remains carefully neutral, although Jenna is sure her reactions have not gone unnoticed. The Russian woman gives the impression that nothing bypasses her. 'The press would go away. Drew would go back to work. All this would be forgotten about. You could carry on with your normal life, in safety.'

'Don't threaten me!'

'This isn't about threats. The investigation has only just started, and look what's happened already. It's only going to get worse.'

Jenna grips the edge of the table. 'You can't buy me, Mrs Merchant. I'd like you to leave.'

'I have said what I came to say. But you should consider my offer.' Natasha stands gracefully and buttons her coat.

'Does Drew know you're here?' Jenna feels compelled to ask.

A laugh that contains no humour leaves Natasha's painted lips, but her eyes spark with amusement.

'Why would he need to know?'

Chapter Twenty-Four

O livia arrived alone, armed with supplies, shortly after 1 a.m., spreading chocolate biscuits and packets of crisps across Jenna's duvet before delving into her pockets and producing her tin while Jenna opened the window on cue. She flinched at the blast of cold air over her misshapen little finger, never properly set.

Michaelmas term had arrived, the second year of their sentences, and half term was already within sight. Holidays had become a minefield – the relief of safety tarnished by the disappointment of home. Sometimes, Jenna wondered if she would ever find somewhere she could be happy.

'Ava's pissed off I've ditched her,' Olivia announced, crunching through biscuit after biscuit with cheerful abandon..

'Did you say you were coming to see me?' Jenna felt a surge of panic at the prospect of upsetting one of her friends. It was such a fragile confidence she had invested in their relationship that she fully expected it to be snatched away from her at any moment, leaving her alone once again.

'Nah, I just said I had other plans tonight. How are you? I mean, I know everything's shit. I wasn't being insensitive. Fuck, sorry, I'm gabbling nonsense now. How do you talk about stuff like this? It's not like there's helpful guidelines in any of those god-awful teen magazines we all used to be obsessed with.'

Jenna couldn't help but laugh at the careless, uncensored stream of words. The sound felt foreign in her ears. When was the last time she'd laughed freely? She inhaled again, revelling in the gentle buzz within her head.

'Want to try a pill?' Olivia asked, producing a clear plastic baggie containing several white tablets.

'What are they?'

'They chill you out, help you sleep. Or I've got some that'll do the opposite, if you fancy an all-nighter.' Her eyes sparkled at the possibility.

Jenna considered it, but eventually shook her head. 'I'll just stick with this for now, thanks.' She took another drag. 'I'm scared of getting expelled, to be honest.'

'You actually want to stay here?'

'I don't want to get kicked out. My mum would destroy me.' She regarded the glowing tip of the spliff, the powerful substance making her reflective. 'I thought life would get better here.'

'And instead, it got even worse.'

'At least I made some new friends.' Jenna risked a smile.

'You're cute,' Olivia beamed. 'Even with all the shit you're going through. You do look like a skeleton, though.'

'I know. I can't stop doing it.'

'You should talk to Matron. You're on the Pill, aren't you?'

Jenna shook her head.

'Fuck, then you definitely need to see her. What if you end up pregnant?'

'I won't.'

'Better to be safe than sorry, even in this situation,' Olivia declared with the superiority of knowledge. 'Go and get a prescription. There won't be any questions, not now you're fifteen. You won't go to hell, promise. Matron won't grass you up to the Brothers to save your soul.'

'You haven't told anyone, have you?'

'I swore I wouldn't, didn't I? I still think you should, though. What about Ava? Or Seb?'

'No one else can know!' Panic stirred, even through the cannabis haze. 'I shouldn't even have told you.'

'You couldn't keep it yourself; you were going to go completely mad. You're already starving yourself to death.'

She tilted her head in reflection.

'That wasn't very comforting. Sorry.'

'I knew what you meant.'

'Are you sure you don't know who it is?'

Jenna shook her head.

'We could find out!' Olivia's voice rose with excitement. 'Though pretty much everyone sneaks around, don't they? I swear no one actually stays in their own bed. It would be impossible to do it on our own. If you tell Ava and Seb, we can take turns to keep watch at night, see who's sneaking around, and Seb can keep an eye on his corridor . . .'

Even though she knew it was a childish plan, Jenna couldn't help but feel the tiniest stirring of hope. If he was unmasked, she would hold the power then. Perhaps it would be enough to make him stop, especially if he realised there were more people who could expose him.

Olivia must have picked up on her glimmer of faith and began nodding enthusiastically. 'It's a great plan, isn't it!'

Jenna nodded back with much less certainty.

'I know it's going to be hard, telling Ava and Seb,' Olivia grasped her hand, 'but I'll be with you. I'll help. You're not going through it on your own.'

She pulled Jenna into a bruising hug. 'You're brave. You just don't know it.'

181

Chapter Twenty-Five

Jenna is back in the Chelmsford interview suite, staring at the yucca plants, wondering if anyone has remembered to water them, before she spots that they are rubber.

She reaches automatically for one of the ever-present water bottles. This time, she manages to open it without revealing the tremors in her hands.

'I'll be honest with you, Jenna,' DS Beckett says, tugging at his tie as if it is garrotting him. 'We're struggling to find anyone who has had any suspicions about Mr Merchant's behaviour.'

'I can't tell you any more! You know everything!' The prospect of more lies makes her voice higher than normal, so it sounds like a plaintive plea. She cringes at her tone. 'It was Drew. I'm not making this up, despite what everyone seems to think.'

Beckett is calm in the face of her panic, allowing her a chance to collect herself before he speaks. 'Why don't you tell us about your school life?' he suggests, his voice gentle and encouraging. 'Help us get a better feel for it.'

Jenna's nostrils fill almost instantly with the smell of oak-panelled corridors, muddy sports pitches, icy-cold winter air creeping through mullioned windows, the ghost of skunk cannabis. She can hear the over-loud laughter of privileged youths, the feverish scratch of pens against exercise books, the rustle of rolling papers being prepared. Her fingertips tap against the water bottle in a fast count as she battles to collect her thoughts.

'I didn't mind boarding at first,' she says finally. 'It got me away from my parents. I was quite academic, though I always felt like I couldn't keep up with the Brothers' standards.'

'Did you make friends?'

'Not many. Didn't have much confidence, didn't know how to make casual conversation. I had a few close friends, and that was enough.'

'Sebastian Byron, Hugo Addison and Ava Vaughan?'

'Hugo was wild, funny. I wanted him to like me so I might seem cool too. Pathetic, really, but it mattered at the time. Seb was scared of his own shadow; he clung to anyone who made him feel better about himself. I was three years below them, but it was such a small school the years didn't separate themselves. I liked having older friends.'

'And Ava Vaughan?'

'Ava's year didn't have many girls – that's why we became friends. Olivia—

She stops too abruptly. Beckett's head rises in interest.

'Who's Olivia?'

'She was another friend,' Jenna stumbles, cursing herself. 'She's dead now.'

'I'm sorry for your loss. When did she die?'

'A year ago.'

'That must have been tough. What happened?'

'Suicide,' Jenna says abruptly. 'Can we talk about something else, please? It's upsetting to discuss.'

Beckett pauses for a couple of beats, letting the subject wane. 'Perhaps you can tell me what sort of school Halewood House was?'

Adjectives fly through Jenna's mind. 'Secretive. Everyone was disciplined in the classroom, but as soon lessons were done and the Brothers had gone into vigil, people knew they could do whatever they wanted.'

'And now it's closed down,' Beckett murmurs.

'I imagine that sort of wild behaviour and lax supervision doesn't fly in modern education.'

'I'm surprised it happened even in the nineties.'

Jenna shrugs. 'The Order had massive influence. The Church protected them and our parents kowtowed in the face of a higher power. If anything went wrong, it was easily covered up. I don't think the Brothers meant any harm, they just weren't equipped to run a school, and someone should have acknowledged that. It felt like they genuinely wanted us to be successful and to love God like they did, but they didn't seem to understand there was more to it than lessons.'

'We've traced the former abbot and your head of house. They gave us the names of a couple of other Brothers who taught both you and Mr Merchant regularly, so we've now got a pretty comprehensive picture from those who were in situ.'

She grits her teeth at the thought of her former self being discussed. 'What did they say?'

'The consensus was you were a troubled pupil. Brother Pius mentioned that you were a heavy cannabis user at the age of fourteen?'

'I'm amazed he looked up from his studies long enough to

184

notice. The school was very good at turning a blind eye to things they didn't want to see.'

'You were offered addiction support several times, according to him.'

'Smoking was the only thing that made me feel better,' Jenna mumbles. 'I didn't want to stop.'

'It would have helped if you'd mentioned this to us during earlier interviews.'

Is she imagining it or is Beckett's voice tighter today, edged with suspicion?

'I didn't want you to think badly of me.'

'It's difficult, Jenna, because you easily recall your general school life, but your repressed memories are much less specific.'

'I can't help that.'

'I'm not saying you can, but you must understand that it won't be enough to warrant charges if we only have those memories to work with.'

'You've not found anyone who has suspicions? No one?'

'Unless you can think of anyone else who was around at the time? Were there any lay staff, any pastoral support for you to talk to, besides the Brothers?'

At the command to think, Jenna's brain immediately begins to whirl in useless circles. 'We had a matron,' she seizes on. 'She wasn't part of the Church.'

'Would you have talked to her?'

'I barely knew her,' she says helplessly. 'It's all becoming a bit of a blur.'

'Because of your habits back then?'

'It was easier to block it all out than face it. It didn't hurt so much when I was stoned or drunk.'

She sees the fleeting expression cross Beckett's face. 'Is there anything else about school you want to tell us?'

'Not that I can think of.' She closes her eyes momentarily, desperate for respite from Beckett's unerring gaze. 'It doesn't look good, though, does it?'

'There's no point me lying to you. No, it doesn't look good. Try and think of anyone else, Jenna, who might back you up.'

Jenna closes her eyes, the voices of her parents ringing in her ears, demanding to know what is wrong with her, why does she insist on behaving like this? Grow a backbone instead of relying on those awful substances. Carry on and she'll find herself in a residential centre surrounded by people with real problems.

Her eyes fly open.

'I saw a psychiatrist. In fifth form, my parents sent me to a shrink in London. It got me out of games – I went every Wednesday on the train and didn't get back till dinner time.' Precious time, free from the chains that bound her.

'What was her name?'

It takes too long to recall. 'Morton. Dr Katherine Morton.'

Back home, relieved to find the house empty, Jenna grabs the iPad and begins a search she is certain will be fruitless. She expects the matron to be retired by now, but Google takes no time to produce the details of a small prep school in Hertford-shire and announces Sarah Turner as the current school nurse. When Jenna clicks on to the school website and finds the attached photo, she realises the woman must only have been in her mid-twenties when she was in charge of Halewood House's medical care. Quite a responsibility for someone early in their career.

If she opens wine, she will drink the entire bottle, so she turns

186

to the freezer and tugs free the bottle of Grey Goose that always nestles in the bottom drawer. Two icy shots bolster her enough to dial the prep school's number and ask to be put through to the sick bay.

'Can I help you?' The voice that answers the transferred call is vaguely familiar.

'Matron, this is Genevieve Alcott.' It hurts to say her old name. 'I don't know if you remember me from Halewood House?'

'I do – hard to forget a name like that! Genevieve, how are you?'

'It's Jenna now,' she feels compelled to say. 'Jenna Taylor.'

There is no sound of a reaction from the other end of the phone. Presumably the matron is not a fan of social media.

'I like the name change,' she replies lightly. 'This is a surprise. What can I do for you?'

'I'm doing a bit of digging into my time at Halewood House.' Jenna remains deliberately vague. Beckett can do the hard explanations if he decides to conduct his own interview. 'I seem to remember I came to you in fourth form to be prescribed the Pill. I don't suppose you recall?'

'You and half the other girls,' Turner says, and Jenna can picture the wry smile on her lips. 'I was young myself, only been qualified a few years. The Brothers would have been horrified at me giving contraceptives to fourth-formers, but I reasoned it was better to make sure you were safe than try to preach abstinence.'

'Did I confide anything in you?'

'From what I remember, it was me who sought you out. People were becoming concerned by your drug usage and drinking habits. That's why I recall it   you were absolutely sozzled when

I came to see you. I'd only met you for a hockey injury before that, so it was a bit of an eye-opener for me. I had to take you to the sick bay to sober you up. I'd say you weren't far off alcohol poisoning. You'd necked almost a full bottle of neat vodka.'

'I didn't explain why?'

'I could barely get a word out of you, apart from when you asked for the Pill.' A pause. 'I rather thought it was because your friends were older than you – you were trying to keep up with them.'

'They weren't to blame,' Jenna says, a little too sharply.

'You spot a lot of little things as matron.'

'Did you spot anything about Drew Merchant?'

'Mr Popular?' A slight upturn of the older woman's tone. 'I made sure he was well supplied with condoms, let's put it that way.' A laugh. 'Girls being admitted to Halewood was Drew Merchant's dream come true.'

Realising there is nothing more to be gleaned from the conversation, Jenna thanks the matron and says a polite goodbye.

That avenue at a dead-end, she hits the Google icon again, entering another name she hasn't considered in many years. Minutes later, after another shot of vodka, she has found a phone number, made the call and booked an appointment.

She will find her proof, one way or another.

Chapter Twenty-Six

Drew

Drew's immediate reaction when the lump of masonry smashes through his study window is to throw himself to the floor. The Persian rug is faintly perfumed from regular cleaning but, in his mind, it smells of fear and despair, now his constant partners.

The missile thumps to the floor, inches from him. It has sent his desk chair flying. Had he remained sitting, it would no doubt have connected with the back of his head. He stares at it in disbelief as it lies, benign now, surrounded by shattered glass, a punishment for his choices.

He has barely scrambled to his feet before Natasha and Elena burst into the room. His daughter lets out a cry that could be fear or fury, but Natasha is emotionless as she assesses the scene – the fragments of glass sparkling softly under the ceiling lights as if entirely harmless, the gaping hole admitting chilling gusts of air.

Drew's instinctive response finally releases him from its protective grip, and he sprints for the front doors, tearing them open and barrelling out on to the driveway. Apart from his own laboured breathing and the traffic sounds from the nearby main road, there is only stillness and silence. He runs on to the street, turning frantically in all directions in search of a culprit he is suddenly desperate to fight, to release every pent-up frustration upon.

No hooded figure emerges from behind the parked cars. No sound of escaping feet pounding against the pavement.

'Drew!' He hears Natasha's urgent call and jogs back across the driveway. His wife is on the steps, glaring out at him. 'Are you crazy? Arm yourself first!'

'With what, a fucking Kalashnikov?'

Natasha stalks back inside, and Drew has little choice but to follow, locking the front doors carefully.

'I've called the police,' Elena announces, appearing in the hallway, waving her phone in evidence.

'You've done what?' both parents cry, almost in unison.

Sarcasm spills from her eyes and lips simultaneously. 'That's what you do when someone tries to break into your house!'

'No one tried to break in,' Natasha insists.

'Why else would they smash a window unless they were trying to get in?'

'Think, for God's sake,' her mother snarls.

For once, Elena does as she told. A moment later, her eyes widen. 'Were they aiming for Dad?'

'Obviously!'

'Then why wouldn't we call the police?'

'Because they don't need to know our business,' Natasha thunders.

Drew seems to have lost the power of speech. He looks down at his hands, shaking with the rush of adrenaline.

'What did you tell them?' he manages to ask his daughter.

'That we were being burgled. They said they're sending officers straight away.' She glows with the drama of it all.

'Then call them back and say you were mistaken.'

'No!' Natasha interjects. 'That will look worse. That will make it seem we have something to hide.' She turns on her daughter. 'Go to your room. If they ask you, you were watching YouTube with your headphones on, or whatever other ridiculousness you do on your phone. Upstairs, now.'

'What if someone throws a brick through my window?' Elena demands.

'You're not their target,' Natasha says dismissively. 'Drew, go and check the rest of the house before they arrive.'

He is about to tell her to check herself, since she is the one with things to hide, but he remembers just in time what he needs to conceal. He hurries through the house. The French windows are unlocked, as always – Natasha at least deigns to smoke outside – but he can't see any sign they have been opened. Upstairs, everything seems to be in order. Their bedroom looks ransacked, but that is a perfectly normal state to find it in after Natasha has arrived home and changed, despite the housekeeper's efforts that morning.

He quickly checks the concealed safe in the floor. He has nothing to do with its contents, but the last thing he needs is to be linked to the business empire of Natasha's family, even though it keeps him in the lifestyle to which he is very accustomed. Natasha's wealth is the sole reason Drew remains married to her, just like his Whitehall ambitions are her motivation.

In the guest room that only he ever seems to sleep in, he takes the older Samsung phone from its usual hiding place on top of the curtain pelmet, concealing the texts of all the women that cannot be allowed to know his real mobile number. The house-keeper doesn't bother to dust up there. He slides it into his pocket, just for now, for safety. He will find a better hiding place later.

'The police are here.' His wife's call floats up the stairs to him, and he can't stop the savage twist his stomach gives, even though his brain knows they are only here about a potential trespasser, not to interrogate him. He swallows acrid bile as he returns downstairs.

Natasha is prepared for battle – her shoulders thrust back, spine ramrod straight, arms thrust down by her sides.

'Do you think the brick is a warning about the accusations?' Drew asks her.

'What else would it be about?' Natasha's scorn burns.

He shrugs, looking away, all the women he has kept hidden from her for so many years flashing through his mind.

She has no idea that he is always waiting for disaster to happen.

The uniformed officers have barely finished offering their flat reassurances as they watch the summoned handyman board up the desecrated window before a second car pulls into the drive-way. Another unwanted visitor makes his entrance.

'What happened here?' He waves his warrant card at the non-plussed PCs. 'DS Beckett, Chelmsford.'

'Bricked,' says the male police officer, unnecessarily gesturing to the window. 'Big chunk of breezeblock. What's Essex doing over this way?'

'Ongoing investigation.'

'Anything we need to be aware of?' The PC eyes Drew with new suspicion, as if he has immediately been elevated from boring but blameless victim of youth crime to a person of interest.

'Not at this point,' Beckett says smoothly, examining the handyman's work with apparent interest. 'Shall I wait outside till you're finished here?'

'No, we'll be off,' the female PC replies before her colleague can. 'Not much else we can do here. We'll pass it on to the PCSOs, Mr Merchant, and see if they can make this street part of their regular patrols, but if you've no idea who would have reason to do this, we can only assume it was teenagers on a dare.'

Beckett raises his eyebrows. 'It's a big driveway. Surely a house that looks directly on to the street would have been a more likely dare target?'

'Plenty of cover in all the bushes. Probably easier than being out in the open road for anyone to see.'

'Fair point.' Beckett says this while looking directly at Drew.

The uniforms busy themselves storing notebooks and zipping pockets. 'This is your crime number, sir, and my card.' The male PC places a business card on Drew's desk. 'Victim support is available on their helpline twenty-four hours a day, if you need it.'

'Unless they will replace a very expensive window, I can't imagine we shall require their services,' Natasha says icily. 'I will show you out, officers.'

The two troop after her obediently and Drew wishes he had offered to escort them, to save him from being left alone with Beckett.

Beckett takes one of the armchairs, uninvited this time, making Drew bristle. 'Were you intending to tell me?'

'I wouldn't have thought a detective needed to know about a bit of vandalism,' Drew snarls, refusing to sit, leaning one hip against the edge of the desk instead.

A flash of amusement crosses the detective's usually impassive face. 'Anything that relates to the investigation is useful to know.'

'It's not relevant to your investigation.'

'A campaign of hatred against you is very relevant.'

'A chunk of breezeblock is hardly a campaign.' Drew doesn't hide his impatient sigh, an effective cover for his racing heart rate. 'Is there anything else I can do for you, DS Beckett?'

'I'd like to ask you about your left collarbone.'

Drew's fingers automatically fly to the bump in the otherwise smooth bone, even though the imperfection is hidden by his polo shirt. 'What about it?'

'You had a fracture, yes?' Beckett pauses for the answering nod. 'Can you remember the year it happened?'

Drew has to stop and think. So many ski trips over the years, an insane ambition to compete at the winter and summer Olympics. Various injuries that ultimately snuffed out both desires. They all blur into one as he tries to recall the information. 'Not off the top of my head, no. I did it skiing, crashing into a slalom pole and putting my arm out to break the fall.'

'In your teens?' Beckett persists. 'While you were at university?'

Drew knows he should refuse to say anything without his solicitor present, but he has no idea what the importance of the collarbone fracture is and he's curious about the casual inquiry. 'I think I was at university. Why don't you check my medical records if it matters that much?'

'Do you give us permission to access them?'

That brings Drew to his senses. 'That's a question you need to ask my solicitor.'

For just a moment, he sees anger in the detective, a rush of frustration, before it is quickly disguised.

'What's my collarbone got to do with—'

'Darling.' Natasha has sauntered, unnoticed, into the study. For once, she has discarded her heels, granting her anonymity. She locks eyes with Drew, pursing her lips, tightening her jaw, momentary actions before she turns to their visitor. 'Detective Beckett, how nice to see you again. Have you been offered tea? The housekeeper has made scones today.'

'I'm not staying, Mrs Merchant, thank you.'

'Of course – you must be so busy.' Natasha shakes her head with a sympathy that would fool a stranger easily, though her husband isn't duped for a minute. 'Did you have more questions for my husband?'

'Just wondering about his old collarbone injury.'

One eyebrow flicks upwards. 'You know him better than I do! I've barely ever thought about it.' She drapes her hand over Drew's shoulder and flashes a smile that would make most mortals cower. 'It is rather obvious, darling. Visible through your shirts.'

Drew resists the urge to shrug her off, even though he understands what she is doing. An entirely phantom pain jabs through the maligned clavicle, sharp enough to make him draw breath.

'Shall I call Henry?' Natasha continues. 'Do you intend to ask any further questions, Sergeant? Perhaps Jenna has accused my husband of something which led to his own injury.'

Beckett's lips tighten. 'I'll be leaving now.'

'Excellent. Do let us know, the next time you wish to stop by.' Natasha has already crossed to Drew's desk, pressing the bell to summon the housekeeper. They stand, united, until the detective is shown from the room.

'What was that about?' Natasha demands as soon as they hear the front door close.

Drew kneads unnecessarily at his shoulder. 'Hell if I know. Maybe Jenna thinks it's a way of identifying me.'

'You did it at school?'

'Can't remember. I had loads of shoulder trouble from skiing. I can't remember which season was the collarbone.'

'Then call the GP in the morning and check your records. Before the police do.'

'What did you think my plan was?'

'I assumed you didn't have a plan at all, since you seemed happy to answer his questions without Henry here.'

'It would have seemed obstructive if I hadn't!'

Natasha's eyes roll ceilingward, unfazed by the threat Beckett brings to their door.

'Not another word unless Henry is with you,' she dictates. The study door clicks dismissively closed behind her.

Drew turns back to the plywood sheet covering the window, hating the shadow it casts over the room at the same time as he is glad to hide within its darkness.

Chapter Twenty-Seven

*T*he moment he left, Jenna lit a joint. With half term only two days away, she had not expected him to come creeping into her room. She had learned his visits tended to happen more frequently after holidays, tapering off as the term went on, and his sudden appearance has left her even more vulnerable than usual.

She couldn't inhale fast enough. The drug was strong and she knew she was imbibing it too quickly, but she couldn't stop grasping the salvation it brought.

The tap at the door made her panic, look for somewhere to hide the roach, to mask the smell, without any obvious solutions from her slow-motion brain. The door had opened before she could move and she let out a laugh of sheer relief as Olivia and Ava sidled in.

Olivia didn't giggle in return. Her face was serious for once, her fists tightly clenched by her sides.

'We saw him!' Olivia was flushed, speaking too fast. 'Creeping down the stairs!'

Vomit rose in Jenna's throat and she nearly choked trying to swallow it down. 'Did you see his face?'

'No, just the back of his head,' Ava said. 'But we followed him, pretended we were going to visit Seb.'

'We saw which room he went into!' Olivia crowed.

The panic was now rising fast within Jenna and she sucked more smoke into her lungs, over and over, until it felt like she was melting into the bed. She closed her eyes, willing Olivia to admit defeat. She had never tried to find out who the shadow was. She couldn't bear to know, to see his exposed face in the dining hall or on the corridors and be forced to acknowledge he was truly real.

'Who is he?' she whispered, because she knew they were waiting for her to ask.

Olivia had been holding her breath, as if she couldn't trust herself not to burst out with the information, and now she released it in a great rush. 'Rory Addison.'

Jenna heard a choked noise claw its way from her throat. 'Rory?' Her thoughts stumble as badly as her words. 'But I barely know him . . . he never speaks to me . . . he stays out of the way . . .'

'I'm going to ruin him,' Olivia declared, a snarl marring her elfin beauty. 'He'll never touch you again.'

Jenna held out the spliff, almost forcing it between Olivia's fingers. The alluring smell was enough to distract the smaller girl, and she fell silent as the drug seeped into her system with each long, slow inhalation.

For once, Ava shook her head when offered a drag. She was twisting a bracelet around her wrist so hard she was leaving marks, muttering inaudibly under her breath. She visibly jumped when the door opened and Seb sidled in, his lips compressed into a thin line, his movements jerky and clumsy.

'What's going on? Why are you running around the corridors like psychos?'

'We've seen who's been hurting Jenna!' Olivia cried before Ava hissed at her to keep her voice down.

The colour drained from Seb's already pale face. 'Who?'

'Rory,' Jenna whispered, unable to raise her gaze, focusing on her own feet.

'We saw him going back to his room,' Ava said grimly.

'Was he wearing the mask?'

The fifth-form girls nodded in unison. Jenna squeezed her eyes shut, her head about to explode.

'Are you OK?' Seb asked, stretching out his hand to her but letting it drop at the last minute, as if he couldn't quite bridge the gap.

'We need to do something,' Olivia said, her voice low, words forced through her gritted teeth. 'Rory can't get away with this.'

'We could grass him up?' Seb suggested.

'What are we, nursery kids? Besides, what if the Brothers don't believe us?'

'They won't believe us.' Ava barked a humourless laugh. 'Nothing bad ever happens at Cell Block H. Expelling a boy would lead to questions. The Brothers don't like questions.'

'So what can we do?' Seb asked.

'We need another way. Fuck, this stuff isn't strong enough. I'm going crazy.' Olivia leapt to her feet, pacing the room. 'Hand over the nug, Ava.'

'I'm saving it!'

'You're getting another delivery tomorrow!'

Ava growled her frustration but slapped a small clingfilm ball into Olivia's demanding palm. Jenna watched in fascination as Olivia held her lighter to the nugget of skunk, caressing it with the flame until she could crumble it into a rolling paper.

'We've got to sort the bastard,' Olivia muttered, as if to herself. 'He's not getting away with this shit.'

She continued to pace as she smoked, talking to herself under her

199

breath, shaking her head and spitting curses when her ideas all fell short of the mark.

Her friend's reaction making her heart thump with fear, Jenna retreated to the corner of the bed, tucking herself against the wall. Rory. She would never have suspected Rory. He had barely seemed to notice she existed.

Was that why he had come to Halewood House? Had he done the same thing at his old school and been asked to quietly leave, to avoid scandal just like the Brothers would do?

'Ava, have you got any pills?' Olivia asked suddenly, her voice too loud in the quiet room.

'You can't mix pills with that skunk – you'll end up in hospital!'

'Not for me!'

'What, then?'

Olivia's eyes shone as she dragged triumphantly on her spliff. 'I've got a plan. Forget about accusing him – let's ruin the bastard's future instead. We're going to plant some of your pills in his room then put a note under the abbot's door saying that Rory Addison is dealing. The Brothers will search his room and he'll be expelled – they won't risk a drugs scandal.' She rolled her eyes at the irony of this declaration. 'Oxbridge won't touch him with that on his record, and we get rid of him so Jenna will be safe. Perfect, isn't it!'

She beamed round, bouncing up and down on her tiptoes. The others digested the slew of information in silence, weighing up the likelihood of success or failure.

'It's a great idea!' Olivia insisted.

'It could work,' Seb said slowly. 'If we don't get caught.'

Ava gripped a hank of her hair, tugging sharply on it as she thought. 'I still think we should just grass him up.'

'We don't have proof,' Olivia hissed. 'It'll be his word against Jenna's.

And it will mean Jenna having to sit down with the Brothers and talk about what Rory did to her. Do you want her to go through that?'

'Stop!' Jenna choked out, her head about to explode. 'I can't tell the Brothers. I won't!'

'You won't need to.' Olivia reached to grip her hand, fierce in her reassurance. 'I'll do it in the morning, when everyone's at breakfast. Ava, you go down and keep Rory talking, he's got to be nice to you. Seb, you come with me and keep an eye on the corridor.'

'No, I'll come with you,' Jenna said quickly.

'You're not getting involved!'

'I'm the one most involved. If you're taking the risk, I am too. Seb can go to breakfast with Ava, then there's not too many of us missing.'

Seb threw Jenna a smile as if approving of her loyalty. She glowed at the acknowledgement.

'You know we love you, don't you?' Olivia threw herself down beside Jenna. 'You're so brave. This shit is all going to be over soon, I promise.'

She wrapped her arms around Jenna's neck, hugging her close, and Jenna relaxed into the warmth of her friend's embrace, knowing it would be the last affection she would receive until half term was over.

The next morning arrived far too quickly for Jenna's comfort. No sooner had the footsteps of other students trooping off for breakfast faded than Olivia was tapping on her door, urging her downstairs to the sixth-form corridor.

Olivia raised a warning finger to her lips, indicating up and down the silent hallway, before opening the door and slipping inside Rory's room. Jenna hovered in the doorway, keeping watch, her breath coming in sharp gasps.

The room was bigger than the attic shoeboxes the girls inhabited, and noticeably tidy. Everything was in its rightful place, bed neatly made, clothes put away, floor and desk surfaces clear. Even the pairs of shoes were lined up squarely against the skirting board.

Olivia took her time choosing the right hiding place as Jenna's internal monologue begged her to hurry up. Finally, Olivia selected her spot, beneath the mattress, right in the middle, placing the little plastic baggie almost reverently on to the divan base.

'Won't he find it when he changes the sheets?' Jenna hissed.

'It's not bed change day till next week. It'll all be over by then.'

Olivia smoothed the sheets back to smoothness and cast one last check round the room. 'He must be weird, being this tidy.'

'Come on, we've got to go!'

Olivia did as she was told for once, closing the door silently behind her. She linked her arm through Jenna's, pulling her close.

As soon as they were out of the corridor, she broke into a bouncing skip, giggling loudly as she dragged Jenna along with her.

'You're free, baby,' she grinned. 'Told you I'd look after you.'

Jenna tried her best to smile back, to show her gratitude. 'Coming to breakfast?'

'Nah, I want a smoke before chapel. You go and eat. You don't need to waste away any more.' Olivia winked. 'Don't think I don't know why you were doing it. Go! Eat everything!'

Jenna hugged her bag closer to her chest and made her way to the dining room alone, suddenly starving. The wood-panelled room echoed with noise, conversations that seemed more urgent than usual.

Loading her plate with overcooked scrambled eggs, Jenna carefully scanned the tables for somewhere to sit, casting around for a familiar face. Seb waved to her across the tables, and she hurried over to him.

'Did you do it?'

'Yes, it's done. Olivia put them under his mattress.'

'Are you OK? You look terrified.' He gave her hand a reassuring squeeze beneath the table.

'I was so scared we'd get caught,' she breathed.

She didn't dare look at High Table, where, as usual, the Brothers were slowly eating in peaceful silence, eyes half closed in meditation. Once grace had been said, they didn't try to enforce their reflection on the pupils.

'You could play catch across the dining room with a stash and they wouldn't notice,' Seb hissed.

'Do you hate them?' She had never heard such venom in his voice before.

'The Brothers? No. They treat me OK, they don't bother me.'

'Then why are you so upset?'

'Because it's half term.' Seb's jaw clenched and she saw his knuckles whiten around his fork as he moved his food around the plate, trying to make it appear he had eaten. 'And I have to go back to my mother's house and face her again.'

'Sorry.' She'd forgotten how much he seemed to dislike his mother.

Seb blew a snorted breath from his nose and looked away from her. She watched him watch Rory Addison and Drew Merchant, who had been named head boy for his final year and was everyone's favourite pupil, holding court further down the table, their raucous laughs louder than everyone else's. Ava was in the midst of the ruckus, her voice louder than all the rest, egging the boys on.

'Does Drew buy from Ava?' she asked, suddenly curious. Anything to distract her from the wrongdoing gnawing at her stomach.

'Surprised he's got the cash to buy from anyone at the moment.'

'What do you mean?'

'He comes from old money, but his dad had a gambling habit, lost the lot a few years ago, and now they're having to sell the ancestral pile. Why do you think Drew's here instead of paying the Harrow fees like all his relatives?'

'You know everyone's secrets.'

Seb shrugged. 'I'm invisible, just like you.'

'Wish I could be invisible at home, then I wouldn't get blamed for so much.'

'I can't imagine you causing much trouble.'

Jenna flushed. 'I never dare do anything wrong at home, but Mum still thinks I'm to blame for every little issue.'

'Mine blames me too.' Seb's voice became quieter. 'I never did much wrong either.'

Jenna didn't know what to respond to that so she concentrated on her plate instead.

'Parents fuck everything up, don't they?' Seb seemed to shake himself and picked up a slice of toast to reluctantly nibble on.

'That's why I never want kids.'

'Same.' He dropped the toast, barely touched. 'I'm going to hide before chapel. I feel sick. Coming with me?'

'No. I don't want to get caught skipping again.'

'God will approve,' he drawled. 'See you later.'

Jenna felt herself flush again when he smiled at her over his shoulder as he left. It was nice to have friends.

Chapter Twenty-Eight

Nearly twenty years have passed since Jenna last stood in this office, and she finds it strangely reassuring to see it is exactly as she remembered it. Fresher paint, more books lining the floor-to-ceiling shelves, a few extra certificates hung. Dr Morton, similarly, is little changed: a few extra pounds, plenty more grey hairs, but still with the deep lines carved by a ready smile and the expressive, flying hands of an undiscovered pianist.

'Take a seat, Mrs Taylor.' The smile is waiting to welcome her, but no sign of recognition flashes in the sharply intelligent eyes. 'What would you like me to call you?'

'Jenna is fine.'

'My name is Katherine. Pleased to meet you.'

'We've met before, actually,' Jenna blurts out in a rush of breath. She winces at her indiscretion, cursing this new inability to control her emotions. It has come from nowhere, defying the walls she has spent decades constructing, refortifying whenever their heights have threatened to be breached, and now her own mind seems determined to destroy them brick by brick.

The clipboard about to be proffered stalls in mid-air. 'I'm sorry, I'm afraid I don't recognise you.'

'I was Genevieve Alcott then. I was at school when my parents sent me to you for treatment. Bulimia and self-harm.'

A moment of careful consideration, the clipboard hovering patiently. 'You were at boarding school? You hid in a bathroom, intending to commit suicide?'

'That's right.'

'I remember you. Forgive me— you look so different.'

'Reinvention was necessary. I needed to leave that part of my life behind.'

'Understandable. It was a troubled time for you.' Morton places the clipboard on her desk, its questions not required for this moment. 'Are you having further issues now? It's quite common for patients to return for further treatment, but rarely after so many years.'

'I'm not here as a patient. I'm hoping you'll share some information with me.'

A frown. 'What sort of information?'

She doesn't know how to word it but, again, her brain responds without a conscious signal. 'When you treated me, did you suspect a reason behind my issues?'

'You were clearly very unhappy at school. You said you were bullied quite badly.'

'No other indications?' Jenna persists with a tenacity she doesn't feel but knows only too well how to project.

'Why don't you tell me exactly what you'd like to know?'

'Is this confidential, whatever I say to you?'

'As long as it doesn't involve placing yourself or anyone else in danger, yes, everything within this room remains strictly confidential.'

That is reassuring enough to give her the courage to explain.

'I've been experiencing the return of repressed memories.' Jenna chooses her words carefully. 'Things that happened to me at school.'

Morton leans forward slightly. 'Are you saying you were the victim of abuse?'

With the reassurance of confidentiality, Jenna is finally safe to make her admittance and she feels the weight of her burden lift, even if just momentarily. 'I can't seem to remember the details myself, no matter how hard I try. Did you ever get the feeling something like that could have happened to me?'

'You can't have given any indication of it; I would have acted on even a hint of child abuse.'

'I'm certain it happened.'

'I'm very sorry to hear it. Give me a moment.' Morton slides her chair across to the desk, tapping rapidly at the keyboard. Her eyes scan the screen, effortlessly absorbing the information it presents. 'I don't have your detailed notes on file any more, not after so long, but your general record doesn't highlight anything. Your conditions were determined to be caused by the stress of bullying. It says you improved greatly once you went to university. You stopped accessing mental health services in your second year. You'd met a boyfriend?'

'Yes, I ended up marrying him.' A smile plays across her lips of its own accord as memories of student Zach push their way to the forefront.

'You were heavily addicted to cannabis at the time I met you. I'd say you were dependent on alcohol as well.'

'I stopped the weed. I never did drugs again.' No need to explain why. She gives a self-deprecating shrug to distract the psychologist. 'Couldn't give up wine, though. It's still my crutch.'

'Your mother was an alcoholic, it says here?'

'She still is. Quite a high-functioning one, to be fair. Most people have no idea, even now.'

'It was a difficult life for you, especially at that age,' Morton murmurs, getting the level of sympathy just right.

'That's why I went to boarding school, and that's why I would never have told my parents what happened to me there.'

'I would have expected you to have shown some signs during your therapy if you had been abused,' Morton says, carefully. 'Something so devastating would have been hard to conceal when you were undergoing intensive treatment.'

'I'm not making it up.'

'I didn't say that.'

'But you can't help me.'

'I'm sorry, Jenna, I have to be truthful with you. I saw no red flags during your sessions. You presented as a fairly typical victim of adolescent cruelty and you were certainly badly affected by it, but nothing more sinister. I wish I could be of more help.'

Jenna leans forward to place her coffee cup down before her shaking hands spill it, her safety net collapsing.

'I really am sorry,' Morton repeats.

It is little comfort. Jenna's mouth is flooded with a bitter tang of regret. She shouldn't have come here. In trying to find proof, she has only compromised herself further.

'If you don't mind me saying so, you're clearly struggling.'

Something broke, a floodgate bursting open deep inside, and the words are out before Jenna can even attempt to corral them. 'My son hates me. I'm a terrible mother and an even worse wife.'

Morton leans forward, direct eye contact that, surprisingly, doesn't feel distressingly intimate. 'I'm sure none of those things are true, however much it feels like they are.'

'I never intended to have a child.' Jenna delivers this admission to her shoes, unable to look Morton in the eye. 'Lando was an accident, just like I was. I knew I could never raise a child successfully.'

'What makes you say that?'

'After everything I went through at school, I shut down. I refused to let anyone get close to me in case they harmed me. I learned to get my attack in first, so I wouldn't need to defend myself.'

'And that's continued through your adult life?'

Jenna drags a shuddering breath into her rigid lungs. 'I hate being touched. I can't dole out hugs and kisses like normal people, not even to my own son.'

'Were you depressed after he was born?'

'No. It was different from depression. Even when he was a baby, I could barely bring myself to touch him, change his nappy, anything like that. I knew I loved him, but I didn't know how to show it. It was like a part was missing.'

'Children who come from troubled family backgrounds often find this. You said your own mother wasn't affectionate towards you, so you missed out on that vital attachment. Consequently, you didn't know how to show your own child love because you didn't have your own example of it.'

'My husband does his best to make up for it, but he can't replace both parents, can he?'

'Better to have one nurturing parent than none. Your son has attached to his father, presumably.'

'Yes, he adores Zach. He actively avoids me. He prefers talking to his sports coaches than to his mother.' A bitter taste floods her mouth at the thought of Lando confiding in Drew.

'That will be his brain's way of coping rather than a deliberate slight.'

'I thought it would get better as he got older, that maybe I'd learn from Zach, but even if I tried to copy him, I got it wrong. Forcing it didn't work, it made it worse. I was acting out feelings rather than experiencing them.'

Morton taps her pen as she thinks, taking her time. 'When trauma is suffered, such as abuse, part of the brain can shut down. It's trying to protect you from further harm, but it can go too far, causing the person to lose certain abilities such as empathy.'

Jenna feels her muscles jump as if an electric current has run through her. 'There's science behind what's made me this way?'

'It's a psychological reaction as well, but scans have shown the brains of abuse victims can work differently to those who never experience that kind of trauma. From the way you've described your inability to form relationships, your defensive mechanisms, I would expect to find some abnormalities if your brain was scanned.'

'So there's nothing I can do? The damage is permanent.'

'You can affect the psychological reactions, if that's what you really want.'

'I want to be normal, like any other wife and mother.'

'It isn't that simple, Jenna. You've said you've been like this for several decades; that can't just be undone. It would take time and work, interventions, therapy, possibly medication.'

'But if I really wanted to change, it would be possible?'

'To some extent, yes, but your circumstances would need to allow you to make those changes. You'd need to feel secure and safe, grounded, and not doubt your attachments so you wouldn't feel such an urge to protect yourself. It isn't a simple process, and some people find they are never able to truly relax their guard. After so many years, it has become their nature.'

'I could try, though,' Jenna interjects.

'Have you talked to your family about this?'

'I can't. I don't know what to say.'

'You've managed with me.'

'This is different.'

'Because your defences aren't necessary in this office?'

Jenna blinks, taken aback. 'Yes.'

'You're carrying a lot of strain.'

'It's my own fault.'

'Is it? You didn't ask to be abused.'

'I didn't ask to become a mother either, but I still should have done better. I should have tried harder for Lando. I prevented there being a bond when he was little and, now he's a teenager, he knows that.'

'And that is why you should talk to him. Like you said, he's a teenager now. He'll have some awareness; he may empathise more than you think. Give him the chance to learn why you are the way you are.'

Without warning, the office walls start to close in on Jenna, cutting off the air in the room. She grinds her knuckles against her sternum, trying to rub away the sudden pain as her chest heaves with the effort to breathe. How can she ever show Lando the true depths of her scars?

She has to get out, before she suffocates, before the psychiatrist's urging smothers her.

'Thank you for your time, Dr Morton.' She grabs her belongings and scurries out of the office before the older woman can form a sentence, cajole her to stay, offer further help.

Jenna wastes no time in leaving the building, hurrying down the street as if being pursued. The window of hope closes with a thud of finality.

Chapter Twenty-Nine

Jenna walks in a slow circle around the park, huddled into her coat, as Loki careens around after his tennis ball, joyfully exploring every blade of grass. Zach has gone to meet his snooker pals for the evening, leaving his dog behind. Loki loves to leap on to the table and steal the brightly coloured balls.

Jenna doesn't notice the man on the bench staring at his phone at first, doesn't see his head lift as she passes him.

He begins to walk in the same direction, a few paces behind, until she pauses in mid-step to throw the ball for Loki again. He steps around her, too close, peering at her face as if assessing.

'I know you.'

'No, you don't,' Jenna snaps, lengthening her stride.

He keeps pace with her. 'You're the woman on Twitter. The one who's accused the headmaster.'

An electric jolt of fear shoots up Jenna's spine. 'You're mistaken.'

'You shouldn't go around making accusations like that.'

She puts on a burst of speed, heart beginning to pound as adrenaline thumps through her veins. 'Are you friends with him?'

'Never heard of the guy before he started trending.'

'So you don't need to have an opinion.'

'It's women like you who ruin men's lives.'

Coming to an abrupt halt, Jenna looks at him properly for the first time. He doesn't look the type for such an abhorrent statement. Floppy dark hair, suit trousers, a laptop bag over his slim shoulder, Joe 90 glasses. He exudes uncertainty rather than confidence, shifting from foot to foot. If she had to guess, she would say mid-level civil servant. His chin is raised, but he can't disguise the slight quiver to it and she is reassured he won't be a physical threat.

'Whatever issue you've got, it's nothing to do with me,' she tells him firmly, a schoolteacher correcting a rebellious pupil. The irony isn't lost on her. 'I can see it bothers you, but my personal affairs are none of your business.'

'Not very personal now you're all over social media.'

She bristles, temper rising. 'Please leave me alone.'

'You're all the same, aren't you? Cause all this trouble, then start crying when you get called out on it.'

Rage and indignation meet in Jenna's head, sparking each other into a sudden blaze. 'Do you see me crying? I've been polite, but now I'm done. Fuck off!'

The change is instantaneous. Suddenly, he is in her face, grabbing her arm, a sneer marring his previously neutral features. She can smell garlic on his breath, and cheap deodorant, and something sharp and feral and toxic. He is taller than she thought and the fingers gripping her flesh are too strong for her to break free.

Jenna looks frantically around the darkening park, for anyone who might be willing to defend her. She scrabbles for her phone, but her panicked fingers are clumsy and she drops it as she tries to pull it free from her pocket.

Her assailant's nose presses into her cheek, his voice dropping to a snarl, an animal about to attack its prey.

'How about I fucking show you what should happen to women who ruin men's lives?'

The steely fingers twist sharply and Jenna cries out at the sharp jolt that runs through her humerus. A moment later, her attacker yells as well, surprise and pain together, and kicks out. Off balance, his grip loosens, and Jenna yanks her arm free as he stumbles, tripping over his own feet and tumbling to the ground.

Loki, growl deeper than she has ever heard it before, keeps his teeth firmly sunk into the man's ankle, shaking the limb like his tuggy toy.

'Loki, leave!' Jenna cries, snatching up her phone and grabbing for the dog's collar. Loki reluctantly releases, looking to her for guidance.

Jenna doesn't wait for the man to scramble back to his feet. Taking Loki in her arms, she runs, and she doesn't stop until she has slammed her front door, locked and bolted it.

She jumps violently when a knock echoes from the other side of the door. Has he followed her home?

'Mrs Taylor?' a female voice calls, vaguely familiar. 'It's Amy Donald. You looked upset when you ran past my car. Is everything OK? Do you need help?'

The reporters haven't gone away – they have just changed tactic.

'Leave me alone,' she manages to say, her voice trembling as badly as her hands. She puts Loki down before she drops him.

He doesn't scramble to check his food bowl as usual but sits before her, watching carefully, ready to defend her again.

'What happened?' Amy Donald asks. 'Are you safe?'

'A man attacked me in the park.' Jenna has made the admission before her brain has caught up with her mouth.

She hears the intake of breath on the other side of the door. 'That must have been terrifying. Why don't you talk to me about it?'

'I don't want to talk to you!'

'Let's go and get a coffee. Bring your dog with you. You'll feel better with a hot drink inside you.'

'I've plenty of coffee here, thank you.'

'I'll throw in a millefeuille as well? Nothing you say will be recorded; it can just be a chat. I can show you I'm not a monster. You've got support, Jenna, even with all that shit on Twitter. People are still prepared to stand by you.'

Jenna can't take the persuasion tactics any longer. She could just retreat to the kitchen, close the door and curl up on the sofa with Loki, but the walls are closing in on her, trapping her. She can't breathe.

'Why won't you leave me alone?'

'Because I know what this feels like.'

'How can you possibly know?'

There is a pause, only momentary, but enough to make Jenna wait to hear the answer, as if she instinctively knows what Amy Donald is going to say.

'Because it happened to me too.'

Jenna has no idea how to respond, but her muscles slacken of their own accord and she slumps against the hallway wall.

'Why do you think I'm writing these articles? I can help other women like me.'

Jenna stands shakily upright and unlocks the front door. Amy Donald's expression assures her that this isn't another journalist trick.

'Wait here. I won't be a minute.'

Amy nods, drawing her coat more securely around her.

'Lando!' Jenna strides upstairs, banging on his door. 'I need to go out for a few minutes.'

'Whatever.'

'Don't answer the door to anyone. Your dad will be home from snooker soon.'

'I'm not stupid. Where are you going?'

'To meet someone in the Elk. I'll be back in an hour. I'll only have one drink.'

He doesn't respond immediately, and she is on the top stair before she just catches his reply.

'No, you won't.'

The local pub is more gastro than local, but the tall round tables reserved for drinkers are mostly empty. A waiter approaches immediately with a welcoming smile and the wine list.

'A Sauvignon Blanc.' Jenna doesn't need to consider her options. 'Large.'

'Anything else?'

'Just a tonic water, please,' Amy requests.

Jenna is tempted to change the order to a bottle, but she restrains herself. The wine is ice cold, sharp with citrus and perfumed with passionfruit. She has to prevent herself from downing it in a few large gulps. A sigh escapes from her as she sips, and she closes her eyes in relief. Amy sips her water, barely taking any in her mouth.

'The police have told me not to speak to any journalists.'

'They can advise you, but they can't actually stop you,' Amy counters. She cradles her glass casually; her lipstick has left a perfect stain on it. 'Police don't like journalists, I'm afraid.'

'I can understand why.'

'I'm not a threat to you, Jenna. I'm trying to help you. Think about what telling your story could achieve.'

'More hatred and backlash?'

'Have you actually looked at the comments?'

'Not since it went viral.'

'Take a look. Like I said, you've got support.'

'From who?'

'Other women. Even some decent men.' Amy produces an iPad from her bag and taps rapidly before turning the screen to show Jenna a Twitter thread. 'Here.'

#drewmerchantinnocent supporters are the adult version of school bullies.

I wish I could be as brave as Jenna Taylor.

Threatening to harm a woman who has already been abused is just sick #jennataylor deserves justice for what she went through.

All women should be able to report #abuse without their lives being ruined.

From nowhere, Jenna feels a warm glow that can't just be from the alcohol. She scrolls to the bottom of the comments, taking in the positive messages and well wishes, evidence that the entire online world is not against her. When she hands the iPad back, her burden seems to be just that little bit lighter.

'Do you believe me?' she asks.

'Of course I do. Why wouldn't I?'

'You're in the minority.' Jenna shakes her head with a bitter laugh. 'I know Drew Merchant hurt me, but no one else seems to believe it.'

'Then this is your chance to make everyone see it from your perspective,' Amy says. 'You're the victim, yet you're being portrayed on much of social media as the villain, despite the supportive comments. You could change that.'

'You can't identify me – I know you're not allowed to do that. So what would be the point?'

'We couldn't print your name or your image – we'd have to take your photo in shadow profile – but readers would know it was you. We're allowed to print Drew Merchant's name, after all.'

'Have you asked him for an interview as well?'

An impish grin. 'He refused in no uncertain terms.'

'I've refused as well, so why are you still asking me?'

'I don't like to see women like me being hung out to dry because they've been brave enough to speak out, particularly against a powerful man.' Amy purses her full lips. 'I've had some great coverage. Just think how quickly I'd be able to get your words out there. You'll be well compensated.'

'I don't want money, I just want to be left alone. You can't give me back my anonymity, so you have nothing else I want.'

'You don't want to change people's minds?'

'As if I have that power.'

'You shouldn't underestimate the power the mainstream media can have.'

Jenna drains her first glass and signals for another. Amy's drink remains almost untouched.

'You won't change my mind.' Jenna traces the ring of condensation left on the table. 'You're wasting your time.'

She takes her second glass and drinks immediately, not even bothering to place it down. It no longer matters how it tastes or how chilled it is.

'I'm finishing this, and I'm going home to my family.'

Amy's sigh is barely audible. Her face remains irritatingly perky as she sets her own glass politely aside and stands, shrugging on her coat.

She places her card precisely on the table.

'If you change your mind, I'm always available.'

Jenna doesn't touch it until she is certain Amy has gone.

She prepares a lasagne once she makes it home, hoping the calming actions of cooking will sober her up. She has to grit her teeth against the temptation of the knife as she watches the cold steel effortlessly dice carrots, onions and celery. Even once she has sweated down the mirepoix, added garlic and herbs and a splash of balsamic to deglaze the pan, it calls to her, beseeching her just to see what it will feel like against her skin.

Feeling beads of sweat gathering on her hairline, she crumbles beef and pork mince into the frying pan, draining the excess liquid before stirring in an Oxo cube and her secret ingredient, a tablespoon of Marmite. She pours in red wine; too much, but it stops her from drinking the remains of the bottle, and crushed tomatoes, perfumed with basil, stirring slowly until she feels the mix begin to thicken.

As it bubbles, she tackles the béchamel, feeding milk bit by bit into the roux, grating generous handfuls of Gruyère, vintage Cheddar and Parmesan, sprinkling mustard powder and the smallest hint of nutmeg. Comfort wafts from the steaming pan, the wooden spoon raising soft, pillowed peaks from the creamy sauce.

When she hears a crash that seems loud enough to shake the foundations of the house, she drops the spoon and béchamel sprays across the tiles.

'Lando!' she cries, shutting Loki in the utility room for safety before running upstairs. 'What was that?'

'It wasn't me!' The indignant roar comes back. Lando appears in his doorway, his hair standing on end as if he has been clutching hanks of it. His chest is rising and falling rapidly, as if he has been exercising hard. 'Sounded like glass breaking. Is Dad home?'

'Not yet.' Inexplicable fear reaches out its icy hand to grip Jenna's heart. She knows she must search the house to find the cause of the crash, but she can't bring herself to do it alone.

For once, Lando seems to understand. He places a finger to his lips and beckons her to follow him. She watches as if from behind a veil as he collects his souvenir Red Sox baseball bat.

'I'll go first,' she whispers as he goes to open the master-bedroom door.

'I'm the one with the bat,' he hisses back and, before she can grab him, he has shouldered open the door and launched himself into the room. It is empty, undamaged, but he checks the wardrobes anyway, as if he is in an action film.

The bathroom and spare room are both clear, and Jenna swats Lando's hand away when he reaches for the cord to pull down the attic steps. It is impossible to pull the hatch closed from inside the dark, musty space.

Besides, she already knows the crash came from downstairs.

As they descend the stairs, she can hear Lando's breathing as well as her own, though she suspects his is now laboured from excitement rather than fear, like hers. The kitchen is clear, but they check it anyway, Lando rattling the patio door handles. There is only the living room left, and there is no reason Jenna can find to avoid it.

This time, she does go first. As Lando hangs over her shoulder and turns on the overhead light, she takes in the cold night air streaming in through the smashed window, sending the curtains rearing like aggressive ghosts. The fragments of glass wink knowingly at her under the glare of the light. On the fawn carpet she has been intending to replace for years, wet footprints stamp a pattern of movement around the room. Nothing else appears to have been disturbed.

'Has someone been in our house?' Lando whispers, his eyes gleaming.

Terror grips Jenna's throat with spindly, vice-like fingers as she imagines the man from the park following her home, violating her only place of safety, but she forces calm into her voice. 'Whoever it was isn't here now. We've checked.'

Lando's shoulders go rigid. 'You're not going to call the police?'

'I don't see the point.' The last thing she wants is more police involvement.

'In case whoever did it has left fingerprints! Come on, Mum, you can't just leave it! You ring, and I'll text Dad.' Her child suddenly sounds so adult, so in charge of the situation.

'Yes, tell him to come home.' Zach never stays out this long.

Jenna's fingers feel too clumsy to use her own phone as Lando taps away on his. She spends too long debating whether to call 101 or 999, hovering indecisively over the keypad numbers.

Finally, she decides the situation warrants an immediate response.

'Someone has been in my house,' she breathes. 'They smashed my living-room window and climbed in.'

'Are they still on the premises?'

'We don't think so.' She doesn't want to tell them about the house search, which now seems ridiculous.

'How long ago did this happen?'

'Maybe five minutes? My name has been shared on social media in relation to a police investigation and I'm scared some-body has found out our address.'

'I've got officers on their way to you. Are you safe to wait for them?'

'Yes, we're safe,' she confirms, even though she isn't sure they are. She threads her arm through Lando's and tries to pull him close, but he rears away, out of reach. She can't blame him, but the rejection still smarts.

'Shall I stay on the line with you till they arrive?'

'No, thank you, it's fine.' She sounds so polite and British, her professional voice.

'Let's look outside,' Lando says when she ends the call.

'No, they might still be hanging around.'

'As if.' The scorn has returned.

He dives into the understairs cupboard, emerging with the powerful torch. Jenna has no choice but to follow him out. On both sides, the neighbouring houses are in darkness, and it doesn't seem that the sound had penetrated across the road, for no one is at their door or window, peering out to see what was happening.

Lando shines the torch on the flowerbed beneath the bay window, illuminating several more shoe prints. They are large, masculine and broad, pressed into the damp soil, more defined than the ones in the living room.

'Have you seen our address being mentioned on social media?' Jenna whispers as she stares at the evidence.

'No, but it's easy enough to find out where someone lives.'

'Jenna!' Zach has arrived, out of breath and barely moving at a jog, dishevelled and sweating in evidence that he has run from the snooker club on Essex Road. He never thinks clearly in times of panic; it wouldn't have occurred to him it would be quicker to flag down a cab.

'We're fine,' Jenna says, tensing as he hugs them both to him. Lando pulls away as his body is pushed against his mother's.

'Have you called the police?'

'They're on their way.'

'Where's Loki?'

'Shut in the utility room. Don't let him out, Zach, he'll end up with cut paws.'

Zach concedes unhappily, reaching to sling his arm around Lando's shoulders instead of hugging his dog. Lando allows him the contact without complaint, eyes darting continually as he takes in the scene.

The police arrive swiftly, blue lights but no sirens. Two tall, bulky men in stab vests, loaded belts cinched around solid waists, one with a bright yellow Taser strapped to his thick thigh. They direct the family back into the kitchen, allowing Zach and Loki to be reunited in a volley of cries and reassurances.

The rich smell of Bolognese sauce is at odds with the cold atmosphere. Jenna leaves it simmering as she makes tea for the officers and avoids looking at the wine rack. Zach offers them the best chocolate biscuits, the Waitrose ones that cost a fortune, and she is inexplicably enraged.

'We've requested a crime scene investigator. They'll be a while, so stay out of the living room and away from the footprints till they've done their work.'

Jenna nods cooperation, although she is surprised they are bothering to be thorough.

'Nothing missing from the house?' the first officer asks.

'Not that we can tell.'

'You mentioned social media backlash when you called? Any idea of names?'

Jenna and Zach shake their heads simultaneously. 'The comments have been pretty unpleasant,' Zach says. 'It's entirely possible someone has taken things a step too far.'

'Have specific threats been made?'

'Mostly just mouthing off, but a few trolls have been particularly nasty. I wouldn't say there's been any direct threats, though.'

'What if it was Drew?' Lando interrupts, the words bursting from his lips as if he has been holding them in for ages.

The officers turn to him before Jenna can seize his arm, demand what the hell he is playing at. 'Did you see anything?'

'No.' Lando raises his chin. 'But what if he wants to scare Mum into dropping the case?'

'But you think the world of Drew!' Jenna is mystified by this sudden about-turn.

'He doesn't give a shit about me now you've caused all this. He hasn't replied to any of my messages.'

'That's the right thing for him to do!' Jenna ignores the officers' questioning looks.

'Lando, we've no reason to think Drew has anything to do with this,' Zach says, with rare forcefulness. 'You can't go around saying stuff like that without proof.'

For an awful moment, Jenna thinks Lando is about to reply that his mother is doing exactly that.

'Go and play your game,' she interjects. 'Let us deal with this.'

Lando's eyes narrow. 'Yeah, just like you deal with everything else.'

He strides from the room with unusual urgency, keeping his gaze averted from the police. Jenna slumps on to a stool.

'Sorry about him. He's at that age.' It's a weak explanation, but the officers don't seem particularly concerned.

'I've got a teenager myself,' one says with a rueful smile. 'Who's Drew?'

'The man I've reported for historic abuse. He was Lando's swimming coach until the investigation started.'

'Who's the investigating officer for your case?'

'He's from Essex Police – DS Nick Beckett. I've got his card here.' Jenna produces it from her phone wallet. The card is always with her now.

Beckett's number is noted down. 'I'll let him know what's happened, just so he's kept in the loop. You can call an emergency glazier once the scene's been processed. They'll make the property secure till you can arrange a new window.'

If only it was so easy to make the rest of their lives secure.

Chapter Thirty

*T*hrough the haze of her hangover, Jenna became aware of urgent, thumping footsteps and loud voices in the corridor outside. Morning had arrived, the sunlight peeping through the thin curtains, making her sensitive eyes water.

Someone was crying, a keening noise that did little to help Jenna's pounding head. Doors were opening and closing, more voices joining the commotion. She pulled the duvet higher and tried to ignore whatever was going on.

As the volume continued to rise, Jenna admitted defeat, her own curiosity getting the better of her. She struggled out of bed and found a thick hoodie to pull on over her pyjamas.

A sudden rush of panic coursed through her as her brain finally began to function. She opened her door to find the corridor full of students, male and female. They were all talking at once, some clutching each other, others with hands slapped across their mouths as if gagging themselves.

'What's going—'

Jenna didn't get time to finish her question before Ava was in front of her, grabbing her hand. Ava's face was grey, her eyes red. Tears had left glistening tracks down her cheeks and Jenna could feel how sweaty her palm was. On her shoulder, Olivia was silently sobbing, her fragile frame convulsing.

'We need to get out of here,' Ava hissed, standing too close, her breath hot and sour against Jenna's face. 'Come with us, quick, before anyone notices.'

'I don't understand.'

'Just hurry up!' Ava's grip tightened and she suddenly seemed twice as strong as Jenna. She was dragged to the door leading to the stairs, and they slipped through, unnoticed by the transfixed crowd gathered at the entrance to the sixth-form corridor.

Ava led the frantic dash downstairs to the side entrance, Jenna stumbling as she was hauled along, trying to keep up. Outside, the bitter cold of the early morning robbed her momentarily of breath and she snatched her hand free, hissing in discomfort as she tried to suck frigid air into her lungs.

Out of the corner of her eye, she saw a flash of colour, the reflective material of a high-vis jacket. Heavy boots crunched against the gravel, heading for the front door of Raleigh, and Jenna heard the mumble of a hand-held radio.

'Ava, what—'

'This way!' Ava was darting ahead again, and Jenna had no choice but to follow. Mist still clung, damp and eerie, as they sprinted across sports fields until they reached the cricket pitch. Only once they were safely under the cover of the pavilion veranda did Ava finally stop, collapsing on to a wooden bench as she fought for breath. Olivia was sobbing and retching at the same time, trying to gulp air between heaves.

'Rory,' Ava managed to gasp out.

'What about Rory?' Jenna heard her own voice rise as Ava's panic became contagious.

'They found him this morning,' Olivia moaned.

Jenna didn't understand. 'Who did? Found what?'

'Rory's dead!' Ava almost screamed, immediately clamping her hands over her mouth as if she could retract the volume. 'My God, Jenna, he's dead.'

Icy coldness flooded Jenna, shooting through her veins, seizing her brain. She was helpless to do anything but stare at Ava and Olivia, opening and closing her mouth as she searched for words that wouldn't come.

'What happened?'

'What the hell do you think? He must have found the pills and tried them.'

'How do you know?'

'Because why else would he be dead?' Olivia cried, sobs exploding from her mouth. She dropped to her knees, rocking and hugging herself. 'He must have had a bad reaction. Oh my God, we've killed him. We killed Rory.'

Jenna could only stand, frozen, as her teeth began to chatter in time with the frantic flutter of her heart.

She saw a shadow across the grass and jumped violently before realising it was Seb, scuttling towards them with his hood tightly drawn around his face.

'What the hell?' he stammered. He was as pale as Ava and sweating profusely, droplets glistening on his clammy skin. 'Everyone's saying it's Rory. It can't be!'

'It's true,' Olivia choked.

She continued to keen, her rocking becoming faster and faster.

'Ava, listen, for fuck's sake!' Seb grabbed her by the shoulders. 'We need to get rid of the rest of the stash. The police are already searching my corridor. You'll be top of the list.'

Jenna squeezed her eyes shut, trying to force calm upon herself.

'We'll be expelled.' Ava started rocking again, a low moan emanating from her lips. 'My parents will disown me. Rory's dead, and my life will be over. What if we go to prison?'

She clasped her hands as if in prayer. Jenna could hear her own breath coming in sharp, shallow gasps as the realisation hit her – she would never see Ava and Olivia again if they were expelled. Never smile at Ava's raucous laugh or listen to the streams of words spilling excitedly from Olivia's lips. Never feel their bodies snuggled up against her, warm and reassuring.

The tears came then, a silent cascade of misery and fear.

'Jenna, you have to help me!' Ava's movements became fast and jerky with panic, her words spilling from her lips in a rush. 'Will you hide the rest of the pills? You won't be suspected. Just for today. Please.'

'Don't get Jenna involved,' Olivia hissed. 'I'll take them.'

'No!' Ava grasped the hem of Jenna's hoodie in desperate fingers, fighting for her attention. 'You'll be on the search radar too. So will Seb. Jenna's the only one who won't be. It's only for one night. I'm begging you, Jenna, please.'

The terrified eyes fixed upon hers broke the spell and Jenna's bright mind fought to focus on the awful problem that had now becomes hers as much as Ava's. That was what friends were for, after all.

'OK,' she whispered.

Ava pulled a pair of tightly rolled socks from her bra, holding them out to Jenna.

'No!' Seb grabbed them, thrusting them into his own hoodie pocket, both hands gripping the bundle beneath the fabric. 'We're not putting Jenna at risk. I'll just get rid of them.'

He turned away, about to go, but Jenna took hold of his shoulder. He resisted for a long minute, threatening to pull away from her, refusing to turn and face her.

'Give them to me,' Jenna said.

Another long moment passed before Seb finally heaved a great sigh and swung round, holding out the socks to her.

'Thank God I've got you to rely on, Jenna,' Ava croaked, her throat punished by her sobs.

The flush of pride, from both the praise and the demonstration of trust, made Jenna glow inside even as Seb glared at her. She shook her head at him, letting him know this was her choice, not coercion. 'I promised Ava I'd help her, and I will.'

'You're the best one of us all.' He gave her a wry smile. 'Never forget that.'

'Why can't we just get rid of them?' Olivia demanded.

'Because if I don't give my supplier his money, he'll break all my fingers,' Ava snarled. 'I can't pay him unless I sell them.'

'But they've killed someone!' Olivia almost howled.

'I've been selling those ever since I got here – no one has died! You two have taken them loads of times! Rory must have had something wrong with him. A heart condition or something – I don't know. Maybe he threw up and choked. There's nothing wrong with the pills!'

Olivia clutched her hair hard enough to pull it out. 'For fuck's sake, Ava!'

Jenna was sharply reminded just how young they all were. It was clear none of them had any idea what to do for the best, and Ava, for all her smart mouth and disregard of rules and laws, was completely out of her depth.

'What the hell are you lot doing?' a male voice rang out, making them all let out muffled cries of shock. None of them had noticed Drew Merchant striding towards them. 'Get back to Raleigh before Pius finds out you've gone!'

The little group broke apart as if about to make a run for it. Jenna hid the socks in her sleeve, swiping at her eyes with it to erase the tears and disguise the lump at the same time. Drew looked from one to the other, his jaw clenched.

'Don't tell me you're hiding your stash, Ava,' he growled. 'And don't fuck me about denying it. Did Rory buy from you last night?'

'No!' Ava wrapped her arms tightly around herself. 'He never gets his stuff from me. He says my prices are a rip off.'

'Whatever he did buy must have been dodgy.' Drew's intelligent eyes were clouded. 'This is a nightmare. The cops are turning Raleigh upside down; the abbot president will be on his way. Cell Block H is fucked.'

'That's not our fault,' Ava whimpered.

'Isn't it? You sure none of you lot gave him anything?'

'We're not the only ones into drink and drugs!' Olivia yelped. 'You're no innocent either! Most of Raleigh has a stash, for fuck's sake.'

Drew raised his chin. 'Swear to me none of you are mixed up in this shit.'

'We swear,' Seb whispered, shaking so hard his teeth were chattering.

Jenna couldn't tear her eyes from Drew, so handsome, so authoritative. She couldn't tell if he believed them. The urge to tell him everything, to beg for his help, to ease her burden on to his strong shoulders, nearly overwhelmed her.

'Get back to the house, all of you, before you're found to be missing. Keep your bloody heads down. Hurry up!'

'Are you going to tell Brother Pius we sneaked out?' Seb asked, standing close enough to Jenna for her to feel him trembling violently.

A muscle jumped in Drew's firm jaw. 'I haven't seen you.'

Jenna's lungs convulsed as she expelled a huge breath, gasping to try and replace the oxygen. Drew's eyes met hers, calm and reassuring, and she felt her panic began to lessen as she looked into their dark depths.

232

'Go,' he told her quietly.

Ava was already grabbing her sleeve and urging her along, back towards Raleigh House and the hell that awaited them.

It didn't come as any real surprise when the police arrived at Jenna's door, two detectives in civilian clothes and one silent uniformed PC. All Raleigh students had been confined to their rooms, and she had waited with a certain finality, sure of what was coming and preparing as best she could.

She would protect her friends, just like they had tried to protect her from Rory's sins.

'Do you know why we're here, Genevieve?' the first officer asked.

'Because Rory died,' she whispered, and the enormity of the words struck her like an icy blow.

'We have reason to suspect drugs were involved. We're searching all rooms in Raleigh.'

Jenna forgot to breathe as her belongings were rifled through, watched over by her tight-lipped housemaster. It took no time or effort to find what they were seeking, and Jenna saw Brother Pius's face drain of colour.

'Are these yours?' the first officer asked, his voice almost gentle.

Not trusting herself to speak, Jenna shook her head.

'Do they belong to someone else?'

'I don't know,' she managed to say around the stone that seemed to be lodged in her throat.

'Did you know they were here?'

She shook her head again, unable to think of anything else to do.

'Genevieve, do you understand how serious this is?' the second officer demanded. 'A boy has died, mostly likely from taking drugs. And now we've found these hidden in your room.'

'They weren't hidden! I didn't know they were there.'

'When did you last see Rory Addison?'

'I don't know. We're not friends. We don't talk.' She cleared her throat. 'I mean, we didn't.'

'Did Rory use drugs regularly, Genevieve?'

'I've no idea. I barely knew him.'

'What about yourself? Do you take drugs?'

'No.'

'Never?'

The housemaster leaned forward, forcing Jenna to make her look at him. 'God will protect you, Genevieve, if you tell the truth.'

Jenna bit down on her lower lip to silence herself.

'Do we need to contact parents before we go any further, Father?' the lead detective asked.

'It's Brother, Officer, not Father.'

Jenna saw that the detective actually looked apologetic. Surely the police weren't cowed by the power of the Church too?

'Do you want us to call them?' Brother Pius asked her, his voice as gentle as always, despite the fear gleaming in his eyes.

'No! Please, Brother Pius, I don't want them here.' Panic surged through her again.

'I will be Genevieve's appropriate adult,' Brother Pius stated to them, clutching his crucifix as if it would save him from the situation he had found himself in.

Jenna held her breath, waiting for questions she had no idea how to answer, counting the frantic beats of her heart.

'So,' the detective finally continued, 'do you ever take drugs?'

'A bit of weed occasionally,' Jenna mumbled, unable to look at any of the adults.

'Nothing stronger?'

Yet another headshake. 'Is Rory really dead?' She knew the answer but, for some inexplicable reason, she needed to hear a person in authority say it.

'He was found early this morning by another student, who alerted Father . . . sorry . . . Brother Pius. But you say you weren't friends?'

'It's still sad he's dead,' she whispered.

'Who are your friends, Genevieve? Ava Vaughan? Olivia Seabrook?' She nodded quickly.

'We've been told Ava and Olivia are best friends.'

Jenna felt the burn of the slight, whether intended or not. 'We're all best friends.' She jutted out her chin. 'Us and Sebastian Byron.'

'Did these pills belong to Ava or Olivia or Sebastian?'

'I told you, I don't know whose they are.'

The second officer looked across at Brother Pius.

'Ava Vaughan and Olivia Seabrook both arrived with drug issues on their records,' he confirmed. 'We believe in second chances here. We wanted to allow them a fresh start, free from judgement, and absolved of their past sins.'

'I don't think these pills are yours, Genevieve,' the second officer said as the first nodded respectfully at the housemaster's words.

'I've already said they're not mine. I've never seen them before, and I didn't put them in my drawer.'

'I think your friends asked you to hide them.'

'They didn't.'

'I think Ava Vaughan is the school dealer.'

'I don't know what you're talking about.'

'Do you buy your weed from Ava Vaughan?'

'No.'

'Who do you buy it from?'

Jenna didn't dare verbally refuse to tell them so she just stared at the thin carpet.

'You're covering for someone, Genevieve, it's pretty obvious. Who are you scared of?'

'I'm not scared of anyone!' It didn't matter who did scare her — it wasn't her best friends.

'Then why won't you tell us the truth?'

Jenna stared back, feeling her chin trembling even as she tried to prevent it. She forced herself to take deep, slow breaths, battling to maintain eye contact, hardly daring to blink.

How could she say she was terrified of losing the only people who had ever shown her acceptance?

Chapter Thirty-One

Drew

Drew watches the electric gates being erected from behind the safety of the Venetian blinds.

'This makes us look like we have something to hide,' Natasha declares behind him.

'Do you want to wait till the Molotov cocktails start being thrown through the dining-room windows?' he demands.

A careless shrug. 'Maybe they will be food parcels instead.'

Her flippancy towards his reference sends acid momentarily coursing through Drew's veins. When he looks down, his fists are clenched so tightly his neat nails are digging welts in his palms. He studies the white crevices as he slows his breathing.

He is afraid. For his family, his reputation. But, mostly, for himself.

'I'm going out,' Natasha announces.

He doesn't bother to ask where she's going. He doesn't care. He watches her Mercedes spin past the gate installers, the mirrored windows preventing them from being permitted even a glimpse of her stunning profile.

Drew twists the blinds' cord, shutting out the outside world. It seems to take a huge effort to drag himself up the stairs and he is short of breath when he gets to the top.

He gets into bed fully clothed, despite it being only a couple of hours since Sunday lunch was served. He curls into a foetal position under the down-filled duvet. Sleep will defy him again, just like it has been doing every night, but he feels safe here, huddled away from the world.

He is going through the stages of grief, mourning the golden life now most likely lost for ever. The plan had been so intricately mapped out, a ten-year blueprint he had never had cause to doubt. For the first time, he has no idea what to do next.

Closing his heavy eyes, he nestles deeper into the pillow, his mind and body numb with exhaustion. He isn't aware of drifting into a fretful doze. It isn't restful sleep – he tosses and turns and calls out denials – and his body aches unbearably when he is startled awake again several hours later.

With no clue as to what woke him, he peers warily out of the bedroom window to see the gates in place but wide open, and the installers gone.

Drew grabs a hoodie, barely able to keep from wincing when he sees it is adorned with the badge of his school, and goes in search of the housekeeper.

'Are the gates finished?'

She nods, eyes wary.

'Then why are they open?'

'They said you or Mrs Merchant need to set the code, and neither of you was available. They left the instructions for you.' She waves a manual and a small box of tiny remote controls.

'You could have woken me.'

'I didn't think you'd want to be disturbed. The men said it was straightforward. Shall I put some coffee on?'

Drew nods shortly, craving the bitter rush of caffeine. 'Natasha's not back yet?'

'She said not to expect her home for dinner.'

As he sips the thick, dark espresso, Drew idly wonders if his wife is having an affair. How wonderfully ironic that would be. He won't ask her. It doesn't really matter if she is. They are tied to each other by anchors much weightier than marriage vows.

He sinks two coffees and leaves the dirty cup on the island, collecting the instruction manual and remotes and striding out to examine the new gates. They are constructed of solid teak panels, reassuringly strengthened with wrought-iron bars, presenting a fortress image he likes. Frowning in concentration, he taps at the little touch pad discreetly attached to the existing pillar and pairs the remotes. The mechanism purrs smoothly into life and he steps smartly back into the driveway as the gates slide home with a definitive clang.

They are safe. He is safe.

He crosses to his BMW to store the remote, already wondering if he should have paid the extra for sensors to be attached to the car dashboards. He can already hear the complaints of his wife and daughter at the inconvenience of having to locate the little device and go to the effort of tapping it.

His car is unlocked. He is certain he would have locked it the last time he used it, out of habit. He has lost a car to London's thieves before, and he is cautious. Though, in his current state of mind, who knows if he would have remembered.

Something catches his eyes as he closes the driver's door. He takes a step back, wondering if it is a trick of the light.

It isn't.

Drew stares in disbelief at the key marks scarring the pristine paintwork of his car, angry gouges driven deep into the enamel. Beside it, Elena's little Fiat 500, her reward for finally bothering to pass her driving test but barely used due to her preferences for Ubers and drinking, is unharmed.

When did he last check the car? He slowly circles it, seeing the lines become letters as he reaches the bonnet. A word, screaming at him.

Liar.

Chapter Thirty-Two

B eckett and Nixon are on the doorstep, looking far too awake for a Monday morning, more alert than Jenna has felt in weeks.

'What's happened?' She allows them across the threshold, where Loki welcomes them like lifelong friends. She glares at the spaniel for his disloyalty, but he is too busy getting ear scratches from the delighted Beckett to notice.

The detectives follow her through to the kitchen, where Zach is buttering his morning toast. He greets them cautiously and she sees him trying to think of a reason to leave the room but, unlike Loki, who is now pressed tight against Beckett's leg, he stays loyal. He moves to stand beside her, sliding his arm around her waist. She resists the unconscious urge to pull away.

Beckett leans his elbows on the breakfast bar, banishing the height difference and winning Jenna's eye contact against her better judgement. His broad shoulders seem to fill the space around him, and Jenna instinctively leans closer to Zach, even though Beckett's expression is benign. Nixon remains at attention, as focused as Loki at mealtimes.

'Sorry about your window. The officers who attended have been in contact with me. Hopefully it was just a one-off, teenage idiots.'

Zach returns to his breakfast and Jenna wraps her hand around her mug of tea, refusing to offer the detectives a drink. 'You came all this way to discuss a smashed window?'

'Not exactly. We need to talk about the statement taken from your friend, Ava Vaughan.'

Jenna feels her shoulders tighten. 'What about it?'

'She says the allegations against Drew Merchant are fabricated.'

Even though she was expecting it, the damning words still wind Jenna. Out the corner of her eye, she sees that Zach has stopped with the butter knife in mid-stroke and wishes she had sent him upstairs.

'She was very much in defence of Mr Merchant. Any idea why?'

'No.' Jenna is too taken aback to wonder why her best friend is defending her abuser.

'My colleague observed that she seemed upset throughout the meeting. Have you fallen out?'

'No, she's been supportive since all this started.'

'She was very adamant in her statement. I would have expected her to side with you.'

'So would I,' Jenna whispers, almost to herself.

'Jenna, I'll have to disclose this to Mr Merchant and his lawyer.'

'Why?' Jenna grips her mug so hard her fingertips turn white against the warm ceramic.

'It's not something I can keep to myself. Ava will most likely be summoned by the defence if we come to court.'

'You think we will?' she dares to ask.

'Fifty-fifty we'll have enough to charge at the moment, to be honest. I don't want to get your hopes up.'

Jenna no longer knows what she is hoping for. She jumps at the sound of footsteps banging against the stairs.

'My son,' she explains. 'Lando, this is DS Beckett and DC Nixon.'

Lando slinks past Beckett to retrieve his lunch, head down, eyes fixed on his shoes. He doesn't return Beckett's hello or Nixon's tight nod of greeting.

'Why aren't you at swimming?' Zach asks.

A shrug. 'Couldn't be bothered. I'll take myself to school.'

'No, you won't.' Jenna nods to Zach, reassuring him that she can manage alone. 'Your dad will walk you.'

Lando's gaze flits momentarily to the detectives. 'I don't need an escort.'

'That's exactly what you need.' Zach rolls his eyes dramatically, trying too hard to create the impression of boring domesticity. 'Or you'll conveniently forget where the school gates are.'

He sweeps his coat and laptop bag from the dining table. 'Loki, come!'

Father, son and dog clatter out as if being chased by wild beasts. If Beckett notices the abruptness of their departure, he doesn't show it. He looks disappointed the spaniel has gone.

Jenna busies herself wiping up toast crumbs and shoving half-full cups into the dishwasher without bothering to empty them into the sink first, anything to avoid looking at the detectives. She swears as splashes of tea rain on to her suede shoes.

'We've been checking the school records,' Beckett continues.

Jenna turns on the tap to flush out the sink, hoping the rush of water will drown out what she knows is coming.

'Why did you change your name?' he asks.

'I got married, obviously,' Jenna retorts.

A steady gaze that brooks no defiance. 'Your first name.'

'You try being called Genevieve. Bloody awful name.'

'And you changed it legally, by deed poll?'

'Yes, soon as I left school. I didn't want to have that name at university. You must have known I'd changed my name when I came to Chelmsford. Why not ask me about it then?'

'We were still making inquiries. Any particular reason for the change?'

'As I just said, I hated the name Genevieve. I wanted to be a different person. Jenna had been my shortened name for years so it wasn't a difficult transition.'

'And what about the fact that Genevieve Alcott was involved in a police investigation? The Brothers must have forgotten to mention that. They weren't very forthcoming about certain things. Why the Order was removed from the school community, for example.'

'The Church protected its own, Sergeant Beckett, and no one had the balls to argue about it.' Jenna feels redness rush to her cheeks as the memory of standing in the abbot's study, listening to his words, echoes in her ears as if it happened yesterday. 'Look, I didn't do anything. I got the blame, but it wasn't me.'

'You didn't supply drugs at school?'

'No, I didn't. Someone else was the supplier and I took the rap for them.'

'Who?'

'What does it matter now? I wasn't convicted.'

'The drugs were found in your room.'

'I didn't know they were there. That's why I wasn't expelled.

It was accepted that I'd been set up, but they never found out who by.' If only it had been that simple.

'Our records show the drug issues came to light after someone died?'

The lump in Jenna's throat is growing by the second and she finds she can't say the name that leaps so readily to her lips, a vibrant ghost who should never have been rendered silent.

'Rory Addison? The cousin of your boss, I believe.'

'The post-mortem proved Rory had a cardiac arrest, that it was an accident. The coroner agreed. Death by misadventure. But you know all that, don't you?'

'Did that make it easier for you?'

'No, of course it didn't,' Jenna chokes, shaking her head so quickly the room spins. 'Look, I wasn't charged. My fingerprints weren't on the drugs. What happened to Rory was awful, but I didn't cause it.'

'Someone at your school did. And you protected them.'

Jenna tears off a piece of kitchen roll, wiping up a spray of water from the tap. 'Misplaced loyalty,' she says shortly.

'Was Ava Vaughan a good friend?'

'I thought she was.'

'She doesn't seem to think you are now.'

'You'll have to ask her about that.'

'Jenna, I'm asking you. There's a lot that doesn't add up in this investigation and I can't help you if you hide things from me. Ava Vaughan is adamant that Drew Merchant did not abuse you. If there's something I need to know about her, you have to tell me.'

Jenna has begun to shred the kitchen roll into tiny pieces. She stares at the little pile she has created.

'What about Olivia Seabrook? You and Ava were friends with her too?'

'Yes.'

'I'm told her suicide note blamed Halewood House for her poor mental health.'

'I never saw the note.'

'What happened at school that had such an effect on her?'

She crushes the pile of tissue shreds with a flattened palm, denying the maelstrom of emotions churning in her gut. 'What has my friend's suicide got to do with your investigation?'

'That's what I'm trying to establish. There seems to have been rather a lot that went on at Halewood House involving you and your friends.'

Jenna snatches up her bag and coat, icy fear coursing through her nervous system. 'I have to go to work. I'm already late. I can't afford to annoy Hugo any more than I already have.'

'We can drop you at work, talk in the car?'

'I'm perfectly capable of driving myself, thank you.' She can't be in a confined space with this man, his size as intimidating as his intelligence.

She widens the gap between them, grabbing a packet of mints from the dining table.

'I need to go, DS Beckett.'

Striding through the familiar, heaving streets of central London, Jenna draws comfort from her anonymity in the crowds of busy people. None of them care who she is, what she has done. She can breathe amid the traffic fumes and narrow pavements and shoulder-barging.

She knows where she will find Ava and Seb – the same place

the three of them go every Monday for a late lunch, true creatures of habit, no matter how strongly they insist on their spontaneity. Her feet carry her to their favourite spot, a tiny French bistro tucked away from tourists. A waiter greets her by name.

'Are Ava and Seb here?' Jenna manages to dredge a smile.

A frown. '*Mais oui*. Aren't they waiting for you?'

'Um . . . no . . .'

He awkwardly indicates the back of a tall booth. 'Sorry. I assumed you wouldn't be far behind. Had a falling-out?'

'No, nothing like that,' Jenna mumbles.

She is rewarded with a smile, equilibrium restored, and he is leading her to the booth before she can make an excuse to leave. The two women lock eyes, mirroring each other's thin lips and rigid shoulders.

'Are you waiting for someone?' Jenna asks as she sits beside Seb.

'No.' Ava's reply is too quick.

'Sorry, Max just assumed I was meeting up with you.' Jenna tilts her head towards the waiter, who has already gone to mix her usual. She feels like that nervous, isolated schoolgirl again, stumbling over her words. Her armour has abandoned her just when she needs it most.

'How are you?' Seb asks, enveloping her in a hug.

'Exhausted. My life's falling apart.'

Ava looks away and sips her drink rapidly. 'What's happening with the investigation?'

'Not a lot, from the sounds of it. Not since you made a statement insisting I'm lying.' Jenna cringes at her own tone, at the neediness that has somehow insinuated itself.

Ava shifts in her seat. 'I didn't put it quite like that.'

'You did according to DS Beckett. You defended Drew.'

Ava's fingers seize her vintage Zippo lighter and begin to twirl it rapidly. 'Simon's seen your name on Twitter. He doesn't want me to have any contact with you. You know what he's like about keeping up appearances.'

Jenna grits her teeth at her friend's determination to avoid the salient issue, hard enough to make pain shoot through her jaw. 'Doesn't want his wife tarnished by my sordid reputation, I suppose? Since when do you give a fuck what Simon thinks or says?'

'My marriage is hanging by a thread already. He'll ruin me if we end up divorcing. I won't get a penny out of him.'

'You really do have the perfect marriage,' Seb sighs. 'You live on opposite sides of the world, Simon bankrolls you, and you meet up for a shag a few times a year. It's a miracle you got pregnant, frankly.'

Ava turns crimson. 'I told you, I'd forgotten to get my implant changed before it expired.'

'If he didn't divorce you after that, I don't imagine he'll dump you for being friends with Jenna – the victim in this scenario.' Seb gives Jenna a gentle nudge. 'Hello? Are you with us?'

Jenna is staring at Ava as if she has never seen her before. Her brain is racing so fast she can almost hear her own thoughts.

'Oh my God, Adeline isn't Simon's,' she whispers.

Ava drops her lighter with a clatter. Seb's body stills, even as his head turns back and forth between the two women as if he were watching a tennis match.

'That's why she goes to Drew's school!' Jenna's words spill out rapidly now understanding has dawned. 'I couldn't understand why you chose to send her there.'

'As if I'd turn down the chance for her to have such a good education!' Ava retorts.

'Is that why you wouldn't let me up when I came to yours?' Jenna refuses to look away from Ava. 'Was he there?'

'Jenna, I don't get what you're talking about,' Seb says plaintively, his expression frozen in discomfort at the tension.

'Drew is Adeline's father.'

Absolute silence. For a long moment, no one moves. Even their breath is hushed.

'You're talking nonsense,' Ava raps out.

'It all fits. Why else would you side with him over me?'

'Maybe because I'm a realist, not a fantasist.' Ava scrabbles to retrieve the lighter from under the table.

'Come on, Ava, tell us the truth!' Jenna presses. 'Are you having an affair with Drew?'

Ava barks out a laugh. 'I wouldn't call it an affair.'

'What the hell?' Seb gasps, his eyes bulging, voice higher than usual. He unconsciously grasps his neck chain, tugging at the delicate links in an attempt to calm himself.

'It's been half a lifetime.'

'What has?'

'Drew and me. It started at school, and it's never really stopped.'

Jenna meets Seb's eyes, hoping he won't see the storm of emotions swirling in hers. He gives a little shrug, no idea how to react.

Ava gulps her cocktail. Her deliberate movements tell Jenna she is already drunk. 'I've been one of his mistresses for years. Natasha doesn't sleep with him, hasn't done since Elena was conceived.'

'Is that what he's told you?' Jenna almost laughs.

'It doesn't matter whether you believe me or not,' Ava says impatiently.

For a long moment, Jenna has no idea what to say in response. Her muscles clench. 'Does Drew know about Adeline?'

'Of course he knows. Adeline and Simon don't, and I intend it to stay that way.'

'Why didn't you tell us?' Seb asks, his tone hushed.

Ava lets out a harsh laugh, 'Would you admit you gave birth to a secret love child? Think about what I've got to lose!'

Jenna stares at her friend as if seeing her clearly for the first time. 'No wonder you didn't want me to report him.'

'I have to protect him. I love him – I have since I was fifteen. I know it wasn't Drew.'

'How?' Seb asks.

'Because he could have me any time he wanted. I was sleeping with him a few weeks into the first term! And he never – he wouldn't – he couldn't . . .'

'That isn't proof!'

Ava looks at her, eyes shiny with unshed tears. 'It is to me.'

'You don't know anything,' Jenna hisses. 'You're just seeing what you want to see. Drew's blinded you.'

'Like you're being rational. Jenna, I've loved you like a sister, ever since school, but you've gone too far.'

'You did too!' The words are out of Jenna's mouth before she can stop them. 'What about Rory?'

'We're all to blame for Rory,' Ava hisses.

'Beckett knows how he died.'

Ava freezes, her knuckles white as she grabs the edge of the table. 'How?'

'He's a detective, for God's sake. I covered for you. I lied for

250

you.' Jenna's mind is racing in circles, a dizzying carousel. 'You were hysterical when you found out he was dead.'

'I thought I was going to prison! Obviously, I was hysterical!'

'Not about the fact that a boy had died, like I was stupid enough to assume?'

'Olivia gave him the pills, Jenna, not me. You two came up with the plan. All I did was provide what you needed.'

There is a long moment of silence as that declaration is processed. Seb looks from one woman to the other, his face white and drawn.

Jenna drops her head into her hands. 'He wasn't supposed to find them,' she mumbles to Ava. 'Olivia promised he wouldn't find them.'

'Olivia was crazy, Jenna. I loved her, but she was out of control.'

'How were we supposed to know what they'd do to Rory? I didn't think you'd have anything really dangerous.'

'Those red-and-yellow ones weren't that strong. They shouldn't have killed anyone!'

Jenna opens her mouth to speak before Ava's words register. She frowns, trying to focus. 'Red and yellow? They were blue.'

'No, they weren't. I always got the same batch because they looked like those paracetamol capsules Matron doled out.'

'I saw them,' Jenna insists. 'The police showed them to me. They weren't red-and-yellow capsules. They were tiny, light blue pills.'

Ava's forehead contorts with the effort of concentration. 'That can't be right. You must be remembering a different time.'

'I'll *never* forget them!'

'But . . .' Ava is shaking her head as if trying to dislodge water from an eardrum. 'But they can't have been. I gave you the socks. The baggie of red-and-yellows was inside them. There were no blue ones.'

Jenna grips the stem of her glass hard enough to snap it, her breath coming in tiny sips of oxygen as her brain starts to understand what this means. She stares at Ava, unable to look away from her. Ava continues shaking her head, unable to stop, her lips mumbling words as if they have lost all sensation.

'Jenna, I swear. I never sold any blue pills.'

Chapter Thirty-Three

Drew

The moment Drew hears the housekeeper on the intercom, opening the gates to reveal Beckett's car, followed by a liveried van containing two uniformed officers, Drew grabs his phone and dials Henry.

'The fucking cops have turned up. Can they keep doing this?'

'Unfortunately, yes. Unless you're formally arrested, they can question you at home.'

'I want you here this time.'

'On my way, old chap. Go out and tell them you won't be inviting them in till I arrive. Let them sit in the cold for a while.'

Drew does exactly that, managing not to smirk at the expression on DC Nixon's face when he informs them of Henry's mandate. Beckett is, as ever, irritatingly impervious, and even pulls out a paperback from the glovebox – *Brave New World*, no less – as he makes himself more comfortable in his seat.

It takes Henry half an hour to arrive, too much time for Drew to be alone with his thoughts, and by the time his friend is shown into the study, Drew's heart is pounding and his shoulders are so taut it feels as though they are touching his ears.

'Ring for the housekeeper to show them in,' Henry instructs, buttoning his tweed jacket and resting one hand against Drew's desk, entirely in control.

Beckett doesn't rush in, and Drew's teeth are grinding together by the time the detective and his shadow deign to join them, followed by two anonymous men in uniform.

'What is it now, DS Beckett?' Henry's voice rings out reassuringly.

Beckett takes a seat, again without being asked. Nixon hovers at his shoulder, notebook poised.

'These officers are from Islington police station.' Beckett indicates the two men. 'They informed me of an incident on Saturday evening at Jenna Taylor's address. Mind if I ask you some questions, Mr Merchant?'

Drew watches the uniformed officers, but they remain still and silent, happy for the detective to take the lead.

'As you wish, Sergeant,' Henry says, magnanimous in his overt cooperation.

'Where were you that day?' Beckett addresses Drew directly.

'Here,' Drew replies without hesitation. 'I didn't leave home. My wife and daughter will confirm it.'

'Do you have any walking boots?'

'Walking boots?' Drew is thrown by the question.

'Sturdy footwear for countryside activities,' Beckett helpfully explains.

Drew doesn't bother to disguise his scowl in return. 'I suppose I will somewhere, yes. There's not much need for them in London.'

'See if you can find them for me? Just to check.'

'Check what?'

Beckett waits, his expression declaring that he has all the time in the world.

Drew gives in, opens the door and yells for the housekeeper. 'Any idea where my walking boots might be?' he asks her.

'Wellies and stuff are on the shelf at the back of the utility room,' she replies immediately. 'Shall I fetch them?'

She trots off at Drew's curt nod. He taps his fingers against his desk until he sees Beckett is observing the movement. By the time he has recognised that the housekeeper is taking too long to retrieve the damn boots, she is back, empty handed.

'They're not there.'

'They must be somewhere else.'

'I haven't moved them.'

'Neither have I.'

'When did you last use them?' Beckett asks.

'I don't bloody know. Months ago.'

'Have you seen them recently?' Beckett directs this question towards the housekeeper.

'Yes, each time I go to the chest freezer in there. They've got a luminous badge on them so they always catch my eye before the lights warm up.'

'And you've no idea where they might have gone, Mr Merchant?'

'Like I said, I haven't used them for months. I've no idea where they are. What the hell is this about?'

'The Taylor house suffered criminal damage on Saturday. We found footprints in the flowerbed, so we want to compare them to any possible matches.'

255

'Why would my boots be a match? You think I did it? As if I'd be that damn stupid. I've no interest in playing games.'

'We still need to do the comparison. It will have a bearing on the investigation if some tit-for-tat retaliation is going on between you two.'

'That will be difficult without the boots,' Drew says between gritted teeth. 'If I find them, I will let you know.'

'That's not the only reason we're here.'

'What the hell else can you want?'

'I need to ask you about a signet ring.'

Drew frowns, struggling to keep up with the sudden change of subject. His brain, usually constantly active, has stagnated recently. He feels sluggish, stupid.

Beckett shows him a rough sketch, the shape and colouring immediately recognisable.

'That looks like my father's ring.'

'He gave it to you?'

'It was passed down to me when he died.'

'When was that?'

'I was doing my GCSEs. But I lost the ring, only a few weeks after I started wearing it. It was too big for me. It must have fallen off, and I never found it again.'

'Did your family claim on insurance? I assume it would have been valuable. That would prove the year you lost it.'

'Yes, of course we did.'

'Mrs Taylor has said she recognised you as her abuser because of the ring you were wearing. She drew the picture. She was very familiar with it.'

Drew's body jerks as if an electric current has passed through his body. He immediately falls silent, realising the trap.

256

'You state that you are no longer in possession of the ring?' Beckett tries a different tactic.

'No, not for decades. I had a new one made that looks similar, but it's not the same one.' He holds out his hand, showing them his wedding ring.

'You won't mind if we search for it?'

'You want to search my house?'

'Do you have a warrant?' Henry barks, as if he is in a TV drama.

'We can obtain one, but if Mr Merchant has nothing to hide, surely he won't mind us taking a brief look round? We won't cause a mess or any unnecessary disturbance. You can be present the entire time.' Beckett makes deliberate eye contact with Drew. 'A warrant would involve bringing more officers for a more thorough search. I'm sure your wife wouldn't appreciate your neighbours seeing that.'

Rage bubbles in Drew's stomach and he has to grit his teeth to remain silent.

'I'd like a moment alone with my client,' Henry declares.

He waits for the door to close and footsteps to move away down the corridor.

'This ring's definitely lost, old chap?'

'Yes!' Drew says defensively.

'So they won't find it at the house?'

'You're going to allow them to do this?'

'To be honest, it makes you look bloody suspicious if you refuse.'

Drew clenches his fists. 'Fine. Let's get on with it.'

While Henry follows the police group around like an attentive bloodhound as they conduct their search, Drew downs a large whisky and tries to force his thoughts into some semblance of order.

His dulled brain struggles to summon the recollections he requires. It takes too long to access the memories of Halewood House, to visualise the ring on his finger .

He had been so careless with it, lost in a cloud of grief for his father, wanting the ring in his possession at all times, even though it didn't fit him and was due to be resized. He could remember the panic quickly turning to rage as he discovered it missing, scouring the wet, muddy changing-room floor, crawling on his hands and knees under benches, yelling at his peers to join the search. Assurances and consolations went unheard as he retraced his steps, ripped his dorm room apart in case he had forgotten to put it on. Turfed protesting boys out of the bathroom so he could search the sinks and shower shelves, just in case. An announcement in the following morning's assembly, a stern warning to keep eyes peeled and return the property immediately if found. No accusations, of course.

That wasn't how it was done at Halewood House.

Brought abruptly back to the present, Drew finds he is rubbing the skin of his little finger, as if expecting to find a faint mark still there. His wedding ring has none of the sentimental value and, once again, he laments the carelessness of his youth.

The troop of footsteps announces the search party's return. It hasn't taken them long to admit defeat. Maybe Henry has convinced them of the futility of the task.

One of the uniformed men is casually swinging a large evidence bag, a paper sack with a clear film window. Drew frowns at the walking boots it contains.

'Sir, these were in your BMW, in the footwell behind the driver's seat.'

'I haven't had them in my car.'

'Who else would have put them there?'

Drew searches for an explanation. 'My car was unlocked when I discovered it had been damaged. You must have seen the scratches. Anyone could have got into it.'

'Does that seem likely? You didn't report anything about your car.'

'It seems very likely that someone is trying to frame my client for the damage done to Mrs Taylor's property,' Henry interjects.

DC Nixon, chin raised as if producing Excalibur, holds up another sealed evidence bag, plastic this time. It contains a small gold object.

'And what about this?'

Drew stares, uncomprehending. 'What's that?'

'It seems to be a signet ring, sarge,' Nixon speaks directly to Beckett, as if Drew wasn't in the room. 'The stone is missing but you can still see engraving similar to that in Mrs Taylor's sketch.'

'But, but . . . that can't be mine!' Drew splutters. 'It must belong to my wife. She has countless rings.'

Nixon hands Beckett the bag. 'I would say it's a male ring. Too large for a woman.'

'Mr Merchant?' Beckett looks expectantly at Drew.

'Any further questions must be asked in an interview room, DS Beckett,' Henry interjects. He has started to sweat, his lips thin and compressed as he shoots Drew an icy glare. 'We won't be making any comment at this moment.'

'Where did you find it?' Drew chokes out, his voice constricted by an invisible hand squeezing his windpipe.

'At the back of your bedside drawer.'

'I didn't put it there.'

'Then who did?'

'Drew, don't say another word,' Henry hisses.

'Maybe your wife would know more?' Beckett suggests helpfully.

'She's not here, and how the hell would she know?'

'Your housekeeper, perhaps? Presumably she would have tidied items away into drawers when she was cleaning?'

'Bloody ask her then!' For the second time, Drew snatches open the study door, and yells down the hallway.

The housekeeper shakes her head uncertainly as she is shown the evidence bag. 'It looks a lot like Mr Merchant's wedding ring, but he's wearing that.'

'Are you sure you don't recognise it?'

'I'd remember it, I'm sure.'

'How often do you tidy the master bedroom?'

'Every day. Mrs Merchant' – a quick glance at Drew – 'isn't the tidiest, and Mr Merchant likes everything in its place.'

'So you know the contents of drawers, things like that?'

'I don't go looking,' she huffs. 'I just put things away as I need to.'

'What belongings of Mr Merchant do you tend to tidy away?'

'Socks and cufflinks, mostly. That's the only jewellery he wears, apart from his watch and wedding ring.'

'When was the last time you needed to put anything in his bedside drawer?'

'I couldn't say.'

'Try.'

'Weeks ago, I suppose. He asked me to put a packet of paracetamol in there.'

'Do you need a written record of each time I've had a headache as well, DS Beckett?' Drew interrupts. Henry lays a restraining hand on his arm, but Drew shrugs him off.

Beckett takes a step closer, his jaw tense. 'Andrew Merchant, I'm arresting you on suspicion of . . .'

Chapter Thirty-Four

'Jenna! Wait!'

Even though she knows it isn't, Jenna still allows herself to hope it is Ava chasing after her as she speed-walks away from the restaurant. Instead, Seb is the one who catches up with her.

'This is crazy.' He pulls her into a hug in the middle of the pavement. 'I had to come after you. We couldn't leave it like that.'

'Why does Ava think those pills were different, Seb? I don't understand.'

'It was a long time ago. She's blocked out Rory as much as you've blocked out Drew. Ava doesn't want to be guilty for his death, but she is, darling. You're not.'

'But I went along with it,' Jenna whispers into his shirt, closing her eyes and counting his rapid pulse. 'I was so sure it was Rory. He died because I got it wrong. *We* got it wrong.'

She feels Seb's muscles go rigid, and he holds his breath for a long moment. 'Do you think Ava's supplier just mixed up the pills?' His voice is unsteady when he finally exhales.

'I guess we'll never know.' Jenna steps back, the physical

contact too much for her. 'What if someone else did? Could Drew have had something to do with it?'

'He'd have had access to the stash if he was sleeping with Ava. He could have switched them. Did you see the pills when Olivia hid them in Rory's room.'

'No, I didn't think to look.' Jenna shakes her head, dismissing. 'Yet another thing we can't prove. I'm going home. Want to come?'

'I'd better get back to Ava. She was crying when I ran after you.'

'Sorry to make you choose between us.' She knows how difficult he finds conflict.

He gives a lopsided smile. 'I love you both, but you were the one who rescued me after New York. You get first loyalty.'

'Thank you.' Jenna sees his need for reassurance and briefly squeezes his muscled forearm.

'I know I'm no one's idea of protection, but I've been trying, I really have. I've been online, replying to those sick comments, backing you up.'

'Really?'

He shrugs. 'I've got lots of accounts. I find it easier to talk to people behind a screen than in real life. I've been posting every day, stoking up support for you. I know the trolls are everywhere, but I thought at least I could do something.'

He trails off as Jenna hugs him quickly, holding him tightly for a brief moment. 'Love you,' she whispers to him.

He smiles as she releases him. 'I'm always here for you.' He turns back unenthusiastically towards the restaurant. 'Text me when you're home safe.'

★

'Why are you home so early?' are Jenna's first words when Zach walks through the door. His arrival hasn't given her time to hide the wine.

Loki leaps up to say hello and she shoves him away, protecting her glass. It is the only clean one left. The house is going to hell around her, something that would usually never be permitted, but, for once, she isn't gripped by the compulsion to restore order.

Loki drops down at her feet, tail wagging uncertainly, as if challenging her unpredictability. One minute she is craving his attention, the next she is rejecting him, and she can see the confusion in his loyal eyes. Eyes not dissimilar to Lando's.

She turns away from him before the scream building in her chest unleashes itself. Dinner. She needs to cook. The house is in an unforgivable state. Everywhere she looks, there is mess: piles of clothes waiting to be washed, clean laundry to be put away, the sink overflowing with crockery because the dishwasher hasn't been emptied. Loki's food bowl needs scrubbing clean, the kitchen floor is gritty with garden dirt and the work surfaces are covered in dried stains.

'I wanted to check you were OK after this morning.' Zach crouches to reassure the spaniel.

'OK with the fact that my best friend has turned against me?'

'Have you tried talking to her?'

'Tried and failed.'

Suddenly too hot, Jenna yanks at her collar, shoving her sleeves up above her elbow.

She follows Zach's eyes to her wrist. In rolling up her sleeves, she has revealed the deep scratches she has etched into her skin. She yanks her jumper back down, denying the evidence, but it's too late.

'You've started hurting yourself again?'

She doesn't want to answer. She wants to hide behind her walls and wait until it is safe to emerge. 'They're just scratches.'

'Do I have to start locking away the sharps, like at uni?'

He has inadvertently given her the perfect excuse to drive him away, and she doesn't hesitate to let her words fly at him. 'Don't talk to me like an idiot. I'm not going to slit my wrists!'

'How can I be sure?'

Jenna has lost control of the defensive fury and retaliates before she fully comprehends what she is saying. 'What does it matter if you can be sure? Just leave me to do as I want!'

'That's not how it works! We're a family!'

'Maybe I don't want to be part of a family that refuses to side with me!' Jenna yells. She slaps her hands in horror across her mouth as she hears her own words.

Zach's body shudders as if she has punched him, his jaw rigid. He opens his mouth several times but can only utter hesitations. He has no idea what to say in response.

His head jerks back to look up at the ceiling. 'I'm going to check Lando didn't hear all that.'

Jenna counts his footsteps against the stairs. What has she done? Her family is the only security she has ever known, and she is destroying it in her clumsy attempts to protect herself. She needs to apologise, make Zach see she didn't mean it.

Moments later, a door slams, then another. Zach's pace quickens, the creaking floorboards announcing abrupt arrival and departure in several rooms. She listens to him call their son's name.

'Did you hear him go out?' He's back downstairs within minutes.

'No, I haven't heard him at all.'

'Didn't you check he was home?'

She hadn't, because she never does. She calls a greeting, receives Lando's silence, and gets on with her chores. Did she notice his shoes discarded in the hallway when she arrived home? Was his damp kitbag dumped, hanging on the staircase's newel cap?

When she checks, there is no evidence of her son's return from school.

'Jenna! Was he here when you got in?'

'I don't know! I assumed he was. He's always in his room with his headphones on.'

'You don't ever go up and see him?'

She shrugs helplessly. 'He doesn't like me disturbing his gaming.'

She can't look at Zach. Instead, she fumbles for her phone and scrolls for Lando's name. It rings out until it goes to voicemail.

'Lando, where are you? Ring or text soon as you get this. We need to know where you are.'

Zach is on his phone too, fingers flying over the screen as he fires off messages on various platforms. 'He's not been active on anything since lunchtime. Call the school. Check he was there for afternoon lessons.'

It takes Jenna too long to find the school's contact number. She's never bothered to store it. Zach gets the text reminders about vaccinations and visits to the Tate Modern.

'This is Lando Taylor's mother,' she tells the neutral voice on the other end. 'He hasn't arrived home from school yet. Can you confirm if he was in classes all day? What? A password? I need to know where the hell my son is!'

'Loki,' Zach hisses at her. 'The password is Loki. They need to confirm your identity before they'll give out any information.'

Jenna obediently repeats the name.

'Thank you, Mrs Taylor. I'll check the registers now. One moment, please.'

The moment takes for ever.

'Lando has been marked present in all lessons today.'

'Are there any after-school clubs going on?'

'Not at this time. There's only admin and senior staff left on site by now. Let me see if he attended any . . . no, he didn't sign into anything. Maybe he's gone home with a friend?'

'Yes, that'll probably be it. Thanks.' Jenna hangs up abruptly. 'Do you know which friends he would be with?'

Zach is still tapping frantically at his screen. 'I've been messaging them. He's not with any of the usual lot.'

'Where the fuck is he, then?'

'He might have his SnapMap on.' Zach thumbs to the app and they both peer at the screen. 'No, he's blocked it.'

'Find my iPhone?' Jenna suggests.

'Should we call the police?'

'Surely not yet. He might just be at the skate park or gone to a new friend's house and not noticed the time.'

She hovers over his shoulder as he logs into the iCloud, unable to keep still. A map appears on the screen, showing a green dot hovering over Camden Locks. Zach expels an audible breath of relief.

'He must be hanging out with a mate. Maybe he forgot to switch his phone on after school. I'll go and pick him up.'

Some foreign instinct tells Jenna there is more to this than teenage inconsideration. 'What if he's with Drew?'

'Why on earth would he be?'

'He feels rejected. There's been no contact between them since the investigation started. What if he's got Drew to meet up with him?'

Zach's eyes meet hers. 'I don't think that will have happened, love,' he says softly. He grabs his phone, smacking the screen urgently with his fingers despite his outward calm. 'Let's go and get him.'

He tries to rest his hand atop hers on the gearstick as she drives, his way of calming her, but his touch only makes her more unnerved. She keeps stalling, grinding gears, behaving as if she has no idea how a car operates. The Audi is contorted into a too small parking space and abandoned as they head for the bridge, urgency turning a fast walk to a jog.

They take a side each, leaning over to peer down at the canal and the towpath. It is too chilly for the regular crowds to be sitting taking in the scenery, but enough people are dotted about, anonymous in coats and hoods, to make quick identification difficult.

'He's moved into the market!' Zach yells from across the road. Jenna shoots to his side, narrowly avoiding being run over by a bike. She doesn't hear the rider's furious curses.

Together, they stare at the green dot on Zach's phone screen. 'How accurate is it?'

Zach shrugs. 'Shall we split up, cover more ground?'

Jenna is already heading for the East Yard entrance, not stopping to check whether Zach has taken the sensible route into Lower Stables. Tourists still roam the narrow gangways, stopping to handle handmade jewellery or test the quality of a woven shawl, their voices a disorientating hum. The scents of a thousand reed diffusers, candles and incense sticks mix with cooking smells – Thai, barbeque, Indian melting together – and bring waves of nausea.

She elbows her way through, head constantly jerking from side to side in a frantic effort to glimpse every face. Deeper into the market, darker paths, stalls crammed more tightly together. A few teenagers in Lando's school uniform; none of them him. They shake their heads in bemused denial when she demands if they know him.

Eventually, her route and Zach's merge at the food court. He shakes his head, grasping his phone like a lifeline.

'Is he still here?' She grabs at it.

'Somewhere.' Zach's eyes roam, never still. 'What the hell is he playing at?'

Before Jenna can find a response, Zach freezes, his entire body stiffening, not unlike when Loki sights a pigeon.

'Is that him?' He jabs a finger towards two people at the churro stall on the opposite side of the court. Both wear dark parkas, fur-lined hoods protecting them from the drizzle that has started to fall. Before Jenna can prevent him, Zach has raised his voice. 'Lando!'

The pair startle immediately. Lando swings round in the direction of his father's voice, but his companion is instantly on the move, weaving their way through the hungry queues with rapid strides. They are gone before Jenna can catch more than a glimpse.

Zach has already reached Lando's side, grabbing him in a hug. Lando allows the embrace for a moment before easing himself free. He doesn't offer his mother the opportunity.

'Mate, what's going on?' Zach keeps hold of Lando's coat sleeve, as if afraid he will disappear before their eyes.

269

'Sorry,' Lando mumbles.

'We need more of an explanation than sorry.' Jenna's fear emerges as anger before she can prevent it.

'Lando, why didn't you come home?' Zach asks, his voice soft.

'I met a mate. Didn't keep track of the time.'

'Your phone's off.'

'Forgot to turn it back on when school finished.'

'Who was that you were with?' Jenna interjects.

'No one you know.'

'Male? Female?' She was sure the answer was male. Too tall for female. Older, almost certainly, judging by their broad outline and polished loafers.

'What's it matter?'

'A friend from school?' Jenna persists.

'Yeah.'

'Why didn't you let us know where you were going?'

'I didn't think, all right?'

'No, it's not all right.'

'We were worried, pal. Your mum didn't even know you hadn't come home till I got in.'

Lando shrugs. 'That bit's not my fault.'

'What made you come here?' Zach indicates around them. Camden Market is not a regular haunt.

'My friend wanted to show me a couple of stalls.' Lando isn't quite quick enough to make sure his coat sleeve covers a new woven bracelet.

'Did you steal that?' Jenna's voice rises.

'No! My friend bought it for me. They got one too.'

'Why would they do that?'

'Because that's what friends do, Mum, for fuck's sake!'

'Stop swearing!' they both say automatically.

'What's their name?' Jenna asks.

'I told you, it doesn't matter. I'm not getting them in trouble as well.'

'You should have let us know where you were going,' Zach says.

'I know. It wasn't planned. We just decided after school to come.'

'Didn't you think we'd notice you were missing?'

A shrug. 'Mum wouldn't.'

Jenna holds her breath to prevent the retort that flies to her lips. 'Lando, did you plan to run away?'

He gives an angry slash of his head. She doesn't believe him.

'Let's get home.' Zach slings his arm around Lando's neck. Jenna watches their son's shoulders tense, but he doesn't pull away. 'You hungry, mate?'

'I had a burger here.'

'Did your friend pay for that as well?' Jenna can't prevent herself asking.

The glares she receives from father and son are identical.

Zach paces the kitchen, picking up objects and putting them down, peering into the fridge but taking nothing out.

'Will you just spit it out?' Jenna eventually has had enough of his avoidance tactics.

'I'm worried about Lando.'

'So am I!' She gets her defence in, just in case he is going to accuse her otherwise.

'I think he needs a break from the city, put a bit of distance between him and this friend, whoever they are.'

'And from me?'

'Why would I want that?' Zach's brow creases. 'You're his mum, Jenna. He loves you.'

'He's only happy when he's with you.'

'He can see how much you're struggling. That's hard for a kid to process.' Zach looks away, uncomfortable with taking charge. 'I could take him to my mum and dad's for a couple of days.'

She hadn't been expecting that. Zach's parents are in the Yorkshire Dales, a six-hour drive away. She loves the little village of Zach's birth, with its stone cottages and quaint pub and winding lanes, safe from threats.

'All that way?'

'I'll tell the school he's got a bug, and I'll work remotely.'

She starts to protest, wants to tell him how much she loves him and how sorry she is that she's wrecked everything, but the words don't come. Her brain still tries to protect her, even from Zach.

'If that's what you want.'

'I want us to be together as a real family again.'

'But you're leaving.'

'Don't say it like that. I'm not leaving you.'

Jenna has to bite her lip to prevent herself hurling back a painful retort she doesn't mean. Even now, her instinctive reaction is to cause hurt before she is wounded, to save her from more scars. She can't bear the thought of being left alone in their silent home.

'Can Loki stay here?' she whispers.

'He won't settle with you.' It hurts that he doesn't trust her to care for their pet, but can she blame him, when she is too damaged to show her own son affection, let alone Loki? She's driven everyone away in her bid to save herself.

'What if I withdraw the allegation?' She is desperate now. 'I could make everything go back to normal.'

'Hasn't it gone too far for that? What about the press? Social media?'

Jenna closes her eyes as reality smacks hard. 'They'll rip me to pieces. Again. I'll probably lose my job. No one will believe me.' She grips her head. 'Maybe we should leave London, be closer to your parents. We could move nearer your parents. Lando and Loki would love that.'

She can't stop the spew of words.

'That won't solve anything, love,' Zach finally manages to interrupt. 'We'll just have to deal with whatever comes next. Together.'

'How can we do anything together when you won't be here?'

'It's only for a few days.' He reaches to grasp her hands, to reassure her with the intensity of his grip, but all he succeeds in doing is making her feel trapped. 'I don't want to leave you on your own, but you've got Seb to lean on if you need someone. I have to think of Lando.'

She snatches herself free. 'Because I don't,' she states flatly.

Zach stares helplessly at her. 'Were you ever going to tell me?' he asks abruptly. 'About your past? If you hadn't started having the dreams, would you have told me?'

She can't will herself to say what he hopes to hear. 'Probably not.'

He regards her with eyes that no longer know peace. 'Are you keeping any other secrets, love?'

She has to look away as she shakes her head.

If only he knew.

Chapter Thirty-Five

*J*enna fixed her gaze on the polished floorboards of the abbot's study, unable to meet Brother Dominic's accusing stare.

'Do you want to remain at Halewood House, Genevieve?' he finally asked.

'Yes, Brother Dominic.'

'And we want you to stay. You're a bright girl. You stand to get excellent exam results.' The abbot began to pace slowly. 'However, if any parents were to find out that you were involved in this awful business, we would have no choice but to permanently exclude you. We would have to make an example of you. Do you understand?'

'Yes,' she whispered.

'We don't want to see that happen. Halewood House has a reputation for academic excellence, Genevieve. We are a highly regarded school. We need to remain so, for the sake of the Order.'

Jenna nodded hard.

'Did you tell the police the truth?'

'Yes, Brother Dominic.'

'I think, perhaps, there is a different version of events.'

She couldn't help but frown, uncomprehending.

'Let me explain what I think really happened last night. If you decide you agree that what I say is the real truth, then the matter will be taken no further. We will mourn the loss of Rory, but your school career will continue untarnished, as will the school's good name.'

Jenna hesitated, waiting for her brain to calm itself enough to absorb what the abbot was saying.

'You want me to lie?'

Brother Dominic clasped his hands together, benign, his gaze focused on the large crucifix adorning the far wall. 'We are men of God, Genevieve. All we can ask of you is to think about what is best for all concerned.'

He raised his fingers, blessing her.

'You are part of our community, and we will forgive you your sins.'

The abbot gazed out over the school community gathered before him in the oak-panelled chapel. He stood high above them, hands resting on the polished wood of the pulpit.

Even though the pupils were forbidden to speak, the chapel was alive with noises: coughs and sniffs, the squeak of shoes fidgeting against the floor, the creak of chairs as the restless shifted, rustling papers tucked under teachers' arms, the odd yawn as the wait became interminable.

Finally, the abbot spoke, and the student body seemed to lean forward as one, knowing that no good news would come. Bracing themselves to have the gossip confirmed, and face the fact that one of their number was dead and their halcyon days were almost certainly over, for fallout would be sure to come.

'It is with great sadness that I have to announce the tragic and untimely death of a Halewood House student.' The abbot's voice was resonant, ringing out clearly. His tone was sombre and tinged with just a whisper of accusation. 'Rory Addison was a popular upper-sixth pupil and member of Raleigh House who excelled at rugby and swimming.'

A pause to let his words sink in and to clear his throat.

A low rumbling began among the pupils, a rolling sea of mutters and exclamations. Some had gone rigid, sitting too upright, while others had slumped in their seats as if trying to sink out of sight. The younger years were flushed with the scandal, whispering frantically to their neighbours. At the back, some of the older girls allowed tears to run down their pale faces as the boys stared at their polished brogues.

'Rory's death was a tragic accident which occurred off campus.' *Clear emphasis on the final two words.* 'He chose to break the rules of our community and, ultimately, his choice cost Rory his life.'

Jenna pushed her clenched fist against her mouth to prevent a low moan from escaping. She didn't dare raise her eyes from the chapel's flagstones.

'We always encourage you to do your best in the eyes of God, and we strive to do the same for all our students. Ultimately, however, the school cannot protect those who decide to take such risks. The risk Rory took proved too great, and that will forever be our regret, that the preventative measures we put in place did not stop him. He was clearly a determined young man.' Brother Dominic cleared his throat, standing taller. 'We will hold a Mass to celebrate Rory's life after half term, but, for now, we will pray for him.'

And with that, all the pupils bowed their heads and the ringing intonation of the familiar prayers echoed around them.

As the chants ended and the wisps of incense smoke evaporated, they were dismissed. Jenna couldn't move. As others pushed their way past her, she was frozen, unable to remember how to instruct her body to stand and walk. She looked desperately around for her friends, but she couldn't spot them among the sea of bodies thronging out of the chapel, desperate to escape.

The chapel had become airless. Her tie and collar had tightened, threatening to strangle her. She had to get out, but she couldn't trust her legs to support her.

Somehow, she found the will to stand, stumbling out into the mercifully cool air, a gentle freeze fanning her burning face.

'Jenna, over here!' a familiar voice cried.

Olivia and Ava pushed their way through the crowds of pupils who didn't seem to know where to go or what to do so had settled for milling aimlessly on the gravel, the crunching of their shoes against the loose stone as loud as their conversation. Seb hovered close on the two girls' heels. His hair was a mess and spots bloomed on both cheeks, betraying the fact that he usually wore concealer.

'Are you OK?' He slipped an arm around Jenna's shoulders and she had to fight a sudden urge to pull away, retain her personal space, as she fought to calm her racing heart and heaving lungs.

'No,' she managed to say. She didn't think she would ever be truly all right ever again.

Ava grabbed her in a suffocating hug, burying her face in Jenna's neck. Jenna stood very still, squeezing her eyes shut, waiting for the embrace to end.

'I'm so sorry,' Ava whispered, her breath tainted with stale whisky. 'I didn't dare come and find you. I saw the police taking you away.'

Jenna clenched her fists as her mind replayed the scenes like an old movie; wobbly, tainted images. 'They took a statement. I said someone had planted the pills in my room, that I'm always being bullied. I think they believed me.'

'What did your parents say?' Seb gripped his tie, tugging on it as if it were a noose.

'They didn't come. Brother Pius was my appropriate adult.' Her parents would never know what had happened. She would never tell

them, and nor would the school. It was a shared secret, one that neither party would dare to reveal.

'Jenna?' Ava released the hug, holding Jenna at arm's length. 'What are you whispering to yourself?'

'Nothing. Sorry.'

'Oh, shit,' Olivia breathed, looking past the group, the colour draining from her face.

Hugo and Drew were heading straight for them. Hugo was grey, his pupils huge and slow to react, and he was noticeably unsteady on his feet. He wasn't in uniform, and his clothes were crumpled and stained. He stank of stale booze and fresh weed. Drew was almost keeping him upright, his broad shoulder rammed into Hugo's body.

'He never went anywhere,' Hugo mumbled. 'He was here all night. Lying fuckers.'

'Not now, mate,' Drew murmured.

'Ava sold him some shit.'

'No, I didn't!' Ava's eyes filled with tears again.

'You, then.' Hugo swung to Olivia, a snarl marring his attractive features. 'You're always involved in something.'

Olivia gulped down a sob, her fingers gripping her tie. 'I swear, Hugo—'

'Fuck you!'

'Easy, Hugo.' Drew threw an arm around Hugo's neck. 'Don't make the Brothers come over. It'll only make it worse.'

'How can it get worse? Are you in on it too, Drew? You know something I don't?'

'No, mate, 'course I don't. You're not thinking straight. Come up to my room. I've got some decent Scotch. Come on.'

Drew guided Hugo away, only just preventing him from stumbling over a stone and falling to his knees.

278

'Why did the abbot say that Rory had left campus?' Olivia asked, as if in a daze, her eyes fixed on the retreating backs of Hugo and Drew. She was biting agitatedly at her fingernails, ripping them off, careless of the blood she was drawing.

'That's what the Brothers are going to tell the parents.' Jenna drank in a long, ragged breath, trying to remember the agreed story. Her memory was dull, clouded by terror, and it was a struggle to form a coherent explanation. 'Rory sneaked out of school, bought the pills and had a bad reaction. He made it back to his room but died before he could get help.'

'Is that what they told you to say?' Seb gasped, his face contorted.

'Either that or I'd be expelled immediately. If I keep the secret, they won't kick me out. I agreed. What else could I do?'

'They're covering it up,' Ava whispered as if to herself.

'They won't let the Order come into disrepute. The Brothers can't allow a scandal like this to get out.'

'So we won't get the blame,' Seb said.

Olivia turned on him so fiercely he shrank back, nearly tripping over his own feet. 'Is that all you can think about, saving your own skin?'

'No one is going to be blamed,' Ava intervened, visibly giving herself a shake, drawing her shoulders back. 'Jenna's made sure of that.'

She turned away from the others, linking her arm through Jenna's.

'I'll owe her for ever.'

Chapter Thirty-Six

Drew

Henry's voice is sombre when Drew answers the phone, and a cold shiver of dread runs through him.

'They're asking us to attend Chelmsford station this afternoon,' Henry says.

'For another interview? I don't have to answer bail yet.' He had been released yesterday pending further inquiries, humiliated by a string of terms and conditions he had seen dished out to hardened criminals on Channel 4 documentaries.

'No, old chap. I'm so sorry.'

'Sorry for what, Henry?' Drew's voice rises in fear.

'They're going to charge you with historic sex offences.'

He can't speak. The words are trapped in his throat, cutting off his air. He's choking. He can't breathe. He's going to die.

'Drew? Are you there?'

He coughs, managing to swallow. His chest is so tight that it takes several ragged breaths before he can reply.

'We'll fight it, old chap, I promise.'

'My career will be over. I'll lose everything. How is this happening?'

'Listen to me, this doesn't mean they have a watertight case. All it means is they've found enough for the CPS to take a punt.'

'What can they have found, when I'm innocent?' Drew almost screams.

'The discovery of your ring didn't look particularly good. Mrs Taylor has identified it as the one worn by her abuser.'

'That ring vanished years ago. I didn't hide it, Henry. I told you!'

'I know, I know,' Henry murmurs soothingly. 'This White-hall inquiry, all the press investigations into the public-school scandal – the charges will have been approved because of that.'

'So I'm being punished because some kids used to grope their classmates?'

'Probably not the best line to use. I'm on my way to pick you up – best we get it over with. Put a suit on and have a quick drink to calm your nerves.'

'It'll take more than a whisky,' Drew grinds out.

He doesn't bother to call Natasha and tell her the news. By the time Henry presses the gate buzzer, he has downed two ice-cold vodkas to prevent whisky fumes on his breath and dug out the Savile Row suit again. He is sure he can still smell the faint traces of fear trapped within the fibres, even though it has been dry-cleaned.

There is no conversation on the journey. Even Henry doesn't know what to say. Drew stares straight ahead, deaf to Henry gently humming along to the quiet sounds of Mozart.

They are led straight through by a uniformed officer who doesn't even deign to look them in the eye. Henry grips his briefcase like a shield, a fine sheen of sweat glistening across his receding hairline.

Beckett is waiting for them behind the hulking beast of the custody desk. He has secured his top button, precisely knotted his tie, and he stands with his shoulders back, at full height. Beside him, DC Nixon is shifting from foot to foot, her eyes darting from one man to the other, her lips tightly pursed as if she cannot trust herself to remain silent.

Drew is shaking his head frantically even before Beckett starts to speak, his ears ringing too loudly for him to hear the words clearly.

'Andrew Merchant, you are charged with . . .'

And even though he knew it was coming, even though he had tried to prepare himself to take the blow stoically, Drew cannot control his reaction. His knees fold beneath him as his entire world crashes down around him.

He can't bear to remain at home after Henry drives him back. Within minutes he has changed, retrieved his beloved Cannondale road bike and is powering away from Wanstead, away from London, school and family, away from the restraints that threaten to squeeze the life from him.

As the city roads change to winding country lanes, he feels his breathing finally ease as his lungs take in the fresh, soothing air. He hits a straight, a well-maintained stretch of empty road that beckons him.

Drew drops his head and pedals furiously, keeping a smooth rhythm despite his rapid pace. The carbon-fibre frame is light and responsive and he crouches low over the triathlon handlebars, trying to time his breathing with the pump of his legs. He is free, flying past the hulking trees of Epping Forest, needing to focus only on the road in front of him and the numbers of his

Garmin. His problems always seem to melt away when he gets on the bike, when it is just him, the tarmac and his own personal goals.

The abject terror coursing acidic darts through his veins is too great to be beaten away by exercise but at least it is being kept at bay for the moment, a struggling beast fighting its temporary restraints. He pushes harder, willing the bonds to hold for just a while, a short respite from this torture.

His thighs are screaming, quadriceps muscles bulging from their tight Lycra cladding, and he gradually slows from the sprint, easing upright to give his lungs a chance to recover. He settles into a steady pace, taking the time to appreciate the lush greenness surrounding him. For the first time in far too long he is calm. He can think.

He hears the car engine approaching from behind but pays it no attention. The road is empty of other traffic; plenty of room to overtake.

Drew only notices how close the vehicle has got when he feels the heat of its engine. Instinctively, he swerves, hitting the brakes to attempt to haul the bike on to the verge.

Too little, too late.

The shriek of metal impacting against metal is momentarily deafening, an awful grinding as the car's grille collapses Drew's rear wheel. His back thuds momentarily against the bonnet, then he is airborne, flying sideways across the gritty road. The bike is catapulted into the sky, crashing to the tarmac in a mangled heap.

The undergrowth is still mercifully soft from the day's drizzle and does something to cushion Drew's landing as his slide across the road surface ends. His helmet thuds against a young sapling, a shock impact, but it isn't robust enough to do real damage. Dazed, Drew can only watch the dark-coloured hatchback speed away. He fancies he sees a pair of eyes in the rear-view mirror, but he can't be sure, and by the time he thinks to look for the number plate, it is gone.

For this moment, he feels nothing.

At last, the anger arrives. It courses through him, molten lava searing his veins and arteries. He doesn't feel the pain as adrenaline spurs him upright. He is invincible as he scrambles to his feet and drags the sorry carcass of his bike to safety.

It is only when he looks down that he sees the pinprick spots of blood rising from road rash, livid purple bruises already starting to form on his swollen skin. He feels the grating of his ribcage with every deep breath, the sharp burn shooting up and down one leg, the stabbing in his left clavicle.

As the pain finally begins to register, he locates his shattered phone and calls the police.

He doesn't go home after he has been assessed, patched up and released from A&E. He had argued vehemently against the attending police officers summoning an ambulance but, once again, his pleas had gone ignored. His humiliation complete, he can't face his family.

Instead, he instructs the taxi to drive west. Natasha's family keep a little bolthole in Knightsbridge for when they have business in London, a discreet mews house that doesn't draw attention. He hates the place, filled with uncomfortable formal furniture, but it is safe and empty, and he has used it for his own devices for many years.

The noise from the busy thoroughfare beyond the mews is

constant, blunting the sound of his own thoughts. The bed is enormous in its emptiness as he gingerly lowers himself on to the mattress. It hurts to be, for once, alone under this duvet, but his body craves rest, and he isn't strong enough to fight the heavy curtain of exhaustion that envelops him. Not that sleep comes. Every time he closes his eyes a kaleidoscope of images plays across his mind.

Thirteen-year-old Jenna, stiff and scared in her new uniform as he shows her around.

His father's signet ring, delivered into his guardianship as the coffin was lowered into the ground.

A woman's eyes gazing up at him, alight with mischief.

Beckett's face as he reads the charges.

Drew makes it to the bathroom just before he vomits. It doesn't feel like a symptom of concussion. Is this his penance for the choices he has made? Maybe he deserves it. He's hurt so many people along the way.

Simply because he doesn't like being told what to do.

He can't bring himself to return to the loneliness of the master bedroom. The second bedroom is smaller and has been used as additional storage space for items Natasha deems clutter. Boxes of paperwork, their Russia wardrobes, Elena's discarded belongings she insists she might need again one day, a couple of small pieces from Drew's ancestral home before it was sold to pay off the creditors.

Something sparks insistently in Drew's tired brain, demanding his attention, but he can't decipher what his instinct is trying to tell him. In recent days, he has lost all ability to order his thoughts, analyse, plan. His usual capacity for quick thinking has abandoned him when he needs it most.

He stares at the stack of archive boxes rammed with old bank statements, mortgage papers, bills and files rescued from his father's decimated study.

He has an idea.

Forgetting his aches and pains, Drew tears the lid off the first box, scattering the carpet with administrative confetti in his haste. Nothing useful. The second box is the same.

The third box contains a manila file neatly labelled in his mother's careful hand. Insurance.

Pulse pounding in time with his breaths, Drew rifles through the contents. Renewals, his mother's diamonds, his father's watch collection, a claim against a Land Rover he vaguely remembers rolling into a stream on a pheasant shoot.

He spots a colour photo clipped to a form.

Drew's heart leaps as he pulls the document free, grasping it so tightly he creases it. It confirms a policy against lost or stolen property, namely one twenty-four-carat gold signet ring set with a Celtic black onyx stone, made in 1884. His own signature confirms the report, which states the item was lost by Master Andrew Merchant at his boarding school in July 1995.

Girls hadn't been admitted to Halewood House until the new academic year in September 1995. Jenna Taylor had not been a pupil there in the July of that year.

She couldn't have identified Drew by his ring. It had no longer been in his possession when she claimed to have seen it on the finger of her abuser.

Chapter Thirty-Seven

The intercom buzzes right on time.

The glaring sunlight obscures the details of the caller's face, but from his smooth, well-spoken voice, she pictures a chiselled jaw and strong cheekbones. He and his wife had booked their appointment just days after returning from several years managing oil money in Abu Dhabi. They hadn't batted an eyelid at the £2.7 million price tag.

'Good morning, Mrs Taylor. I'm afraid my wife has been delayed. Are you comfortable with it being just me for the viewing?'

It is considerate of him to ask. Most female estate agents are wary of lone viewings with male clients – too many historical horror stories for comfort – but Jenna can't afford to be fazed. Her buyers expect their requests to be accommodated without fuss, and her sale figures are in such a slump that she has been forced to find some semblance of professional determination before she ends up jobless.

'Absolutely. Please come up. I've left the door on the latch for you.'

She positions herself by the floor-to-ceiling windows so his gaze will be immediately drawn to the views across the Docklands, chrome and mirrored buildings dappled with sunshine, the river glinting invitingly.

'Your timing is impeccable,' she says brightly as the door swings wider. 'Property in this building very rarely comes up for sale . . .'

She isn't so much stunned into silence as suddenly rendered unable to speak. Her throat closes as if gripped by a strong hand, cutting off her air as well as speech. The door closes softly, the expensive lock clicking securely into place.

Drew Merchant moves gingerly across the room, bearing most of his weight to one leg. His left arm guards his ribs and his shoulders are at uneven heights, but there is still danger in his movements. His chin bears angry grazes, peppered with spots of purple bruising.

Jenna's eyes dart, seeking escape routes as her body tenses, ready for the dash to the door.

'Don't.' The single word is weary, heavy with the weight of exhaustion.

'Drew, please . . .'

'If you scream, I will hurt you.' He must notice the swell of her chest as she gathers the deepest breath she can. 'Put your phone down. Throw it on to the sofa. *Now.*'

She finds herself instinctively reacting to the authority, just as she had in her tiny dorm room. Her phone bounces on the plump cushions.

'Don't come near me!' she hisses as he steps closer, wincing when he treads too hard. 'You can't be here! You're not allowed to contact me.'

'Tell me what else I'm supposed to do then? Stand back and let you continue destroying me? Was it not enough that you cost me my reputation – do you now want my life as well?'

'I don't know what you're talking about.'

'You hit my bike with your car. Left me lying in the fucking road like a half-dead animal.'

She stares at him, uncomprehending. 'You think I'd do something like that?'

'Someone has a vendetta against me, and I can't think of many other likely suspects. What's the next plan? Shove me off a Tube platform? Pour petrol through my letterbox?'

'It wasn't me! I swear.'

'Forgive me if I don't believe you.'

Jenna makes her move, lunging for the door. Her heels slide on the polished floor as she scrambles for freedom, her nails hampering her attempts to wrench the latch open. She cries out sharply as Drew's right hand closes painfully around her wrist, squeezing until it seems the bones will crack.

He drags her back, pinning her against the wall, his forearm bruising her throat as he leans his weight forward. Jenna gasps, desperate for air. She tries to knee him in the groin, flinching as he swings his flattened palm, awaiting the blow.

'Let go of me, Drew! You can't behave like this!'

'What have I got to lose?'

She manages to trap his gaze. His eyes gleam unhealthily, but she sees as much fear as anger in their depths. She speaks more quietly this time, letting the force of her words penetrate. 'Let. Go.'

He follows the instruction almost automatically, not quite registering that he has released his grip until Jenna has shot behind the relative safety of the sofa.

Drew is gasping for breath, chest rising and falling hard enough to make him wince. She watches his right hand press against the opposite collarbone. His eyes seek hers.

'I broke this after I graduated,' he says, fingers tapping softly against the bone. 'There was no lump at school. You couldn't have seen it then. You've seen it much more recently, haven't you?'

'I'm not discussing anything about the case.'

He produces a folded piece of paper from his inside pocket. 'More proof, Jenna. The insurance claim on that fucking signet ring, made months before you joined Halewood House.'

'You could be showing me anything!'

'You've tripped yourself up. Beckett will know you lie now, once I've taken this to him. Between this and my medical records, you've not got a leg to stand on.'

She reaches over the sofa to snatch up her phone, trying to keep her breathing even, determined not to show him the tremors wracking her body at the realisation of what his evidence means. The case against him is collapsing. She has nothing left to convince a jury, or Beckett, of Drew's guilt.

'I'm leaving now. If you come near me again, or try to make contact, I'll call the police.'

'Wait!' He throws his palms up. 'You can't go yet, not till you tell me why. I have to know why you've accused me of these awful things. Why are you doing all this, Jenna? What harm have I ever done to you?'

'You know exactly what you did!'

'You're wrong! Christ, you know me! Why would I do something so terrible to anyone?'

He begins to pace, fists clenched, and suddenly the large, airy space feels claustrophobic.

290

'It's very convenient you suddenly remember just as I'm about to move into politics. Did you think I'd pay you off to shut you up?'

Jenna blinks. 'Why the hell would I want your money?'

'Why else would you do it?'

'Because you shouldn't get away with it!'

'I did nothing to get away with!' he shouts, his handsome features contorting into something much less palatable. 'This is fantasy, Jenna. It never happened! If you really think it did, you need help.'

'Don't try to twist it! It won't work, Drew, you won't convince me I'm mad. I won't let you.' Jenna shook her head so hard the room swam. 'I'm not listening to you. You can try to manipulate the investigation, but you won't convince me I've got it wrong.' She can't let his words get to her. One person has already died because of her mistake; this time she must be right.

'Manipulate it? I've been charged!' Drew collapses on to the expensive sofa, wincing as he jars his tender body. His head drops into his hands, but not before Jenna sees his eyes are shiny with tears. 'I'm the one whose life is in tatters.'

Jenna is shocked by the urge that rises in her to reach out and comfort him, to smooth his hair back and hold him close. Even after all these years, after everything she knows about him, he is still breathtaking in his beauty, and she is thirteen again, gazing longingly after him as he carries her suitcases up the Raleigh stairs.

'Yet your Twitter trolls still support you,' she spits, forcing herself to summon anger again.

'Christ, you're not still looking at that shit, are you?' A protective tone, as if he feels the urge to shield her from the foul tide.

'Forewarned is forearmed. Maybe it'll be me getting run over next, or worse.'

He barks a laugh. 'Bit dramatic, to arrange your own hit and run after mine.'

'I didn't arrange anything!' She howls.

'What does it matter? I've got evidence against you, and a lot more besides this piece of paper, as you bloody well know.'

She doesn't know what to say. There are no words to describe the maelstrom of emotion, fear and dread that is churning within her.

'Jenna, whoever it was wearing that ring in 1995, it wasn't me.'

'You could have lied about it being lost!'

Another, more immediate issue slaps her in the face and she is mumbling without realising she is speaking aloud, trying to establish some order in the tornado wreaking havoc inside her skull.

'So, if it wasn't you . . .does that mean . . .was it . . .really Rory?'

'Rory?'

Drew's incredulous tone penetrates the maelstrom and she slaps a hand across her mouth in horror, watching his expression change as his keen mind starts to join the dots.

'Rory Addison's death was labelled a teenage experiment gone wrong,' Drew says softly. 'But we all knew there was more to it than that. Is that why you work for Hugo, out of guilt? Because you and your friends killed his cousin? You were convinced Rory was your abuser?'

'No!' Jenna shakes her head so hard the room spins. 'You're wrong. We didn't do anything!'

'I'm not crazy enough to think you meant him to die. Did he

292

OD accidentally, or did you want him to be caught with a stash and expelled?' Drew is almost talking to himself, trying to work it out with his own answers. 'Olivia Seabrook killed herself because she couldn't live with the guilt. Is that why Seb Byron came back to London, because he was terrified you or Ava would crack with her gone?'

The strength of his tone is like a punch. 'You can't prove any of this.'

'Do I need to? I can show you're completely unreliable. That will be enough.'

'Do you love Ava?' she asks desperately.

Drew's jaw tenses. 'As I gather you've worked out, she's the mother of my daughter.'

'So you won't risk her being exposed.'

'Don't try and play games!'

'You don't need to bring Rory into it,' she whispers. 'The case will be thrown out with the evidence you've already got. You'll be free. You'll get your life back.' She isn't sure if she is placating him or reassuring herself.

Drew rakes back his hair, showing angry scrapes across his palms that clearly sting. 'Mud sticks in education, even after every attempt has been made to wash it off. I imagine the school will want me to resign and slink away quietly, and I can't see anywhere offering me another headship. I can certainly kiss goodbye to Whitehall.'

The urge to apologise is almost overwhelming, and Jenna has to clamp her back teeth together. He looks so broken, physically and mentally, that she struggles to prevent herself from going to his side.

'Please, Drew . . .'

Abruptly, he shakes himself, his attention returning to Jenna, and he suddenly looks more like the Drew she used to know.

'I'd better go. Sorry about forcing my way in, but I knew I'd never get to talk to you otherwise. It won't happen again.'

He hauls himself up and limps past her, maintaining a respectful distance.

'My solicitor is in court today. The last thing I wanted to do was wait, but apparently the cogs of justice are slow movers. I've got an appointment with DS Beckett tomorrow. Brace yourself.'

She almost expects him to kiss her cheek in farewell, as if they are leaving a party. She wants to say something cutting, to remind him that she has the upper hand.

Except now she doesn't.

She has barely taken off her coat and sat down in her office before her mobile rings. Beckett's name flashes on the screen and nausea swells instantly in her throat, even though she knows he can't have seen Drew's evidence yet.

The temptation to ignore the call is strong, but it will only leave her creating imaginary scenarios of the conversation that will torment her for the rest of the day.

'What now?' she demands as she answers, forcing strength into her voice that she doesn't feel. She can't let him know how close to breaking point she is.

'Hi, Jenna. Have you time for a couple of questions?'

'Not really.'

'I'll be quick.' Not even a hint of apology. 'Mr Merchant has been in an accident. He was knocked off his bike by a car yesterday. Deliberately, he says. The driver didn't stop.'

As if she didn't know. 'What's that got to do with me?'

'What car do you drive?'

'An Audi A1.'

'And the colour?'

'Navy blue. Why are you asking me these questions?'

'Can you tell me where you were around four o'clock yesterday afternoon?'

'I was at work. Where else would I be?'

'In the office?'

'In and out. I can show you my appointments diary. Or do you need my clients to vouch for me?'

'You used your car to get around?'

'Obviously. And no, I haven't lent it to anyone and I have the only set of keys. Do you investigate road accidents as well as sexual abuse?'

'You're right – it's not my investigation at all. Call it satisfying my own curiosity. I thought you'd prefer speaking to me rather than to a stranger, so I offered to contact you.'

'I don't prefer anyone asking me if I'm stupid enough to run over Drew Merchant.'

'You haven't asked how he is.'

'I don't care how he is.' Another lie.

'He was lucky,' Beckett continues, as if she hasn't spoken. 'Some soft-tissue damage to one leg, a couple of cracked ribs. The car didn't stop.'

'Maybe it wasn't deliberate. Perhaps the driver didn't see him.'

'He attempted to get out of the car's way. It steered towards him. We're treating it as a targeted hit and run.'

Jenna grits her teeth against the frustrated tears springing to her eyes. Yet another spoke thrown into the wheel that has become her life. 'I can't be his only enemy.'

Beckett's sigh is audible. 'Just be careful. There's a lot of unsavoury things happening at the moment. None of it will help your case.'

'I haven't done anything wrong.'

'I hope not. I'll be in touch soon. Take care.'

Jenna is left with the distinct feeling he doesn't believe her. But what can he prove? She replays his words in her head, his description of Drew's injuries.

A jolt of power runs through her.

Hugo appears in her doorway. 'Get a deal?'

'Hardly.' She barks a laugh to disguise her fear. 'The client was Drew Merchant.'

Hugo's eyes widen. 'I thought he wasn't allowed near you!'

'He's been charged, so he figured what else has he got to lose.'

Hugo crosses to her desk in a couple of long strides. 'Did he hurt you?'

'No.' She rubs her wrists, even though Drew hasn't left marks. 'But he scared me.'

'Bastard.' Hugo moves as if to put his arm around her and she cringes away, stepping to the filing cabinet to pull out some completely unnecessary papers. 'You've told the police?'

'There's no point.' She is overwhelmed by tiredness. 'There doesn't seem much point in anything any more. Maybe I should just drop the complaint and let all this rest.'

'I think you need a break. I can see how much you're struggling. It's all getting on top of you.'

'I'm fine.'

'I know you, Jenna, and you're not fine. No one would be fine in this situation.'

'Hugo—'

'I'm telling you to take some time off. Give yourself a chance to process everything. Take care of yourself.'

'Are you suspending me?'

'As if. I'd never have got Addison up and running without you. I couldn't believe my luck when you agreed to ditch Foxtons for me.'

She forces a smile. He can never know the real reason she jumped ship for him. Drew had been right about one thing. She had agreed to work for Hugo out of guilt.

This time, she allows him a hug and she silently makes the apologies she can never say out loud.

'Go home,' Hugo says softly, his toned arms holding her close. 'Your job's safe, don't worry. Get this mess dealt with. Find yourself again. Therapy might be an idea.'

'I thought everything could be solved with Xanax.'

'This has gone a bit far even for Xanax.'

Chapter Thirty-Eight

Jenna doesn't want to be here, in this airless interview room deep in the bowels of Chelmsford station. Seb isn't answering her calls or messages. Zach hasn't responded either and Lando hasn't even bothered to view the Snapchats she's sent him, and she can only kid herself for so long about the unreliable Wi-Fi and phone signals in Yorkshire.

She is slowly losing every good thing she has in her life that she has never fully appreciated before. She doesn't have time to hear what DS Beckett has to say.

She wonders if Drew sat in this room too, earlier today. Can she smell the ghost of him?

'Why do I need to be here?' Jenna looks nervously around the interview room, feeling the grey walls closing in on her. 'You've been turning up at my house, so why make me come all this way?'

Beckett rests both hands on the table, linking his fingers together. 'We felt it was better to record this conversation. We've quite a few things to discuss with you.'

She waits, tensed, waiting for the blow to be struck.

'Mr Merchant granted us access to his medical records. His broken collarbone occurred when he was twenty-one. So how can you have seen it when he was seventeen?'

'I must have been mistaken.'

'But you were quite adamant that is how you were able to identify him, together with the signet ring. How else would you have known your abuser was Drew Merchant?'

'I knew.'

'We've had another piece of evidence come to light now. Mr Merchant had claimed his signet ring had been lost before his lower-sixth year, *before* you joined the school, but he couldn't find a way to prove it. He's since found insurance paperwork, confirming a claim was made against the lost property in July 1995.'

Jenna unscrews the cap on her water bottle and drinks until there is none left.

'Jenna, what year did you start at Halewood House?'

'In 1995.'

'September 1995?'

'Yes. That's when a school year always starts.'

Beckett doesn't react to the dripping sarcasm. 'You've stated the abuse began soon into your first term?'

'Yes.'

'And your abuser wore the signet ring, which you recognised as belonging to Drew Merchant.'

There seems no point in saying yes again, so Jenna just nods.

'Then you see our problem.'

'Drew could have lied about the ring being lost. You found it in his house, for God's sake! I identified it!'

'Mr Merchant insists the ring was planted on his property.'

'But he has no evidence to prove that!'

'We'll move on to our next point, Jenna.' Beckett won't be distracted. 'Mr Merchant asked to make a statement when he brought in the insurance documents.'

Jenna remains silent. There is nothing she can say. This is it, the moment she has dreaded.

'He claims the two of you slept together shortly before you made your allegation.'

Jenna can't move. She can't even blink. Even though she knew what Beckett would say, her brain has frozen in shock at hearing the words spoken aloud.

'Can you confirm if that's true?'

Lie, her brain orders, finally whirring into action, disorientating her even further. But she can't add more lies into the mix. There are too many already.

'Yes,' she whispers. 'It's true.'

Beckett presses his back against his chair.

'Jenna, why would you sleep with a man you thought had abused you?'

Jenna dug her fingernails into her palms. 'I didn't know it was Drew then,' she finally admits. 'I didn't know who the abuser was at the time.'

'So how did you reach the conclusion, twenty-five years later, that it was Mr Merchant?'

'I saw his wedding ring,' she forces out. 'After we slept together. That's when I made the connection. I was so sure the dreams were true—'

'Dreams?' Beckett interrupts. 'What dreams?'

'I didn't remember all those details,' she whispers, because there is no point in continuing to lie. 'They were dreams.'

Beckett's eyebrows knot together momentarily, but he allows her to continue.

'I don't have many real memories.' She forces her voice to be strong, doesn't let it waver, even though her throat is so constricted she feels she can barely breathe. 'The details all came from dreams, until I saw Drew's wedding ring. I did remember the signet ring, but that was the first time I made the connection.'

'You understand what this means, don't you? We won't be going to court, Jenna. The charges will be dropped against Drew Merchant.'

She knows. She nods.

Beckett's face is expressionless, but she sees how tight his grip is on his pen. 'Do you realise how serious this is?'

Jenna nods. 'For what it's worth, I'm sorry.'

'We've put a huge amount of time and resources into this investigation. You know you can be prosecuted for deliberately misleading us?'

She dares to look up at him. 'Will you do that?'

'I'll certainly be looking into the possibility,' he says grimly.

'I never intended it to go this far.'

'Then why not stop it before it did?'

Jenna squeezes her eyes shut, hiding from the accusing gaze.

'I didn't know how to.'

She has no recollection of the drive back to London, operating the car on autopilot. Beckett's solemn words echo in her ears, mixing with Drew's familiar tones, which can still send shivers down her spine.

Somehow, she makes it home, to her silent, empty house that

may never know the sounds of a family again. If a family is what they actually are.

She grabs her phone, dialling Seb's number again. This time, her call goes directly to voicemail, the phone switched off. She tries Zach, to tell him she has done as he wanted and the hell it has unleashed. He doesn't answer. It doesn't seem worth typing out a message.

As she cancels the call, her thumb hovers over her contacts, over Drew's name. She unblocks him, composing a text, deleting it, starting again, deleting that one too. Her finger hovers over the call icon.

Jenna slams the phone down and strides across the kitchen. Sliding open the cutlery drawer, she closes her fingers around the smooth surface of the Sabatier handle. She draws the knife slowly from its protective sleeve, the light glinting off the wickedly sharp blade. She holds it out in front of her, feeling the lightness, the balance, as if it belongs nestled in her palm.

The map of blood vessels run intricate routes up the underside of her forearm, a web of red, blue, green and purple weaving their way just beneath her skin. She traces their path with her finger, feeling velvet and heat and the thud of her own pulse.

When she draws the blade across her arm, she does it so gently that she almost expects it to leave no mark. For the first moment nothing is visible, then the skin seems to spring apart effortlessly. She yields the knife once more, just below the first cut.

This time she applies pressure, not too much, but enough to make her gasp in ecstasy. All the old feelings rush back as if they'd never been away. The relief, the immediate sense of release. Her brain is silent for the first time in for ever, pacified by endorphins, and she feels warm, liquid relaxation running through her nervous system.

The bleeding stops eventually, like it always did. Jenna applies antiseptic cream and a bandage before thoroughly cleaning the knife, returning it safely to its sheath. She is about to put it back in its usual drawer but stops herself. She climbs on to a breakfast-bar stool to put it high out of reach on top of the cupboards. Maybe the difficulty of access will be enough to prevent her next time.

She almost reaches for the phone to tell Zach, like she always used to, but she can't burden him with this, not when he's trying to look after Lando. The memory of his reaction to the mild staple scratches brings red shame rushing to her cheeks. She can't let him know how far she has fallen.

When the noise in her head builds to an unbearable crescendo, she fills a glass too full of Malbec and takes the bottle upstairs to run a scalding bath. Her skin screams in protest as she climbs in, taking care to keep the bandaged limb clear of the water, but she welcomes the burn.

Zach's razor calls to her until she has to sink her head below the surface to block it out. Even when she is forced to resurface, it glints alluringly, inviting her to grasp it. It would be easy. The bath has cooled to a delicious warmth and she is loose from the wine. She could do it.

Her fingers reach, beyond her control, for the razor. She dips it in and out of the water, taking her time soaping her shins, running the blade slowly across the stubbly hairs. On each run, she presses a little harder. She studies the metal each time she rinses it.

It takes an inordinate amount of control to return the razor to its place and haul herself out of the bath. Once she is wrapped in a cold towel, she has to close the bathroom door to block out the temptation.

She hurries to roughly dry herself, dragging her clothes on over damp, chilled skin. She can't stay in the house. The walls are closing in around her, even though only hours earlier she had craved the sanctuary they offered.

If she stays, the call will overwhelm her. She is not strong enough to fight it.

And she doesn't trust herself not to press just that little too hard over a vein.

Chapter Thirty-Nine

It is only when she arrives at Seb's faded front door that Jenna realises she has never been inside his flat before. She has poured Seb out of a cab on her own way home or grabbed him from the doorstep en route to a night out but never gone beyond the threshold. They've never needed to socialise here – she and Ava much prefer to host in their larger properties.

He lives on the edge of Somers Town, on the ground floor of one of the sixties-built low-rise council blocks typical of the area. She can smell unemptied bins and cannabis in the air, and the sound of grime music floats from the top floor. Graffiti announces gang territory and childish arguments with equal artistic skill.

Seb takes several minutes to open the door and she can't miss his double-take when he finds her standing there, awaiting entry.

'What are you doing here?'

'Why have you gone to ground?'

'I haven't. I just needed some time out.' His eyes are glazed. 'I've been struggling. The bad thoughts are getting stronger. I can't stop them.'

'Then you shouldn't be alone. Are you going to let me in?'

He blocks the doorway with his body. 'Can we go to yours?'

'I can't stay in my house. I'm losing it. Zach's gone, taken Lando with him. I don't even know if they'll come back.'

He acts as if he hasn't heard. 'Shall we go out, then?'

'Please let me in. Have you got someone here?'

'No, just me.'

'Then why are you keeping me on the doorstep?'

'Because we don't come to mine. We go out or to Ava's, or to yours.'

'I can't go to Ava's, not after she chose Drew over me. Let me in, Seb!'

For a split second she thinks he is going to slam the door in her face. She can see his mind racing, his eyes flitting continuously as he searches for another reason to prevent her entry.

'What is it?' she asks, deliberately softening her tone. 'Have you got a dead body in there or something?'

'It's just such a mess. It's embarrassing.'

'At this moment I couldn't care less if your carpet's so mouldy it's growing mushrooms.'

A sigh whispers from his lips. 'Don't say I didn't warn you.'

He steps aside and she crosses the threshold, down the dark, narrow hallway into his living room. The air is still and stale, windows not opened in far too long. It smells of male bodies and expensive aftershave she recognises but can't place, of old take-aways and fresh cannabis. She sees Seb is stoned; she can spot the looseness of his limbs as he moves and the redness of his eyes.

Jenna moves past the threadbare sofa that may once have been a vibrant red, now faded and worn to a colour resembling strong tea, reaching for the window catch. She can feel the grittiness of the carpet through the thin soles of her ballet pumps and avoids stepping on several darkened patches.

'OK to open the window?' She feels she has to ask permission, even though she doesn't know why.

Seb gives a shrug, watching as she wrestles with the unyielding lock, eventually managing to admit a welcome breath of breeze. He makes an effort to clear the coffee table of several pizza boxes, crushed cans of Heineken, half-full tumblers stained with lip marks. A mug grows a protective blanket of blue-and-green mould alongside a piece of congealed toast, abandoned after a couple of bites, uneven teeth marks stamped into the bread.

'When did you sack the cleaner?' Jenna attempts to lighten the atmosphere.

'I've never been able to afford a cleaner.'

He has regularly made references to having one, but Jenna decides it isn't the right time to raise that point.

'Told you I've been struggling,' Seb says with a laugh that contains no humour. 'Kind of given up trying to keep the place tidy.'

'You should have said things were getting on top of you.'

'Didn't want to be a mood-killer. It gets harder when work's scarce.'

'At least there's the Disney prospect.'

Seb's jaw tightens and he shakes his head. 'Didn't get it.'

'Oh, shit, I'm sorry.'

A shrug that means to be careless but falls short. 'Hey ho, shit happens.'

'Nothing else on the horizon?'

'I'm sure Ava will find me something. She always does.' His voice has become artificially bright. 'Let me get rid of this crap and we'll open the wine. The corkscrew should be lying around somewhere.'

He staggers through the archway into the galley kitchen, struggling to balance his armload. Jenna doesn't follow – she doesn't want to see the state of the surfaces. Instead, she searches for the corkscrew, choosing to ignore a rather graphic porn magazine and scribbled notes that seem to be sexualised poetry, finally finding it on the dusty TV stand.

Seb returns with two wet glasses, freshly but carelessly washed, as she twists the synthetic cork free from the bottle neck.

She holds the bottle out to pour, but as she fills the glasses his gaze falls on her bandaged forearm.

'Have you started cutting again?' His expression is uninterpretable.

'Not really. Just a few scratches before tonight, then I couldn't stop myself. I had to do it.'

'I still do it,' he says abruptly.

His hand indicates his groin area and she involuntarily recoils. Seb's eyes darken at her flinch, lips tightening as a shadow crosses his face, but it's gone before she can be sure it was ever really there.

He grins suddenly, his perfect teeth very white against his sunbed tan, but it doesn't reach his eyes. 'Screw it, let's get wasted. I've got some gorgeous Afghani hash – want to try?'

Jenna hasn't smoked since university, but the dark chunk of soft resin Seb shows her is so fragrant, spicy and earthy and enticing that she finds herself nodding. She watches, fascinated, as he prepares a small, patterned glass pipe with the ease of regular use.

He inhales first, long, deep breaths that he holds until his chest is quivering. By the time he sends a cloud rushing to the Artex ceiling, his mouth has relaxed into a smile. Jenna willingly takes the pipe, comforted by the heat of it as she holds the lighter to the little bowl.

The first hit makes her cough until she is gasping for breath and her eyes are streaming. The second calms her racing pulse. The third brings the warmth, the slowing of time, the embrace she once knew so well.

She feels herself sinking deeper into the collapsing sofa, her limbs growing leaden and her head fuzzing until the room seems to waver as if it is melting before her eyes. She hears herself moan softly as the sensation of being caressed by a heavy velvet blanket creeps over her and she allows her weighted eyelids to close.

She has no idea how long she lies there, somewhere between sleeping and waking, unable to move and with no motivation to try. Whatever state of being she has reached, she is dreaming.

Zach has come back to her. She can feel his breath hot in her ear as his lips caress her lobe, nipping gently. Beside her, on their own Chesterfield, his body is pressed against her. She feels his hand caressing her breast, fingers stealing under her top and inside her bra to tease her nipple. Her body responds to him and her back arches, a mewl escaping from her lips at the sensations running through her, tiny electric sparks making her fizz with pleasure.

Zach pushes up her top, pulling it over her head with much less gentleness than normal and snatching at her bra until he manages to free the clasp. She gives a yelp as a hangnail catches her delicate skin, hears his sharp intake of breath before his ministrations continue, firmer and surer this time. She feels his teeth, and pleasure becomes pain as he bites down.

Jenna's eyes fly open. Not a dream. And not Zach.

It isn't Zach on top of her, tearing at his jeans with one hand as the other grasps her hair.

'Seb!' Her own hands fly, acting on their own instinct. She shoves him hard enough in the chest to make him sit back. 'What the hell are you doing?'

'You were enjoying it a minute ago!' He rubs his sternum.

Jenna struggles upright, scrabbling for her top to cover herself. 'I had no idea what was going on.'

'You wanted it! You were moaning!'

'From the bloody hash high, not because I wanted you to start groping me!'

Sweat is beaded on Seb's forehead, his breath coming in urgent pants. 'I thought you liked it.'

'You're my best friend – I don't see you like that. And I'm married, for fuck's sake!'

'Where's Zach when you need him? It's me you've turned to, not him.'

'He's still my husband!'

'But you don't trust him! You tell me your secrets, not him!'

'I do trust him. Just because we disagreed about the investigation doesn't mean I love him any less.' She sees Seb flinch at the word 'love'. 'I'm going. We need to forget this ever happened.'

Abruptly sober, her self-preservation finally kicking in, she leaps to her feet, grabbing for her coat. She can still feel him on her skin, like ants crawling over her body, and it nauseates her that her personal space has been so casually disregarded by a man she trusts.

'Don't leave!' Seb's eyes are stretched wide, so much white visible around his dark irises. The veins stand out in the lean ropes of his neck muscles. 'I didn't mean to do it. I'm sorry. I'm so sorry. It was a mistake.'

A sob breaks from his throat and he sinks into the corner of the couch, drawing his knees up to his chest to rock gently. He suddenly looks so young, so vulnerable. He stretches a shaking hand out, his expression begging her to take it. She squeezes his fingers, feeling the erratic fluttering of his pulse, and when he tugs her to sit down again, she doesn't resist.

Tears stream down his face. 'I just want someone to love me. You've got Zach and Lando and Loki; Ava's got Adeline. I've no one. My own mother didn't love me.'

'I'm sure she did.' Jenna has never met Seb's mother, so has no idea if this is true, but surely every mother loves their child deep down? She thinks of Lando and how little she shows him this and feels the guilt burn her heart.

'She told me she did,' Seb sobs. 'She told me all the time. But you don't hurt the people you love, not like she did. And now I've no one. I just want someone to come home to like everyone else, is that so much to ask?'

'You'll find someone,' she says, helpless in the face of this unexpected outpouring of emotion.

'I won't. Women don't like me.'

'Seb, you're good looking, you're charming and you're good fun. The right one will come along eventually. Maybe you just need to explore different options than clubs and dive bars.'

His jaw hardens momentarily. 'You make it sound so easy.' He sits upright, pulling his hand free as if she was the one who had asked for the comfort. 'We're out of wine. Whisky?'

She should go, she knows she should. Something has changed

between them and she is not sure she likes it, but he's her best friend and she can't leave him like this. He wouldn't leave her.

'Bring out your best bottle,' she says with a careful smile.

Jenna wakes in a bed that is too soft and thin to be her own mattress. She can feel the cheap springs digging into her. There is no duvet, only blankets that feel rough and scratchy against her skin and the smell of stale body odour and something musty and earthy. The pillow is squashed flat and her body aches from the position she's in.

She can hear heavy breathing beside her, the weight of a body, but she can't bring herself to look. She slides a hand under the blankets, even though she already knows she is naked. She is damp with sweat, her skin releasing the toxins she consumed.

Eventually, she can avoid the reality no longer and she turns her head to look at Seb. He is deep asleep, sprawled on his back. She takes in the angry red weals rising from his waxed chest and her own skin begins to burn, and she peels back the covers and takes in the scratches, the bite marks, the bruises. The aching intensifies, running deep inside her.

Nausea swells in her stomach and she recoils, almost tumbling out of bed. She scrambles unsteadily to her feet, wincing as she makes contact with the sticky laminate floor. Seb sleeps on as she rushes to find the bathroom. She must have used it yesterday but she has no memory of doing so.

The toilet has no seat and the porcelain is cold enough to make her draw a sharp breath as she sits, fighting the urge to vomit. She drops her heavy head into her hands, a pounding headache reverberating through her skull. Her mouth tastes vile, bitter and metallic. How much did she drink? She doesn't remember hash having this effect before. Maybe it is stronger these days, or it was laced with something else.

It stings when she urinates, undeniable evidence of what happened last night. She has betrayed Zach again, with a man she has never felt a moment's attraction to. Why was she so determined to make a mess of her life these days? She doesn't remember the end of the night, no memory of the act itself. Another example of blocking out whatever she finds too hard to face? Or had she just sunk so much whisky that her recollections have drowned in a sea of bad decisions?

Beginning to shiver, she returns to the bedroom. Seb doesn't stir, even when she takes a blanket to wrap around herself and sits on the edge of the bed to wait for the waves of nausea to calm enough for her to get dressed. Her clothes are scattered across the floor, mixed with Seb's. She clutches her head as she imagines undressing him, mouths clashing together as they reached for each other.

How could she have been so stupid? Was it pity, or had she been fuelled by alcohol lust?

As she establishes the location of each item of clothing, she spots that one wall of the room is decorated by a collage of photographs, mostly colour, some black and white. Pictures of Seb, from childhood and teenage years up to early twenties. The same woman is present in each image, always embracing Seb as he stares into the camera. There is something about her poses that makes Jenna feel deeply uneasy.

It takes too long for her to recognise the woman is Seb's mother.

Chapter Forty

'You hate your mother,' Jenna finds herself whispering to Seb's sleeping form as she stares from photo to photo, feeling the eyes of the immaculately groomed woman boring into her as she holds her son with a tenderness usually reserved for lovers.

She doesn't have time to understand. She needs to leave. She needs to get out of this place, call Zach and beg him to come home, and never return here again.

'Jenna?'

She starts violently at the raw, scratchy voice, very loud in the silent room.

Seb props himself up on his elbows. He examines the marks on his chest with interest. 'You don't give in easily, do you?'

Jenna stares at him.

'No memory at all?' he asks. 'Maybe it'll come back to you.'

He reaches for an object on the cluttered bedside table. He shakes a tiny bottle that looks like the eyedrops Zach regularly has to wrestle into Loki's gritty eyes while Lando wraps the spaniel in a bear hug. A wave of nausea washes over Jenna at the sudden thought of her family, so far away from her.

'Most of them don't remember the next morning.'

Jenna stares at the bottle. 'You put that in my drinks?'

'Easy enough to do. No one ever realises, they just think they've had too many doubles. You lose count when you're dancing all night. Worse if you've dropped a pill too.' Seb checks his watch and exaggerates surprise. 'Two o'clock! We slept late.'

'Why the fuck would you do that? What the hell is wrong with you?'

'Do what?' He looks at her as if genuinely puzzled by the question.

'Why did you drug me?'

'To help you sleep.'

'Did we have sex?' She can barely bring herself to ask.

A slow smile spreads across his lips. 'You don't remember?'

She spins away from him, grabbing at the clothes scattered around the room, dragging them on, hands shaking so badly she can barely do the zips and buttons. He watches her in obvious amusement, a stranger in her friend's body. She can't look at him any longer, striding out of the bedroom in search of the rest of her belongings.

Her handbag is in the living room, her purse and keys safe, but no phone. She scrabbles for it along the edges of the cushions, feeling down the back of the sofa, but instead of the solid rectangle of her phone her fingers find something metallic. She pulls free Seb's familiar neck chain, its clasp broken. She must have snapped it when she was trying to fight him off.

She lets the fine chain slip back and forth between her fingers,

315

counting the links. It is light and delicate, a round pendant hanging from it. The pendant is set with a polished stone, very dark against the silver metal. Black onyx.

Jenna's breath stalls in her throat as she pinches the pendant between her thumb and forefinger, bringing it closer to her face.

She knows this stone. It doesn't belong on this neck chain.

It belongs on a gold signet ring.

'What are you looking for?' Seb's voice is very loud in the silent room. She hadn't heard him step up behind her. He is too close, towering over her, still holding the little bottle. For the first time in their friendship, she is afraid of him.

She jumps away from him, her fist closing around the chain. 'My phone. I need my phone.'

'Are you leaving?'

'Obviously I'm leaving!' she almost shouts. She scrabbles in her handbag as if still searching for the phone, taking the chance to drop the chain safely into it.

'You don't have to shout.' His mild tone doesn't match his taut jaw and clenched fists. He is holding out her phone. She has no idea where he has produced it from.

She snatches it from him, switching it on. 'Why have you done this to me, Seb? I trusted you.'

'We had sex, that's all. It happens all the time.'

'You drugged me!'

His upper lip lifts in something close to a snarl. 'You wanted it, Jenna. You were leading me on all evening, snuggling up to me.'

'I didn't mean it like that! I pushed you away!'

'Only out of guilt. It's hard for married women. I know that.'

'How do you know?' She gapes at him in disbelief.

'They all resist at first, say they love their husband.'

316

'What the fuck are you talking about?'

'I'm talking about all the slags that lead me on! Wedding ring on their finger, but it's not enough for them!'

Jenna backs slowly away from his fury. 'Seb, I'm going home. I don't feel safe—'

His face contorts. 'That's what all the fucking bitches say.'

For some reason, she can't look away from him. 'What do you mean?'

'Women don't have a problem with me when I'm buying them drinks and dancing for hours with them. Oh no, it's all great then. But soon as we go, doesn't matter if it's my place or theirs, they change. Tell me I'm scaring them. Tell me they don't feel safe being alone with me. You're all the *fucking same*.'

The last words are hissed into Jenna's face with such venom that she feels tiny droplets of his spittle spray on to her skin. She tries to inch away from him, but she is trapped by the wall. She presses painfully into it, trying to buy herself even a few millimetres.

'*Don't hurt me!*' he cries, an uncanny imitation of a female Glaswegian accent. '*Just let me leave and I won't tell anyone.* I hadn't even touched the stupid whore.'

'I don't understand, Seb,' she whispers. 'What the hell is going on?'

'You rejected me too, Genevieve, when I tried to get close to you. When girls came to Cell Block H, I thought it was my chance to be normal, but you all fucked up my life even more.'

Jenna flinches at the sound of her old name. 'I didn't see you in that way.'

'Clearly. Neither did any one of the other girls that suddenly invaded us.'

'I didn't know it made you feel like that.'

317

'Of course you didn't – you were too busy getting stoned out of your mind.'

She flinches as Seb strides past her, but he only grabs the whisky from the coffee table, carelessly dropping the little bottle on to the stained surface. There is almost no whisky left, although Jenna is sure it had been full yesterday evening. The fumes rising from the open neck makes her feel sick, but Seb drinks without hesitation. He tilts his head back, over-acting, the ropey muscles of his throat bulging as he swallows.

Jenna snatches the little bottle from the table and shoves it into her bag before he can look at her.

'Fucking women,' he hisses as he takes another mouthful of whisky.

Jenna takes the opportunity and hurries for the front door, fumbling in her haste to open it. The Yale catch yields obediently, but the deadlock holds strong.

'Unlock the door!' Jenna yells, panic fully unleashed now. She kicks at the wood. 'You can't keep me here!'

Seb strolls down the hallway towards her. He seems to fill the narrow space. 'Don't tell me what I can and can't do!'

'Open the door!'

He watches her casually for another long minute, as if watching a kitten playing with a ball of yarn.

'I saw you with Drew, getting into his car, all over him. Just another whore fucking a married man. I'd tried so hard since you came back into my life, to make you feel loved and wanted, and you still chose that prick over me. For fuck's sake, how much more could I be expected to take?' He barks a laugh. 'It was perfect, really. I could deal with you and with Mr Golden in one fell swoop, just like I dealt with Rory.'

318

The unexpected sound of the name on his lips freezes Jenna's blood. She spins round, fear gripping her heart with an icy fist.

'What do you mean, *dealt with Rory*?'

Seb shrugs, his lips twitching with amusement. 'It was easy to switch those pills.' At last, he moves past her, producing the deadbolt key and turning it slowly in the lock. He holds the door open for her, his forearm muscles straining against a woven leather bracelet around his wrist. 'I couldn't risk him proving he was innocent, could I? What if he had alibis for those nights?'

'Why are you telling me all this? Why now?'

'Because I want you to see what you caused. I'm safe now. You can't accuse me, not after what's happened with Drew. You've told too many lies already.'

She doesn't move. She doesn't quite dare walk past him.

'Off you go. Tell whoever you want about last night.' Another laugh. 'No one will believe you, Jenna. You're a proven liar. There'll be no trace of anything in your bloodstream apart from enough alcohol to fell a giant. If anyone does bother to look into your ridiculous claims, I'll admit we've been having an affair. You're good at those, aren't you? I'll tell them all about how we both like it rough, how we enjoy hurting each other a little. That sometimes we get carried away and leave marks but it's always consensual.'

'What the fuck is wrong with you?' she screams, sure she is loud enough for the neighbours to hear. But this is London. No one will come to help.

'Maybe I'll post a few photos I took of you last night. I've done pretty well at getting you internet attention recently.'

'What?' She can't grasp what he is saying.

'Told you I've got quite a few social media accounts. It was

319

pretty easy to start the #Drewmerchantinnocent. So many idiots who'll jump on the bandwagon. It was harder to post the positive messages, actually. I really got ripped for supporting you.'

Jenna doesn't wait to hear any more. She runs, clutching her bag to her chest, blindly making for the busiest road. She doesn't dare look over her shoulder in case he is following her, her breath burning in her throat as she sprints through the estate, eventually emerging on to the Caledonian Road.

She almost leaps into the street as a black cab approaches, orange light illuminated, waving both her arms until it stops.

'Everything all right, love?' the driver asks as she scrambles into the safety of the back seat. The locks click reassuringly as they engage and she slumps in relief on to the vinyl.

'Yes,' she manages to say. 'Camden, please.'

She waits until they are trundling along and the light indicates the driver has turned off the back speakers before scrabbling in her bag for her phone. She desperately wants to call Zach, hear his reassuring flat vowels and his calming voice, and ask him to put Lando on so she can tell him she loves him. But that is not for now. Later, she will do those things and maybe, finally, she will feel safe, but for now there is someone else she needs to talk to, the last person she thought she would speak to again but the only one who may be able to make sense of all this.

She doesn't expect Ava to answer, grits her teeth waiting for the call to be diverted to voicemail, but after what seems like for ever, Ava picks up.

'Are you at home?' Jenna doesn't give her the chance to speak first.

'Yes, why?'

'I need to meet you, now.'

'I don't think we should see each other, Jenna, not after last time.'

'I'm not going to tell your secrets. Ava, please listen to me, has Seb been in touch?'

'What? No. Why would he? I've not heard from him for a couple of days – he'll be sulking about not getting the Disney job. What's wrong? You sound strange.'

Jenna drops her voice to whisper even though the speaker light remains off. 'Seb attacked me last night.'

Ava is silent for a long minute and, when she does speak, she struggles to form a sentence. 'What? I don't . . . What are you talking about?'

'I'm in a cab to yours. Don't answer if Seb calls you.' She has to pause to swallow the salvia that floods her mouth. 'I've just left his flat. You can't imagine it, Ava. We don't know him at all.'

She hears Ava take a long breath. 'Go straight to the police, not to me!'

'I can't, not yet. I need to get my head straight first. I need to be sure about him.' Jenna rubs her temples hard, trying to squeeze out the pulsing pain. Any further words are lost in a gasp as her lungs constrict.

How could she have been so blind?

The moment the cab pulls up opposite Ava's warehouse, Jenna is out of the car and almost running to the intercom. Her buzz is answered immediately and she flies up the stairs as if expecting to be confronted at every turn, unable to face being trapped in the lift.

'Jesus!' Ava's hands fly to her own face as she opens the door. She takes Jenna's arm and pulls her inside, straight to the bathroom. The windowless room smells of faint ghosts of citrus perfume and a woody male aftershave, blending together.

'Look in the mirror.' Ava sinks on to the edge of the bath.

Jenna steps to the sink, bending close to peer at her reflection. What she sees shocks her. Her eyes are so bloodshot barely any white can be seen through the web of redness. Her skin is grey, hair a wild tangle, lips swollen as badly as the rims of her eyes. She can smell herself, a feral scent of stale whisky and unbrushed teeth, and something acidic, chemical.

'Bloody good thing you didn't go straight to the police,' Ava murmurs. 'Tell me what happened.'

Her tone brooks no argument, but for a long moment Jenna doesn't know where to start. She pulls off her coat and lifts her top to reveal the bruises, strangely vulnerable in front of her friend. 'I don't know what happened.'

'Were you pissed?' Ava asks bluntly.

Jenna struggles back into the garments. 'Absolutely hammered.'

'Did you have sex?'

'He said we did. It feels like we did. I don't remember.'

'Nothing?'

'He came on to me when we were sitting on the sofa. I pushed him off. He didn't like it. He was stoned, drunk, but he's been in that state around me plenty of times. It was like he wasn't Seb, not the Seb we know. He was so angry, so aggressive.'

'Did you want to have sex with him?'

'No! That's what I'm trying to tell you. I didn't consent. I wasn't aware of what he was doing to me.'

'Because you were so drunk?'

'Because of this.' Jenna holds out the little bottle she had snatched up. 'He was taunting me, wanting me to know he's used it on other women.'

Ava closes her eyes for a moment. 'What is happening to us?'

'Our friend drugged and assaulted me last night, that's what's happening. I think he's been interfering in the whole investigation into Drew.'

'That makes no sense. How could he?'

Jenna delves into her bag, scrabbling until she finds the damning evidence, and pulls it free. She lets it hang, dangling from her fingers, in front of Ava's face.

'I'm sure this is the stone from Drew's ring. He said he'd lost it at school. Seb's had it all this time.'

Ava's face drains of colour, her eyes moving in rhythm with the gentle swing of the pendant, hypnotised by it.

'So Seb did get revenge, after all.'

Chapter Forty-One

Ava visibly jumps at the sound of another door opening and closing out in the hallway, echoing around the industrial surfaces of the conversion. A burst of conversation can be heard.

'I need a drink.'

She strides through to the kitchen, mixing them both a large glass of gin, before moving into the living room, Jenna trailing helplessly behind her.

'I don't understand.' Jenna's legs feel as if they are about to give way beneath her, but she remains standing. 'What do you mean, revenge?'

'Drew and Seb, they were sleeping together at school, before we all arrived. It happened all the time before girls went to Cell Block H – boys locked away for weeks on end, frustrated. Seb must have helped himself to a souvenir after Drew dumped him.'

Jenna has begun to shake uncontrollably as she struggles to process all the information, trying to piece the timeline together.

'So if Seb had already stolen the ring, that means it wasn't Drew who was wearing it.'

Ava stares at her. She starts shaking her head rapidly, opening her mouth, but no words come out.

'No,' she eventually whispers. 'It can't have been.'

'It wasn't Drew who abused me.' Jenna grabs at the wall for support, the room spinning.

'But you said—

'They were a similar height, similar build. They both smoked, wore the same aftershave.'

'No way.' Ava's head-shaking grows even more violent, as if she doesn't know how to stop. 'Seb wouldn't do that.'

'He's fucking twisted!' Jenna yells back. 'He was talking about Rory, about how he switched the pills. Seb killed Rory, not us!'

'Why would he do that?'

'So we'd never have a reason to think that it wasn't Rory who abused me. With Rory dead, Seb was safe—'

She is interrupted by her phone ringing. She jabs at the screen to cancel Zach's call. She can't speak to him at this moment, not when she and Ava are face to face, breathing as if they've run a sprint, fists clenched and faces flushed.

The phone beeps insistently, telling her she has a voicemail waiting. To avoid having to look at Ava, she taps to listen to it.

Zach's voice. 'Jenna, where are you? We're home – Lando insisted on coming back. A mate's birthday he can't miss, or something like that. Reckon he was just fed up with the lack of gaming. Anyway, he's just off out to meet the boys. Let me know when you're coming back.' A pause. 'I've missed you. Let me know you're safe. Love you.'

Those two simple words, ones he has said practically every day of their marriage, are enough to make Jenna's throat close up. Zach still loves her.

She hasn't lost everything.

She sees Ava has her own phone out, fingers flying as she types a message.

'Are you messaging Seb?' she cries.

'I'm messaging Drew.'

Jenna goes hot and cold, feverish in an instant, and the urge to snatch Ava's phone from her rises uncontrollably. 'Stop, Ava!'

'He needs to know! This affects him too. This is more proof of his innocence. He can get his life back!' Ava pockets her phone as if reading Jenna's mind. 'Sit down and I'll get you another drink and we'll decide what the hell to do.'

'I don't want another drink!' For the first time in what feels like for ever, she doesn't crave the comfort blanket of alcohol. She wants clarity and precision, not the blurred confusion that has protected her for too long. 'I need a shower. I need to get clean.'

She stands under the shower until the hot water runs out, scrubbing her body over and over again. Ava has left leggings and a warm jumper for her to change into, but she is still cold when she returns to the living room, wrapping herself in a blanket that still doesn't stop the shivers.

She isn't aware she has drifted into a doze, her mind and body equally exhausted, until she hears the sound of a key scratching in the front door. She leaps to her feet, certain it will be Seb, even though she knows he doesn't have access.

She doesn't feel much better when Drew's athletic figure appears in the doorway. He stops dead when he sees her sitting before him. Their eyes lock, neither of them able to look away.

'You didn't tell me you had company,' he says tightly to Ava.

'If you knew, you wouldn't have come.'

'Whatever game you two are playing, I don't want to be involved.' He turns to leave.

'Drew, wait! You'll want to when you hear what Jenna has to say,' Ava says. 'Pour yourself a drink. You'll need it.'

Drew hovers, clearly torn between storming out and his own inevitable curiosity. His dark eyes burn into Jenna and she has to fight equal urges to flinch away and reach out to him.

Finally, he limps to the kitchen, casually familiar with the apartment. The touch of Ava's hand against his arm is so subtle Jenna would have missed it if she hadn't been looking for it.

'What's this about?' He returns clutching a glass of whisky. He doesn't sit, choosing to lean against the furthest wall. The scrapes on his face are fading but still visible.

'Tell Jenna about you and Seb Byron,' Ava says.

Drew's jaw visibly tightens, as does his grip on his glass. His hardened eyes flick between the two women.

'She already knows. Please, it's important.'

'How can it be important?' Drew demands.

'Because of what happened to Jenna last night.'

His glass stalls partway to his lips. His eyes search Jenna's, questioning, and she is sure she doesn't imagine the spark of concern.

'Seb spiked my drink. I woke up in his bed today.' It is difficult to admit this to the man whose body she had explored so willingly.

'Did he hurt you?' Drew's voice is rough, suddenly gravelly.

She can only nod. She can't say the words.

'We don't think it was the first time,' Ava says for her. 'Show him, Jenna.'

Jenna produces the neck chain, allowing Drew to take it. Electricity sparks as their fingers momentarily touch and she almost jumps away. Drew's throat bobs as he swallows hard, his breathing quickening as he touches the onyx stone, tracing its lines.

'Seb Byron had this?'

She nods again. 'You didn't give it to him?'

'Of course I didn't give it to him!' Drew rakes his fingers through his hair, his reluctance clear. 'Seb and I fooled around for a while in fifth form. I broke it off when it was confirmed Cell Block H was going to be accepting girls. It had only been a bit of fun, something to do.'

'Seb didn't take it well?'

'He didn't like being rejected. Kept trying to win me back, but I wasn't interested. He was a mess, to be honest. Obsessed with how much he hated his mother.'

Jenna takes a gulp of gin, even though she doesn't want it. 'And you lost the ring in July? You definitely didn't have it in the lower sixth?' Her voice is barely audible, but she has to confirm.

Drew is shaking his head as realisation hits him. He stares at Jenna, his fist pressed to his stomach as if it pains him. 'Your abuser wore it,' he states. 'Jesus. What the fuck?'

'Seb thinks I rejected him at school too.'

'My God.' Drew has sunk his whisky seemingly without even noticing and now tries to drink from the empty glass.

'What do we do?' Ava asks.

'Why are you asking me?' Anger replaces the shock again.

'Because Jenna can hardly report it now, after everything.'

'You're expecting me to do it?' he asks incredulously. 'Not a chance!'

'If not, he gets away with it.'

'Don't put it on me, Ava. I want no part in this shit after everything I've been through.'

'I understand,' Jenna murmurs. 'I've ruined your life I know.'

'He did those terrible things to you,' he hisses, stepping closer to her. 'He let me take the blame for his twisted mind. How can you not have realised?'

Jenna almost leans into him, desperate to apologise for all the harm she has done, but Ava is watching them too closely.

'I'm so sorry,' she whispers. 'I had no idea what was really going on.'

He turns to Ava as if Jenna hasn't spoken. 'Where's Adie? She shouldn't hear this shit.'

'School, it's Friday.'

Drew's face momentarily contorts, as if it pains him to hear about his school, and he slumps into a chair. Jenna wonders if he will ever return to the job she knows he loves, which she may have ultimately robbed him of.

'Drew,' Ava says softly. 'Do it for me and Adie, if you can't do it for any other reason. You have to keep us safe from Seb.'

His head jerks up, his lips moving silently as he processes his lover's words.

Jenna's phone beeps and she automatically grabs it. Seb's contact icon flashes on her phone screen, a WhatsApp picture message. Against her will, she opens it.

She studies the photo, the selfie Seb took the night they all gathered at Jenna's house and had Thai takeaway. At first, she doesn't understand why he has sent it. There is no text attached.

Then she sees it.

Lando is on the edge of the picture, unaware he is in shot. His eyes are fixed on Seb, an expression of anguish etched on his face.

From nowhere, a memory sparks. Seb's hand reaching for his front door, a woven leather bracelet around his wrist. An identical bracelet to the one Lando had been bought at Camden market.

And Jenna finally understands what has caused her son's behaviour to change so drastically.

Chapter Forty-Two

Nearly dropping the phone, she leaps to her feet. 'I need the bathroom.'

She almost runs into the small room, locking the door for safety. Unable to keep still, she paces the few steps back and forth across the floor till Zach answers her call.

'Where did Lando say he was going?' she demands the moment she hears his voice.

'Are you OK? You sound strange. Where are you?'

'Where's Lando?'

'With his mates at the skate park. What's the matter? Are you coming home?'

'Are you sure?'

'That's what he said.'

'Can you check? Find his phone's location.'

'Jenna, what's going on?' Zach's voice rises. 'Why do you think he's not where he said?'

'Just do it!'

She hears the sounds of Zach lowering the phone, opening the app, his even breathing at odds with her panicked snatches of air.

'Bet he'll have turned it off after last time . . . ah, no, he must have forgotten. He had to use location for the map in Yorkshire . . .' He's put her on speaker. 'Fuck, he's not at the skate park.'

'Does it say where he really is?'

'Camden, just off the high street. Will you tell me what's wrong, for Christ's sake?'

'Meet me there. I think I know who he's with.'

'Is he in danger? Should I call the police?'

'No, just get there!'

She cancels the call before he can speak again, running back into the living room, scrabbling to grab her belongings.

'What's wrong?' Drew asks, drawn to his feet by her panic.

'I've got to go.' She can't take the time to explain. All she needs to do is find her son.

'What's happened?' Ava asks.

'I've got to go!' she repeats, almost a scream now. She has ripped open the door and is running down the stairs before Ava or Drew can move.

On the street, she thrusts a hand out, waving frantically, trying to attract a cab's attention, but none of them stop.

Her phone goes. Zach again. 'Lando's turned the tracker off – he must have remembered about it. I've no way of telling where he is now.'

'What do we do?'

'I don't know!' He's in full panic mode; she can tell by how brittle his voice is.

'Hold on a second.'

Jenna puts Zach on hold and opens her Snapchat app. Tapping Seb's icon, she hisses a triumphant breath as the map opens, pinpointing his location.

'Zach, they're on the canal off the high street. By the construction site next to the railway. I'll meet you there.'

She continues her frenzied signalling to cabs that don't seem to see her, her terror rising with each one that passes by.

'Jenna, tell me what's going on.' Drew has appeared without her noticing and she starts violently when his hand grasps her shoulder.

'I need a cab. Or an Uber. Anything. It can't wait.'

'What can't?'

'Lando. Lando's in trouble. I think he's in danger.'

'Tell me why?' His hand doesn't move, his grip reassuring in its strength, and she feels her pounding heart begin to slow.

'Because he's with Seb.'

Drew's expression freezes as he processes the information, just for a moment, before she sees the leadership figure visibly rise within him. 'Get in the car. Quickly.'

He grabs her hand and runs across the road without hesitation, his injuries ignored, pulling her with him as horns and yells ring out around them. He opens the door of his BMW for her, helping her up into the seat. For just the briefest of seconds, he grips both her hands in his.

'Lando will be fine, I promise.'

He drives with authority, carving his way through the traffic, but it is still too slow. The five-minute journey seems to take for ever, a languid speed made worse by traffic lights and cyclists and tourists forgetting they're no longer in the pedestrian market. Darkness has already fallen, a cloudy sky hiding the moon and the stars, making the evening heavy and foreboding by the time they draw into the side of the road.

'It'll be OK.' Drew pulls into the kerb. The urge to cling to him almost overwhelms her, but she knows she can't.

She presses the little bottle into his palm and moves back, out of reach.

'What is it?'

'Show it to the police. They'll know what Seb used it for.'

Drew slips it into his pocket with a nod, as if reassuring her of his decision. He goes to open his door but she grabs his sleeve, hauls him back.

'Don't come with me.'

'You can't go on your own.'

'I told you, Zach will be here.' Another lie. Zach won't have made it yet, not from the other side of Islington. 'We'll be fine.'

'I'll wait here then, to be sure.'

'Just go, Drew!' Her voice rises abruptly. 'Go back to Ava, or Natasha, or whoever else you want to be with. I need to get to my son.'

With that, she leaps from the car, slamming the door, and runs.

The steps down on to the towpath aren't worn like the ones by the lock; they haven't known thousands of feet descending them. The path is silent, deserted. The ghostly shadows of the construction site loom above her as she begins a rapid walk, her breath burning in her throat.

Beside her, the canal water looks inky black, cold and threatening. She begins to shiver violently. Her nose and fingertips prickle, with cold or with a sixth sense she never knew she possessed; she can't be sure. Her phone buzzes continually, but she ignores it.

On a bench, barely visible in the weak beam of orange light from the single streetlamp several yards away, she spots the fur hood of her son's parka. He sits close to another, taller, person, the clouds of his breath visible in the chilled night air.

'Lando!' she screams, her voice echoing around her.

Both figures leap to their feet.

'How did you know I was here?' Lando cries, looking frantically about him as if the source will be revealed.

Jenna clutches her phone tighter in her hand, waving it at Seb. 'You haven't turned your fucking SnapMap off.'

Seb smiles, spreading his arms wide. 'We're just chatting, aren't we, Lando? We're not doing anything wrong.'

'Come here,' Jenna implores her son.

He rears up as if she has slapped him. 'Just fuck off, Mum!'

'Get away from Seb!'

Lando throws her a look of defiance, raising his chin as he steps closer to Seb. 'Leave us alone. Seb understands me. He knows what it's like having a mother who doesn't love you.'

Jenna's mouth falls open and it takes too long for her to scrabble for the right words. 'Of course I love you.'

'You've always resented me for being born. You told Seb you wished you'd never had me.'

'I did not!'

'He's told me everything, Mum! How I've been nothing but an inconvenience all my life!'

'That's not true, Lando. I've never told him these things. He's trying to turn you against me, can't you see?'

'Why would he? He's the only one who gets me!'

'Listen to me. He's not what you think he is. He doesn't care about you, it's just an act, a way to get back at me for something I didn't do!'

Even in the dim light she can see Lando's face darken, a ferocious scowl contorting his features. 'I'm better off without a mum than one who hates me!'

'I don't hate you! I've loved you since the moment I held you!' Her voice trails off into a gasp. 'I just don't know how to show it. My parents never showed me.'

'So let's all feel sorry for you,' Lando snarls. 'That's what you want, isn't it? The attention.'

'That's all she's ever wanted,' Seb murmurs. 'And now it's turned on her. All those people, baying for her blood. You've seen it all, haven't you, mate?'

Rage rises inside Jenna. 'You sent him those links! He didn't stumble across the posts by himself!'

Seb smirks. 'You should see how long our Snap streak is.'

She wishes she didn't know what that means, that it is proof of daily contact between her son and this monster. 'Why are you doing this?'

'You know exactly why.' He is so calm, smiling as if they are chatting over coffee.

'But you helped me, Seb! You wanted Drew to be charged.'

'Oh, I hate Drew, don't get me wrong. I've always wanted to get my own back for how he made me feel, and you just made it worse fawning over him like you did back then.'

'So why make me look like I'm crazy?'

'Because I hate you even more, Genevieve. Can't you see? I finally had the chance to screw over the two people I despise the most. I could see Drew lose it all, even if he didn't end up in prison, and I could see you exposed as the lying, manipulative bitch you really are.'

'What did I ever do to you?'

'You led me on. You made me feel like we had something special.'

'I didn't mean to! I was a child – I only wanted friends!'

'I thought Drew could make me forget everything women had done to me. Then he dumped me and I had nothing left until I met you. You were different. Or so I thought, till I saw you only had eyes for Drew.'

Lando's head jerks back and forth between them, his confusion palpable. Jenna sees him tense, squaring his shoulders.

Seb is oblivious. 'Women have abused me all my life. My own mother! I've hated women since I was a little boy.'

'Your two best friends are women!'

'Ava? She's useful. I have to be nice to her or I'd never work again.'

'What are you talking about?' Lando cries. 'You said if you smashed our window it would help Mum's case because the cops would think it was Drew! You said you wore his boots so he'd get in trouble for it! I thought it was something she'd actually approve of, for once.'

Her son's plaintive words make Jenna feel sick. How badly she has failed him. 'As if you wanted to help my case,' she snarls at Seb.

Seb shrugs. 'I'd have enjoyed Drew being done for witness intimidation, though. I didn't go to his house intending to nick the boots, but the opportunity presented itself so nicely.'

Jenna drags in a sharp breath. 'You went to Drew's house to plant the ring, didn't you? Couldn't you bear to give the stone up?'

'That stays close to my heart.' Seb beams like a proud parent. 'I'd like it back, please. I know you have it, Genevieve.'

'I haven't got it.'

'More lies. But never mind, there's plenty of time for that.'

'What about the brick through Drew's window? His bike accident?'

Another nod. 'Made you seem like a nutjob and Drew like a

337

man with something to hide. I borrowed Ava's car. She's not as observant as she likes to think she is. She never noticed it was missing for a few hours.'

'I don't understand!' Lando almost shouts.

'I couldn't tell you the truth, Lando, don't you see?' Seb changes tactic with terrifying ease, his manner instantly becoming conciliatory, his tone and body language softening. 'I had to be sure I could trust you, that you wouldn't tell. But I know for sure now, don't I? I know you can be trusted.'

'Lando, look at me,' Jenna whispers.

Her son's eyes jump instinctively to her, and she sees rage darken Seb's face as he realises he isn't fully in control.

'It was Seb who abused me at school, not Drew,' she says to Lando. She squeezes her eyes shut, desperate to protect her son from the awful knowledge she must give him, to show him once and for all. 'I was at his flat yesterday. He drugged me. Then he hurt me again.'

For one awful moment, no one reacts. All three are frozen, staring wildly at each other. Lando's eyes dart and she sees the teenage facade fall away, revealing the child beneath it.

'Did you?' He looks up at Seb, his voice faltering. 'Is it true?'

Seb throws an arm around Lando's neck, pulling the boy against him, stepping nearer to the edge of the towpath. 'It's more lies, I swear.'

Lando's head turns back and forth, uncertainty tightening his face.

'Come here, sweetheart.' Jenna quietens her voice, reaching her palm out to her son. Her phone begins to buzz again. Maybe

Zach is close. Lando will go to his dad; she is sure of that. 'It's OK, you're not in trouble. I just want you to be safe.'

She sees Lando's confusion at the rare endearment, indecision making him shift from foot to foot.

'Think you can ruin me too, Jenna?' Seb takes another step towards the water, pulling Lando with him. 'I'm happy to leave this world. It's done nothing but fuck me up.'

'Get away from my son!'

Lando begins to struggle as he spots how close they are to the edge, trying to free himself from Seb's grasp, but Seb is too strong. Jenna throws herself at the two, trying to separate them, trying to put herself between Seb and her son.

Seb's fist hits her square in the nose, a punch hard enough to make her face explode with red-hot pain. He swings again, catching her ear, and the world tilts alarmingly, throwing her off balance.

A noise erupts from Lando's throat, partway between a snarl and a howl. He throws a punch that connects with Seb's jaw, an agonising crack that throws the man off balance. Jenna stumbles as her son seizes her coat, dragging her away from the looming threat of her former friend. She falls backwards as her legs give way, refusing to support her.

From the darkness, another figure emerges. Long, athletic strides eat up the distance as they charge past Jenna, head down, feet crunching hard against the towpath. She sees a pair of strong arms spread wide, a rugby player preparing to tackle.

There is a cry and a thud, something solid striking stone, a dull sound that still manages to echo.

A splash.

Then silence.

Jenna scrambles to her feet, looking desperately for her son in the black water. She can just see the surface disturbance from the body that has sunk beneath it.

'Mum!' Lando is on all fours, leaning over the edge. She grabs for him, hauling him back from the brink, struggling to move his dead weight.

She doesn't need to ask where Seb is.

Drew is sprawled on the ground, grasping his left shoulder as he eases himself to his feet, covered in mud and gravel and splashes of canal water. He staggers to Jenna and Lando, shielding them with his own body.

Together, they watch. They wait for Seb's head to break the surface, gasping for air.

The water stills.

'Mum,' Lando croaks. He cradles one hand, knuckles red and starting to swell.

Jenna reaches for his uninjured hand, squeezing it as tight as she can. 'I know.'

'What do we do?'

She has no answer. She can only stare at the black water, unsure of what she is hoping for. Drew is shaking uncontrollably beside her, his breath coming in sharp gasps.

'You need to go,' she whispers urgently to him. 'Now, Drew.'

He looks wildly at her, not understanding.

'You were never here,' she tells him. 'It was just me and Lando.'

Comprehension finally dawns in his eyes and he begins to shake his head. 'I can't let you do that. You didn't do anything. You didn't hurt him.'

'No one saw what happened apart from us. Go.'

'There's no point, Jenna. The police will see me on CCTV.'

'There is no CCTV,' Lando interrupts, his voice raw. 'Not on this part of the towpath. The steps aren't covered either.'

'How do you know?' Jenna asks.

'Seb told me. That's why we met here if we wanted to smoke weed or have a drink.'

She feels sick at the thought of her thirteen-year-old son sharing beers and spliffs with Seb but a strange calmness is descending on her, her thought process clear and agile for the first time in far too long.

'Lando.' She squeezes her son's arm urgently. 'It was just you and me here tonight, you understand?'

Lando looks between the two of them, torn, and her heart aches for what she is asking him to do when he has already been through so much.

'But why?'

'Because I owe Drew a debt bigger than I can ever repay. Do you hear what I'm asking you to do?'

'Drew was never here,' he repeats obediently. 'I won't tell.'

Drew looks between mother and son for a long moment.

'Go,' Jenna pleads and, finally, he turns. The darkness swallows him in seconds as his hurried footsteps fade away.

Jenna guides Lando to the bench, gently pushes him down. He starts violently, lunging to prevent her as she pulls out her phone. She gently bats his arm away and taps in three digits, ignoring the tens of missed calls from Zach, just for now, just until she has done this one last thing.

'Trust me,' she whispers.

Chapter Forty-Three

Zach arrives to blue lights illuminating the towpath in their ghostly flashes. He has no idea yet of just what has happened, but his priority is clear as he grabs his wife and son, holding them tight against him as he whispers reassurances. The time for questions will come but, for now, Jenna clings to her husband, unable to release her grip on him or her hold on Lando's hand.

'I'm sorry,' she croaks. 'There wasn't time to answer your calls.'

She wraps her foil blanket more tightly around her, avoiding the expressions of concern from the paramedics as they watch the powerful police torches futilely search the canal surface. She doesn't want their treatment and has already batted them away from Lando, determined they will not glimpse the evidence of his swollen knuckles.

Her teeth chatter as shivers wrack her body. Lando's face is drained of colour, his eyes wide and staring in shock.

'Do you need to get checked out?' Zach touches a gentle finger to her swollen, throbbing face.

'I'm OK. I just want to go home.'

'Lando?'

Lando takes a moment to acknowledge he is being spoken to. He shakes his head rapidly, sliding his bruised hand into his coat pocket before his father can see it. 'I'm fine.'

'Let me ask if we can go.' Zach heads over to the liveried police officers, the reflective material of their jackets blinding against the darkness. An earnest conversation starts, each person indicating the water, speaking rapidly. Jenna hopes he is getting some answers to the questions he has been considerate enough not to hassle her with.

She turns urgently to her son, before Zach can return.

'Lando, did Seb ever hurt you?' She can barely bring herself to ask the question, but she must. She has to know.

He stares, uncomprehending, for a long moment, then colour rushes to his cheeks. 'No! He never touched me.'

'You swear?'

He nods frantically. 'All we did was hang out. Talk, you know. He seemed to get everything that was bothering me.'

She wants to ask him why he couldn't talk to them, except she can't, because she knows why. She knows this is her fault.

'They've said that now you've given your initial statements they don't need anything else from you tonight,' Zach reports as he returns.

Relief courses through Jenna's tired, aching body and, for once, she can't stop the tears from falling. They stream silently down her frozen cheeks, cathartic, undeniable.

Zach leans down to press his lips against hers. 'I love you,' he whispers. 'I love you so much.'

He takes her hand in his, grip firmer than normal, and links his arm through Lando's. Together, a family, they turn away from the search and begin to walk back down the towpath.

Jenna's phone pings with a message.

On way to Chelmsford. Going to show Beckett the proof.

The whole story? She quickly types back.

The three dots waver for a long minute.

Only what he needs to know.

Even the next morning, Jenna still can't get warm. Even after a scalding shower, dressed in several layers and wrapped in a blanket and huddled close to the log burner, she is chilled to the bone.

She knew Beckett would visit, but she hadn't expected him to appear before the Islington officers arrived to take her and Lando's second statement. He is tense as he perches on a stool, shoulders taut and grip tight on his pen. Lando eyes him warily from across the breakfast bar, trying to butter his bagel too quickly.

'Lando, go upstairs,' Jenna tells him quietly.

'Let him stay a moment,' Beckett interjects.

Lando hovers, unsure what to do, until Jenna nods reassurance. He resumes buttering, eyes fixed on his food.

'Police divers recovered the body of Sebastian Byron from the Grand Union Canal last night,' Beckett says.

Jenna closes her eyes, waits several heartbeats until she is sure she can speak. 'Do you know how he died?'

'The initial pathology report suggests he was unconscious from hitting his head when he went into the water. He drowned.'

Jenna has to breathe very slowly to avoid being sick. She grips the edge of the table until the dizziness retreats to a manageable level.

'I spent yesterday evening in a very long interview with Drew

344

Merchant,' Beckett continues. 'He's given us a statement regarding the abuse you suffered at school and evidence to suggest Mr Byron's guilt. Mr Merchant tells us his information came from you, but you weren't willing to come forward.'

'After everything that's happened, I didn't dare.'

'If you'd have come to us yesterday, we'd have been able to conduct a medical exam, take blood to check for any drug traces still in your system, find proof that he'd attacked you. I assume you've showered since?'

Jenna nods, drawing the blanket tighter around her, knowing what Beckett is about to suggest. 'I don't want to be examined.'

'The drugs will have left your system by now, but we could still find forensic evidence from other samples.'

'No. I don't want to. He's dead. What does it matter?'

'You were so fixated on getting justice before. What's changed?'

Jenna shakes her head. 'Everything.' She looks at her son. 'Go and play your battles, Lando.'

Lando needs no further urging. He doesn't even bother to take his breakfast with him.

Jenna sits down opposite the detective, not convinced her legs will support her much longer. Her head aches unbearably, matching the throbbing from her swollen nose and cheekbone. 'How did I not see Seb was involved in it all?'

'I gather he was an actor. It seems he treated most of his life like a role he was playing. You can't blame yourself for being fooled.'

'I was so stupid,' she whispers.

'There's also a suggestion that he may have been responsible for a series of date-rape attacks in Soho in the last few years. The bottle you gave Mr Merchant has been identified as GHB.'

Jenna stares at the detective. The thought of a man she had loved and trusted committing these crimes is something she isn't sure she will ever be able to truly comprehend. 'The boy who died at school, Rory – Seb mentioned him yesterday. He said he had given him pills that night.'

'For what reason?'

Jenna catches her confused reply just in time, before she incriminates herself. 'He didn't say,' she mumbled. 'Yet another imagined rejection, maybe?'

'It's not likely we'd ever be able to prove it, with both of them deceased,' Beckett says softly.

'No,' Jenna whispers, but in her heart she knows the truth. She knows now why the pills were blue, not red and yellow, as Ava had insisted. She knows why Seb was in such a hurry to leave breakfast the morning they had planted the drugs.

Jenna, Olivia and Ava had not been responsible for the death of Rory Addison.

Beckett closes his notebook, lays his pen down beside it. 'What happened by the canal last night, Jenna?'

'I've already made an initial statement.' It is a struggle to bring herself back to the present.

'I've read it. You say that only you, Lando and Sebastian Byron were present.'

'That's right.'

'Yet CCTV from further up the high street shows Drew Merchant dropping you off, then getting back into his car and driving away.'

'He offered to help me when I found out Seb was with Lando, but I wouldn't let him. I made him go home.'

'But he didn't go home. He parked up a couple of streets away.'

'Maybe he had something else to do. I don't know. I was only with him because I needed to show him that bloody neck chain.'

'Jenna, I'm not investigating Sebastian Byron's death,' Beckett says with surprising gentleness.

'Then why are you asking me these questions?'

'Because I want to tie up my own inquiry, even if the perpetrator is now deceased.'

Jenna gets slowly to her feet, taking her time pouring a glass of water from the filter jug. 'Drew wasn't there. He gave me a lift, that was all. I couldn't risk Lando being with Seb, not after what I'd found out about him. My son was just another tool to him.'

'Tell me what happened at the canal.' Beckett's tone is almost hypnotic, lulling her into a sense of security that is almost certainly false.

The water glass is empty, but she can't put it down. She doesn't have time to rehearse her lines in her head, as she had planned to do before giving her second statement to the Islington officers, and she has to fight her panicked brain.

'Seb was stoned, drunk – I don't know. He was ranting like a madman. He tripped and hit his head against one of the mooring bollards when he tried to run away.'

'So how did he end up in the water?'

'He landed right on the brink. His weight must have dragged him over the edge. He couldn't have saved himself if he was unconscious.'

'And that was when you called 999?'

'Lando wanted to jump in after him, but I wouldn't let him. The water was pitch black and Seb hadn't resurfaced. Lando could have drowned too.'

'I understand.'

Jenna raised her eyes to Beckett's. 'There was nothing we could do.'

'Just a terrible accident.'

'I didn't wish him dead.'

'I'm sure you didn't.'

They hold each other's gaze for just a moment too long.

'How is your son?'

'He's OK. Shocked.'

'Not an easy thing for him to witness.'

'No,' Jenna agrees.

'His hand must be sore.'

Jenna's spine goes rigid. 'His hand?'

'I noticed it was badly bruised across the knuckles.'

She forces a laugh. 'Oh, that was from rugby. He's always coming home with some scrape or another.'

'Rugby's my sport too. Decent player, is he?'

'From the little I know, yes. I'll be making it to more of his games from now on.'

'Making some changes?'

'I've decided to go part-time when I return to work, maybe think about a career change next year.'

Beckett nods. 'Priorities change, don't they?'

'Yes, they do.'

He stands, stretching his long arms out before slipping into his coat. 'I'll be going, Jenna. The Met officers will be in touch, keep you informed of the situation, and I'll let you know about the file I prepare to close my investigation, but I don't imagine we'll need to meet again.'

Jenna releases a breath she hadn't realised she was holding as

Beckett extends his hand. She takes it, acknowledging how gently he grips, despite his size.

'Good luck to you and the family,' he says.

'Thank you.' And she means it this time. 'I'll show you out.'

He follows her down the hallway, nodding his thanks as she holds open the front door for him. As he steps past her, to leave her life for good, he pauses on the threshold, as if seeing something for the first time.

'I meant to ask, when did this happen?' He indicates her bruised face.

'Seb hit me,' she says.

'On the towpath?'

'No. When I left his flat the morning after he drugged me.'

'There was no fight last night?'

'I said in my statement. No one hurt anyone on the towpath.'

'No one hit Mr Byron? No one pushed him?'

'I told you,' Jenna repeats forcefully. 'He tripped. He hit his head. He fell into the water. That's it. Nothing else happened.'

Beckett nods thoughtfully. Jenna waits for the next question, for the challenge. It doesn't come.

'Goodbye, Jenna.'

'Goodbye, Sergeant Beckett.'

She watches until he is safely in his car and driving away. Waiting to check he is really gone. To be certain he is out of her life for good.

This time, her lie is justified.

This time, it won't keep her awake.

349

Epilogue

EXCLUSIVE: JENNA TAYLOR AND THE REAL STORY OF
CELL BLOCK H

BY AMY DONALD

When Jenna Taylor found the courage to report the abuse she suffered at her troubled boarding school in the mid-nineties, she had no idea her world would fall apart. She was certain her abuser was her former house prefect, Andrew Merchant, but she hadn't dared speak out for twenty-five years. Finally deciding to take action, she didn't expect the maelstrom that would be unleashed.

Not only was Drew Merchant innocent, he had been set up by a man both he and Jenna had regarded as a friend. Actor Sebastian Byron held deep grudges that lasted decades, worsened by his unstable mental health. During his time at Halewood House, he stole, misused drugs and, ultimately, was responsible for the abuse Jenna Taylor suffered. Suggestions that he was involved in the tragic sudden death of student Rory Addison must remain unproven. Sebastian Byron is now deceased, an accidental drowning, and the full extent of his crimes may never be revealed, but at least the other parties now know the true perpetrator.

Jenna Taylor was vilified for her bravery, as so many other women have been when speaking up about abuse. She acknowledges that Byron fooled her completely. She did not accuse Drew Merchant out of spite but from a determination to make sure no one else would have to go through the ordeal she suffered. She is at pains to say she was wrong, and she remains guilt stricken over the trauma caused by Byron's deceptions.

Today, Jenna finally knows the truth and can begin to rebuild her life. Drew Merchant is back on track, on his way to Whitehall and, while Jenna's path is a quieter one, she can now sleep easy for the first time in decades.

Acknowledgements

The second book of an author's career is widely acknowledged to be the most difficult you will ever write, and *What We Did* proved that legend to be entirely accurate. This has been a team effort and I'm eternally grateful to every person who has steered me and the book through the often-choppy waters. My heartfelt thanks to:

My agent, the wonderful Liza DeBlock, who never hesitates to rescue me when I'm in danger of drowning, but equally throws me back into the deep end when I'm lolling in the shallows. I can't wait to continue the journey with her by my side.

My editor Bea Grabowska, who has been nothing short of a dream to work with, even when I have proven entirely unable to recognise the days of the week. I am very lucky to have benefitted from her insight and her guidance.

The team at Headline Accent and Lisa Brewster for a cover that really is so sharp you could cut yourself.

Mushens Entertainment, the dream agency, for mugs, tote bags and the hippest office ever.

The alpha team for fizz, cheese, beige buffets and patiently allowing me to witter endlessly about this book. I'd be lost without you all (literally, you are the ones who can navigate the road trips).

Caravan Man, for thrashing out the original idea all that time ago, and for letting me know absolutely everything I have done that annoys him.

All the bloggers, booksellers and reviewers who have continued to provide their invaluable support.

My parents, who have always gone above and beyond, and continue to do so every day. With their love and support, no achievement feels impossible.

The fur family, including our newest baby Indiana, who listen diligently to plot twists and character arcs between chasing squirrels, provide the best snuggles in exchange for bacon, and love the attention of a Zoom meeting.

And to Lee, who knows edits can only be interrupted by pizza or wine, who generates excellent titles, and who never wavers in his belief in me. I can follow this dream because he is by my side. This is the way, together.

What if everyone you love is lying to you?

THEY SAY YOUR BABY ISN'T REAL.
BUT YOU KNOW HE IS.

BELIEVE ME NOT

'Compelling and
tightly plotted,
the story twists
relentlessly'
DEBBIE HOWELLS

NATALIE CHANDLER

When Megan wakes up in a hospital bed, her first
question is: where's my baby?

But her husband, her sister and her doctor say he doesn't exist.

Megan's not in a maternity ward, she's in a psychiatric unit.

Convinced that they're lying to her, Megan is determined
to find out the truth.

But how can you prove your baby exists when you
can't trust your own memories?

Available to order

ACCENT